MR PEPYS

AND

THE PRIMROSE HILL MYSTERY

MR PEPYS
AND
THE PRIMROSE
HILL MYSTERY

In Restoration London
Samuel Pepys
becomes ensnared in a
Murder Investigation

Malyn Bromfield

Published by Clink Street Publishing 2022

Copyright © 2022

First edition.

The author asserts the moral right under the Copyright, Designs and Patents Act 1988 to be identified as the author of this work.

ISBNs:
978-1-914498-92-3
978-1-914498-93-0

"It's a crime we've got to solve. Go back to the past to solve it — to where it happened and why it happened."

Spoken by Tuppence in *Postern of Fate*
by Agatha Christie

CONTENTS

AUTHOR'S INTRODUCTION

On Saturday 12th October,1678 Sir Edmund Godfrey, a justice of the peace, left his London home and never returned. Five days later his body was discovered in a ditch at Primrose Hill, run through with his own sword. The mystery of his death has never been solved but intriguing clues remain for aspiring detectives. Travel with me back in time to Restoration London where we will visit the crime scene and meet the men who found his body. We will attend the coroner's inquest and hear evidence from Edmund Godfrey's friends and neighbours who spoke with him in the hours before he went missing.

Victimology is at the centre of any murder investigation and Edmund Godfrey may, as our protagonist, hold the vital clue to the mystery of his strange death: that fatal clash between the individual and his world, for the annals of history are full of such tragedies. To understand what may have happened to Godfrey, we must meet the man in his time and try to understand his world. So that you may get to know him, our journey begins thirteen years before Edmund Godfrey died. We will meet King Charles II, a most amiable king, who loves his dogs and his women, and Mr Samuel Pepys who loves a good gossip in London's fashionable new coffee houses. Soon he will become ensnared in the murder investigation.

Gentlemen, wear a long curly periwig, a coat with great skirts and a sword. Ladies, you may wear a fashionable beauty patch in the shape of the crescent moon and a silk gown in the latest French style, but remember, ladies, inside your muff hide a pistol, for Edmund Godfrey has died in a time of great terror. There are rumours of a Jesuit plot to start a rebellion, cut Protestants' throats and assassinate King Charles. But beware. In Restoration London you will confront a much greater danger than plots, pickpockets and cut-throats; a danger against which your swords, your pistols, or even a blunderbuss will be useless.

London, 1665. The plague year.

THE CAST AND EXTRAS

EDMUND GODFREY'S FAMILY, HOUSEHOLD AND ASSOCIATES

Edmund Bury Godfrey, justice of the peace and businessman.

Michael and Benjamin Godfrey, Edmund's brothers.

Jane Harrison, Edmund's sister and her son, Godfrey Harrison.

Sarah Plunknett, Edmund's sister and her husband, Christopher Plunknett,

Mary Gibbon, Edmund's cousin and her husband, Captain Gibbon.

Judith Pamphlin, Edmund's housekeeper from 1677.

Elizabeth Curtis, (Betty) Edmund's housemaid.

Henry Moor, Edmund's clerk from 1677.

Richard Adams, a lawyer.

Sir Thomas Bludworth, Lord Mayor of London.

Edward Coleman, a courtier and a Roman Catholic.

Valentine Greatrakes, (The Stroker) an Irish faith healer.

John Grove, a Jesuit lay brother.

William Lloyd, vicar of St Martin-in-the-Fields.

Richard Mulys, a gentleman's steward.

John Oakley, a neighbour's servant.

John Parsons, a coach maker and churchwarden at St Martin's-in-the-Fields.

Lady Margaret Pratt, a widowed gentlewoman.

Joseph Radcliffe, an oilman and vestryman at St Martin-in-the-Fields.

Thomas Robinson, Edmund's old school friend and justice of the peace.

George Weldon, a taverner.

Thomas Wynnell, a business associate.

THE STUARTS

King Charles II and Queen Catherine of Braganza.

James, Duke of Monmouth, Charles' eldest, natural son.

James, Duke of York, Charles' brother and Lord High Admiral until 1673.

Henriette Anne (Minette), Duchesse d'Orléans, Charles' sister.

ROYAL MISTRESSES

Barbara, Lady Castlemaine.

Nell Gwyn.

Louise de Kérouaille, Duchess of Portsmouth.

AT THE NAVAL OFFICE

Samuel Pepys, naval clerk and after 1674, Secretary of the Naval Office.

Elizabeth Pepys, his wife.

Sam Atkins, Pepys' clerk.

THE OATES FAMILY AND ASSOCIATES

Samuel Oates, an Anabaptist, later an Anglican clergyman.

Lucy Oates, his wife.

Titus Oates, their son, inventor of the Popish Plot.

William Parker, a young Hastings schoolmaster and his father, Captain Parker.

Christopher Kirkby, an amateur chemist.

Matthew Medburne, an actor.

Sir Richard Routh, Captain of the frigate Adventure.

Israel Tongue, an Anglican clergyman.

THE KING'S MEN

Sir Henry Coventry, Secretary of State for the South.

Sir William Coventry, M.P., Henry's brother.

Sir Joseph Williamson, (alias Mr Lee) Secretary of State for the North.

The Earl of Danby, Thomas Osborne, and his servants Lloyd and Sergeant Ramsey.

OPPOSITION POLITICIANS

The Earl of Shaftesbury, Anthony Ashley Cooper.

The Duke of Buckingham, George Villiers.

Robert Peyton, M.P., leader of a gang of discontents.

INTELLIGENCE AGENTS/SPIES

Thomas Blood, (alias Dr Ayliffe)

Colonel John Scott.

WHISTLE-BLOWERS – also including Titus Oates above.

Captain Atkins, a disgraced seaman.

William Bedloe, a self-confessed rogue.

Francis Corrall, a hackney coachman.

T.G. an anonymous person.

Miles Prance, a silversmith/goldsmith.

JESUIT PRIESTS

Father Strange, English Provincial until 1678.

Father Whitbread, English Provincial from 1678.

Father Kelly and Father Le Phaire.

Father Walsh, a character possibly invented by Titus Oates and William Bedloe.

The young Priest, the author's imagined character.

AT THE INQUEST

John Cooper, Coroner of Middlesex.

Nicholas Cambridge, Richard Lazinby and Zachary Skillarne, surgeons.

James Chase, the King's' apothecary and his son, young Mr Chase.

AT THE TRIALS

Sir William Scroggs, Lord Chief Justice.

Sir William Jones, Attorney General.

Sir George Jeffreys, Recorder of London.

Henry Berry, alehouse keeper and porter at Somerset House.

Robert Green, cushion layer in the chapel at Somerset House.

Lawrence Hill, a servant, later a victualler and Elizabeth, his wife.

Mr Chiffinch, King Charles' gentleman.

Mr Warrier, Robert Green's landlord and Avis, his wife.

AT PRIMROSE HILL

Constable John Brown, a victualler,

John Rawson, landlord of the White House tavern and Margaret, his wife.

William Bromwell, a baker,

John Waters, a farrier.

Thomas Grundy, a gentleman.

James Huysman, a painter.

Young Baker, a farmer's son.

Edward Linnet, a butcher and his dog.

ADVERTISED IN THE LONDON GAZETTE

Black Tom, a lost servant boy.

PROLOGUE
17TH OCTOBER, 1678

In summer, London families like to escape the stink and dust of the city to let their children take the air at Primrose Hill. They might bring a pasty or fruit from a street seller, and after their walk into the countryside find a shady spot under a tree for a picnic. There is a tavern nearby where folk may have a drink of ale, if they are not too proud to give their custom to such a poor place. It is only a short walk from the primrose fields where they watch their children run and play in the fresh country air and where, at first dawn on May Day, wives and maids collect the morning dew to dab upon their pretty faces to make them even prettier. Close enough, indeed, to carry a sleeping child in your arms or, on one wet and muddy October night, lug a grown man's corpse between two watchmen's staves by lantern light.

The White House tavern has few wall hangings and hardly a pane of glass in the windows to keep out the draughts, but landlord, John Rawson, is kept busy in the summer months, and during the rest of the year he keeps a good fire burning in the hearth to welcome his regulars.

On a blustery autumn day under heavy clouds, William Bromwell, a baker, and John Waters, a farrier, have walked through the fields from the parish of St Giles-in-the-Fields, and are warming themselves on the settle by the fire shortly after one in the afternoon.

'A man of quality carries a silver topped stick,' Waters is saying. 'It's worth more than a shilling or two.'

'Better to leave well alone,' Bromwell says, in a low voice. He eyes Waters silently and Rawson knows that look: they have secrets they don't want to share with the landlord. But this is only the baker and the farrier and after another drink or two they tell him that they have discovered a scabbard, a belt, a pair of gloves and a gentleman's stick with a silver top lying beside a ditch in a field on the south side of Primrose Hill.

'You should have brought them here,' Rawson says.

'We thought maybe the gentleman had gone into the ditch being hard pressed to relieve himself,' Waters says, 'so we left him to it.'

'Goods of quality, like these, don't fall into the hands of a workingman every day,'

Rawson says eagerly. 'Come, take me to where you found them.'

'Not in this rain,' Bromwell protests, for by now it is pouring down.

'I'll give you a shilling apiece for drinks.' Rawson reaches into his pocket.

The baker gives the farrier that look again. They know more than they are telling, Rawson is sure. Eventually, Bromwell gives Waters a sly nod and they consent to return with him to the ditch but only if the rain stops before it gets dark. It is almost five o'clock before the weather clears. Bromwell complains that the light is fading but Rawson knows that now they have their shillings in their pockets they have no choice but to go along with him.

They walk through fields strewn with hay through gates that are usually locked but have been forced open and they come upon the place where the goods lie. On such a blustery night, Rawson has to hold the lantern inside his coat to keep the candle from blowing out. At the time he thinks nothing of how Waters and Bromwell stand back by a thicket and let him go forward alone towards the ditch, but he thinks much of it later, after he has recovered from the shock of what he sees when he stands at the edge of the ditch.

A hand lies on the bank. A ring on its finger glitters in the lantern light.

'There's a dead body in this ditch,' he shouts to his companions through the wind and the dark.

The body lies on its belly covered with brambles and Rawson sees the tip of a sword protruding several inches through its back.

It is eight o'clock by the time they have fetched Constable John Brown from his home in St Giles' Pound with a dozen or so of his neighbours on foot and on horseback. They pull away the brambles and in the dim lantern light they see the dead man lying face down with his coat pulled over his head. The constable climbs into the ditch with another man and they lift out the body and carry it a short distance in darkness, for the wind has blown out nearly all their lanterns. He pulls the sword out of it with a great wrench and a sickening bubbling sound that turns Rawson's stomach.

'God rest his soul,' Brown says, as Rawson holds his flickering lantern over the dead man's face. 'I fear I may know this gentleman, but we will know better when we see him by candlelight.'

He doesn't ask Rawson if they may remove the body to the White House, only tells him that this is what must be done and the landlord cannot argue.

They need to take note of the position of the corpse, Brown tells them: how it lay with the left hand bent underneath, the knees together at the bottom of the ditch, the feet raised and resting on brambles and the hilt of the sword sticking through the ribs about three inches from the ground. Rawson helps the constable's men retrieve the dead man's hat and periwig from the ditch and collect his stick, belt, gloves and scabbard from the bank. The men are muddy up to their saddle skirts after they have lifted the corpse onto two watchmen's staves, transported it through the fields in the rain and laid it on the table in the White House.

By the light of a couple of Rawson's tallow candles they examine the body. He is a tall, lean man, past middle age.

'Yes,' Constable Brown says, sadly. 'It is as I had suspected. This is the magistrate who has been missing these last five days: Sir Edmund Bury Godfrey.'

'Has he killed himself in that ditch with his own sword,' Rawson wonders aloud, 'or did somebody murder him?'

Part 1
Restoration
1649–1669

*"And all the world in a merry mood
because of the King's coming."*

Samuel Pepys (31st May 1660)

1

THE DEVIL'S CHILD
1649–1660

In the preacher's cottage, in Oakham, Rutlandshire, behind the pillory, in the year of King Charles I's execution, Lucy Oates has ceased to scream.

'I will die bringing forth this child, and welcome,' she says and closes her eyes. Her travail has been longer and more painful than even she, a midwife, could ever have imagined. She has hardly slept for months, for to slumber is to dream that she carries the Devil's child.

He comes with a great surge, tearing his way into the world. Lucy does not die.

'He's not a big baby,' the neighbours say, 'see his little legs. It's the size of his head that gave you so much trouble.'

'Did you beget this boy of a vagrant beggar?' preacher Oates asks of his wife. 'Look at him: his legs don't match. One leg is shorter than the other.'

'Only a little,' Lucy says.

His father names him Titus, after his grandfather.

Lucy cuddles her newborn son and puts him to her breast. He sucks and snorts and pulls away howling and kicking. 'It's the mucus that causes it,' Lucy tells her husband. 'He can't breathe through his nose.'

Little Titus has to be weaned early. As soon as he can toddle on his bandy little limping legs he is afflicted with convulsions. Lucy fears for his life; she holds him, strokes his tufty brown hair and watches him more carefully than her other children.

He does not die.

He is a sickly child aside from the fits: his nose runs and runs and he slavers at the mouth.

'Go play with your friends,' his mother tells him.

The other boys call him *Filthy Mouth* and run away when he approaches them. Soon they begin to taunt him that his chin is growing too big. Little Titus hides in the chimney corner and thinks that a friend is a horrid thing to have, although it is a mighty good thing to be if you know the right words to say to show the other boys that you are stronger than they.

Lucy tries to teach him his letters but there are too many of them and he stamps his foot when she opens the hornbook. 'But he talks well enough,' she tells her neighbours. 'Lord, how that boy can talk.'

Each time his father comes home from his travels with Cromwell's army, he being their chaplain, he never calls Titus by his name. 'Take away that snotty fool and jumble him about,' he tells his mother, many a time, and Titus sees her weep.

The family move to London and Titus listens to his father preaching at the Baptist meeting-house. Titus wants to be like his father. He wants to be the man standing before the congregation telling them what to believe. His father says that every man, however humble, may speak out if it be that he is inspired by the Holy Ghost, just as if he were a vicar or a priest, and he says that the civil magistrates have no authority to prevent a man from doing this. And sometimes, when another pastor is preaching, his father shouts out, *Antichrist!* And the people gasp and stare wide-eyed and some people shout things that Titus doesn't understand

and others call his father a blasphemer. His father doesn't care because crowds of people flock to him and beg him to baptise them. When Titus is old enough, he will be dipped naked into the Thames at midnight, and afterwards, the Holy Ghost will fill him up with things to say.

When he is eleven, something happens.

King Charles II rides through the streets of London on a white horse with golden trappings. He wears a high hat with tall plumes and is dressed all in gold. The next time Titus asks how long it will be until he is immersed in the Thames his mother tells him that this can never happen, not now: because of the King. His father is cursing all day long because he used to get ten shillings for dipping rich people and two shillings and sixpence for the poor. The family plans to move to Hastings, to the parish of All Saints where his father will wear the garb of an Anglican clergyman and Titus and his younger brother, Constant, will be baptised with a little trickle of water into the Church of England.

2

PLAGUE

1665

They have begun to carry away the dead by daylight, there are so many: nighttime is not long enough. A bellman comes before, the driver leads the horse, and the buriers throw the bodies into the cart. They could be shovelling the night soil except that they are puffing tobacco pipes against the plague. They used to cry 'Bring out your dead,' but there's no need anymore: the dead are waiting on the streets. A few lie in coffins, others lie on the ground in winding sheets. Some are naked. And the nearly dead? They drag themselves to the cart as if to lie amongst corpses will the sooner end their agonies.

Only the rich dare to venture onto the streets, if they must, hiding inside their carriages with their perfumes and their tobacco. And the desperate poor, of course. They have no choice but to leave their homes to beg alms or to steal. Most of the shops have been shut up for months, their owners having either fled or perished and there are no horses to be had. There are no wandering cats or dogs either; they will be killed if they are found on the streets. And the pigeons. People think animals are spreading the contagion. On the Lord's Day every sermon is of how the people's sins have brought down God's judgement.

In the parish of St Martin-in-the-Fields, there is a plague

house in Clay Fields at Soho Gardens. A red cross is painted on the door and the plea, *Lord have Mercy upon us*, is inscribed below. A watchman stands before. He grips his red warning-wand as a soldier would hold a sword ready for combat. There is knocking from within and he hastens as far from the door as he dares, puffs hard on his pipe and watches the small, sad procession that has been played out before him for weeks at every plague house he has guarded. A nurse-watcher drags the body of a young woman out of the house. Another carries a dead child and lays it on the ground beside her. 'Stay away, there's more,' one of the women calls to him.

'Why bother to tell me?' the watchman mutters. 'Of course there's more, I know that. There always are. The plague increases weekly.'

He doesn't know which are filthier, the dead with their stinking buboes or the nurse-watchers wearing aprons stained with the black vomit of the dying. They used to say a prayer for the dead, but not anymore. Everyone is praying for themselves: that they will not be the next to lie stinking in the heat waiting for the carts. The watchman turns away and mumbles a prayer to God for mercy for himself and his young wife and child. He dare not go home until the pestilence is gone. Anyway, if he deserts his post he will be sent to prison. God's mercy is a long time coming.

His prayers are interrupted by cries of 'stop thief,' and a man carrying a bundle of filthy cloth comes running from the direction of the graveyard pursued by constables.

'Have pity, have pity,' the man cries as he leaps over the bodies and bolts into the plague house before the constables can grab him. Seeing the dead, they back away and beckon to a tall gentleman who hurries towards the house, but the watchman is ready at the door with his red wand barring the way.

'Let me pass,' the gentleman orders. 'I am a justice of the peace and this man is a thief.'

'I know you, Mr Edmund Godfrey, sir,' the watchman says. 'I swore my oath to you, remember? when you took me on to keep the plague houses safe. And now I will do my duty and bar your way to keep you safe. Leave the rogue to perish amongst the sick; that's punishment enough.'

'I will see justice done.' Edmund Godfrey grabs the red rod and pushes the watchman out of his way. He enters the plague house and emerges moments later, his tall frame bent over the little man clutching his big bundle as he pulls him by the arm.

'Have pity, sir, in the Lord's name, have pity,' the man cries throwing his bundle at the justice's feet. 'I used to sell old clothes. No one durst buy them now. How shall I feed my family except I take winding sheets from dead men who surely will not miss them?'

'I know that you have also stolen new shrouds from shops deserted by their owners,' the justice says. 'You have robbed the living and the dead and filled a warehouse with your spoils.'

'There's a good market for winding sheets these days,' one of the constables shouts from a safe distance.

The watchman takes a step towards Godfrey. 'He wants food for his children. Will you help him, sir?'

'There's food aplenty,' Godfrey says. 'Pears, plums and cherries from the country, and beef, and fewer each week to eat it. The Parish gives relief to the deserving poor as the law requires. Why does he not seek employment in one of the new workhouses?'

'But sir, folks are afraid to mix with others for fear of the contagion,' the watchman says.

Justice Godfrey is still holding the thief firmly by the arm and there is no sympathy in his eyes.

'I was gulled of all my money by a wizard selling plague

water,' the man says, spitting in his rage so that the watchman jumps aside. 'It was filthy Thames muck and would have killed us faster than the pestilence. Forgive me, sir, I beg you, let me go. You have the shrouds. Your constables will return them to the graves.'

The constables look at the filthy heap of cloth and at each other, and shake their heads.

'No harm's been done to any living person,' the man pleads. 'The nurses here will make good use of the sheets.' He pulls cloths from the heap and begins to cover the dead. 'See, I've done my public duty and helped the poor wretches go to heaven decently.'

'I will see justice done according to the law,' the magistrate says. 'When you come to court, I shall sentence you to be whipped around one of the churchyards you have robbed.' He drags the little man to the constables and orders them to throw him in prison.

'Have your justice,' he screams into Godfrey's ear, making him start. 'Have your fair justice. You deserve it for all your snooping. I've seen you, Mr Justice Godfrey, creeping in alleys at night, seeking to discover criminals who are only poor men and women trying to stay alive. I've seen you going home to your nice little business selling wood and coal; to your warm hearths and your good dinners while poor people shiver and starve; I've followed you all the way …'

'That was a rash thing for Justice Godfrey to do: to handle dead men's clouts and to come after the thief into this pestilent house,' a nurse says to the watchman after the constables have taken the man away and Godfrey has departed. 'Does he not value the life that God gave him?'

'He's not a young man, and being a bachelor, I suppose there's no one to suffer overmuch if he drops dead of the plague,' the watchman says.

'Oh, so that's it, he has no wife nor family to worry about.'

'Aye, unlike the rest of us.'

'We're all of us mere mortals waiting on God's mercy, while more good people die each day, thinking that God forgot them.'

'It's a wicked way to send good Christian men and women to their graves, in stinking heaps, like animals, without a proper prayer to their names,' the watchman says bitterly.

The nurse-watcher is used to offering comfort to the woeful. 'I suppose God knows who everyone is and will save the souls of the good,' she says gently.

'What I fear most is a lonely death for my little son, with no one left alive to grieve for him.' The watchman's voice trembles. 'It makes me sick to my very soul to think of it.'

'You and me,' the nurse replies, 'being poor as we are, we have no choice but to leave our families and take work when it comes our way, plague or no. A gentleman like Justice Godfrey could have gone into the country until the pestilence is over, like people of quality, and tradesmen too, yet he chooses to stay. I'll say this for him: he's either a foolish man or a very brave one.'

'I suppose he thinks the Lord Mayor needs his help to keep the peace while there's still a few folk left alive willing to wander the streets looking for shops to loot, or looking for people to rob or murder,' the watchman says.

The nurse-watcher gathers the bundle of shrouds into her arms. 'These will come in handy. No need to wash 'um, where they're going. I'll air one or two by the fire against the infection, and put them aside, 'tis a shame to waste good woollen cloth; the dead won't mind sharing a shroud or two.'

'Well, goodnight to you, watchman,' she says kindly, 'your vigil will soon be over. I dare say you'll be glad that you don't have to do the night watch since the mayor ordered that after nine of the clock all healthy folk must stay within, to let the sick take the air.'

The watchman is left alone with his pipe and the dead.

***

Samuel Pepys has never lived so merrily as through this plague year; he has written so in his diary. Not that anyone else is likely to read it. He uses shorthand, and a few words in Latin and other languages. Every day he writes in secret, for there are passages that his wife must never read. She walked out on him for a short time in the early months of their marriage; that must never happen again to disgrace him.

He's been doing mighty well for himself for five years now; more than anyone would expect from *a prick louse,* the son of a poor London tailor. He's Clerk of the Acts to the Navy Board and well respected for his hard work by His Highness the Duke of York, the Lord High Admiral. The Duke's secretary has presented him with a silver pen for his labours. He's a justice of the peace in the counties of Middlesex, Essex, Kent and Southampton: the naval dock-lands. He's been invited to dine with the Lord Mayor, and these days ordinary men take off their caps to him.

Keeping your spirits up is the best way to fight the con-tagion: this, Pepys firmly believes, and also, of course, now and then drinking plague water or buying a roll of tobacco to smell and chew. He has been able to afford three new suits of clothes this plague year – he had to buy the third, a woollen suit with close knees, because his wife didn't like the look of him in the coloured silk – and he has begun to wear a lace band about his neck. A while ago, he'd promised his wife twenty pounds for new clothes for Easter but when she reminded him of his promise he boggled at parting with the money. Lord, but she knows how to get her way with him; she pestered and pestered one morning when they had just become friends again after a quarrel, so, of course, she got her money. In May, he had his hair shorn and acquired a fine, fashionable periwig of human hair that he bought in Westminster. What a noble couple they make: he in his black silk suit and Elizabeth, so pretty in her new clothes of flowered, ash-coloured silk with her yellow birds-eye hood that is all the fashion now.

Yes, this plague year has been mighty good to him. He's been invited to become a member of the Royal Society where he meets the most intelligent people in the land: mathematicians and scientists. It cost him forty shillings admission to the discourses and experiments and he fears that he hasn't the philosophy to understand them properly. But he's there, at the heart of new discoveries, and that's what's important.

The plague had first touched Pepys on a hot afternoon in June. After a meeting at the Lord Treasurer's house he had taken a hackney coach down Holborn to his home at the Navy Office on Seething Lane, near the Tower. He knew that the bills of mortality were increasing in the city, with unusually high numbers dead of fever, spotted fever and teeth, and had suspected that folk were concealing deaths from the plague under the guise of these other diseases to prevent their houses from being locked up. He was pondering that the nurse- searchers need to be more vigilant when his coach came to a sharp halt and the coachman climbed down and grabbed at his horses' reins, barely able to stand.

'I cannot continue Mr Pepys,' he cried. 'I am struck sick of a sudden, and blinded. I can barely see.'

Pepys had walked away to find another hackney carriage, very sad at heart for the poor man and his family and greatly worried for himself, if indeed it was the plague that had taken the coachman. He must finish writing his will, for his wife's and his elderly father's sakes and make arrangements to send his wife away from the city, to stay with people he knows in Woolwich.

By mid-August the death bells are tolling every five or six minutes. The Navy Office finally moves to Greenwich and Pepys is able to leave the city and its sickness. By that time, the King and court have removed to the safety of Oxford.

Lord, but this plague year is as dull as Cromwell's time, Pepys complains to himself. There's no fun, no entertainment in the empty streets: no puppet shows in Covent Garden, no maypoles and worst of all, no theatres. Sometimes when he walks Pepys likes to read a play. He has dreamed a wonderful dream that King Charles' beautiful mistress, Barbara, Lady Castlemaine, was in his own arms and she permitted him to use all the dalliance he desired with her. It was only a dream, but he has taken such real pleasure from it. He thinks of Shakespeare's Hamlet asking what dreams may come in the sleep of death. Oh, what a happy thing it would be, he writes in his diary, if I could but dream such dreams as this for all eternity; I wouldn't need to be so fearful of death, even with the plague all around us.

In September, he has to visit London for naval business and to check upon his plate and his money which he left at his house. He's greatly cheered to hear news that the fleet has taken thirty-five Dutch ships, but he's feeling a little unwell. He calls at the Bear at the foot of the bridge to take a gill of sack with a biscuit and a piece of cheese, to settle his colicky stomach. Making his way over the bridge he spreads the joyous news of victory at sea but wonders to see so many people, around two hundred men at the Exchange but just plain men, no wealthy merchant or gentleman of fashion. They tell him cheerfully that the bill of mortality has decreased by five hundred souls this week.

Not within the city walls, it hasn't, Pepys discovers. Here, the plague is spreading fast and coming closer to his house. He's much relieved to find his money and his plate safe, but, Lord, what should he tell his wife of the misery he's seen within the city this day: of meeting dead bodies being carried to burial at noonday on Fenchurch Street; of peering inside a hackney coach and seeing a person covered in sores; of taverns he used to visit being shut up? Should he tell his wife that the waterman, who carries him daily, fell sick as soon as he had landed him last Friday morning, and now he is dead?

Elizabeth has prepared a tench for supper to sooth his queasy stomach. 'What news of London?' she asks, 'and where is your periwig?'

He tries to put aside his melancholy and talks of rich Dutch ships and how overjoyed everyone is at the Navy Office talking of prizes of great worth.

'But where is your periwig?' she pesters. 'Why aren't you wearing it? Does it have lice?'

'I dare not wear it,' he confesses, 'for fear that it was made of hair cut from a person dead of the plague that is rife in Westminster.'

'Perhaps wear a woolly one,' she suggests. 'You can't go about with that mangy cropped hair; it will spoil the look of your new clothes.'

He'll grow his hair, he says. Periwigs may not be the fashion after the plague.

***

While the dead-carts rumble on the cobbled lanes and London's graveyards heave and spread into the fields, justice Edmund Godfrey reads a pamphlet that his friend the Lord Mayor, Sir Thomas Bludworth, has recommended: *Wonders if not Miracles*. The author, Lionel Beacher, claims to have witnessed wonderful cures performed by an Irishman, Valentine Greatrakes. Edmund is astounded: more than sixty people have been healed by this man they name The Stroker, just by the touch of his hands. Men and women troubled with the falling sickness were cured even as they foamed at the mouth and wallowed on the ground. Poor cripples stumbled to him, and being stroked, walked away forgetting their crutches. Wherever The Stroker travels, crowds flock to him with their sick and their maimed. He has been invited to demonstrate his cures for the amusement of King Charles, and will, no doubt, have to do God's work with a litter of yapping spaniels around his ankles and a gaggle of whores looking on.

Edmund would have crossed the sea to Ireland to witness for himself this healer at his work but that the mayor needs him to help to keep the peace in the plague streets and alleys. Watchmen are being attacked for locking up houses of the sick and for guarding barriers at the city gates to prevent people from leaving and spreading the disease. The King has taken most of his guards with him to Oxford leaving only a few soldiers to guard Whitehall and the Tower. London is a place forsaken except by the sick, the poor, and, of course, the lawless: those bold and daring men who fear the contagion less than they relish the thrill of law-breaking.

Edmund reads the pamphlet again and again. He has no doubt that the plague is God's vengeance upon the people for their folly, their ignorance, their debauchery and their ungodly ways. He can see now that ordinary physicians are impotent against such divine judgement. Believing that they are protected by their black masks with long beaks, their wide hats and flapping black cloaks, they hover over the sick and the dying like giant ravens. But this is all they can do: watch families die, for they have no better remedies against the plague than his housekeeper with her vinegar bottle, the mayor with his concoctions of rue and garlic, or the jailer of Newgate prison who puts his faith in drinking water from the skull of a hanged man.

But this man in Ireland who works his miracles with a touch of his hands: Edmund cannot wait to meet him.

3

A SPRING OF MIRACLES
MARCH, 1666

It is a time of wonder. A spring of miracles.

Here, in Edmund's own home, verses from the New Testament are being played out before him as if his parlour were God's theatre. Walter Dolle, a goldbeater from the Hand and Hammer on Pye Corner, a man Edmund never knew until today, is weeping and laughing and hugging his son in the presence of physicians, clergymen, the mayor, Edmund's two brothers and the celebrated scientist and founder member of the Royal Society, Robert Boyle, a good Christian man who has written theological tracts and devotional essays. Young Walter, an apprentice engraver, has staggered into his father's arms, drunken with happiness, whole again, freed from paralysis on his right side. Edmund had almost expected Greatrakes to say, 'arise and walk,' as the Bible tells that Jesus did when the paralysed man was lowered through a roof on a pallet because his friends could not penetrate the crowds outside the house. And indeed, multitudes are gathered at Edmund's door pressing for entry, crying out for The Stroker to cure their sick and their maimed.

'Is this the end of my great trouble, for evermore, Mr Greatrakes?' young Walter asks eagerly.

'All will be as the Lord pleases. I am but God's instrument

and humbled to be so,' Greatrakes answers, bowing his head.

'I shall advise our sister Jane to wait upon The Stroker, to be cured of the wen on her side,' Edmund tells his brothers.

'Shall you tell her that Greatrakes will use a dead man's hand to perform his miracle on her cyst?' Michael asks. 'My wife has told me that this is how he does these things.'

'The jailer of Newgate is charging up to ten guineas for the severed hand of a hanged man, to use for medicinal purposes,' Benjamin adds.

Edmund glares at his brothers. 'I have heard that Greatrakes' spittle has cured deafness,' he says.

'Aye, and his urine smells of violets,' Benjamin replies. 'Lord, whatever does the man drink?'

'His urine has been proven to cure dropsy,' Edmund retorts.

Valentine Greatrakes is an imposing man, just as Edmund had imagined: a Protestant gentleman, strong in the body, self-confident, a magistrate like himself, being a clerk of the peace in County Cork. He is one of those men who surprises you when you realise that he is not as tall as he appears. The mayor will, of course, have informed Greatrakes of the great respect that he, Edmund, has earned in Westminster and Middlesex as a justice of the peace who goes well beyond the call of duty, dragging lawbreakers out of alleys at night like rats from a sewer. A man such as Valentine Greatrakes, with a mission to heal the afflicted, will surely understand his own mission to assist the deserving poor and the destitute. It occurs to Edmund that Greatrakes might like to sit in on the next vestry meeting at St Martin-in-the Fields, to see how well his parish charities are administered. There's very little real starvation in the city and Edmund knows that this is due to the efficiency of parish vestries and conscientious justices such as himself.

After the last of the sick has been stroked and his guests take their leave, the mayor turns to Edmund. 'It is your turn now,' he says and at last Edmund is alone with the healer.

'I have suffered with a little deafness all my life,' Edmund says. 'It is natural to me and of no great consequence but if you have time between treating the wretched poor people in my parish who have greater need than I...'

Oh, but it would be marvellous, indeed, if Greatrakes' spittle could open his ears and let him hear as other men. Edmund has rather got used to turning away when he doesn't want to even try to hear what his gossipy house-keeper or an angry thief is saying to him, but he wishes he could hear everything that's being said when he dines out in company. People get impatient when they're asked to repeat something and this makes him cross. There have been times when he has wished he was born blind instead of deaf so that he could have proper conversations with people even though he couldn't see them. Sometimes he feels so isolated, so cut off from other men. He copes well at the Woodmongers' Company meetings and at St Martin's vestry because he's the one doing most of the talking, leading the conversation, so he knows where it's going. But he's stopped visiting the coffee houses. He'd sit there reading the latest tittle-tattle in broadside publications, drinking his dish of the bitter tasting liquid that he was supposed to enjoy whilst his friends and his brothers talked politics with serious faces or laughed at jokes he couldn't understand. When he pointed to a paper that interested him he couldn't interpret their responses through the clouds of tobacco smoke and the continuous din of shouting and rattling of bowls. Sometimes, the effort of making conversation in company is just too much, especially when he has his bad days.

'I see that you are troubled by more than a little loss of hearing,' Greatrakes replies gently. 'Do not deny it, my friend. I see before me a man with eyes of sadness: very great sadness. You have been bled many times, I think, but bleeding has given at best, only temporary relief.'

'How do you know me so well when we have barely spoken?' Edmund asks, and hears his voice falter.

When you meet him face to face, this sober Irish gentleman in his dark attire, wearing his own long hair with a plain white collar about his shoulders, you feel that you may trust him with your secrets. Edmund begins to speak of the terrible worry that darkens his life. 'I am the only one of my father's many children to have inherited... another affliction, indeed, a malady... of sorts.'

'Ah, you are a man living in the shadow of his father.'

'I am a man who lives in fear of his own shadow,' Edmund replies, almost in a whisper. He isn't sure quite how much he wants to confess to Greatrakes about those dark days when the world becomes a wretched, melancholy place. He's not sure that the healer will understand. How could he? How could anyone understand? Edmund doesn't understand them himself. He doesn't know why they come nor what he can do to prevent them. He only knows that one day he will be walking by the Thames exhilarated by the vibrancy of the city and the big ships bringing wares from all over the world: sugar from Jamaica, naval stores from the Baltic, tobacco from Virginia. And so many fine ships leaving the port carrying wool, tin and lead to northern Europe and Iberia – and trade with the New World expanding. Another day, he'll be standing on the stinking riverbank in the silt, wishing that the Thames would swallow him up and it is hard, oh, so very hard, to drag himself away when what he really wants is to drown the terrible misery in his soul. How could Greatrakes stroke away that kind of pain? He wouldn't know where to touch.

'Sometimes,' he tells the healer, 'when I was a boy, I used

to dream that I lived another life in a distant place across the sea where I was not my father's son... not myself, even.'

'To be afraid of yourself: this is a terrible burden for a boy and for a man.' Greatrakes places a comforting hand upon Edmund's shoulder.

'It is how I am forced to live, by day and by night... waiting for the worst... especially by night.'

Greatrakes doesn't ask what the worst might be and Edmund says no more.

'We cannot have you living the rest of your days in this state,' the healer says and his vehemence makes Edmund start. 'A surfeit of black bile, that's at the root of your misery, my friend. I shall lie you on your back and stroke the upper left side of your abdomen, where the spleen lies... when you are ready, of course, calmer than you are after the excitements of today.'

Edmund visits his friend, Colonel George Weldon, at his tavern in York Buildings on the Strand. The Stroker has performed his miracles here too. Many have been stroked and healed in the presence of physicians. George Weldon is still a young man but he has been cured of an excruciating fit of the stone.

'I was in agony until Greatrakes stroked away the pain,' Weldon tells him.

'I know you were,' Edmund replies, 'and now you will live your life without pain. The Stroker has the power of God in his hands when he works his miracles.'

'You and I believe this to be true,' Weldon says, 'but we know that there are others who insult him and name him a quack. A man was drinking here the other day: Samuel Pepys, a clerk from the Navy Office. Do you know him? He's a short man who gossips like a woman and he was most dismissive of my cure.'

'I know of him, of course; he's a justice of the peace, but we rarely meet.'

'Well, he had the audacity to sit here drinking my beer whilst he flirted with my wife. If you had a wife, Mr Godfrey, I would advise you to keep her well away from this man. He told me that he suffers from the stone himself, which is how we got into conversation, and it happens that he passed two small stones last year. He believes that I would have voided my stone regardless of Greatrakes' stroking and he boasted that eight years ago he had a mighty great stone removed from his bladder by a physician. I was invited to his home to view it later in the month, on 26th, the anniversary of his surgery.'

'Will you go?'

'I'm tempted. He says it is the size of a tennis ball, more than two inches around; but if I do go, I won't take my wife.'

'You should have invited him to come to see Greatrakes' cures for himself.'

'I did, but he told me that he carries a hare's foot with him everywhere he goes, against his colic, and that is all the magic he needs. A roll of tobacco or two got him safely through the plague year.'

Edmund's stroking is a private affair: just the two of them in his bedchamber.

When his new friend has returned to his homeland across the Irish Sea, Edmund will remember the warmth of Valentine's breath and the wetness of his spittle dribbling into each ear; the firm but gentle kneading of the healer's hands on his body.

'Those who are not cured?' Edmund asks, 'Why is this so?'

'Only God knows,' Valentine answers.

In the silence and the candlelight Valentine's hands caress Edmund and he cannot remember ever being so close to any other person, even as a child with his nurse. Except of course, that one time.

But that was a foolish mistake, when he was young. He will not let it shame him in his age.

4

FIRE

SEPTEMBER, 1666

Charles allows Pepys to speak and does not interrupt him with questions. Neither does his brother, James, Duke of York, Lord High Admiral who promoted Pepys to be surveyor-general of victualling for the navy in December. Last week, Pepys had been summoned to the Green Chamber here at Whitehall to explain himself after a complaint by the generals that the Dutch fleet was at sea and English ships were not ready to sail. Pepys had spoken of the desperate lack of supplies for our sailors, and Parliament could not but be impressed by his oratory, yet still they pull the purse-strings tight. Charles is furious. Always, always, there is never enough money. How can England fight her enemies at sea if she cannot afford to feed her sailors? He had first invited Pepys to kiss his hand when he was part of the escort which brought him to England upon the Restoration of the monarchy. After several days of bad weather they had finally weighed anchor and set sail from the States of Holland and Charles will never forget how it felt to be coming home after all those years of being a king with no kingdom; to have set in motion orders for the trials and executions of the men who had signed his father's death warrant. He remembers Pepys, young and eager, standing on the quarter deck of the *Royal Charles,* listening with tears in his eyes, while he, wearing his new king's clothes, which in his poverty he had been obliged to allow others to acquire for him, told the story of his escape from the battle of Worcester: four days and three nights up to his knees in dirt, disguised in a peasant's green coat, the biggest that could be found, and wearing labourers' shoes slit at the sides to try to make them fit. Charles leans back in his chair, stretches his long legs and wiggles his big feet inside his soft court shoes. God knows that of all the hardships he endured when he fled his homeland, he will never forget his wretched sore feet.

Mr Pepys is all of a fluster. 'Your Majesty, Your Highness, three hundred houses have burned down in the night,' he cries.

'We heard cries of "fire" and the ringing of bells but did not believe it to be so serious,' Charles replies, suddenly guilt-ridden. The people were calling for God and their king to help them. They were calling for his help and he lay idle in his bed.

'This morning, from a high place on the Tower, I saw houses at the end of the bridge all on fire and an infinite, great fire beyond,' Pepys says, all in one breath. 'St Magnus' Church is gone and most of Fish Street. The fire ran towards the Steelyard at great speed with the easterly wind mighty high and driving it into the city, and everything proving combustible. Even the very stones of the churches crack in the heat. The people throw their goods into lighters, or whatever craft is to be found on the Thames, or else they throw their bundles and their chests into the river itself. Sir, the sick are carried out of their burning homes in their beds and the Lord only knows where they may be taken. No one is quenching the fire, only saving themselves and their valuables and leaving the conflagration to run wherever the wind takes it.'

'I have written to the Lord Mayor and his aldermen warning of the danger of fire,' Charles says with anger. 'They were given my royal authority to pull down such overhanging timber houses that put the city in peril and to imprison those who contravene the Building Acts. And now this happens. The Lord Mayor has much to answer. He knows that fire is a persistent danger to the city.'

'The people stay in their houses until the fire touches them,' Pepys continues, 'and only then do they run to the river from one set of stairs to another to try to find a boat. Even the poor pigeons are so loath to leave their houses that they hover about the windows and balconies until they burn their wings and fall down.'

'Where did the fire begin?' Charles asks. He walks to the window. 'We cannot see the spread of it here at Whitehall because of the bend in the river.'

'I have it from the lieutenant of the Tower that it began on Pudding Lane, at Farryner's bake-house,' Pepys says.

'I think I know this man, Farryner,' Charles says. 'I remember speaking with him on one occasion about the price of flour. Is he not the baker who provides bread for our sailors?'

'Indeed, I believe he is, sir.'

'Find my Lord Mayor,' Charles orders. 'Tell him to pull down houses at once to make firebreaks before the fire consumes all of London. If soldiers are needed, he shall have as many as he needs. I will send my own guards also. Go, tell him so.'

'First the plague and now this conflagration,' Charles says to his brother after Pepys has departed. 'Odd's fish! England's enemies will be laughing.'

'Oh, do not trouble yourself about King Louis,' James says, in that lazy, arrogant manner of his that Charles finds so exasperating in times of crisis. 'Little sister Minette, will surely keep her brother-in-law sweet for us. And you can leave the Dutch to me: my ships are not burning.'

'Not yet,' Charles warns.

Pepys finds the mayor with his aldermen on Canning Street. A gang of firefighters have formed a line from the river.

'We might just as well spit on it,' one of the men says as he passes a bucket to the next.

'I never thought that it would come to this. It was such a little fire at the beginning,' the mayor says. 'A woman could have pissed it out.'

'You should have pissed it out yourself,' Pepys mutters.

The mayor wipes his face with his neckcloth which is all wet and sooty. 'Lord, what can I do? I am a man spent. People will not obey me. I have been pulling down houses, but the fire overtakes us faster than we can do it. Go tell the King that I need no more soldiers. I have done all I can and now I must go refresh myself, having been up all night.'

'Lord, but he's no better than a fainting woman,' Pepys says to himself as the mayor walks away. He has no time to stay to help the mayor's band of firefighters with their shovels and their buckets. He must hurry home. His house in the east near the Tower is safe from the fire. He has done his duty and told the King the worst of it. Let the soldiers and the guards do their work; he has a dinner party at noon. His friends have been invited especially so that they can admire his collection of books in his new closet with the expensive new window.

Through the smoke, the mayor sees Edmund Godfrey hurrying towards him.

'I have organised rosters for buckets and hoses for your bands of men,' Edmund says. 'Every engine is out in the streets and the men are working them to exhaustion.'

The mayor grabs Edmund's arm and pulls him aside. 'Take care for your life, you are too close. The flames are spreading fast along the row; another house is about to fall.'

'I cannot stand aside and watch my city burn and its people suffer,' Edmund cries above the crackling and crashing. The flames have leapt to the adjoining house and already the front has tumbled. Beside him, a woman holds a baby in one arm and a bundle under the other. A man with a crate upon his back has his arm around her. Standing there, like pilgrims, the little family watch the flames lick the bright flowers painted on the wall in their sleeping chamber before they devour the bed and the pretty embroidered hangings.

'We have nothing,' the man says. 'My shop, my home, my goods; all are gone. We never thought the fire would run so fast. We did not even have time to roll up the featherbed and throw it out of the window. We were taking in my poor brother's goods just hours ago, now both our houses are burned. My Lord Mayor, pray tell me, where shall we go?'

The mayor shakes his head.

'Take your wife to the fields, beyond the gates,' Edmund says. 'There will be tents by the end of the day, and something to eat. Biscuits are being brought from the naval stores. You are not alone, countless businesses are ruined. The Hanseatic merchants of the Steelyard have watched their hall and their goods turn to ashes after centuries of trading in London.'

'Wealthy merchants can afford to rebuild,' the man says as he leads his wife away. 'What will become of us? Everything I own is here, on my back.'

'You must blow up houses to make bigger firebreaks before all of London turns to ashes,' Edmund tells the mayor.

'Sailors have brought powder from the Tower, but the aldermen will not let me do it. It is their houses that will be sacrificed. Who will pay the cost of compensation if I blow up their houses? Now, forgive me, Mr Godfrey, I must leave you. I need to rest.'

Edmund has been out in the city since his maid awoke him at the first desperate cries and the ringing of bells in the early morning. He was forced to draw his sword at Newgate, where people were fighting for carts and carriages. There is so much to be done and too few to do it. Should he stay to help the men wield the buckets, or make his way to the Thames to keep order amongst the throngs of people pushing on the steps to get a boat for their goods and hindering the fetching of water? He is thankful that his home is in the far west, near Charing Cross, some distance from the fire.

All afternoon until dusk, Edmund follows the fire as it runs westwards, lifting bucket after bucket with the mayor's men and boys from Westminster School where he was once a scholar. He has forgotten to eat and does not know that he is exhausted. It is the Lord's Day but there have been no sermons or prayers in London; the churches are filling up with people's goods. He makes his way home despairing of the stupidity of Londoners who, desperate to find a source of water, were everywhere tearing up the paving and cobbles to hack into the elm water pipes, but in doing so, made the pressure too low to get water for the engines. He finds his woodyard crowded with people begging for carts, drays and horses. He tells his housekeeper to give food to homeless families and instructs his men in the woodyard to allow poor folk to use his wood wharf to transport their goods by water or borrow his coal carts to take their chattels out of the city. Carts have been arriving from the country to be loaned for up to forty pounds. Edmund would never do this: make money from others' misfortunes. It is every man's Christian duty to help the miserable wretches who have lost everything in the fire.

Pepys just cannot keep away from the fire, from the spectacle of it. His dinner guests are not interested in his house renovations nor his books. All talk is of the fire. In the evening, he takes his wife and some friends on a boat on the river. With the wind in their faces they are almost burned by showers of fire-drops. When they can bear the smoke and the heat no more they a find a little alehouse on Bankside and stay there until the fire glows in a great arch over the city. It makes Pepys weep to see it.

Suffocating, choking smoke darkens London's days, but the nights are fire-bright.

Edmund's neckband is tied around his nose and mouth and he has pulled his wide brimmed hat well over his forehead to try to prevent his eyes from smarting. The hot ashes burn his feet through the soles of his shoes despite several pairs of stockings. He has lost his way more than once. This isn't the London he knows. Rows of houses — with their board signs that were so low riders had to duck to avoid them — have been reduced to smouldering foundations. The sounds of street vendors have been replaced by the cries and wails of the people, the snorting and screaming of horses, the roaring of the fire and the intermittent thunder of the blowing up of houses. And above all this, the running firemen pull their engines and roar, 'Hi-Hi-Hi; Hi-Hi-Hi.' Edmund's ears are bursting. He finds a little lost child with his cat in his arms standing before a row of flaming houses and he's screaming for his mother. Edmund can see that he has been lowered to safety from a window; a rope dangles from his waist and trails in the rubble. Edmund isn't used to children. He doesn't know what to do. He decides to take him to St Paul's Cathedral which is sheltering the destitute; he will surely find a family there who will take care of him. He holds out his hand but the boy backs away and screams and screams and clutches his cat. When the cat wriggles free the child bolts after it into the mass of people with their chests and their carts and their terrified horses with rolling white eyes.

Edmund feels useless.

Alleys he used to frequent in search of the lawless are filled with rubble. Gone are the old familiar smells of London's streets: fresh bread, new leather, fish, apples, the roasting of coffee beans. Now there's one pervading stench: smoke and burning, and something else, something intangible: fear. And he wonders if he will ever clear his nose of it.

He's hardly eaten since the fire started. He pushed away the mutton dinner his housekeeper served yesterday evening and asked for whey. All he wanted was liquid to dry the ashes in his mouth. Thankfully, his own home and wood-yard are safe for the time being. The Swan Inn in Fulham, and the lands around it on the north bank of the Thames, which he bought more than a decade ago, and his properties in Brewers Yard and Blue Cross Street in Westminster are safe, but he knows that he has lost properties in the town. The vast warehouses close to Pudding Lane had fuelled the fire at its outset with their stores of turpentine, brimstone, oil, pitch, tar, tobacco and more. Supplies of coal and timber in nearby wharves did what they are supposed to do: they burned furiously, so this side of his business will suffer. He must call a special meeting of the Woodmongers' Company. The other woodmongers will look to him, their master, to decide what must be done.

The King has ordered that an inner ring of fire posts be set up by the constables and Edmund inspects these to make sure that the men are doing their work and not hanging around drinking beer with the five pounds the King has given them for refreshments. Everywhere, he sees the homeless with their children and their bundles wandering amongst the smouldering foundations. Some of the destitute are weeping. Others are screaming their anger. Someone must take the blame. Rumours are spreading that the French started the fire.

He treads his way through the fog of smoke, lost again in streets of glowing ash and rubble. In a street of fire two men work an engine, pumping the shanks, while a soldier stands atop directing a hose at the flames. Edmund recognises the two men immediately. One is the Duke of York. He saw him several times on Monday, riding around the city keeping order. The other, a very tall man, relinquishes his post to one of the soldiers and walks into the crowd. He is wet up to his ankles and covered in soot. Edmund sees that he is handing out coins of some worth, for several of the men are putting down their bundles. 'Good man, good man,' the tall man says, when they accompany him to houses adjoining the burning building, and he pats their shoulders and hands them ropes and hooks. 'Let us pull down houses where we must, to save what we can.' It is King Charles.

Edmund grabs a water bucket, runs to the front of the line of soldiers, climbs the ladder and hands the bucket to the man on the roof. And there, within the arc of flame, while golden fire-drops cascade like angels' wings, euphoria overwhelms him. He is London's saviour at the pinnacle of his life's work. Every act of duty he has ever discharged is but the harbinger of this moment in time. His Moment in Time. He becomes aware that time is passing very slowly and wonders why this is so when the task is so urgent. It seems to take minutes for the man below him to reach up with a bucket and for Edmund to lean down to take it from him, as if they are actors and they have forgotten what scene they are performing. The last thing Edmund remembers is letting go of one bucket and reaching down for another and after that, his foot slipping on the wet ladder and a great weight falling upon his back.

5

BLAME

AUTUMN, 1666

'Of course you will accept it, Edmund,' cousin Mary says.

Michael takes the paper from her. 'You must accept it for the family's sake, and there's an end to it.'

'You earned it for doing your duty as a magistrate while others fled the city. Why would you not want it?' Benjamin asks. 'You might have died of the plague last year, and have managed almost to kill yourself fighting the fire.'

Edmund's lost count of how many days he's had to lie in his bed and put up with a continuous trail of visitors: physicians, apothecaries, friends and family. And people he hardly knows, men to whom he would only give a brief, 'good morrow,' when he meets them in the street, now think that they can sit in his bedchamber and make him put up with their chatter. Yesterday, his sisters brought a piss-pot physician who applied ointment to his back compounding his pain with unbearable irritation and assaulting his nose with a noxious smell as if his bed were a nest of dead mice.

'His Majesty has seen fit to reward you. If you refuse, you will insult him,' cousin Mary says. 'Oh, Edmund, your poor father would have been so proud.'

Michael turns to Benjamin. 'No one in their right mind would refuse a knighthood.' He speaks loudly and clearly, so that Edmund will hear.

'One more insult won't worry the King,' Edmund says. 'He knows what the people think of him and his whores.'

'The people are saying that he is very brave to risk his life trying to save poor men's homes, and they say the same about the Duke of York,' Mary says.

'Good Lord, but that was foolish. If they had both killed themselves, who would take the throne?' Michael asks.

'Pray, let me be,' Edmund demands and closes his eyes. His brothers should be with his clerk, overseeing his affairs for him, not here with his cousin fussing over the King's letter. He has asked his clerk write to Valentine to invite him to come and stroke his injured back, but the letter cannot be sent, for the Post Office burned with all the rest of London.

'A lady of quality might want to marry a man with such a fine sounding title,' cousin Mary ventures rather timidly. 'No, Edmund, pray, do not wave me away. Please listen to me. I have told you before that it is not too late for you to take a wife and have a family to cheer you when your bad times come. A pretty widow, just into her thirties, with a little child or two to prove that she is fruitful...'

Edmund groans but she persists.

'You are not yet forty-five, the difference between the ages would not be too great.'

He has nothing to say to his cousin. How can he tell her that he is not like other men? Women are distasteful to him. Their wombs float around inside their bodies making them emotional and volatile. Their humours are cold and watery. And they bleed. And when this happens they can turn wine sour and sugar black. When he was a young man he tried very hard to like women and get close to them, but they smell different from men and he didn't like it.

'Pray, do not trouble yourself to find me a wife. I have no desire to marry, and even less to become a father,' Edmund says simply. 'Now, go, all of you, let me rest, the sooner to heal my back so that I can take myself on the streets again and do my work.'

'The knighthood,' his cousin asks, 'Edmund, dear, you will accept it?'

'No,' says Edmund. 'Now let me be.'

He sleeps. He awakes to find his friend, John Grove, reading his Bible. Amongst the Jesuits he is known by his alias, Honest William, and Edmund cannot think of a better sobriquet for the lay brother. Grove insists that after his long sleep the nurse be called to tend to Edmund's needs and he refuses to answer any of his urgent questions about the state of London until he has eaten his supper.

'You must eat a little of what your housekeeper has prepared for you, in gratitude for her trouble, and while you sup, I will keep the good lady company.'

'Women always think they have to feed people to make them happy,' Edmund grumbles as Grove leaves the chamber. 'I'm not hungry, let me be,' he tells the nurse.

'Take a spoonful or so, sir, if you please, and a morsel or two of bread,' she says firmly. 'The poor homeless wretches living in tents and shacks in fields outside the city would be glad of such victals. The Duke of York sent them naval biscuits crawling with weevils. They couldn't give those to their children so His Majesty has had to send for food from the country.'

Edmund lets her prattle on and does not try to listen.

'The broth is greasy,' he complains. How many times must he tell his housekeeper that fatty food makes him bilious.

'Your housekeeper is only trying to put a bit of fat on these bones,' the nurse says, patting his arm. She hands Edmund a chunk of bread. 'Pity the poor sailors who have to fight the French and the Dutch with a belly full of weevils.'

'What is that you say about the French and the Dutch?' Edmund asks, suddenly alert.

'Well, Mr Godfrey,' says the nurse, 'lying here, quietly in your bed, you won't have heard of the great rumour that was spread about lately: that fifty thousand Frenchmen had landed and were coming to cut Englishmen's throats and steal what few goods are left, and the Dutch landed too, in retaliation for their ships and the little town near Amsterdam, I forget what it's called, that our men burned in the summer...'

'What is that you say, woman? You talk too fast. The French landed? And the Dutch also?'

'Nay, nay, prithee don't upset yourself, sir, rest quietly,' the nurse says, seeing Edmund's disquiet, for he is trying to raise himself up by his elbows. 'Our enemies did not really come, but in the fields of St Giles and Moorfields and all around the city, men took up the call to arms with whatever weapons they could find amongst the rubble, and ran in search of foreigners and beat them and kicked them and dragged them to the magistrates and put them in jail, even though they'd lived here for years and London is their home. And His Majesty had to send his own guards and troops of soldiers to calm the people, for they believe that our foreign enemies started the fire, especially the French, being Catholics...'

'What?' cries Edmund, 'Men were fighting in the streets, say you?' He has not heard every word but clearly heard her talk of a call to arms, of weapons, soldiers and the French. 'London streets in turmoil, and I not there to keep the peace. John Grove, John Grove,' he shouts. 'Come upstairs instantly, if you please, and advise me what news my brothers did not see fit to tell me as I lay abed and in pain all these days.'

'I did not wish to alarm you, Mr Godfrey, really, sir, I did not,' the nurse pleads.

'Take your bowl and your tittle-tattle and let me be,' Edmund orders.

John Grove smiles, and sits beside the bed in the nurse's chair. 'It was all a little tempest in Queen Catherine's dish of tea.' He speaks slowly and clearly watching his friend's eyes the while, alert to his loss of hearing. 'Nothing serious, Edmund, no harm's done. All is quiet now. The King spoke to the people in their little makeshift hovels at Moorfields. "The judgement that has fallen upon London is immediately from the hand of God and no plots by Frenchmen, or Dutchmen or papists have any part in bringing you such misery," he told them. And he promised to defend them from any enemy and take care of them all. And they believed him. And so all was quiet again.'

'All quiet?' Edmund asks. 'What of the prisoners who fled when the iron bars of Newgate jail, thick as a man's wrist, melted like wax? I should be out on the streets keeping law and order and helping the destitute. Poor families who live in tenements beside the warehouses near Pudding Lane will surely have perished. How many have died in the fire?'

'Folk are fleeing the city in droves. Who's to say who is dead and who has gone to the country? There has been no bill of mortality for that week.'

Edmund remembers the little boy who screamed for his mother whilst the flames devoured his home. He cannot fool himself any longer. The child would never find his mother. She was inside that house, burning. And this the child knew. His voice trembles when he tells his friend how he lost the child.

'Human kindness will prevail,' says the lay brother, 'Some gentle soul will have taken him into her family, in charity.'

'I see very little kindness or charity in my line of duty,' Edmund says. 'Only felons.'

'You will find goodness in men's hearts, Edmund, if you

take time to seek it and it will cheer you to see it.' Grove speaks slowly and clearly watching his friend's eyes the while.

'What became of the King's baker, Farryner, at whose house the fire started?' Edmund asks.

'Farryner got his children out on the roof and saved them, but his maid died in the fire. She was afraid to climb so high.'

'Farryner must take the blame for the fire,' Edmund says severely.

'No one speaks ill of Farryner now, nor of your friend, Mayor Bludworth, and surely both are culpable. If the French and the Dutch did not cause the conflagration, our Catholics must take the blame. This is now the people's thinking.'

'Why the Catholics?' Edmund asks. 'If they find comfort in the old Roman ways what harm is done to anyone? Why should they wish to burn their own city?'

'Ah, but the people do not forget Guy Fawkes with his gunpowder and his dark lantern nor Queen Mary and the burning Protestant martyrs. In their eyes Catholics must always be plotting against our Anglican king to put a papist on the throne. King Louis would like this very much and he will join the papists in their plotting, so they say. And perhaps he would.' John Grove's fingers stroke the crucifix that hangs heavy and golden-bright from his rosary beads. 'English Catholic families are not interested in plots and politics. As you say, they only want their saints and their masses, their daily prayers and the comfort of the confessional.'

'My father loved to stay with the Jesuits at St Omer College when he travelled in France. They gave him peace when he was troubled in his mind.'

'Are you...' Grove hesitates. 'Are you troubled in your

mind, Edmund? These days of lying abed. Have they brought on your... your bad times?'

'Only that the uselessness of my endeavours against the might of the wind and the fire has saddened me. Only that. I am thankful that I have not awakened in daylight to find that all is darkness.'

'Surely the King's great honour to yourself will have cheered you mightily. Do not shake your head so, Edmund. Tell me you will accept. Of course you must. The good work that you do to keep the streets lawful and safe will be much enhanced by a knighthood.'

Grove thinks he sees the beginnings of a spark in his friend's eyes and the possibility of a faint smile. 'When you are a knight of the realm, Edmund, people of quality will support your call to duty.' He rises to depart just as the housekeeper gives a little knock at the door and pops her head around.

'Mr Edward Coleman is here to pay you a visit, sir. Shall I tell him to come another day when you're more rested and have partaken of a proper meal?'

'Let Mr Coleman come up for a while,' Edmund says.

'Now, here's a new convert to the Roman faith who would be zealous enough for a plot if one were brewing,' Grove says, when the housekeeper's footsteps can no longer be heard on the stairs.

'Do you warn me, Honest William?' Edmund asks, his voice tense and rather too loud.

The Jesuit lay brother puts a finger to his lips and takes his leave.

It pleases Edmund that Coleman does not enquire after his health. He is heartily sick of being asked if he is in pain, if he has eaten, of being told that he looks pale and ill, that he must rest, that he must not worry about London flattened and in ashes. Coleman is all smiles and charm and compliments, as usual, which is just what Edmund needs; he has a way of seeing the best of everything. An injury to his back from a heavy falling timber is just a setback. Edmund will recover sooner than he thinks. And the properties Edmund has lost in the fire? It is the tenant's responsibility to pay for rebuilding; Edmund will make good in the end, Coleman is sure of it. He perches on the edge of the bed.

'I will ask the Duke of York if we may take a look at the plans that Mr Wren and Mr Evelyn have both submitted for making London into a fine city, better than it was before. London will rise again, Edmund, London will rise.'

Edmund eases himself up against the bolsters and if his back pains him he is not aware of it. Edward Coleman's enthusiasm always grabs him, pulls him up from the sucking quicksand of despair towards his good work.

'Plans, say you? So soon?'

'Whose plans will be accepted has yet to be decided. They want to rebuild London with avenues, squares and piazzas. But, this will cost a great deal, and who will pay?'

Edmund shakes his head. 'Bah, the King has no money, Parliament has little more. Such grandiose schemes will never come to pass. What of the homeless poor, how do they fare?'

'The mayor and the aldermen expect great sums of money to come from the provinces for housing and feeding the poor. Already, the homeless have left the fields. They are clearing away the rubble and putting stakes in the ground to claim the land where their houses stood. They have begun building new homes upon the old foundations, even little shacks and sheds. Tradesmen have begun selling their wares from tents and booths, the Post Office has been set up in...'

'Why was I not told of this?' Edmund pulls back the blankets and groans as he tries to rise from his bed. 'Help me downstairs to my desk, Edward, if you please. I must write to The Stroker this instant, to request that he come and heal the pain in my back.'

'All in good time, Edmund. All in good time.' Coleman gently lifts Edmund against his bolsters and straightens the blankets. 'Your housekeeper will never allow me to cross your threshold again if I help you out of bed. Oh, I forgot to tell you: my dear wife sends her best regards and to hasten your recovery has bade me bring you jumble cakes, for the sugar, cream and new-laid eggs and the pound and a half of butter in this recipe will aid your digestion wonderfully, she has no doubt of it. She has fashioned them into pleasing little shapes, I know not what, and I have given them to your good woman downstairs with instructions to lay them upon plates and cook them carefully in the oven for just a little time, and to serve them freshly baked, the better for your enjoyment.'

'Pray, thank her for her kindness,' Edmund says.

Coleman laughs. 'I know you are not fond of such foods, Edmund. Your servants will enjoy them very much and my wife will feel that she has helped you to recover.'

'John Grove tells me that Catholics are being blamed for the fire.' As soon as the words leave his mouth Edmund regrets having spoken. How could he have been so lacking in tact? His young friend's dark, intelligent eyes fix upon him and he mutters words that Edmund cannot hear. He fasts too much, Edmund thinks. He's getting too thin. To look at him, you would not think of the sumptuous dinners he offers to the courtiers, judges and members of Parliament who are his house guests.

'Come closer, Edward, and tell me what is amiss,' Edmund cries.

'An idiot, Robert Hubert, son of a Rouen watchmaker, has confessed to starting the fire by throwing a fireball into the baker's house; says he was hired in Paris to do so. The fool did not step onto English soil until two days after the fire began. He was a Protestant when he set sail from France and did not convert to Catholicism until he was incarcerated here.'

'So, the Pudding Lane baker will be excused from blame whilst the mad, lying Frenchman will bring much fear to English Catholic families, including my friends and my dear cousin, Mary Gibbon,' Edmund says.

'Only bad will come of this for us, I'm sure,' Coleman says angrily. 'I know our king. I know his impotence against Parliament. How can he allow existing laws against Catholics to be ignored after such a confession? He will protect his Catholic mother, his Catholic wife, Catholics in his household, Catholic lords who are his friends, Catholic farmers who helped him escape from Worcester, but that is all. Parliament will revive the anti-Catholic laws and demand that justices put them into practice. Roman priests, and Jesuits like your friend, John Grove, will be forced into exile and your cousin Mary and all the other English Catholics will have to hide their crucifixes and their rosaries and worship in secret.'

Edmund sinks into his pillows and feels a great gloom coming upon him. 'You know that I believe that all men should be allowed to worship according to their faith, whether Anabaptists, Catholics, or Protestants, like myself. I will not seek out Catholics for punishment provided they are good, honest citizens.'

Coleman's voice rises. 'All of London blames Catholics for the fire.' His chest is heaving now, and his face is set hard with anger. 'They say we Catholics cackled like devils when the great bells of St Paul's melted and the leaded roof ran like a stream through the rubble. They say that the Queen Mother's Catholic chapel at Somerset House was saved from the hellfire of our torches. But I tell you this: King Charles was right when he told the people that the great fire was an act of God, for it began upon the Lord's Day. And I ask you this: why did God save the Catholic chapel but let the Anglican cathedral burn? England will become a Catholic country again, Edmund, according to the will of God. The true religion will…' Coleman sees Edmund's hand raised as if he were making an arrest.

'Hush Edward, your voice hurts my ears. It is not safe to speak of such things, even here, in the privacy of my own home.'

6

FOR THE LOVE OF
BEAUTIFUL THINGS
1668

Pepys finds Elizabeth in the dining room kneeling before Christ on the cross. 'This is the most beautiful painting you've ever bought, Samuel,' she says, and closes her eyes in prayer.

'Lord, but it has become the most dangerous possession I own,' he says. 'We must take care who sees it: people will think we are Catholics.'

'Will you read to me, tonight?' she asks, unperturbed, 'perhaps a little from the Mass book, like you used to do.'

Pepys had bought the book of the Mass several years ago, out of curiosity. He's interested in religion but that's as far as it goes. He's a Protestant, of course – what choice does a man have these days? – but it's obvious to him that the Anglican religion came out of Henry VIII's codpiece, and this is a witty comment to make at supper with friends. He can't remember when he last took Holy Communion but he likes a good sermon, although if there's work to do in the office on a Sunday he'll readily give church a miss.

'I'll read you something else,' he says, 'a play perhaps?'

She is stubborn. Tonight neither a comedy nor a tragedy will divert her: she must hear the Mass. Lord, but will she never cast off her Catholic upbringing — her education in a French convent?

'You were a Protestant when I married you,' he says bluntly. 'Your family were Huguenot Protestants when they fled France and came to England.'

'Please read the Mass, Samuel,' she says quietly. 'In my heart I will always be a Catholic and if I die before you, remember this: it is my wish to die in the Catholic faith.'

Lord, but why ever did I buy that crucifixion painting, Pepys muses, except that it is so beautiful that I can never part with it.

Pepys knows that he has a weakness for beautiful things – fine clothes, sweet music and pretty women – but of these three, only music can transport his soul. Singing, dancing, playing his wind instruments and his fiddle, Lord, but he thanks God for the Restoration of the monarchy. How he grieved for the loss of so much music in the republican years. Last February he took Elizabeth to see a rather indifferent play, *The Virgin Martyr*, by Massinger but nothing in the world could ever please him more than the music of the wind instruments as the angel came down. Little Nellie Gwyn played the angel who descended so beautifully bearing a basket of fruit, but it was the music of the wind instruments that ravished him and held sway over his very soul all night. It made him sick with love, just as he was when he fell in love with Elizabeth.

Sometimes Pepys goes to the King's chapel, not to pray, but to listen to the choir, and he has begun to go to Mass in the Queen Mother's Catholic chapel at Somerset House; the music here is far superior. He never takes the sacrament of course, neither does he pray: he just listens. What harm can that do to a man's reputation, so long as he goes to St Olave's Anglican church near his home now and then so that the vicar will remember him there.

7

BEYOND THE LOVE OF WOMEN
1668–1669

Since the fire, and his knighthood, people are always asking Edmund to do things he doesn't want to do. He never really wanted the knighthood and he has recently had the devil of a job refusing the office of sheriff. Then there are dinners and suppers and these invitations he cannot refuse, even though amidst the clattering of cutlery and crockery, the laughter and the raised voices, he can barely hear one word of what the man beside him is saying.

George Weldon has not stopped bragging since his wife was delivered of another lusty boy and now that she is up, she is prancing around the tavern with the baby in her arms smiling and pleading and Edmund has had a great to-do to refuse her. 'No, madam,' he says, 'pray, do not ask me again. I would not know what to do for the child, having no children of my own.'

Edmund can only conclude that Weldon is thinking of the prestige it will bring to himself, his wife and their new son to have a knight of the realm connected to their family.

'Weldon doesn't really know what he is asking,' he tells cousin Mary. 'Yes, he knows me to be a melancholy man, but a busy man in St Martin's vestry and the Commission of Peace. A man who dines with the Lord Chief Justice, the

Attorney General and the judges. A man with connections at the royal court, well known to the King and the Duke of York. He sees me as a businessman, a wealthy man, and I suppose he would expect a costly gift: silver spoons or a bowl or whatever men give on such an occasion.'

'Oh Edmund, can't you see that it is a great compliment that your friends have asked you to be godfather to their boy,' Mary says. 'Colonel Weldon and his lady will be sorely disappointed that you refused them.'

'I have no desire to be any kind of father. I am not fit for such responsibilities.'

'Oh Edmund,' Mary says, 'of course you are, that is why you have been asked.'

There is a cosiness here in his cousin's parlour that Edmund feels but does not understand. The overmantel cabinet is overfull of fussy china, shells, and little curios that women like to collect even though you can't see them all because there's not enough space. Thick sheets of badly coloured wallpaper depict scenes of women doing things they rarely do, like fishing in ponds, standing by fountains, or leaning against incongruous Greek columns whilst posing as shepherdesses. There's always sewing or knitting to be removed before he can sit on a chair, and pairs of stockings drying before the fire, and why does Captain Gibbon leave so many papers lying around when they should be tidied away? Yet Edmund likes to come here each week, and if he is prevented because of business or travel he is sorry for it and wonders if, without his cousin's company, he will manage to shake off the melancholy that is always waiting for him. For when the bad times come and neither walking the streets, nor suffering the ministrations of physicians or bloodletters and their leeches can lift his spirits, here, in this parlour with dear Mary, there is always some little relief. She listens, unlike most women; lets him talk and doesn't interrupt until he's finished.

Being here with his Catholic cousin, it's like being in the confessional, for the solace it brings to his soul.

'However could I make George Weldon's little son happy when my father's malady comes so suddenly and heavily upon me,' Edmund says. 'It is a great evil thing that smothers me and drags me away from myself and I fear that one day it will impel me to do the Devil's work and I will be impotent to prevent it. With such a legacy, how could I even think that I could do right by the child.'

'The Stroker did not cure you?' Mary asks sadly. 'After all our hopes?'

'My hearing was a little better, for a time, but as for the other matter, he never knew the worst. I didn't tell him everything – about my father – not about that terrible time when I was a little trembling child and...' Edmund pauses and wipes his mouth with his handkerchief several times before he continues. 'Oh, cousin, how could I tell him when it is painful for me to speak of it even in your dear company? He never really understood the malady he tried to stroke away. How could he ever understand it when I don't understand it myself?'

'You do not know that you will ever be as your poor father was,' Mary says.

'No, cousin,' Edmund says firmly, 'I do not know. And that uncertainty is a great canker that fills my soul. And if it is never to happen to me, only on my death day will I know this to be so.'

'Pray, do not talk so of your death; it grieves me to hear you speak so,' Mary says, alarmed. 'It bodes ill. Only God knows when that time will come for all of us. Think only of what you hope to do with the life God gave you. Come, tell me of your plans to travel to Ireland to visit your friend, The Stroker. It will cheer you to plan your journey.'

Edmund wipes his mouth again and shakes his head. 'I

have passed some of my business enterprises into the care of my nephew, Godfrey Harrison, and I must wait until I am confident that I may trust him to deal with my affairs in my absence.

***

To Valentine Greatrakes from Edmund Godfrey 12th February 1668:

> *I do intend, God willing, to disengage myself from my great encumbering employments, whereof I hope, if God permits, to have leisure and opportunity of coming and seeing you in Ireland within less than two years' time.*

Edmund has so much to write he doesn't know where to end. Valentine has written so enticingly of the peace and contentment of his country life in Ireland that it puts him in mind of Paradise. Surely, Edmund writes, Valentine's wife could never be as other women: another Eve tempted by the Devil into debauchery. She must be a miracle of miracles, a woman next in virtue to the Virgin Mary. His friend must never bring her to London, for the corrupt ways of that city and of Whitehall would enter her fancy and spoil her. He must keep her at home always, in her country innocence and enjoyments.

Edmund wants to be with Valentine. When he began his letter, twelve months or a little more didn't seem so very long to wait. Now, as his quill travels across the paper, he cannot wait. He was half staggered, he says, to read of Valentine's fears that he, Edmund, expects too much; that he might leave Ireland disappointed. He promises to snatch the moment and come to Valentine, all of a sudden, when the time is right, when business and duty permit.

He signs himself:

Your most affectionately united friend and servant next to the relation of a wife. Edmund Godfrey.

Edmund walks to the Post Office through streets of sickness. Everywhere, he sees poor souls blemished from smallpox who have left their beds to return to their work before their families starve. He cannot remember a time when the disease has been so rampant in London. Many families have lost their breadwinner and he resolves to give money to St Martin's vestry for the widows and children, as is his custom in times of need.

Edmund does not have to wait a year to visit his friend. Only months. In early summer he takes the coach along the Great West Road to Bristol. The Stroker is visiting the West Country for a month or so to perform his healing miracles.

During the journey Edmund opens his Bible at the second book of Samuel, chapter 1 verse 26, and reads David's lament for the death of Jonathan:

Thy love to me was wonderful, passing the love of women.

Early the following year, on 6th February, Edmund begins another correspondence to Valentine:

Most worthy honoured and good friend,
    Yours bearing the date the 8th of January was more welcome unto me than ever the most kind letter from an amoroso his mistress, there being such an established rooted & flourishing friendship in my heart & soul towards you beyond the love of women.

Part 2
The King's
Great Secret
1669–1671

"… but for the great secret, if it be not kept so till all things be ready to begin, we shall never go through with it…"

King Charles II (1669)

8

HOPE

MAY, 1669

Charles II to his sister, Minette, in Paris:

My wife has been a little indisposed some few days, and there are hopes that it will prove a disease not displeasing to me.

Catherine rests on her bed propped up with bolsters and lets her ladies fuss about her with dishes of tea and biscuits. Yesterday she vomited terribly and Charles was all concern and fetched towels from her closet and somehow managed to clean up the mess on the bed with his long, lace-fringed fingers, all the while keeping his spaniel bitch tucked under his arm to keep her from licking it up. Only when he was sure that Catherine had ceased her retching and he had told her in his low, musical voice – which she had loved from the very first time he had spoken to her – to ask for any little thing that she needed and to heed whatever the physicians advised, only then, did he call for her ladies to attend her. Oh, how tenderly he kissed her cheek and stroked her damp curls and promised to return to see how she fared.

She has not had *those* for weeks, not properly; just a little spotting of blood. She has gone almost as long before but this time it is different. She's never been so sick and she feels as if she carries a wonderful secret inside her, which is silly, because everyone at court knows that she has not bled for more than two months; probably, even the whole of England knows. And France too, where Charles' sister, Minette, who is married to King Louis' brother, is also with child. They are praying the same prayer to the same papier-mâché saints that Minette has sent to her from Paris shops: a prayer for a son for their husbands.

Catherine is sure that finally, her time has come. After all the disappointments – the babies who slipped away when they were no bigger than a fingernail, the hurt of seeing Charles loving his mistresses and their children, after all this unhappiness which has turned her pretty face puffy and sad – God and his saints have been merciful. In a few months she will present Charles with his firstborn legitimate son and heir, and the royal whores who breed like vermin will know that one day their sons and their daughters will have to make obeisance to her boy, the King.

Seven years ago, the cruel and beautiful Barbara, Lady Castlemaine, she with the sultry eyes and the arrogant manners, was carrying her second child for Charles when Catherine and her Portuguese ladies came to this foreign Protestant land where the water tastes like poison. Every bride dreads having *those* on her wedding night, and it had happened to her. While she cried herself to sleep, Charles spent their wedding night in Barbara's bed. And in the morning, Barbara flaunted her big belly in Catherine's face and laughed. Surely, soon, he will rid himself of this woman; she has grown old and is losing her looks. These last two years he's behaved differently with his women. He used to love only one at a time but these days he keeps two or three or even more and if they squabble he buys them pretty things to cheer them up or gives them tasty things to eat, as he does with his dogs.

Charles has always been kind to her, and she has learned to accept that she loves him, and he her, in a different way to his whores. He spent time teaching her to speak English in their early days and he likes to take her riding and to be with her for picnics and archery because he understands how much she enjoys these activities in his company. Catherine knows that she is special to Charles and not just because she's his wife and carrying the child that will continue the sacred royal bloodline from father to son. He has told her his Great Secret. A secret shared by people he trusts: his brother, his little sister Minette, and the French King. When the secret bursts, the English and their Parliament will know Charles for what he really is.

9

A WHIPPING

MAY, 1669

The first bailiff groans when the whip cracks on his back. The other closes his eyes and tries to take his punishment silently, but little yelps escape from deep inside his chest.

'We did as the justice commanded,' the first says when it is over and he is putting on his shirt. 'We could not refuse.'

'Where is Edmund Godfrey? Is he to be whipped?' the other asks. 'The fault is his. We were obliged to do our duty as he commanded. We could not say nay. I tried to tell him that it was against the law to make such an arrest and would anger His Majesty. He turned away. Refused to listen.'

'Aye, as is his habit,' the other replies. 'Godfrey hears what he wants to hear and pretends deafness when it suits him not to listen. And since he became *Sir* Edmund Godfrey it suits him to hear less and less.

'Find Edmund Godfrey and give him a whipping,' he tells the King's man who is cleaning blood from his whip with a bunch of straw.

***

'Is Edmund Godfrey a simpleton, or is he mad?' Charles says angrily. 'This meddling, Middlesex magistrate thinks he can arrest my physician for a paltry debt of thirty pounds for coals: a debt to himself. He has even tried to justify his actions to the judges and has persuaded my Lord Chief Justice to show some sympathy for his arguments.'

'Surely he is aware that our royal households are beyond the law,' James says.

'Mine is,' Charles replies pointedly.

James pinches his long nose. There's a strong whiff about his brother today that the odour of dog and perfume cannot hide: he's been playing with his pet fox again. 'I wonder at Edmund Godfrey's impudence,' he says, as he wafts his fashionable silk handkerchief about. 'Whatever was he thinking, to have his bailiffs arrest your physician and expect to get away with it?'

'Whitehall comes under his jurisdiction in the Commission of Peace,' Charles explains. 'He is our justice of the peace for the court and the palace and he supposes that he may dish out his accusations and make an arrest in my house as if I were a shopkeeper on Cheapside. Odd's fish! the pigheadedness of the man.'

Two years ago, Charles had entrusted Sir Alexander Frazier with the trepanning of Prince Rupert's skull. It was a tender operation, using the drill, because of his cousin's old war wounds. Last year, when his dear little sister Minette suffered a painful obstruction, he would not allow Monsieur, her husband, to summon a French physician to treat her and hastily dispatched Dr Frazier to Paris.

'Does Godfrey flout the law habitually, I wonder?' James asks.

'Shortly after the city burned he was summoned before the Commons Committee enquiring into coals and fuels, and found guilty, with other traders, of selling overpriced coals. As Master of the Woodmongers' Company, Godfrey took the blame. They were making a profit of around two shillings a bushel. He was filling his own pockets and those of his fellow coal merchants at the expense of the poor and he expected to get away with it. He tried to argue that the increased coal tax helped to fund the rebuilding of the city. The Woodmongers lost their charter but they remain a powerful company.'

James sniffs and wafts his handkerchief about again. 'Do you have to give that fox free run of the palace, Charles?' he asks. 'It stinks.'

'He's difficult to train. He's not like the spaniels, he doesn't come when he's called.'

'That's because he isn't a dog,' James says dryly.

'I understand from my Lord Chief Justice that Godfrey narrowly avoided being whipped last year whilst travelling in France,' Charles says. 'No doubt the man was poking his nose into matters that were none of his business. I very nearly had him whipped alongside his bailiffs last night.'

'You should have done,' James retorts. 'This is an arrogant magistrate who dictates matters to suit himself.'

'I find his manner very tiresome and strange, indeed I do,' Charles muses. 'My Lord Chief Justice has also brought to my attention a certain leniency Sir Edmund shows towards Catholics, fanatics, and other dissenters who worship otherwise than by the doctrines of the Anglican Church.'

'How very peculiar,' James says. 'Surely not a usual attitude for a justice of the peace.'

Charles strokes the spaniel that nuzzles up against his legs. 'Indeed, yet it seems that Edmund Godfrey and I have some theology in common. You know that when I was restored to the monarchy, I promised liberty of conscience for my people in matters of religion, but Parliament is not ready for this. I have been obliged to give a royal pardon to a congregation of Anabaptists in Aylesbury who were condemned to death. There were women amongst them. I couldn't let women climb the steps to the rope for wanting to worship in their own way, whatever the Protestant laws proscribe.'

'When we were children our mother taught us to practise Christianity in the Roman way, according to her faith,' James quietly reminds his brother.

'I am obliged to heed our martyred father's advice and say my prayers in the Anglican Church, because I am monarch of a Protestant country,' Charles says pointedly.

The spaniel has climbed onto his lap and is licking his face. James notices a twitching of the dark moustache and the beginnings of a smile working at the corners of his brother's mouth.

'Godfrey respects others' faiths. I like that,' Charles says. 'It reveals a tolerance, a kindness even, that is not incompatible with the duties of a justice. Odd's fish! but he is an odd fish of a man, don't you think, James? For sure, he is a brave man, remaining in London during the plague to assist the mayor. And remember how amazed we were to see him running up a wet, slippery ladder with a bucket of water to save a poor man's home from fire, taking no heed of his own safety. A gentleman with a strong sense of duty, I perceive. I like that in a man.'

'How shall you punish him?'

'Godfrey shall remain incarcerated in the porter's lodge whilst he considers the error of his ways. And he will forfeit his place on the Commission of Peace.'

'He won't like that.'

'Oh, he shall be reinstated to the Commission when I see fit. He is far too conscientious a justice to be absent for many years, but I shall not tell him so. I shall let him brood upon the error of his ways. My Lord Chief Justice and the judges must go promptly to their friend, tell him of my high displeasure, and try to talk some sense into the man.'

***

Edmund refuses food and drink, even though cousin Mary has brought pies and jellies and he is nauseous with hunger and faint with thirst. He sits at his table, straight and proud in his big stiff collar and his new itchy wig. He was right to arrest Sir Alexander Frazier. He will do so again if he finds another of the King's people refusing to pay their debts. And he will starve himself to make his point. It is his duty to suffer for the cause of the people; the law must be obeyed by all, even people of quality, even the King's friends. He will show King Charles that his disregard for the law is not to be tolerated.

When he is told of the King's decision to put him out of the Commission of the Peace, Edmund has nothing to say.

***

At Edmund's home near Charing Cross, a maid polishes the great silver drinking vessel, all eight hundred ounces of it, which His Majesty presented to him upon his knighthood. His clerk and his nephew, young Godfrey Harrison, are working in the office. The two of them almost fill it up what with two big writing tables, the little truckle bed for the clerk and a mule chest overflowing with long scrolls of legal documents.

The clerk opens an account book and points to figures in pounds, shillings and pence. 'Sir Edmund put you in charge of the business,' he says. 'He expected you to make a good profit but it seems that large sums of money have vanished into the air like candle smoke.'

Edmund's nephew is defiant. 'There were debts when I took over the accounts. Uncle Edmund knew this. The business was already suffering from the loss of his London properties in the fire, and the price of coals was fixed lower than he wanted.'

'Yes we know all this,' the clerk says with derision. 'Sir Edmund brought you into the business to help put things right.'

'The Dutch fleet sailed up the Medway, destroyed three of the King's ships and towed away the *Royal Charles*, the pride of the navy, the vessel that had brought King Charles home from exile,' young Harrison retorts, 'and in the process they damaged the saltworks in which Uncle Edmund had invested money for himself and Mr Greatrakes. What was I supposed to do about that? I have worked hard with what little training my uncle saw fit to give me before he applied himself to other matters, leaving me to make shift in his affairs as best I could. He is never around to give me advice. He spends his time wandering around the streets all day and most of the night, amongst vagrants, footpads, sodomites and whores. Goodness knows what he's up to with those kind of people past midnight, I don't.'

'Sir Edmund's duties for the Commission of Peace are not confined to the quarter sessions…'

Young Harrison cuts him short. 'And then there's his politics.'

'What politics?' The clerk slams the account book shut and stares at young Harrison.

'Anti-French,' says the nephew, 'he's a fanatic, like Uncle Michael, only perhaps maybe a little less so, or maybe more, for all I know.'

'Nay,' the clerk says, 'Sir Edmund's politics are local: St Martin's vestry, the poor, that sort of thing.' He opens another book and after a great deal of tut-tutting and mumblings of losses, continues to check through the figures.

'Think what you like,' says young Harrison. 'I know what I know about my uncle's politics; and then there's his business dealings with the Duke of York on behalf of his friend Mr Greatrakes who wants to acquire lands and properties in Ireland. Everybody knows the Duke is a closet Catholic, but Uncle Edmund doesn't seem to mind.'

10

MAKING AMENDS
SPRING AND SUMMER, 1669

Pepys is giving Elizabeth a home she should have been proud to show off to her friends. Lord, but it is has cost him a fortune to have the whole house newly decorated in the latest fashion. After all the weeks of dust and dirt the plasterers and upholsterers had almost finished their work when his marriage hit the lowest place it had ever been.

'Of all the false rotten-hearted rogues in the whole world, I married the worst,' Elizabeth cries, all day, every day.

She should have been dancing from room to room laughing, throwing her arms around him, telling him what a wonderful husband he is to have provided so well for her. She should have been so excited about inviting their friends to come for suppers, for music, for dancing. But he found her sobbing by the new hangings in the dining room, ranting at him in the blue room and lying in her dirty clothes upon the new bed in the best chamber. She is filthy, never having washed since that terrible day when she discovered him with the maid doing what they shouldn't have been doing.

She has taken no pleasure at all in the hanging of his pictures, except for the crucifixion painting, which has turned into an excuse for declaring, yet again, just to worry him, 'I'm a Roman Catholic; I've received the Holy Sacrament.' Nearly every night, she puts a candle in the chimney and wakes him, ranting on and on about his unfaithfulness. How can he tell her that it is not his fault that he fell in love with her maid? What man wouldn't welcome a pretty girl about the house whose breasts have begun to swell; a good-humoured girl who combs his hair and dresses him of a morning ready for the office; who blushes when he sneaks a kiss while his wife lies abed in pain with toothache and a swollen cheek? Lord, but he's no worse a husband than the King, and Queen Catherine doesn't seem to mind so much, but this has brought him the greatest sorrow he has ever known in his whole life.

He has had no choice but to confess everything, to his shame. Still, there is no peace at home. For weeks nothing has cheered Elizabeth: not even Easter Day, when they drove out in their new coach in St James' Park for the first time; not even the Duke of York eyeing her mightily and smiling, and why shouldn't he? She's a pretty woman and Pepys has always loved to show her off to his friends. On May Day she seemed to be a little happier, excited about setting out in their coach again with their two new fine black horses with green reins, and their manes and tails tied with red ribbons. She was up early and dressed in her best flowered tabby silk gown, two years old, but hardly worn at all, and very prettily laced for this occasion. She told him to wear his new silk suit with gold lace at the bands. He'd never worn gold lace before and was embarrassed to be so blatantly showing off his wealth: what he, a *prick louse,* a poor tailor's son, driving out dressed like a lord?

The outing was not a success.

'There are too many hackney coaches. Why do they have to be painted bright yellow, with those garish red wheels?' she moaned. 'Gentlemen's coaches, like ours, cannot be properly viewed for all this traffic.'

When they alighted to refresh themselves and take

syllabub she whined that the wind would spoil her topknot and the drizzle would spoil their clothes.

These days she complains about everything. It's because she's unhappy. Pepys understands this and knows that it is all his fault for being a bad husband. It's a great sadness for both of them that she has never borne a child, and every month Elizabeth takes to her bed, miserable with disappointment and pain, but the shock of discovering his infidelity has caused her more misery than ever before and he wonders if she will ever forgive him. There's one last thing he can do to cheer her, to show her that he can play the good husband. What a wonderful surprise he has for her, if only the Duke of York will allow it.

'The Duke was all kindness,' Pepys tells Elizabeth. 'I told him all about the pain in my eyes when I write by candlelight and how red and watery my eyes have become. He wanted to know what remedies I'd tried so I told him about the green spectacles, the paper eye roll for reading, the special silver candlestick to keep the light from my eyes, even the optical water from the King's own apothecary. He was surprised that none of these had any good effect but was most sympathetic and straightaway went to find the King and they agreed to me being absent from the office for several months to rest my poor eyes.'

'Well,' says Elizabeth, who is fiddling with a heap of ribbons in her lap. 'That was kind of them both. Whatever will you do with yourself without the office to keep you busy?'

She's thinking that I'll be running after the little maid, Pepys thinks, seeing the sulky look on her face. He's planned a wonderful surprise for her and she won't even look at him. Well, so be it. He'll tease her awhile.

'I'm going on a journey.' He waits for her response. There is none. Elizabeth has not even glanced at him.

'Where are you going?' she asks at last, in a rather bored tone.

'To Holland on naval business. And from there to other places. Paris, maybe,' he adds, as if Paris were Southwark or Greenwich, nowhere particularly exciting.

'Whatever will you find to do in Paris to please the King and his brother?' she asks. 'There are no shipyards there.'

'Oh, but I shall have my wife for company,' Pepys says, and she runs to him, ribbons and all. Her arms are around his neck and ribbons of every colour are falling around his shoulders like rainbows. Lord, but if they were black or white, he'd have thought he was in mourning.

'I shall need new clothes,' Elizabeth says.

'Of course you shall.'

'Shall I take you to see the house where I grew up and the convent where I was taught by the nuns?' she asks.

'Yes, there will be time to do everything you wish, but remember this: our vacation is a secret. You must tell your friends only that we are going into the country.'

'Why so?'

'My purpose in Holland is to secretly observe their shipyards.'

'Ah, so my husband has become a spy.'

'Who better to assess the state of the Dutch vessels?'

'What about King Louis?' Elizabeth asks with a cheeky grin. 'Will we go to the French court to discover his secrets?'

'Oh, there's no need for that,' Pepys replies, with a wry smile, and a wink, 'but hush, not a word of this to anyone.'

11

SECRETS AND SADNESS
SUMMER, 1669

<u>6th June.</u>
Charles II to his sister Minette, in Paris:

> *… but for the great secret, if it be not kept so till all things be ready to begin, we shall never go through with it and destroy the whole business.*

Pepys knows all about the King's secret, how could he not when he rubs shoulders with the Duke of York and the great lords who are close to the King. A few weeks earlier he had written in his diary of an offer of an enormous sum of money from King Louis to buy Charles' break with the Dutch. Charles is greatly tempted to take the money, thereby being out of necessity of calling Parliament again. Lord, but it will make Parliament mad, for how will His Majesty spend the money except to wanton his time in pleasures?

<u>7th June.</u>
Charles sits at his desk by candlelight writing to Minette. He will only send such a letter by a messenger he can trust, and the elderly Catholic Lord Arundel, he knows to be devoted to him. Even so, he uses a cypher as he writes. It is enough, he tells his sister, that the French ambassador

should be acquainted with the friendship between himself and King Louis without knowing the real reason why:

> *...remember how much the secret in this matter imports, and take care that no new body be acquainted with it till I see what Lord Arundel brings me in answer to his propositions and pray let the ministers in France speak less confidently of our friendship than I hear they do, for it will infinitely discompose Parliament.*

He finishes his letter with sad news of Queen Catherine.

> *I have no more to add, but to tell you that my wife, after all our hopes, has miscarried again without any visible accident. The physicians are divided whether it were a false conception or a good one, and so good night, for 'tis late.*
> *I am entirely yours. CR*

There is gossip around the court that Catherine's miscarriage was brought on when she was startled by his pet fox running into her bedchamber, jumping onto the bed and scrambling over her face. Charles hopes that this rumour has not found its way across the channel. He will be ashamed if his sister hears of it. This time he did not trouble to ask the doctors if his wife is likely ever to bear an heir for him. He knows the answer they will give, if they are honest.

12

PIGEONS AT HER FEET

OCTOBER, 1669

After two months on the Continent Pepys was ready to go home. His eyes were much improved and there was no real reason to stay. He was anxious to get back to the office: Lord knows what had happened in his absence. There was also the upcoming election in Aldeburgh, Suffolk. The Duke of York had recommended that he stand for Parliament and he needed to be there to speak with the electors. No one could do that for him better than he himself. He knows his powers of oratory are beyond the skill of most men. He's always been a good talker; persuasive, making his point succinctly. Also, he's entertaining, people like listening to him; he can easily persuade men to vote for him.

Elizabeth had loved being in Paris. They climbed to the top of the Tour Saint-Jacques and saw the whole city below and she was so excited; pointing out to him the streets where she grew up. He'd allowed her to visit the nuns in the convent where she was taught as a child and she was delighted that her brother was able to join them for the last few weeks. They'd strolled across the pretty Pont-Neuf bridge and thought that, by comparison, London Bridge was far too crowded with houses. How Pepys had loved the bookshops, the galleries, the libraries. How Elizabeth had loved walking in the parks and gardens of Paris where ladies and gentlemen of quality paraded in the latest fashions. Lord, but it had been a holiday full of contentment and as he afterwards recalled, in his wretchedness, excellent health for both of them. His colic had hardly bothered him at all.

On the journey home Elizabeth was taken ill. When their carriage arrived at their home on Seething Lane, she was burning with fever and went straight to bed. The physicians tried everything but still the fever burned. After three weeks, in desperation they cut off her hair and put pigeons at her feet. These remedies had worked well for the Queen when she had been dangerously ill, but not for Elizabeth.

No one's prayers could save her life. Lord, but for evermore Pepys will wonder whose prayers saved her eternal soul. She had wanted to die in the Catholic faith but what choice does a man have these days but to have his wife buried in an Anglican church?

He lost the election of course, being unable to present himself to the electors at Aldeburgh. His bereavement has numbed him: his body and his mind. It will be weeks before he will feel able to return to the office. Elizabeth was only twenty-nine and she had fought for three weeks to stay alive. Pepys can hardly bear to unpack the souvenirs she brought back from their vacation – a few precious stones, embroidery wools and French books.

Oh, the frailty of human life: how readily the body surrenders.

13

SEDITION

NOVEMBER, 1669

The jailer of the Gatehouse Prison asks Edmund who he has come to visit. 'A prisoner who came before you accused of felony, Sir Edmund?' he asks, and begins to make his way through to where petty criminals await their trials.

'Take me to the place where state prisoners lie,' Edmund replies. 'I need to speak with one, Richard Adams, a lawyer.'

'He who is accused of speaking seditious words?' the jailer asks. 'Well, come this way, sir.'

The meeting is brief. Edmund sees that Adams has a good fire and a clean shirt. He can afford hot dinners and wine.

'Prithee, speak for me with my Lord Chief Justice, I beg of you,' Adams pleads.

Edmund nods. 'You know that I am no longer in the Commission of Peace and have less influence than I used to. I will do what I can but I make no promises.'

'Many men think as I do about the King and the Duke of York but they are not indicted,' Adams says petulantly.

'We do not speak our minds where we will be overheard,' Edmund retorts. 'You are a lawyer; you know the consequences of what you have said. You must learn discretion or others will be indicted. I have told you before, the King and his secretaries have their spies everywhere: in coffee houses, taverns and clubs and their ears itch for republicans at their plotting. Packets are intercepted at the Post Office. Codes are broken. Many letters never reach their destinations. When you write to your friends who share our opinions, use an alias, as I do, and only hint at the matter you communicate.'

'Trust me, Sir Edmund, if I come to trial I will name no names. But I will not give up the cause. Tell the others so. We did not welcome the Stuart King back from exile to do King Louis' bidding, to spend French money on mistresses and horse racing, and to allow the Dutch to destroy our fleet. Our country was in better hands with Oliver.'

'Indeed, but control your anger until the time comes to use it wisely,' Edmund charges the lawyer, and departs.

14

A FAMILY REUNION

MAY–JUNE, 1670

Pepys wonders why he has come. He's sure to catch cold. His mourning clothes are sodden. The rain is dripping from his hat, and the white silk weepers dangling from the brim are whipping across his face with every gust of wind. His black woollen stockings are soaking through to the costly silk ones underneath and they will be ruined. Already, he feels a sore throat coming on from fires on the beach where farmers are burning seaweed to make ashes for their fields. Lord, but he would have thought they would leave off their noxious burning out of respect for His Majesty. He regrets his decision to wear his periwig which hangs soggy and burdensome about his neck, despite his wide brimmed hat. It is as well that he has taken out an agreement with his barber to keep his wigs in good order for twenty shillings a year, for it will stink mightily of smoke by the end of the day.

He watches the King escort his sister up the steep hill to Dover Castle followed by his brother, their cousin Prince Rupert, and all the rest of the English and French entourage. How dissimilar they are, Charles and Madame, Duchesse d' Orléans: the brother, strong featured, some might even say ugly – although women seem to like him – and over two yards tall without allowing for the huge ostrich plumes in his high hat. Beside him, the little sister, pale and pretty, hardly reaches his shoulder. Charles seems very fond of her, even though they haven't met for many years. He has his arm around her waist and keeps bending down to kiss her cheek; he cannot stop himself.

It always cheers Pepys to look at a comely woman. He first saw Madame in Queen Henrietta Maria's presence chamber, ten years ago, when she was a princess of England, a few months after King Charles was restored to his throne, and he thought Elizabeth to be much handsomer than the little princess. He had allowed her to wear one or two black patches on her face for the occasion, and she couldn't stop smiling, so joyful was she to be there, standing behind the Queen Mother's chair in her best clothes, with her new white lacy whisk pinned to her topknot. She had wanted to visit St Cloud while they were in France, for a public audience with Madame and Monsieur and when Pepys cut short the vacation she had been sorely disappointed.

When they have done with the business of drawing up the treaty that is supposed to be secret – pity the poor Dutch with England and France allied against them – the royal party are going to enjoy themselves on board the royal yacht. Why such merriment? It is indecent. Little old Henrietta Maria died last September in France. The King and his brother and sister are supposed to be mourning their mother.

His Majesty plans to take his sister to Canterbury and has brought his own musicians for her pleasure. The King likes French music: violins, something to make him tap his foot. The royal brothers and their sister all love music, as Pepys does. The King sings a most pleasant bass and the Duke plays the guitar more than tolerably well, which has encouraged His Majesty to send an Italian master to Paris to instruct his sister in the instrument. In Canterbury, there's to be a ballet to entertain Madame, and dancing of course, in the fashionable French style.

Pepys has told the Duke that he may not be able to follow the court to Canterbury. Made some excuse about work, the office. He will be sorry to miss an opportunity to hear the royal musicians, and he is mightily tempted to attend the royal party but he's not sure that he will be able to listen to music without tears. Not yet. He wonders if he will, ever again. He hasn't played his flageolet or his fiddle in months so distracted is he by sorrow and the suddenness of his bereavement. He tries to cheer himself by looking at the young French ladies following Madame; one of them is remarkably pretty with little curls dangling onto her plump cheeks. Each time grief threatens to overcome him, if his new lady friend, Mary Skynner, is not nearby to comfort him, a good conversation usually helps to divert his thoughts. Pepys turns to a tall, stooping gentleman standing beside him.

'Ah, Sir Edmund, good day to you. I believe we have met before, at dinners and suppers, but have never been properly introduced. I'm Samuel Pepys, secretary to the Naval Office.'

Pepys recalls writing of an incident in his diary, a year ago. This is the bold justice who was dismissed from the Commission of Peace because he had the effrontery to arrest the King's physician because he owed him money for coals.

'Pleased to meet you,' Godfrey replies but he doesn't look pleased, with that sorrowful and somewhat foreboding look on his long face.

'The weather has not been kind for Madame's visit, Sir Edmund,' Pepys says, tipping the rain out of his wide hat brim.

'The weather? Indeed, it could not be worse.'

'Good weather for tailors: clothes of quality are not suited to heavy rain,' Pepys remarks, remembering the cutting room at the top of his father's tailor's shop near Fleet Street, where he lived as a boy. 'My late wife ruined her flower tabby gown in the drizzle and it cost me twenty pounds to buy her new clothes.' She always does this, Elizabeth: almost every day she slips into conversations, even though she's gone. Godfrey looks perplexed. I should not talk about my bereavement so much, Pepys thinks. People are embarrassed. They don't know what to say.

'I dare say sailors do not mind getting wet, being used to storms at sea,' Godfrey says of a sudden, and rather too loud in Pepys' ear.

'His Majesty and his sister are unlucky. In an English summer, good weather is always a matter of chance,' Pepys says.

'What is that you say, sir? Good weather? In France? I hear King Louis awaits in Dunkirk. He sends his people across in boats to see how the King and Madame are getting along.'

To see how the secret Treaty of Dover is getting along, more like, Pepys thinks. Being so close to the Duke of York, he hears things; you do, if you put yourself in the way to discover them.

'What is that you say?' Godfrey asks. 'Forgive me, Mr Beeps, I have been afflicted with a little deafness all my life, and amongst these crowds, and the rain and the wind, it is difficult for me to hear what you say.'

'Sir, I am sorry for your affliction, indeed I am,' Pepys replies. 'You have my sympathies. I have been sorely troubled with my eyes these last months and I fear that I may be going blind. I used to keep a diary but no longer do so, for it has been the undoing of my sight every time I take a quill into my hand: the black ink upon the white paper dazzles my eyes.' Pepys begins to tell Sir Edmund of the operation he had, years ago, to be cut of the stone in his bladder, but he can see by the blankness of his face that Sir Edmund has not heard much of what he has said. Best to change the subject, use fewer words and speak slowly.

'Will you follow the court to Canterbury, Sir Edmund?' he asks.

'Perhaps I may, although maybe, whilst I'm in Dover, I may take the opportunity to cross the Channel to Calais for a day or two, if the storm abates. A short voyage always does one good.'

It didn't do Elizabeth any good, Pepys reflects. 'Good day to you, Sir Edmund,' he says, 'enjoy your journey.'

'Good day to you Mr Beeps.'

Pepys – Beeps – France – chance – tailor – sailor, Pepys chuckles to himself. A poet could make a mighty pleasant ballad from Sir Edmund's misunderstandings. He wanders away to seek someone with whom he might share more engaging and witty discourse.

'I've never got on well with jovial, chubby-faced men who talk too much,' Edmund tells his brother, Michael, while they dry themselves by the fireside at their inn. 'He was far too cheerful for a man in mourning. It was obvious from the white ribbons dangling from his hat that a female relative has recently died, probably his mother.'

'What was his name, this clerk from the Navy Board?' Michael asks.

'Beeps.'

'Oh, you mean Samuel Pepys. I know of him,' Michael says. 'He took his wife on a journey to Europe and upon their return she was taken ill and died. Did he speak of King Louis and the French?'

'I heard him speak of his eyes and his bladder, but little else amongst the hubbub of the crowd. I should have recommended that he call upon Valentine Greatrakes when the healer is next in London.'

'You should have asked him what he knows of the King and the French,' Michael says severely. 'What a wasted opportunity. If you chance upon him again, court his friendship. A loose-lipped man like that, in daily contact with the Duke of York, could be made to be somewhat indiscreet with a little coaxing.'

Edmund dismisses Michael's advice with a wave of his kerchief and wipes his mouth several times. 'He will not want my friendship until the King restores me to the Commission of Peace.'

'The King will reinstate you sooner rather than later if you ask your friends who have his ear to intercede for you. The Lord Chief Justice will readily put in a good word. Learn to use your friends for your own gain, and for goodness sake, Edmund, put that wretched cloth away. This damned habit of yours is getting worse and it is most distracting.

'We need to discover what is going on between Charles and Louis,' Michael continues. 'The French King has no need to be wasting his time in Dunkirk if Madame's visit is only a family affair. He would doubtless be in his palace at Versailles, at his pleasure. I have no doubt that our king and his brother are conspiring with Louis, and that Madame is the ambassador for England and for France. The Duke of York is a church Catholic, you know, of course, Edmund. He does not go to the Anglican church, except at Easter. It is no secret.'

'The Duke must worship according to his own con-science.' Edmund turns his back on his brother goes to sit on the settle. He occupies himself flicking through the pages of his rather soggy pocketbook.

'The Duke should remember that he is the sole heir of a Protestant country,' Michael says and goes to sit beside him. He speaks fiercely and slowly, face to face with Edmund to make his meaning clear. 'Listen Edmund, look at me. Hear what I say. Louis is up to something, of this I have no doubt. He is wealthy, whilst Charles cannot even afford to feed his sailors. Some of the menial servants at Whitehall Palace have not received a farthing in wages since the Restoration, did you know that, Edmund? Louis is able to give Charles all the money he needs for his whores and his horses at Newmarket, even, should he desire it, the cost of disbanding the English army, and for Louis it will be like throwing pennies to a beggar. I don't doubt that they are plotting something. Your friend Edward Coleman is often in York's company. Speak to him, Edmund, discover what he knows.'

Edmund wipes his mouth again and looks away. He has no list to talk of treason in this public tavern where any pot boy or maid could be listening at the door.

'You must discover what Coleman knows,' Michael says. 'For God's sake, Edmund, look at me, and listen. Can you not see what harm an alliance with France, with Catholics, will do to our country, our Parliament, our businesses?'

'Edward Coleman boasts that it is he who converted York into the Catholic faith,' Edmund says, matter of fact.

'The vanity of the man,' Michael exclaims. 'York's mother converted her little son when he was a child in skirts, and unlike his older brother, he has not grown out of it.'

'Coleman covets a position in York's service and would travel to France as his ambassador.' Edmund regrets offering this bit of information as soon as the words are out of his mouth. It will only fuel his brother's anger.

'If your friend can charm his way into that position, which I doubt not, we will soon get to know what is brewing between Charles and Louis,' Michael says. 'With very little encouragement from you, Edmund, he will boast of the important business he conducts. The man has no common sense.'

A serving girl comes to set steaming dishes upon the

table. They take their places and Michael dismisses her. No, they want no more ale and they will serve themselves, thank you kindly, but please to ask his wife to come to dinner, when she is ready.

'It is your duty to ask questions,' Michael tells Edmund, and puts a large slice of pasty onto his plate.

Edmund helps himself to stewed carp and salmon. 'Coleman is very intense about his Catholicism and his politics. I will ask no questions of him because I do not wish to know the answers and there's an end to it. No, do not push me upon this matter. You know that I will turn away if I do not like what Coleman says.'

'And if he should write to you, after he succeeds in acquiring this position of confidentiality with York that he so covets, what will you do about his letters? His letters full of self-aggrandisement, for make no mistake, Edmund, Coleman will waste no opportunity to inform his friends of his achievements in the Catholic King's court. You may pretend not to hear when it pleases you, but the letter in your hand, the written word before your eyes, these surely, you cannot deny, and you must do your duty accordingly.'

Edmund uses the excuse of his sister-in-law's entrance to leave his seat and his brother's unwelcome conversation and escort her to the table.

15

TWO SISTERS
JUNE, 1670

Catherine finds Minette alone, lying on her bed in her shoes and dancing clothes. Her sister-in-law has been so lively since she arrived in England, with her love of music and her excitement at seeing her brothers after ten years apart, it is such a shock to see her tonight, so thin and ill, her complexion as white as when she disembarked, seasick, at Dover.

'We have worn you out with our chatter and our entertainments,' she says. 'The banquets, the gavottes, the minuets, and the Duke's Company with their comedies, making us laugh until we are exhausted. Let me fetch your ladies to prepare you for bed.'

'No, no, not yet. I cannot bear to have them fussing about me.' Minette reaches out to take Catherine's hand. 'Come, sit with me while I lie quietly to ponder over these last happy days so that every minute will stay in my memory to cheer me when I am returned to my husband, as indeed I must, although most unwillingly, as Charles knows.'

Minette speaks her native English with a heavy French accent. Her letters to Charles are always written in French because her English is so poor. You wouldn't think that her father had been a king of England. She is very beautiful with her bright intelligent eyes and her fine straight nose. And being so much the French Madame, with a little bit of the coquette, in a teasing way, it just adds to her charms. Catherine has felt obliged to use more cosmetics than usual: a little white paste to hide the dark shadows below her eyes; blue crayon on her lids to give her eyes a sparkle; Spanish paper to put a flush on her cheeks. And when she smiles, she has to remember to open her mouth only a little to hide her buck teeth.

'I wanted to thank you for all the little things you have sent to me from Paris and to tell you, one last time, how very pleased I am that we are together at last,' Catherine says.

'It must be hard for you, poor dear sister, a Catholic, living in a Protestant country. England is so different from your home in Portugal. The English do not take kindly to foreign queens, especially if they are Catholics. But they like you,' Minette adds hurriedly. 'The people have taken you into their hearts. Charles has told me so.'

'Charles is forever kind. He has given me Somerset House, and the Chapel there, which was your mother's.'

'I miss her.' Minette's lower lip trembles. 'We were very close. The horrible murder of my father made it so.'

'Let me make you more comfortable.' Catherine slips off Minette's shoes and removes the heavy earrings cascading with three long pearls. It takes some time for her to untangle the wired frame which supports the long ringlets of false hair mingling with Minette's own tight curls which dangle in bunches on either side of her head.

'I am too tired to have my maids put in my curl papers tonight. They will have to do their best with the tongs, tomorrow,' Minette says, letting her chestnut tresses fall across the pillows.

Catherine has noticed how little her sister-in-law has eaten these last days. She questioned Minette's maids in secret, and the pretty young one with the chubby cheeks confessed that Madame had taken nothing, only milk, on the journey through France to Flanders with Monsieur and King Louis, and Monsieur had told Madame that she looked so ill she had not long in this world, an astrologer having recently told him that he would have many wives.

'I fear you are unwell, dear sister,' she says. 'I shall summon Charles' physician.'

'Oh no, no, I pray you, do not trouble Charles, for he worries so already and is miserable that we must part tomorrow. It is merely the sadness of leaving that wearies me. The Lord only knows when Monsieur will allow me to visit my brothers again. He is the most jealous of husbands. He tried to make me pregnant again to prevent my coming, but thank God I am not.'

Catherine blushes and looks away. When fruitful women talk like this, as if having babies is as easy as growing roses in the garden every summer, she feels dried up, barren. Charles no longer expects that they will have a child. Minette has been married for nine years, just a little longer than Catherine. She has miscarried once and has two daughters. Catherine has heard gossip that when her first child was born she was so disappointed that it was not a boy, she told her maids they might as well throw it out of the window. She gave her husband a baby son for a short while until the infant died, but another son will follow, surely. There is plenty of time: Minette is not yet twenty-six.

'It was kind of King Louis to allow you to stay for longer than planned,' Catherine says, to change the subject.

'My brother-in-law is a generous man when he has got what he wants, and Charles signed the treaty,' Minette replies. 'And, yes, he is very kind. He was very, very good to me in those early days. Monsieur could hardly wait to marry me when I was a girl living at the French court. Louis willingly gave his blessing to our union and Charles too.

I thought Monsieur Philippe to be so handsome with his big eyes full of tears when he declared his wish to have me for his wife. Our courtship was sweet, and short, and all the while he couldn't stop looking at me, and kissing me. I did not know then that what he really likes is to mingle amongst ladies wearing feminine attire, the better to attract the attention of the gentlemen and be admired by them. And one gentleman in particular, more beautiful than any woman, held great sway upon him even before we were wed: le Chevalier de Lorraine. But I will not speak of him, for you will not wish to hear it.

'Before two weeks of marriage had passed, my husband's love for me had turned into fierce jealousy of every man who looked at me, and Louis, seeing my loneliness...' Minette giggles and her pale face flushes. 'He became rather more than a brother, for a while. I suppose Charles has told you everything, there are no secrets between us.'

Catherine doesn't like to hear Minette talk like this. She shakes her head and tries not to listen.

'Louis has a way of looking at a woman that makes her melt. He doesn't need to say anything; he seduces her with his eyes, and those lips of his, always pursed as if ready to kiss... and I was so very young, and lonely, and miserable, and spurned by my new husband who was really in love with le Chevalier...'

Catherine wants to stand, make some excuse to leave, but Minette is still holding her hand. 'Oh dear,' she falters. She doesn't know what else to say. These Stuarts, how unchaste they are. The sister is even more shocking than the brothers and their mistresses.

'There was a time when...' Minette giggles again, 'the Comte de Guiche, how shall I say... he wanted both of us, myself and my husband, to be his valentines – and it wasn't February – so it wasn't just for fun.'

'I must summon your maid to prepare you for bed. You have a long journey tomorrow,' Catherine says firmly.

'Monsieur will be glad to have me back within his eyesight and Louis will be pleased to see me, and delighted with the Treaty of Dover. Oh, Catherine,' Minette declares, 'how clever we have been, the three of us, Charles, myself and Louis, and you of course, dear sister, to hide the Great Secret inside the treaty, like a nutmeg inside the mace. If our enemies or Charles' Parliament come looking, they might find the Treaty of Dover, which is privy and shocking enough, especially to the Dutch, but the real secret will be safe.'

'Yes, until the time comes to reveal it,' Catherine adds. 'Charles is determined that the time must be right, and this Louis knows.'

Minette hugs Catherine. 'Oh how well we have done, you and I, to persuade Charles to agree to it.'

Catherine knows that it is Minette who has done the persuading. Charles has begun to speak of it as the Treaty of Madame.

'And one day soon,' Minette whispers, 'Louis will be so happy because England will once more be…'

'Hush, sister, say no more. I hear footsteps.'

The little Breton maid who comes to tend to Minette has been crying.

'What is amiss, Louise, ma chérie?' Minette asks.

'Am I to remain here, Madame, or return with you to the French court?' she asks sulkily.

'Why, Louise, you will sail with me tomorrow,' Minette says sweetly. 'Why ever should you not?'

'Madame, you know that His Majesty, the King of England, has asked for me,' the girl replies, glancing slyly in Catherine's direction.

'His Majesty, the King of England, had no right to ask. You are too young; I told him so.'

The girl stamps her foot and Minette laughs. 'Whatever will your parents say if I tell them I've left you behind to be my brother's whore?'

'Dear Charles is such a one for the ladies. I knew he would like Louise with her baby face, and her curls and her chubby cheeks, and the way she narrows her eyes so enticingly when she is petulant,' she tells Catherine when they kiss goodnight, as if they are blood sisters.

Catherine knows that Charles will have Louise sooner or later. She is surprised to find herself laughing. Poor Nellie, the tiny actress with the smallest feet in London, who disrespectfully calls the King of England *Charles III* because he is her third lover with that name; she will not like to be pushed out of Charles' bed for this little Breton maid. They will fight like puppies. And later, they will cuddle up together to share their secrets. How Nellie will love to tell stories to La Belle Bretonne about Barbara Castlemaine who was so cruel to the Queen; what an old hag Barbara is, now that she has lost Charles' love and is to be pensioned off with duchess of this and countess of that and baroness of somewhere else, and a belly that will bear no more of Charles' bastards.

16

POISONED

JULY, 1670

'Your Majesty.'

Oh, the many ways to address a king with these words. Charles remembers the first time: the words spoken so softly, almost in a whisper, when he was a young man. How to tell a firstborn son that his father, God's anointed King, lies on a scaffold awash with blood, his royal head smitten from his body, his countenance, so beloved by his queen and his children, made stony in death? Two words.

'Your Majesty.'

His father's gentleman of the bedchamber would have trimmed his beard and waxed his moustaches that morning like any other, surely.

Charles, eighteen years old, had burst into tears and fled the chamber.

'Your Majesty.'

These words, spoken again, so quietly with sadness. The young courtier, Sir Thomas Armstrong, has come in haste from the French Court.

'What is amiss?' Charles asks. 'Tell me, sir, be quick about it.'

'Your Majesty, I have to tell you… Madame, your sister, the Duchesse d'Orléans… she is dead.'

Sir Thomas had been present at the death. Charles

demands that he tells everything he saw in the ten hours it took Minette to die. Madame complained of a pain in her side at around five in the afternoon of 29th June after bathing at Saint-Cloud. Feeling thirsty, she called for a cup of iced chicory water and having drunk, she cried out in agony that she was poisoned. After eight hours of torment in her stomach and her bowels everyone knew that she was dying. His Majesty, the French king, held her in his arms sobbing. Finally, Monsieur, her husband, wept. Madame called for her confessor, and two hours later, she died.

Charles has shut himself away in his bedchamber, refusing to see Louis' official envoy. Catherine wants to throw her arms around her husband, kiss his tears away and comfort him, but he lies prostrate on his bed clutching his favourite spaniel bitch and his face is buried in her fur. She tries to tell him that Minette was very sick, that she would not see a physician. She reminds him how concerned he had been about how little his sister had eaten in Dover and at the feasts in Canterbury.

Charles does not listen. 'Monsieur is a villain,' he snarls again and again into the fur. 'Minette was poisoned.'

Five days pass before Charles emerges from his bedchamber. Private grief must give way to foreign diplomacy. He allows Louis' envoy to offer his official condolences. He reads the letter the French King has sent and acknowledges his grief at the loss of his sister-in-law. He dispatches his own man to Paris for Minette's state funeral, carrying with him a copy of the Treaty of Dover which will conceal the true Treaty of Madame.

The Great Secret has become more than a promise which seals an alliance with a powerful, wealthy enemy: it is a sacred vow to his dead, beloved sister, and to his God.

Part 3
Converts and
Conspiracies
1673–1678

*"The Devil is never so Dangerous
as when he presents him-
self as an Angel of Light."*

Roger L'Estrange (1687)

17

BONFIRE NIGHT
17TH NOVEMBER, 1673

Pepys has walked along Tower Street, Cannon Street and Watling Street, seeing fires everywhere. There must be more than two hundred, in the city, surely, on this anniversary of Elizabeth's accession to the throne. He passes the newly built church of St Mary-le-Bow, still waiting for Sir Christopher Wren's new spire, and as he reaches Cheapside it is a shock to see what is being burned here. It is not Guy Fawkes with his dark lantern and his gunpowder barrels. Oh no, the people don't want him tonight. Effigies of a pope with his red cap and cope and white lace cassock with a couple of devils at his shoulders and red-robed cardinals at his side are being consumed by flames.

Tonight the people remember the Protestant martyrs who burned in Queen Mary's reign more than a hundred years ago. They remember civil war and the execution of King Charles' father because he wouldn't do what his Parliament wanted. King Louis XIV of France is an autocratic Catholic king who heeds no Parliament. Lord, but these common people out on the streets tonight are determined that England must never have a monarch like that and this is their way of letting the King and the Duke of York know it.

The Duke is a widower now, like Pepys, and he desperately needs a new wife to get himself a male heir; all his first wife gave him was two daughters. His new Italian bride, Princess Mary of Modena, is on her way to England, sea-sick and weeping, because surely she knows that the English people don't want her. She's a Catholic and they hate her, even before she's set one foot upon English shores. She's fifteen, poor wretch, only a little older than Elizabeth was on their wedding day. York still goes to Communion on Easter Sunday, but not for much longer, he has confided as much to Pepys, and he's resigned from the Admiralty because everyone knows that really, he is a Catholic too, like his dead mother and this new little wife. Pepys has tried to persuade the Duke to remain a closet Catholic: to go to the Anglican church every Lord's day but to take Mass privately with his confessor.

'Give your advice when it's requested,' the Duke told him bluntly, 'and about what you know best: the navy.' Then the Duke said something very worrying.

'You surprise me greatly, Mr Pepys. Your own religious faith is most ambiguous, and is obvious for everyone to see. Surely you must know this. I have seen you many a time in the Queen's chapel wiping the tears from your eyes. You are an emotional man and I see that the Catholic Mass has a profound effect upon you.'

'It is the music, sir,' Pepys had stammered, astounded at the Duke's assumptions. 'It is far superior to any I have heard in an Anglican church. It always moves me thus.'

'When did you last attend Anglican communion?' the Duke asked, without waiting for a reply. 'A man must be true to his faith.'

Pepys understood then that the Duke had no intention of keeping his own religious faith a secret. Being the King's brother, the Duke does not have to comply with the new Test Act which came into being in March, so he has not had to declare disbelief in transubstantiation, nor leave the country, as Catholics are supposed to do, although it's clear to Pepys that this is not happening because there are still so many Catholics in London that a new law has been made to ban them from Whitehall and St James' Park. Nevertheless, the Duke is frequently to be seen enjoying himself there, walking with his brother and their dogs and playing the fashionable new game, *pell mell*, which the King nearly always wins because he's so tall he easily hits the ball through the loop. Although the King has begotten children on his mistresses ever since he was a teenager in exile abroad, everyone has lost hope that Queen Catherine will ever bear Charles a son. York is heir to the English throne, but Lord knows what will happen if the King should succumb to a fever or to the smallpox. The people don't want a Catholic king: they don't want James of York and he knows it, but it doesn't appear to worry him at all.

Pepys owes everything to York: all his promotions. He's recently been appointed Secretary of the Naval Office. The King and the Duke are desperate for someone to represent the Navy Board in Parliament and Pepys will be entering the Commons in January as the member for Castle Rising. When he presented himself for election at this safe seat there were cries of 'bloody papist' from the crowd. He's too close to the Catholic Duke and it is a mighty great worry for him.

There are hogsheads of wine on Cheapside and already people are merry, as if they are celebrating a happy occasion, May Day, perhaps, or the King's birthday. One man has followed Pepys from bonfire to bonfire. Over the roar and crackle of the flames he wails, 'My little church, my parish, all gone, all burned to cinders by Jesuit dogs.'

The people stare. He is an old man with a filthy long beard. First they laugh, then they listen and take up his refrain. 'Papist pigs, Jesuit dogs,' they shout with every stick they throw onto the fire where the pope and his devils burn.

'They are here amongst us, plotting,' the ancient clergyman shouts into the noise of the rowdy crowd. 'Jesuit dogs who hide behind their false names and their layman's gear, papist pigs, who fired our city, dare to sneak into the Queen's chapel to eat and drink their god. They are here amongst us, conspiring to set London ablaze again and to murder our Protestant king. They eat their god, I tell you. They eat their god.'

Children are holding hands, chanting and dancing in a circle.

'They eat their god,
They eat their god,
Spew, spew,
Spew out their god.'

They fall to the ground gagging and giggling.

The old clergyman watches the children and spits in the direction of the pope's effigy. He settles himself on the ground with surprising agility for such an ancient man, pulls a notebook and writing materials from his pocket and begins to scribble frantically.

'What missive do you write in such haste?' Pepys asks.

'I am making new words from old to the glory of God Almighty and the demise of papists and Jesuits,'

'New words from old?' Pepys queries. Does the old fool make his living trading words like a peddler?

'God has given me a wonderful task,' the old cleric cries excitedly. 'To shuffle words like a pack of cards to find the word of God within the individual characters. Therein lies the mystery: a word is jumbled, then another, and another, and a new phrase appears like alchemy, telling of the power and the glory of Almighty God, and the damnation of Jesuit heretics.'

Pepys recalls the strangest sermon he has ever sat through. This is Israel Tonge, the stark raving mad cleric who lost his church and his sanity after the Great Fire. He becomes aware of two men standing beside him. The tall, stooping presence of Sir Edmund Godfrey is unmistakable.

'Good evening, Sir Edmund.'

'What is that noise?' Godfrey asks, pointing towards the fire, 'It is terrible to hear, and most hurtful to my ears.'

'It is the wailing of cats, sir,' Tonge replies excitedly.

'Cats, you say? Cats?' Godfrey asks, putting his hand to his ear.

'The animals are howling dreadfully. Why so?' Pepys asks, alarmed for the poor creatures.

'They're inside the belly of the pope: burning. The noise of their howling mimics the devils cackling their evil blasphemies into the pope's ears.' Tonge laughs, an angry, guttural, laugh. 'Catholics, Jesuits, bloody papist vermin, all of 'em. Parliament and the King can't rid us with their laws and their fines for not going to church, so it's up to us to smoke 'em out.'

'You should go home, Honest William,' Edmund advises his friend in the overloud voice of the deaf. 'It is unsafe for you out here on the streets.'

Godfrey's companion is Jesuit layman John Grove. Pepys has seen him several times taking the Mass at the Queen's chapel.

'It is unsafe for you, also, to be standing here beside your Jesuit friend,' Grove replies, 'but you will not go home.'

'It is my duty to keep law and order when multitudes gather, and to do it conscientiously now that I have kissed the King's hand and have returned to the Commission of Peace.'

'Come, gentlemen,' says Pepys, sickened by the wretched burning cats. 'We should all go home. This is no place for us.'

At Fish Street Hill they part: Grove, to walk across London

Bridge to his home in Southwark; Edmund Godfrey, to go west, probably, Pepys guesses, to keep order on Cheapside now that his friend is safely away from the mad cleric. Pepys makes his way to his temporary, rather fusty lodgings, near the Tower, for he has no home.

Last January Seething Lane burned – the whole row – the naval offices and twenty houses. His beautiful home with its costly furniture and haberdashery crackled and tumbled to the ground: his best bed with its costly hangings; the marital bed that he had shared with Elizabeth; his fashionable clothes with their gold and silver lace, but worst of all, his irreplaceable collections of books and paintings. Thankfully, his diary and the portraits of Elizabeth and himself were amongst valuables that his clerks and his maids managed to save.

Soon he will move to the best living accommodation he has ever had: to the West End in the new Admiralty headquarters at Derby House between Whitehall and Westminster.

How dear Mary Skynner will love the view over the river.

18

A LEWD AND WICKED LIFE
JANUARY, 1674

Pepys watches the Duke of Buckingham stepping nimbly along the aisle in his marvellous blue suit, with silken bows at his shoulders, gold lace at his neck and his wife at his side – poor wretch! He is all elegance and grace and charm; he might as well be dancing a French branle as attending Sunday service here in fashionable St Martin-in-the-Fields. Who would think that this great lord has no more sobriety than to dangle actresses under the King's nose when he has tired of them himself? And worse: to fight about a whore. Buckingham? Oh no. Duke of Fuckingham; this is how courtiers refer to him these days behind his back. His long affair with his mistress, Countess Shrewsbury, has been nothing but a scandalous history.

During a performance at the Duke's Theatre, Countess Shrewsbury's other lover, Killigrew, had hit Buckingham on the head with his sword, fortunately – or maybe not – in its sheath. And Buckingham caused chaos, chasing him over forms and boxes. But brawling is not the worst of his offences.

Lord Shrewsbury, the cuckold, challenged him to a duel the way they do it in France: the seconds also taking part, three men against three. One man died, Buckingham was injured and he put his sword through Shrewsbury's shoulder.

Weeks later, Shrewsbury died and Buckingham shamelessly brought his widowed mistress to live in his house. If his wife didn't like this arrangement, she should go to her father's house, he told her. There are even rumours of bigamy: a secret marriage to the Countess.

Three times, at least, the King has put him in the Tower but he loves the Duke more than his own brother, they having been brought up together and he being much more fun than the sober James of York. So he treats Fuckingham like a bucket in a well: for his brawling and duelling and worse he goes down but he knows that the King will always forgive him, free him from the Tower, pull him back up again.

As Buckingham and his lady pass by, Edmund Godfrey opens his prayer book and concentrates upon the text so that he doesn't have to acknowledge them. This depraved duke has led a lewd and wicked life and parading himself like this is an insult to the vicar. This is the great lord who once spent thirty thousand pounds on a jewelled suit for the King's coronation; who is always sluggish about putting his hands in his pocket for the poor money he owes to the parish.

Bah, it is time His Majesty was told what he, Edmund, knows about Buckingham, his new friend Lord Shaftesbury, and their politics.

19

HOSTILITY

JANUARY –FEBRUARY, 1674

Pepys wears his fine silk suit of brown with his best lace about his neck and a new full-bottomed dark wig reaching past his shoulders and onto his chest. Who would ever have thought that the day would come when he, a *prick louse,* son of a poor tailor, would enter Parliament; would be driven there by his own coachman in his own coach to take his seat in the House of Commons? He isn't nervous at all. Lord, but the electors of Castle Rising in Norfolk have done him a great service and this he will not forget.

From the moment he enters the House, hostility almost overpowers him. But speechless – no. Not he. He came to the Commons expecting to defend the Navy Board and this he does well. He's a good speaker, better than the King, but then, who isn't?

He outlines his argument confidently. He knows that no one can argue with his facts and figures. It is what comes next that is so completely unexpected. He's unused to the Commons and its ways. He had expected handshakes and a welcome; not a cannonade of untruths and a threat to remove him from the House.

'Do you deny that you are a Catholic, Mr Pepys?'

'We have evidence to the contrary: that you have an altar and a crucifix in your house.'

The accusations become hurtful, of a personal nature. Pepys, always an emotional man, feels tears stinging his eyes. Lord, but he has enemies here, in the House of Commons, enemies he never knew of until this day.

'We have heard that you broke your late wife's heart by trying to convert her to Catholicism on her deathbed.'

I should have done, I know I should, Pepys reflects. It was what she really wanted.

His tears turn to suppressed laughter when he hears the evidence upon which the accusations rest.

'We have witnesses who have heard from your own lips that the Anglican religion came out of Henry VIII's codpiece.'

And now, thankfully, he finds that he has one friend in the House: Sir William Coventry, one time secretary to the Duke of York and the Navy Board. These days he's the member for a neighbouring Norfolk constituency, Great Yarmouth.

'Do we really expect Mr Pepys to defend himself against this remark?' Sir William asks. 'It is a joke, surely, which he may have used at supper occasionally, to entertain his guests.'

Nobody is laughing now. Have I, unbeknown, invited secret enemies into my own house all these years? Pepys wonders.

There is worse to come.

'These witnesses who accuse Mr Pepys of papism,' Sir William Coventry challenges the house, 'who are they? They must be named.'

Members look to each other and a murmur fills the house but no one comes forward to name the source of the accusations. The Speaker insists and one man's name causes a mighty stir: Anthony Ashley Cooper, Earl of Shaftesbury.

Pepys is shocked. He had invited this man to his home

in Seething Lane years ago, on more than one occasion. He remembers ordering a handsome supper that cost him a mighty fortune. Shaftesbury was only Lord Ashley then; not yet an earl, only a baronet, but an honoured guest for a mere naval clerk.

Alias Shiftsbury, to those who do not like him: since the execution of Charles I, Lord Shaftesbury has been loyal to whatever political faction was in power. At the Restoration, he stepped out of his plain republican clothes, put his fine point lace around his neck and sailed to the States of Holland, as did Pepys, to bring Charles II home from exile. The King and the Duke of York have little liking for Shaftesbury. He is alias Little Sincerity, to the tall royal brothers. He's a short man, like Pepys, and Pepys has always felt a certain affinity towards him, being, like himself, a man who has survived a dangerous medical procedure. Shaftesbury is into his fifties now jaundiced and in pain, and is only kept alive by a copper tube that leaks poison from a wound in his side where he had an operation around five years ago to remove a cyst on his liver.

Despite his poor health Shaftesbury has decided that he's important enough and strong enough to stop shifting and he's appointed himself leader of the Opposition. It's no secret that he wants rid of the Catholic Duke of York and the French influence. The King's eldest, most beloved natural son, James, Duke of Monmouth, would be an ideal Protestant heir presumptive, and Shaftesbury has tried to persuade His Majesty to declare that he was secretly married to the boy's mother when they were both barely more than children.

Lord, but it is mighty arrogant of him to think that he can manipulate the King like this however much he dotes upon his handsome bastard son. 'I have a small table in my closet,' Pepys explains to the House, 'with my Bible and the

Book of Common Prayer, and my late wife's painting above it. I think this might be what Lord Shaftesbury supposes to be an altar.'

Lord Shaftesbury must be asked to explain his allegations, but members of the Commons may not send for a great lord. They must go wait upon him and request that he presents his evidence. The Earl needs time to think and remember but eventually he sends a message to the Commons. He admits to his memory being imperfect and consequently he would be uneasy about giving testimony under oath. But he has a somewhat imperfect memory of seeing something of papist origin in Pepys' home: a crucifix he thinks, but whether of wood or painted or carved he cannot remember.

Oh, Lord, Pepys thinks. It is my beautiful crucifixion painting of which he speaks. I remember showing it to him.

***

In the end it is His Majesty who rescues Pepys, or looking at it another way, it is ironically, Shaftesbury and his anti-Catholic Opposition peers who save him. They introduce a bill demanding that any children of the Duke of York should be raised as Protestants and propose new legislation preventing the King or any prince of royal blood from marrying a Catholic without Parliament's permission or else they will be excluded from the royal succession. Soon there are rumours that Shaftesbury and the Opposition are talking of accusing the Duke of York of treason. The King has to move quickly to protect his brother. He prorogues Parliament.

When Parliament sits again Lord Shaftesbury's accusation is old news. Pepys feels safe within the friendship and protection of the Duke of York. Safe enough to consider inviting a Catholic musician to join his household. Cesare Morelli composes, sings beautifully and is mighty proficient on the lute. Presently in Lisbon he is anxious to return to London. Oh, what blissful evenings they will have making music in his grand new home.

20

THE SEA CHAPLAIN

MAY–JUNE, 1675

Captain Sir Richard Routh can hardly bear to look at the man. If ugliness pronounces evil then surely his new chaplain is the Devil incarnate: chin so long his mouth is in the middle of his big red face. His foul-mouthed utterances to the men have been learned in a common tavern, not at Westminster School, nor at Cambridge where, he had boasted to Routh, he had been educated. Lord knows he must have stuck out like a sore thumb at those institutions with his coarse ways; for he is certainly badly placed here, on the frigate *Adventure*, taking responsibility for the spiritual health of the seamen. There is not so much as even a hint of the manners of a gentleman about him. His habits are disgusting: he spits and pisses wherever the fancy takes him, although he has been given a chamber pot like all the other seamen. The content of his sermons and his high strident voice hardly recommend him for a man of the Church. He stands before the men affecting the speech of a gentleman, bleating like a goat, and each time he intones 'Almaighty Gaad,' Routh hears suppressed sniggers from the seamen. He would never have believed it possible for a clergyman to use the vulgar phrases that spill out of Titus Oates' mouth. Lord Inchquin, travelling to his new post as governor of Tangier, had remarked that the language of the chaplain's sermons was most inappropriate to the Anglican Church. The Earl was being tactful. 'Yon chaplain learned to talk with the rats in the gutter,' the ship's surgeon had uttered in disgust during his first sermon and he refused to attend another.

'Take Chaplain Oates below, give him a drubbing and tie him neck and heels until we reach Tangier,' Routh orders.

Routh knows his sailors: knows what some men will do when there are no women around, or even when there are women. Such are the secrets of seamen. This time it is different. He is ashamed to admit to such wicked goings on at sea under his own command.

'You'll get no pay.' Routh tells the chaplain. 'You'll be expelled from the navy when we dock.'

Titus Oates is a young man, not yet thirty. He has the eyes of an old dog; brown and wary. 'How am I supposed live without my pay?' he demands in the whining voice of a sulky child.

'Sodomy is a capital offence. I would have you swing from the yardarm this very minute,' Routh declares, 'but that I may need someone to bury the dead.'

The boy, of course, has said nothing: not to Routh nor to anyone. If you speak to him he stares at the deck, won't look you in the face. And he was such a lively lad, so excited about coming to sea, and not seasick at all. For the last two days he's stayed mainly atop the rigging. He won't sit to eat his food and sleeps fully clothed. But there's no privacy aboard ship; the men know what had happened. Routh is deeply ashamed. He had promised the boy's mother to take good care of him.

What horrifies him about the whole matter is the attitude of the chaplain. Where is his guilt, his shame, his remorse? He showed no surprise at his punishment, nor anger. Just a flinch of fear when he knew that he was discovered. He eats, he sleeps, he shits, he is alert to danger and he buggers without a care for his victim. The man is an animal. Routh can't wait to be rid of him.

The sea swells, the waves crash, the timbers creak. Below decks, Titus has nothing to do but to try to quench his nausea with thinking. Fantasy, that's what life is: a play, something you make up as you go along. He isn't getting along well enough. He's got to get better at it.

'Snotty little fool, always a disappointment,' his father had said when he was expelled from Merchant Taylors' School. He wasn't stealing, or cheating, he told his father. He was a free scholar, wasn't he? The tutor, William Smith, had no right to the entrance fee.

'Master Smith was kind and patient with you,' his mother gently reprimanded.

Titus remembers hearing boys who were his junior, by many years, sniggering whilst the master sat beside him slowly explaining the lessons, as if he were an infant still, in skirts.

'They spewed you out because the other boys didn't like you and the masters neither, because you would not learn.' His father had whipped him and told his mother to take him out of his sight. She sent him to a dame school to learn from a horn-book with little children. He was fifteen years old.

'A great dunce,' one of his Cambridge tutors had said later, to his face. 'Why are you here? You'll never learn Greek or Latin.'

Titus knows that he has gifts his tutors couldn't comprehend: his vast memory, his imagination. He was expelled from Gonville and Caius College after only two terms, and two years later, obliged to go down from St John's College without a degree. What? He, a thief? Never! It was that damned tailor's fault, accusing him of debt, that's why he was sent down, he explained to his father.

'Thief, liar, fool,' his father said, and slapped his head. 'You stole a coat from a tailor, sold it to a second-hand dealer and told your tutor that your mother gave you the money. Stop whining and make something of yourself.' He'd been a self-taught chaplain in Cromwell's New Model Army, his father had, from being a common weaver.

Now that Titus has taken Holy Orders he's a man to be respected. And truly, his father was proud of him when he acquired a curacy at Sandhurst, and later, a living at Bobbing in Kent. He doesn't remember using indecent expressions to expound the mysteries of the Christian religion, nor being drunk. Can't a cleric take a drink now and then like any other man without being thrown out of his living? A man shouldn't be taken to account for what the Devil puts into his mouth. And no, he did not steal poultry and pigs from his neighbour. He's a man of God. His parishioners should expect to provide him with his victuals, in charity.

His father was pissed off when he turned up at Hastings, penniless, expecting to be given a curacy. Whenever he goes home, he's that ugly, limping, snivelling little child cowering in the hearth, fearing his father's insults more than his clerical boot.

'Cease your blubbering and cook me a handsome dinner, not this pile of turds you've put on my platter,' Titus had scolded his mother.

Black rats scamper between barrels and sacks, over his legs, even over his face when he sleeps. Nothing matters anymore, Titus tells himself, nothing is real, only what's inside his head; that's what's important. Telling the truth won't earn him any favours, won't make him a living. Yes, a man can change the world by words alone. If you imagine a thing deeply enough you can make it happen. This he believes, more than the

Bible, more than God or the Devil. Inside his head he, Titus, can alter men's lives. The mind is a powerful thing for a man with a long memory and a wonderful imagination. You must have the skill for it, of course, and not many men do. He knows he does. He just needs to work at it: what happened in Hastings must never happen again.

They were in the stable behind the tavern, himself and William Parker, the young schoolmaster. They'd been drinking late, and he's helping William to mount his horse. He thinks he knows young William. Thinks he can make him be what he wants him to be. In the darkness of the stable William's thigh is hard and muscular for such a slim young man. Titus lets his hand wander as if it has a will of its own. William slaps his face, calls him a molly, tells him sodomy is a sin and the penalty is death. Tells him, in his gentleman's arrogant, cropped accent, to go fuck the horse. Hot tears sting Titus' eyes and his throat feels lumpy.

When you're trapped in a corner like that, the only way to defend yourself is to attack. There was no other recourse but that Titus should accuse young William of being the guilty party; of practising sodomy in the south porch of the church, no less, adding blasphemy to his crime. When the schoolmaster is found guilty, Titus will get what he really wants: William's position as master at the school.

His father had quarrelled with the Parkers who think mightily highly of themselves, the elder Captain Parker being a magistrate and an ex-mayor. No one tells his father what to do, especially a magistrate, but Parker tried to. Now, if Titus could bring down this arrogant family and do it properly, through the law, it would please his father, mightily. So, with his father's blessing, Titus accused the Captain of speaking treasonable words in his hearing. There's money to be made from giving evidence of high treason and indeed, his father was pleased. And Titus was pleased with himself. He's a man of God, a curate of the Anglican Church, who would doubt his word?

Secretary of State, Sir Joseph Williamson and the Privy Council declared Captain Parker to be innocent and Titus returned to Hastings amidst the ringing of bells and lighting of bonfires for the Parkers. The local magistrates likewise disbelieved Titus' accusations against the son. Young William Parker sought damages of a thousand pounds, and furthermore, Titus had accused one of his father's churchwardens of threatening to beat him and he was bound over to the sum of forty pounds for perjury. He had to hide indoors away from the womenfolk of Hastings, his mother's friends, who whipped him and threw buckets of water at him when they found him on the street.

'Fool, liar, runt of the litter,' his father called after him as he slunk away one night to board the frigate *Adventure*.

One day his father will know who he really is, what he can do. He will conjure something audacious, and they will believe every detail of his fantasy, all of them, these people who have scorned him, and it will be the making of him. He will not let the law get the better of him again. He will make himself rich. And his enemies will dread his anger.

He loves it when people look at him with fear. It happens sometimes during his sermons. He can see that the people are terrified of the word of God coming out of his mouth. How distorted and ugly their faces appear in the candlelit church, like goggle-eyed gargoyles.

The boy didn't cry out; how could he with Titus' big hand over his mouth. He thought the boy was writhing in pleasure until he saw his eyes full of fear. The ship creaked and the sea swelled and Titus' other hand fumbled awhile before he pushed the boy onto his belly.

'If you tell, you will die. Think how your mother will weep when she hears how you fell overboard. She will weep for years. She will never stop weeping.'

Oh, the power of words, if you know how to use them.

21

THE UNGENEROUS SILVERSMITH
1676

It is Middlesex quarter sessions at Hicks Hall, and Edmund Godfrey regards the man who stands before him. The slightly stooped posture, so typical of a craftsman whose work requires close attention to detail, defies the blatant arrogance of the silversmith. 'Miles Prance, did you think you could walk away from this court with your parish duties forgotten?'

'But Sir Edmund,' the other justice says, 'this man is Queen Catherine's servant. I think a discharge would be appropriate in this case, for all concerned.'

The accused is quick to respond to the sympathy of Edmund's colleague. 'My family have been Royalist supporters since the reign of our blessed monarch's martyred father,' he says. 'My own father was imprisoned for his loyalty to the crown in the past troubled times.'

'Your father is not here accused,' Edmund declares angrily. 'It is your loyalty to your parish that is in question today.'

'What is your religion?' the other justice asks.

'I am a Catholic, sir, as is the Queen, and have been so all my life.'

Edmund gives his colleague a cold stare. 'The man's religion is irrelevant to the matter in question.' He turns to

Prance. 'You are a skilled craftsman?' he asks. 'It must be so, or Her Majesty would not patronise your business.'

'Indeed, sir, I am proud to say so. It has pleased Her Majesty to appoint me to design personal trinkets for her use from time to time, in silver or occasionally in gold. I also serve as a verger in the Queen's chapel in Somerset House, where I snuff the candles and polish the silver.'

'The Catholic community has need of your skills, I think, Mr Prance,' Edmund says.

'I have crafted chalices and candlesticks for worship and other necessaries besides, for gentlemen of quality and their ladies.'

The other justice nods his approval. 'You are obviously well respected for your craft, Mr Prance.' He turns to Edmund and whispers, 'Perhaps, a little leniency in this instance might be politic, don't you think, bearing in mind Mr Prance's connections to the Royal family? You would not wish to displease His Majesty again, surely not, Sir Edmund. It is several years now since you kissed the King's hand and returned to the Commission of Peace. Do not, I beg you, put yourself in the way of being obliged to forfeit your place on the Commission a second time.'

'Bah,' says Edmund and turns to the accused. 'The Queen has no power of protecting her servants whether Catholic or Protestant; you are as liable for your duties to your parish as your neighbours and you can well afford it. You must comply with the law or else take the consequences. Your refusal to do so is a great unkindness to the deserving poor in your parish and your greed and selfishness in this matter is very much to be despised.'

22

A SAD SONG

SPRING, 1677

Pepys hasn't looked at his diary in years, not since Elizabeth died. While Cesare Morelli is busy composing mourning music, he finds the page where he had written the names of his siblings and writes, *mort*, against the name of his last brother, John.

'Shall you sing with me at the funeral?' Morelli asks.

'Of course.'

How very strange, Pepys thinks, that I, who all my life have had such ill health, should survive my poor brother. I might have died years ago strapped to a table whilst the surgeon cut the stone out of my bladder.

These days Pepys is again plagued with pain in his bladder and also his bowels, for which he has to insert suppositories. Thankfully, all his worries about his eyes have proved unfounded. He has not become blind, although he has severe pain in his eyes each morning when he rises until he drains his head by spitting and blowing his nose. Even so, close work of any length has become almost impossible and his clerks have to read and write for him. And as for the pains in his hip and knees, shoulders and wrists, and itching all over his body that occasionally happens, Lord, but he never lets these interfere with his work. He makes sure he is bled in the arm at least once a year and is careful what he eats and drinks, which is no real problem because these days, he can barely taste his food.

This year has been good for Pepys. In February, the King sent Lord Shaftesbury to the Tower. Parliament hadn't sat for fifteen months but how dare Shaftesbury and his friends claim that the new Parliament was illegal?

Pepys still fights hostility in the Commons and has been accused of speaking more like an admiral than a secretary. Well, so be it. He's managed, by his oratory, to persuade Parliament to give an enormous sum of money to the navy: millions of pounds.

There have been remarks that Pepys is filling his own pockets; for example, from fees for granting passes to ship owners. It matters not. His conscience is clear because he's happy to help other men who are his social inferiors. The new overseer of the *Northumberland* cannot thank Pepys enough for this promotion although he knows that it only happened because his pretty, and very persistent wife did the pleading for him.

Yes, Pepys is proud of his promotions and his good works these last two years. He is Master of Trinity College and also governor of Christ's Hospital and Bridewell prison and it is thanks to him that child inmates there now have a school-master. He plans to ask His Majesty for money for Christ's Hospital School, to endow a maths department where boys will be prepared for the navy. Education and intelligence are more important than family background. Pepys wouldn't be where he is today without his Cambridge education and every boy of intelligence should have such opportunities. The Jesuits are good teachers and their English schools abroad are reputedly excellent. What a pity, Pepys laments, that the increasing anti-Catholic climate prevents such schools from being established here, in London.

23

THE NEW CONVERT

APRIL, 1677

'I understand that you were received into the Catholic Church in March. This is so?' Father Richard Strange, the English Provincial of the Society of Jesus, speaks slowly, making long pauses inside his sentences, as the elderly do when memory is sluggish but the mind is keen. He stares through narrowed, liquid eyes at the stunted, shadowy figure of the man standing before him. He tells the novice to come closer, pull up a chair by the fire, so that he can see his features clearly; see whether the man speaks from his heart, or if he lies, the better to infiltrate the Jesuit Society and discover their secrets. Father Strange sees an ugly man. The convert's face is wide and ruddy with a low forehead and a great long chin sprouting a filthy red beard. The eyes are brown and dull, yet defiant.

'On Ash Wednesday,' the convert replies, 'after instruction and prayer, I perceived that the Devil himself had kept me from the True Faith and I was accepted into the Roman Church.'

'You wish to leave the security of the Anglican Church and come to us? Are you a spy, sir? For you must know that Parliament does not want us to practise our religion in this country and there are severe penalties…'

'I was searching for the Truth, Father,' the convert

interrupts. 'Our blessed saviour calls me to be a son of the True Church of Rome. I have weighed everything seriously and considered the consequences. Matters of God are not to be understood by men of straw with little imagination but by men of imagination and vision, like myself, who –'

'Be quiet,' the Provincial hisses. The man's arrogant manner is incompatible with the humility he expects from a mere novice of a few weeks who has everything to learn about the ancient Catholic faith. He pulls up his blanket and sips a warm draught from a silver cup. The fire's heat reddens the side of his face that is closest to the flames yet still he is cold; the dead could not be more frigid. 'Pray, move your chair a little further away,' he says, for he shrinks from close proximity to this man he cannot understand. 'I am a man older than my years and feel the chill of death creeping into my bones, but I see that you are uncomfortable in this heat.' Indeed, sweat drips from the tip of the convert's nose onto his collar, for he has little neck.

'From what I know of your career, to date,' Strange says, 'you have been something of a man of straw yourself.'

He sees the hurt in the man's eyes before ill temper hardens them. 'Did you think that I would agree to this interview without asking questions?' The convert does not reply and Strange makes him wait for more than a minute before he cuts to the quick. 'Your father was an Anabaptist preacher. As a child, you were indoctrinated into this blasphemy? Of course you were,' he adds when no reply is offered. 'However, upon the Restoration of the monarchy, your father became an Anglican clergyman as eventually, did you yourself, becoming a curate in his parish in Hastings. So why was your father obliged to flee to London from this comfortable living and become an absentee rector? And you yourself? You vanished quite suddenly from Hastings to go aboard the *Adventure* with Captain Routh. But you did not stay long at sea, did you? One voyage, and they had had enough of you. It took my men some time to discover what became of you when you returned to England. Why was this, Mr Oates? Where were you hiding?'

'I was attending to my devotions and to a study of the Bible, being sorely troubled about my religion and my eternal soul, for I began to understand that the doctrine of the English Church is indeed blasphemous, as you say, and a man with my intelligence, imagination and vast memory should use my talents to the glory of God within the True Catholic Church.'

'Either you lie to me,' Strange says, heaving a great sigh, 'or your vast memory has let you down, for you cannot remember where you were less than a year ago. Let me remind you, Mr Oates. You were incarcerated in...' he pauses. 'Now where was it? I forget, but it will come to me in a moment. Was it Newgate? No, no. Ah yes, now I remember; you were arrested and taken prisoner to Dover Castle concerning incidents in Hastings and lies that you told.'

'It was a misunderstanding, a small matter of –'

'A serious matter of perjury, as I understand, and another of defamation of character.'

'Father, I beg you, listen whilst I tell you the truth of –'

'I know what happened,' Strange says, and stays silent for a while watching Oates fidget in his chair like a child who has an urgent need to urinate.

'The schoolmaster at Hastings wanted a thousand pounds from you to compensate for your lies,' Strange says at last. He is having difficulty keeping his temper. 'You departed again, rather suddenly, from Dover, Mr Oates. Your jailers missed you, I've been told.'

'I have been with the Catholic Earl of Norwich at Arundel House, here in London. I was his chaplain.'

'His Protestant chaplain,' Strange says. 'As you are well

aware, the Catholic nobility are, by law, obliged to educate their children and their servants into the Anglican religion. But again, you did not stay long in this household; a matter of months only. Why was this?'

Titus wipes his nose with his sleeve and begins to answer. 'Father, the Earl and I—'

'Enough, enough, no more lies. The Earl did not like you, Mr Oates. I will not ask you why. He did not wish you to stay in his house, and there's an end to it. The impending question is this: what am I going to do with you? Be quiet, I pray you, Mr Oates, and let me think.'

The heat of the fire and the potion in the silver cup have made Father Strange drowsy. Soon his chin has fallen on his collar and his high black Jesuit hat is all askew. Titus watches the rising and falling of his chest and sniggers at the accompanying music of his thin, droning snores. If the fool hadn't shut him up every time he wanted to deliver the speech he's been rehearsing at his lodgings for days, he knows that he could have explained himself better, presented himself as a man more zealous, more passionate about his newly found faith and his mission to serve God with the Jesuits. He thinks he's given the dull-witted old man reason enough to give him what he wants. If he hasn't, if Strange refuses him, he knows what he has to say to compel him to change his mind in less time than it takes for the senile old fart to beshit himself.

Titus hasn't planned to tell Father Strange about what goes on in Fuller's Rents at the Pheasant club amongst Catholic and Protestant members, but if he must, he will tell all, and blame it on the Catholics. Strange won't like it. The acts of sodomy at the Pheasant in Fuller's Rents will shock the English Provincial, or maybe not. Perhaps the celibate old man enjoys a bit of buggery himself, now and then. It's what Titus knows, or pretends to know about Catholics doing it, Jesuit priests in particular, that will force him to be a generous patron. It's the shame of it, the disgrace that it brings. He isn't surprised that there's so much of it going on; some men, like himself, well, women don't like them. So what else can they do? It's how things are, how it's intended it to be. He doesn't fear the rope; sodomy is such a great sin that few who discover it would dare admit to it happening in their own houses, let alone to themselves. But for him, Titus, knowing that a man is a molly means that he's got a hold on him. When you haven't a penny for lodgings, food, or a jug of ale, such knowledge is worth more than a curate's living. It's worth as much as it suits Titus to demand.

He and his father have finished with the Anglican Church, his father having returned to his old Anabaptist ways. 'See what misery you've brought upon your mother,' his father told him. 'She was happy in Hastings. The women respected her because of her profession and she earned money by it, pulling their babies out of their bellies. Her friends don't speak to her now, knowing that her ugly son is a convicted criminal. God alone knows why he's saddled me with a useless runt, for I don't.'

'Oh, Samuel, prithee, do not speak to him like that,' his mother pleaded, 'for he is my child, you know, and it grieves me to the heart to hear you say these things.'

Titus likes to wear clerical garb, likes the respect it brings being a man of the Church. It's no matter to him whether it happens to be Anglican or Catholic. It was Catholic members of the club at the Pheasant, actor Matthew Medburne especially, who had assisted him to obtain his position with the Earl of Norwich. Strangely, he'd never thought of seeking a way out of this mess his life has become by approaching the Jesuits until he happened to meet Israel Tonge, who had befriended his father. Listening to the mad old Yorkshire clergyman ranting about the Jesuits and their secrets got Titus thinking. Where there are secrets there is always a bargain to be made for keeping those secrets.

Titus tiptoes to the sleeping priest, takes the silver cup and drains the dregs. He had expected that someone in Father Strange's position, being head of the Jesuit community in England, would have offered his guest some repast. Titus has had spells of near starvation these last years. Living off the charity of others he's always wondering where he will find the next meal. He even resorted to begging at Queen Catherine's chapel at Somerset House, pretending to be a converted Catholic clergyman. And the priests were keen to help him, leaving him alone with the Host. If a man's left alone with something he's a fool not to take it. He didn't eat it, he didn't need to on that occasion, so he used it as wafers to seal his begging letters.

Father Strange awakens to the sound of hissing and spitting at the fireplace and groans when he sees the new convert relieving himself into the hearth.

'I am not sure that you fully understand the mission of the Society of Jesus, Titus Oates,' Strange says when Titus has returned to his chair.

'Jesuits have a duty to go out into the world to teach the mysteries of the True Faith to ignorant boys.' Oates speaks ponderously as if to emphasise the importance of his statement.

'Ah, so you desire to be a schoolmaster, Mr Oates. Why go abroad? Are there no schools in England that will have you?'

'You know that there are no Catholic schools in England, Father Strange. I have already told you that I am converted to the Roman Church.'

'I wish to save another soul from damnation before I retire,' Strange says, with a sigh of resignation. 'The Earl of Norwich recommends that you be sent abroad to study; why,

I cannot imagine. I shall send you to Spain, to our college at Valladolid, where you will study philosophy and theology. The term is nearly over and lessons will resume in October, so you will have several months to prepare yourself. With your Cambridge background, there will be no need for you to study Latin, you will be perfectly proficient already, but you should take the opportunity to learn Spanish before lessons start in autumn. The Society of Jesus will pay for your travel and subsistence, and you will adopt an alias, which is usual for Jesuits abroad. Henceforth you will be Titus Ambrose. Remember, you have a lot to learn before you will be fit to teach boys of tender conscience: lonely, homesick boys who have been forced to leave their families and their homeland where education in the Catholic tradition is under severe penalty. And mind your manners,' he adds, looking towards the hearth. 'It is mainly the sons of the Catholic gentry who are educated at our colleges abroad.'

Strange sees the beginnings of a smile on the convert's face, although his eyes are not smiling when he says, 'You will not regret your decision, Father, I promise you. For to induct another novice into the True Roman Faith is to fart in the face of the Devil.'

24

HIGH TREASON
LATE SUMMER, 1677

In a corner booth at White's coffee house, near the Exchange, two men smoke their pipes and sip their coffee.

'So, that's it, Mr Lee, that's everything I've discovered,' one of them says in a low voice after glancing around to ensure that he will not be overheard. He's a stout man, past middle age, wearing the woollen garb of a common man. 'The conspirators plan to march on London in October with armies from three counties, seize the Tower, kill the King and the Duke of York and establish a republic.'

Mr Lee, a dark gentleman appears to be unsurprised by this news. 'You have names for me, I hope, Dr Ayliffe?' He speaks with the accent and the confidence of a gentleman but it is possible to detect a hint of the northern counties in the timbre of his voice.

'Sir Robert Peyton's gang of discontents have joined Opposition politicians to stir this mischief. I think you'll be surprised by one or two of the men who have joined his gang.'

Mr Lee leans closer and nods each time his companion whispers a name. 'Here are your guineas, as promised, Dr Ayliffe,' he says, without further comment, after twelve men have been accused of high treason. He passes a heavy girdle under the table.

The informer fastens the girdle under his coat and whispers behind his hand, 'Well, I'll be in touch, Sir Joseph, as usual, when I discover more.'

In his office in Whitehall, Secretary of State for the North, Sir Joseph Williamson, alias Mr Lee to his informers, takes a scrap of paper out of his desk drawer and stares at a dozen names.

It was no surprise to learn from his informer today that the known republican activist, Sir Robert Peyton, has joined forces with other dissatisfied antimonarchist groups. This he had expected. When the King is told of their plotting, Peyton and some of the others will doubtless be stripped of their offices. The King has already found an excuse to send Lord Shaftesbury to the Tower. Thomas Blood, alias Dr Ayliffe, is one of his most reliable, if disloyal, informers: being a man who serves many masters, he discovers information less diligent spies might miss. Williamson stares at the name that is fourth on his list. He was hoping that after his visit to White's coffee house he would be able to strike it off. Yes, he knows that this man dislikes the profligacy and debauchery of the royal court. He has complained to Williamson of the huge sums of money King Louis uses to bribe Charles into an alliance against the Dutch, and he will never stop moaning about the needless expense of a gift in return for the French King: toys for a spoilt child – two little pleasure yachts Mr Pepys has organised for Louis to sail on his lake at Versailles. But who would have thought it? Edmund Godfrey has joined Robert Peyton's gang of republican plotters.

25

THE CONVERT RETURNS
EARLY DECEMBER, 1677

'I had hardly thought to see you returned to me so soon.'

'I did not expect to be here either, but circumstances have made it so, Father Strange.'

'I forget your name, pray do not tell me, let my aged memory recall... ah yes... it is coming to me... Titus Oates... Ambrose is the alias I gave to you. I remember your face, of course. You came to me fresh as a summer peach, newly converted and wanting to learn our ways, and I sent you to Valladolid to learn Spanish and to become a priest and a schoolmaster. Yet here you are, covered in snow, bringing icy air into my chambers. Don't you like warmth and sunshine, Titus Ambrose?'

Titus removes his shoes, shows Strange the holes in the soles and puts them by the fire. He pulls off his soaking stockings, throws them onto the fire irons and rests his filthy bare feet on the hearth. Steam rises from his shabby grey horseman's coat.

'In Spain,' Father Strange continues, 'you learned our Jesuit ways in comfort without fear or penalty, but you come to me again, here, in London, where it is dangerous to declare your faith. Tell me, why have you returned so soon?'

'As I have told you, Father, circumstances were not in my favour. I studied until the new term began, when, to my great disappointment, it was discovered that there was no place for me.'

'We paid for your place. You departed because…? Come, come now, no more of your lies, give me the truth.'

'The tuition was in Spanish, Father,' Titus mutters.

'Speak out, sir, I cannot hear you.'

'I could not understand the tuition, which was in Spanish.'

'I see. Clearly you did not work hard enough to learn that language.'

'What? In just a few weeks I was supposed to understand the blabbering idiot tutors who would not speak slowly for me? They knew English but they would not translate.'

'Cease your whining,' Strange says, putting his hands to his ears. 'The fault was yours. The tuition was mostly in Latin, admittedly spoken in a Spanish dialect, but you could have learned to understand it, given the time you were there. Clearly, you are not proficient enough in that ancient, Christian language either, yet you told me that you had studied at Cambridge University. Your education is sorely lacking, it seems, although my priests have informed me that whilst at Valladolid you have somehow managed to acquire for yourself a doctorate of divinity from Salamanca University. However did this occur?'

'I have lately been presented with that honour and am properly to be addressed as Dr Ambrose these days. The tutors at that well respected institution believed that I deserved to be rewarded for my vast intelligence and considerable hard work.'

'A doctor of divinity who knows little Latin?' Strange shakes his head and sighs. 'Pray, give me no more of your lies, but tell me plainly, what do you want of me?'

'Father, I have told you that our blessed Saviour calls me to the True Church to be his advocate. A man with my intelligence, imagination and vast memory should use my talents to the glory of God within the True Catholic Church.'

'Yes, yes, yes. I heard you last time and I gave you opportunity to train and money for sustenance within our Society.'

'That is another matter,' Titus says. 'I believe the Society of Jesus will, in charity, help its own members when they have need.'

'Surely you are not going to tell me once again that you are penniless and starving?'

'I was robbed of my money by one William Bedloe, a bad man whom I happened upon in Spain and trusted to be a friend, having made his acquaintance when we were both employed by the Earl of Norwich who is now the Duke of Norfolk. I thought Bedloe was one of us, Father, for he used to carry messages between Catholic households. I could not be expected to foresee what a cheating rogue the man was. He was touring on the continent purporting to be a peer of the realm on the Grand Tour with his brother posing as his servant. They travelled through Spain living like lords, swiving every doxy in every whorehouse–'

'Pray, save me the details,' Strange interrupts. Melted snow is dripping from Oates' soggy coat and the chamber stinks of old wet wool and his filthy bare feet.

Titus ignores him. 'William Bedloe and his brother travelled like lords, eating handsome dinners, sleeping in the best beds the taverns keep for gentlemen of quality. When I discovered him in trouble for horse stealing and other matters, I did what any good Christian man would do for a friend. I helped him out of this little mess.'

'I will not ask how you did this, Titus Ambrose,' Strange says wearily. 'I would not wish to know that Jesuit funds were used to assist a fraudster and a thief.'

'Aye, a thief, a figging cutpurse. That bastard stole ten pieces of eight from me. Whilst I was fetching a dinner for the three of us, he and his brother departed with my money. Christ's blood, if I ever discover his whereabouts, that man will get no more fucking Christian charity from me.'

'Pray, cease your blasphemies and do stop whining,' Strange says, frowning. 'Tell me, how have you subsisted in London these last weeks without funds?'

'The Catholic Church refused to help me when I went begging at their door,' Titus tells him testily. 'Thomas Pickering, a Benedictine, who gave me sustenance last time I was homeless, turned me away. Only one man came to my assistance: Israel Tonge, an Anglican clergyman whom I hoped to convert. He kindly opened his door to me...' Oates voice trails away as the aged Provincial glares at him and makes several attempts to raise himself from his chair which is creaking from the pressure of his hands on the arms.

'What say you? You stayed with Israel Tonge, he who has become the rector of St Michael's on Wood Street?'

Titus nods.

'That insane cleric who speaks ill of our Society, nay, invents evils to blame upon us?'

'Father, I did not know...' Titus stammers.

'He who writes venomous and prolific papers against us?' Strange manages to pull himself onto his feet. 'Titus Ambrose, I see that you do not choose your friends wisely. If you count this man amongst your confidants, I have to tell you that you are not fit to name yourself a Jesuit. Goodbye, Mr Oates. I have done my best for you and wish you well, but your future is not with us.'

Titus faces Strange. His lips are smiling but his eyes are cold. He fumbles inside his coat and brings out a plug of tobacco, never taking his eyes from the Provincial's bewildered countenance. He waits, young and strong, chewing his tobacco, until the old man's weak legs begin to tremble and he is forced to sink into his chair. Titus moves closer and puts his face so close that Strange has to turn away. 'I am the lame dog who is not worth helping over the stile, eh, am I? Is that what you think, Father Strange? What if I say that there is some truth in what this man Tonge says of fires, treason and plots? What if I should tell you also about my leisure hours at the Pheasant club in Fuller's Rents? Shall I tell you what I discovered there of the gross sins performed by Catholic men, with Catholic men, in the Devil's name; of evils fit to hang a Catholic man or a Jesuit priest if my Lord Chief Justice should hear of this. And there are other matters I could disclose, for I kept my eyes and my ears open at Valladolid.' Titus spits out his tobacco onto tiles that are puddled with melted snow. 'I have told you before, old man, if your ears are sharp enough to hear me, and you are not too weak in the head to understand. I have a long memory and I never forget the name of any man, nor the deeds he has done, especially those who have shunned me.'

Ten minutes later Titus Oates has given himself a new Jesuit pseudonym, Samson Lucy. Titus, son of Samuel and Lucy.

Father Strange's watery eyes are fixed above Titus' shoulder onto a blurred stack of precious books which he has collected during his career with the Society of Jesus. He hopes to read them all again at leisure if God grants him a long retirement and his eyesight does not fail him. He speaks slowly and carefully in his old man's wavering voice. The tone is flat, showing no emotion, as if he is speaking only to his books and expects no argument.

'I have decided what to do. You have asked me to allow you to complete the education you failed to take advantage of when you were a student. You shall travel at once to the province of Artois in France, to our school there, Saint Omer. The character of this institution is as English as it is possible to be abroad, so it will suit you well. Its purpose is to educate children from English Catholic families, but occasionally adults are accepted. You will not object to sitting in the schoolroom amongst young boys of fourteen years or so?'

Titus lowers his gaze. 'It will be a humility I will be pleased to accept in the service of the Almighty and the Society of Jesus.'

26

WHERE IS THE MASTER?
EARLY SPRING, 1678

Edmund Godfrey's s home these last five years is a house
on Hartshorne Lane, a narrow, busy alley, not far from
Charing Cross, which leads down to his wood and coal
wharf on the Thames. This morning he did not waste
time sitting in his bachelor's parlour drinking his dish
of chocolate and reading the London Gazette as he does
occasionally when business permits. Neither is he in his
woodyard.

By mid-morning, the smell of a good dinner has brought
his clerk into the kitchen.

'It's a hare, hashed and steeped in claret overnight, Mr
Moor,' the maid, Betty, tells him. She's an elderly woman
with strands of grey hair straggling out of her cap, but she
stands straight and tall beside the little old man as she skims
the froth from the pot with her brass scummer. 'There's
onions and lemon and ginger and nutmeg; that's what you
can smell.' She dips a spoon into the pot. 'Here, have a taste.'

Edmund's housekeeper, Judith Pamphlin, snatches the
spoon from Betty's hand. 'They'll be nothing for you,
Henry Moor, until Sir Edmund has eaten his fill.'

'We may as well eat our boots as wait for the master,
you silly fool, for the hare will be dry as old leather when
he returns, whenever that might be,' Henry says, smirking.

Judith starts and turns red in the face. 'What? Sir Edmund gone away and me not told of it.'

'Nay, missis, you forgot that he told you so yesterday.'

'I did not forget,' Judith says. 'He never told me he was going anywhere. If he had, I'd have set Betty here to do the washing whilst he's gone. Shame on you; you lie to get a taste of my good cooking. Get back to your office and your work. The master won't be pleased when he comes and finds you dallying in my kitchen.'

'Sir Edmund ain't a coming home for his dinner, I tell you. Not today, nor tomorrow and perhaps not for days after, so set the table, missis, and let us eat the dinner that you and Betty have put your hard work into.'

'Why did he say nothing to me?' Judith grumbles.

'He went of a sudden after he'd had his morning draught and a slice of bread and butter. "Henry," says he, "look through these papers whilst I'm gone," and that was that.'

'Nay, you should have told me that he was going away,' Judith complains.

'Now don't you get upset, Mrs Pamphlin,' Betty says kindly. 'You and Mr Moor, you've not been a year in this household; you don't know Sir Edmund like I do. I've come in and charred for him on and off these last seven years and he's been a good master to me. But he does have a habit of wandering off now and then. He would've expected you to tell Mrs Pamphlin,' she says severely to the clerk. She pulls him aside and whispers, 'You shouldn't go distressing a poor widow woman like this.'

'Sir Edmund didn't mention anything about telling anyone else in the house that he was going on a little journey,' Henry says, and sits at the table with his hands in his lap waiting to be served.

'It wouldn't have made any difference, Mrs Pamphlin,' Betty says gently. 'We started doing the hare yesterday evening, before the master decided to go away, of a sudden.'

'He's supposed to be dining at Lady Pratt's the day after tomorrow,' Judith complains. 'I've washed and starched his best cravat, ready for him, the fancy one trimmed with point. He likes dining with Lady Pratt. She'll wonder where he's got to if he don't turn up and she'll be cross that he's let her down so sudden leaving a seat with no backside on it at her table.'

'If he's not come home by mid-morning, the day after the morrow, I'll hurry over to Charing Cross, myself, and give his apologies to Lady Pratt,' Henry says. 'Now, Mrs Pamphlin, shall we eat your good dinner before it spoils. Sir Edmund wouldn't wish it to be wasted, knowing what it cost for the wine and the spices and all.'

'Did Sir Edmund say where he was going?' Betty asks, while she sets the table for three and brings out the remains of yesterday's pullet pie and a cheese, to complement the hare.

'No, he didn't say, so we're not supposed to know,' Henry says, 'and it ain't my business to ask him. But I'll say this: he wasn't dressed proper for going to visit folk of quality, just in his old coat and breeches and all. No fancy linen at his neck.'

'Oh,' says Judith, 'so we know where he's gone. His sisters won't be pleased when I tell them this.'

'It hasn't taken you long to get a-gossiping with the master's sisters,' Henry says shaking his head.

'It's not right, not right at all,' Judith grumbles, ignoring the clerk. 'Sir Edmund, a knight of the realm, who sits at table with the Lord Chief Justice and the Lord Chancellor: at the best tables in the land, I dare say. And such a sweet, kind person as Lady Pratt, looked up to by all the gentry, and a good friend to him too, inviting him to her table spread with fine dishes to tempt him, with his poor digestion, and then he don't turn up. And if she knew where he's gone instead, and what company he's keeping, well, what an insult to the good lady. Only last week, I heard his cousin ask him why he takes the trouble to go to Richmond for his sport when he's got St James' Park here at his doorstep.'

'Listening in doorways, as well as gossiping,' the old clerk mutters, shaking his head. 'No wonder Sir Edmund don't like women.'

***

Edmund runs up the green and bends his long body until his left knee is almost resting on the freshly scythed turf. His cupped right hand grasps the stone sphere and his left rests on his bent knee for balance. A footman and the man who rolls the green watch from a bench. Three apron-men stand in a group, each with their hands clasped behind their backs, intent upon the game. When Edmund releases the bowl there is silence. The serving woman bringing tankards of ale stops short in her tracks and she too watches Edmund's bowl roll straight and steady. Even the geese have ceased their honking.

This is what Edmund loves most. The silence. These moments when he and his companions watch the progress of their bowls, and afterwards, no talk, just frowns of disappointment or grins of excitement, and the counting and holding up of fingers. Edmund's bowl comes slowly to rest beyond the others and very close to the jack. He calculates his score: nineteen, he's in the lead. The man who tends the green pats his back. The footman rises to take his turn and gives Edmund a wink. If his bowl comes to rest nearer to the jack than Edmund's, they will be equal. Either of them could win with their next two bowls.

The footman takes longer than any man to eye the jack, so serious is he about his game, and he would never allow

Edmund to win because of his social status, he being a gentleman and a knight. Afterwards, all talk in the tavern is of the game. These common men communicate in facial expressions, gestures and a simple vocabulary slowly spoken. Listening is easy: Edmund knows the context, he misses nothing of the conversation. His companions are jolly in their defeat and he joins them in their laughter and adds his pennies to their own when they place their bets for the next game. And how wonderful it is to become absorbed in conversation about the course of the game from start to finish; about what might have happened if the butcher's bowl hadn't halted where it did in the first round, or if the taverner's bowl had rolled just one inch further, or if Edmund's last bowl hadn't stopped short so unexpectedly?

Whenever his brothers ask him why he debases himself on the bowling green with such mean people, Edmund can never make them understand that company of his own kind is irksome to him. Running up and down the green, absorbing himself in the game; this is the best medicine he knows for those times when melancholy overpowers him. He will be let blood in the autumn as always, to balance his humours, for autumn and winter are bleak, melancholy seasons for him. Only when he is on the green, and the game is all that matters, only then is he free of the world and its heaviness.

27

THE MURDEROUS PEER
SPRING AND SUMMER, 1678

'You have been thinking of this for some time,' John Grove tells Edmund. 'It would not be a hasty decision. And you say that Valentine Greatrakes has the approval of his lady for such a move?'

'The invitation is from Valentine only: his wife passed away in January,' Edmund says. 'Valentine writes of such peace and contentment in his home country that I think I could happily retire to Ireland, to be with my friend when my work on London's streets is done.'

'If you wait for vagabonds, fraudsters, thieves, drunks and whores to repent of their ways and become honest, hard-working citizens, your dream of a tranquil retirement will only ever be that, Edmund, a dream.'

'It is not my public duty that prevents me from…' Seeing Grove look towards the door Edmund stops speaking.

Betty enters the parlour carrying a tray. 'Mrs Pamphlin made them especially, knowing that they are your favourites, sir,' she says to Grove as she puts two dishes of chocolate and a plate of oatmeal cakes on the table.

'Please thank her kindly, from me,' Grove says, whilst Edmund waves his hand impatiently towards the door.

'That woman is always creeping into my chambers and taking me by surprise, I keep telling her to knock louder.

Women never listen. I was saying, before we were interrupted, that matters other than my public duty keep me
here in the capital; another man may kiss the King's hand
and join the Commission of Peace in my place. It is my
private businesses that prevent me from leaving. If my
nephew had proved himself to be the worthy business part-
ner I expected him to be, I might have left him in charge
of my English enterprises and taken the crossing to Ireland
years ago. That a member of my own family should treat me
with such unnatural unkindness is a great sorrow and disappointment to me. No, I will not let it go, so do not ask me
to. I will see this matter resolved in Chancery before I retire.
I trusted that boy. His father taught me much that I know
about business. Valentine cured his mother you know. Jane
had a great wen on her side and it has not returned since
he removed it. She has been well and in good spirits these
twelve years except for the distress young Godfrey has
caused her through his incompetence and his deceit. That
boy is a disgrace to my sister, nay, my whole family, and it
is a pity that his mother does not tell him this, for I have,
often enough.'

'The boy is married with a family to support and in much
anguish. He needs the annuity he claims should rightly be
his. And you, Edmund, you will wear yourself out with the
worry of it all, and to what purpose? You know that you will
never regain all of the money that is gone.' Grove speaks
quietly, face to face so that Edmund reads every word he
says. 'And all the while you could be living tranquilly in
Ireland, looking after your business interests over there and
enjoying the company of your friend.'

'I will not give in until I the matter is settled,' Edmund
says. 'Also, I would need someone to attend to my business
ventures here, in England. My clerk, Henry Moor, is getting
old, but he's competent. It is not yet time to replace him.'

'Let go of the lawsuit, employ a steward and go, join Greatrakes,' Grove says.

'I am not yet sixty, I can wait awhile.'

'Time is a precious commodity and should be used wisely, Edmund. The weekly bills of mortality do not lie. You have a vision of happiness, my friend, snatch it now,' Grove gently urges.

'Honest William, you speak plainly as always, but prithee, do not press me on this matter. Even if the lawsuit were settled in my favour, even if I found a true and honest steward…' Edmund's voice falters, he pulls out his handkerchief and wipes his mouth several times. 'Whenever I consider my retirement, it always comes to this: being the way I am, however could I go to him?'

'Your Father's legacy?'

Edmund nods. 'One time… when I was boy…' He pauses awhile before he continues, 'I pray that I shall never have to know such terror again. My father was taken by the Devil, there can be no other explanation.'

Grove says nothing, but silence is never heavy when friends know each other well and Edmund begins to talk of the terrible fear that has haunted him since he was a boy.

'The servants had to tie my father to his bed, you know, after they took the cleaver from him. I was a little trembling child hiding in a corner watching everything. He wasn't the father I knew any more with his eyes all bloodshot and staring and his mouth open wide and howling like a hound. I had to cover my ears for the sound hurt them badly. Afterwards, a surgeon was called, for he had hurt three of his children and I could barely breathe.'

Grove eats his cake and observes Edmund for some time until he catches his eye. 'You have never suffered as your late father did. In your many bouts of melancholy over the years you have never harmed a soul, nor threatened to hurt another being but yourself.'

'I fear that one day I might,' Edmund mutters to himself.

***

'Edmund, dear, prithee, calm yourself; let matters be when nothing can be done,' Cousin Mary says.

'I will not watch our nation being spoiled by peers of the realm who, far from setting an example to the common people, are heedless of the law,' Edmund replies.

'Hush, you are shouting.' Mary glances upwards. 'Mother is sleeping.'

'I beg your pardon,' Edmund lowers his voice, 'I should have inquired sooner. How is your mother?'

'Yesterday, she was quite her old self, but today she suffers badly.'

Edmund picks up his hat. 'Then I hope her end comes soon. Forgive me; I should not intrude upon your hospitality at such a time.'

'Nay, Edmund, stay awhile and tell me what it is that troubles you so.'

Edmund sits with his hat in his hand and his head bowed, staring for some time at the bright square of matting on the polished wooden floor. The smell of smoke and tallow is ever present in the homes of ordinary Londoners, but sitting here, in his cousin's cosy parlour in Old Southampton Buildings, there are other odours too, both sweet and calming, that kindle memories of his nursery when he was a very little child in the time before his father's malady changed everything; a mixture of lavender, jelly, honey and other things Edmund cannot recognise. He sighs and straightens himself into his tall chair.

'Philip Herbert, that violent, drunken, murderous man,' he spits out of a sudden.

'I do not know of him, should I?' Mary asks.

'He is a titled peer, the Earl of Pembroke. His wife's sister is the King's French whore.'

'The young lord who keeps a London home at Leicester Fields? I thought the King had put him in the Tower.'

'So he did. But the House of Lords voted to let him out, and thus he found his way to a tavern and to drunkenness again and there he found a man who had done him no harm, except to quarrel, and the Earl knocked him down and jumped upon him and kicked him, even as he lay helpless. The poor man has since died of his injuries.'

'Such wickedness,' exclaims Mary Gibbon. 'Surely the young lord will hang for his evil deed.'

'No, he will not,' Edmund retorts. 'He came before a jury where I, as their foreman, pronounced him guilty of wilful murder. And that should have been the end of the matter. Today, he pleaded benefit of the clergy, as is his legal right as a peer. The House of Lords has reversed the judgement to manslaughter, and it being, supposedly, his first offence, which, as is common knowledge to every honest man and indeed, every rogue hereabouts, is not the case, he has been let off to drink at any tavern in the city at his pleasure, and kick to death whoever he likes. Oh, cousin, how it wearies me when my efforts to keep the peace are fruitless. Of what use to the people of London is a jury that is impotent to convict a wild man who is a danger to others?'

'Are you yourself in danger from this man?' Mary asks. 'Will he seek revenge for your part in his conviction.'

Edmund shrugs.

'Maybe you should leave London for a while,' Mary says as she offers him cake and pours a glass of brandy, an expensive treat which she buys especially for him with the coal money he will not take from her. 'Your work incites hatred towards you, Edmund, you know it does. There was that gardener who was fined for calling you a knave, and there was that person who was brought before the justices for directing a scandalous paper against you because of a woman whom you sent to a house of correction. And what of all the cases in chancery? You have even made an enemy of your own nephew. Oh, Edmund, remember that your enemies do not forget you. And now this mad peer is amongst their number. I worry for you, Edmund, ever since you were threatened in an alley…'

'Bah, that was long ago, in the plague year. I had the rogue whipped around a churchyard for looting shut up shops and stealing shrouds from the dead and he bore me a grievance. I drew my sword, called for the constables, and the felon put down his cudgel and was taken away. For this and worse offences he was transported; fear not, cousin, he is no danger to me now. You know that I have never paid heed to men who hate me for doing my duty to keep good order on London's streets.'

'Maybe the time has come when you should,' Mary Gibbon says gently.

***

After a year in the Tower, Lord Shaftesbury's health has worsened. He struggles to walk without the use of two sticks, his complexion is yellow, but he is not lily-livered in his political aspirations. He has finally been invited to kiss the King's hand and beg forgiveness. In London's boiling summer, while the skies threaten a thunder that will not come, he seeks the company of his friend, Philip Herbert, Earl of Pembroke, at his home in Leicester Fields.

'The arrogance, the audacity of that man, Edmund Godfrey,' Pembroke declares in a rather slurred accent. 'How dare he accuse me, a member of the aristocracy, of such a dire crime as the murder of a man and expect to get away with it.'

'I hear that he has run away to France, to escape your anger,' Shaftesbury says.

'He can't hide away on the continent for ever. I'll wager he'll be back before Parliament sits again in the autumn.'

'I know the two younger Godfrey brothers well,' Shaftesbury says. 'Michael and Benjamin are loyal supporters of our Opposition faction: they are staunchly anti-French and abhor the prospect of having the papist Duke of York for their king when Charles dies. I've always thought Edmund Godfrey, unlike his brothers, to be a rather odd, unpredictable, miserable man; far too easy upon Catholic recusants to be a loyal follower of Opposition politics, but surprisingly, he's shown his hand, having joined Peyton's gang of republicans.'

'You do surprise me,' the young Earl says.

'I'm suspicious,' Shaftesbury replies. 'Is Edmund Godfrey as loyal to the cause as he pretends to be? Or has he wormed his way into Peyton's gang to discover our plans? Is he one of Williamson's spies? Or maybe his friend the Duke of York has set him to it. Godfrey has been doing some business with the Duke relating to land in Ireland.'

'That man, Godfrey has made a career of poking his nose into places it doesn't belong,' Pembroke retorts. 'Get one of your men to dog him when he goes about his daily business. Sooner or later we will discover something serious enough to get him kicked out of the Commission of Peace again.'

'Good idea, I'll have him followed when he returns to London.'

'You'd better see to it quickly before I kick the life out of him,' says the young inebriated Earl and laughs.

Part 4
The Hellish Popish Plot
August–September, 1678

"We shall all rise in the morning to find our throats have been cut."

Alderman Player (1678)

28

TRAVELLERS RETURN
EARLY JULY, 1678

Edmund disembarks at the docks after a channel crossing bringing him home from a visit to Europe where he has admired the great canal in construction at Montpellier. Upon sniffing the air, he puts a cloth to his mouth and hails a hackney carriage, directing the driver to Hartshorne Lane. He had travelled abroad for his health, his wellbeing, but seeing London in such a state he fears that his return may negate any good it has done. London is scorching and dry as a desert. The dirt that always covers London's streets, the animal dung, ashes and the filth that householders throw out of their windows; it has all turned to dust, and it is everywhere. Edmund sees the people walk in it leaving footprints as if it were sand. It settles on the silly white lace that ladies wear upon their topknots and in the rims of men's hats. A convoy of carts with their outrider bringing goods from the wharves has blocked Thames Street and the journey home takes longer than it should. On his slow progress through the busy streets Edmund sees dust soiling goods on the counters of the open fronted shops. A butcher boy swatting flies from carcasses hanging outside his master's shop beats a hail of it onto himself. Bah, what a homecoming, Edmund says to himself. London will suffocate me.

Even before the busy autumn, when the law courts will

resume for the Michaelmas term and the King and court return to Whitehall Palace, London is bustling. The hackney cab enters Hartshorne Lane and proceeds with difficulty, for the narrow thoroughfare is clogged with a convoy of carts. Edmund steps out of the carriage to watch them pass, for they are his own carts carrying his timber and coal. At his door, his clerk, old Henry Moor, awaits.

'Welcome home, Sir Edmund. I trust you have had a pleasant journey.'

He's no sooner walked through the threshold than Judith Pamphlin starts fussing around him. 'I've prepared a light meal of cold meats and curds and cream, Sir Edmund. Just what is needed for a traveller with a queasy stomach after a channel crossing from France.'

'The sea was calm,' Edmund says curtly. Reading the dismay on her visage he adds, 'The curds and cream will be most welcome to dry my mouth.'

Another man returns to London that summer wearing a wide-brimmed hat, grey and dirty, and Spanish leather shoes down at heel. He carries all his possessions in a bag slung over his shoulder. Even if he had enough money to send his luggage on ahead in a cart, he would have nowhere to direct the driver, having no home. He barges his way through a huddle of goodwives who are sorting through baskets of summer fruits, grabs a small basket of strawberries and hides it inside an old grey horseman's coat that is draped across his arm. A stray goose stretches its neck, opens its beak and hisses at his shins. He kicks it and swears at the countryman who is trying to hook the offending goose with his crook to return it to the trailing gaggle that he is herding to market.

Sweat pours from the traveller's face. It runs from his short hair onto his forehead, into his eyes, and drips from the end of his nose down his long chin. His shirt is soaking. He wanders up and down the little streets between Cheapside and Walling Street and finding himself on Cornhill and seeing a coffee shop, avails himself of a complimentary pipe and sits on an empty form awaiting his beverage.

'Back in London so soon, Mr Oates?' The proprietor holds the dish in his apron corner and makes a show of holding the coffee pot high and pouring the dark liquid in a long aromatic stream. 'Thought you'd gone to Spain?' he asks. 'Or was it France?'

'It's Dr Oates, to you. And of course I'm back. What a damn fool question. You can see me can't you?'

'Only I thought you told me that you were going away to study for a year or so,' says the proprietor. 'And just a few months later, here you are again.'

Titus blows on his coffee and swallows it in one gulp. 'It tastes like a foreign fart,' he complains and sends a cloud of smoke from his long clay pipe into the man's eyes. 'Pour me another.'

'Aye, I will, with pleasure, when you've paid me,' the proprietor says, holding the pot aloft ready to pour. Titus throws a coin onto the table.

'English coinage if you please, or one of our house tokens, I don't take foreign change.'

'It's all I have, so take it, pour my coffee and fetch me something to read.'

Titus sips his coffee and turns to the advertisements on the back page of *The Gazette*. There's a ten shilling reward if he can find a little lost spaniel that has run away from Somerset House, and twenty shillings for returning a black boy of around sixteen years, originally from the East Indies, who has run away from his master. The lad answers to the name of Black Tom, wears his hair long and is handsomely dressed in a blue edged suit of clothes and blue stockings.

Titus sniggers. If he should discover the boy, he knows where to take him for a greater reward than the mere twenty shillings his surgeon master is willing to pay.

A gentleman, wearing clothes of quality and colour and a long fashionable periwig of dark brown, approaches. He sweeps his arm in a wide arc with several flourishes of the wrist, making his lace ruffles flutter. 'I give you good day, Titus Oates. Well, now, tell me, how do the Jesuits abroad?'

Titus inclines his head in a curt bow. 'Matthew Medburne, well met. How does the Duke's Company?'

'Good, good, good. I write, I entertain. The King honours our theatre occasionally with his presence. He laughs at our comedies, he eats his oranges, and he has an unfortunate habit of departing with our wenches.' Medburne puffs on his pipe and waves an impatient hand to a waiter for coffee. 'So, you do not answer my question: how do the Jesuits abroad?'

Titus picks a strawberry from the basket on his lap and chews. 'I have no idea,' he says sulkily.

'Thrown you out again?' Medburne asks. 'Didn't want you for a schoolmaster to their little boys?'

'Sodding little Jesuit devils broke a pot over my head.'

'What, a piss-pot?' Medburne laughs raucously. 'Whatever did you do to deserve that? Come, come, you can tell me.'

'What, for you to make a play of it?'

'Hardly. Even the King would not countenance such an entertainment. What would it be, comedy? tragedy?'

Titus puffs out billows of tobacco smoke to mingle in the fog that always hovers above customers in the coffee houses. 'It wasn't a piss-pot,' he says sulkily. 'The boys there were vicious. A little boy whipped me up and down one day with a fox's tail.'

'Oh, so the young scholars didn't like you. Now I

understand,' Medburne says. 'You've left that institution rather hastily, for reasons of... now let me guess... was it, by any chance, an act of...?'

'Hush,' Titus hisses. 'You speak too loud being an actor and used to projecting your voice. Do you wish to have me arrested?'

Titus drinks his coffee alone, whilst Medburne wanders around the booths waving his silver-topped stick to groups of men he knows.

'Ah, Mr Pepys,' he cries, and seeing that gentleman alone in one of the booths, sits beside him. 'I saw you where you shouldn't have been on the Lord's Day but you did not follow your Italian friend to the altar?'

'You know that I come for the music,' Pepys replies tersely. 'I have told you more than once that I am not of your religion.'

'Ah, now I understand. Our Catholic Mass is rather like a play to you, Mr Pepys: an entertainment.'

'I will confess to you that I love your music perhaps just a little more than your comedies. But understand this, both lift my soul and take me to a mighty happy place.'

'The former will take you to a very dismal place, should the Earl of Shaftesbury hear of your visits to the Queen's Catholic chapel,' Medburne rejoins. 'He would greatly enjoy putting another gentleman in the Tower which he himself has only recently vacated.'

'Are you not afraid, Matthew, for your family and your Catholic friends?'

'Who am I for a great lord to notice? But you, Mr Pepys, member of Parliament, member of the Royal Society, Secretary to the Navy Board; do you dare to make an enemy of Lord Shaftesbury?'

'The King and the Duke of York will protect me from Shaftesbury's accusations, as they have done before.'

'Well, I wish you well. I dare say I may see you at the theatre later in the week. Good day to you Mr Pepys.'

Medburne returns to the solitary Oates. 'Where do you stay? Walk with me if it is in my direction.'

Titus runs his fingers down his long jaw, from his ruddy cheeks to his unshaven ruddy chin. Two or three times he does this, like a man deep in thought. 'I've lost my patron, Father Strange having recently retired,' he says in a low voice, looking Medburne in the eye. He throws the contents of his purse onto the table. 'This is all I own: a few fucking foreign coins.'

'Of little worth, I see.' The actor shakes his head with exaggerated exasperation and adjusts his features into a lugubrious stare but says nothing, only reaches into his pockets and passes a few coffee house tokens across the table.

'The new English Jesuit Provincial, Father Whitbread, dismissed me from Saint Omer as soon as he arrived on a tour of inspection,' Titus says grabbing the tokens. 'My Latin wasn't good enough,' he adds hastily.

Still, Medburne does not speak, just heaves great sighs and shakes his head whilst looking around as if he is on stage and inviting the audience to share his point of view.

'Bloody Jesuits were supposed to be giving me tuition,' Titus continues in a whine. 'I'm finished with the Society of Jesus and their promises. Papist pigs, all of them; Strange, Whitbread, I never forget a name. Papist bloody plotters. There's things I could tell...'

'You forget who I am. I find your remarks most painful to my Catholic ears.' Medburne reaches into his pocket again and throws a few shillings onto the table. 'Here, take these, they will buy you a dinner or two and a bed without fleas. Never let it be said that I did not help a man in need who was once my friend. I found you a patron, the Earl of Norwich. Through my Catholic influence, I acquired you an excellent position in his household. But you did not please him. I cannot this moment think of another who would suit. I would offer another invitation to the Pheasant but there again... perhaps not.' Medburne slaps his elegant ringed fingers on Titus' fat hand as he reaches to grab the coins. 'You saw and heard nothing of any matter contrary to the Law at the Pheasant. Remember that, Dr Oates. I expect no lies from you concerning things that were said or done at that club whilst you were there as my guest.'

'What is a lie?' Titus asks, while he counts out the shillings in his hand. 'I've forgotten. In fact, Matthew, if I'm honest, I think I never knew.'

***

After a clean bed and a good breakfast Titus must think clearly: make a plan. He walks the city streets past new churches waiting for their spires; past post-fire, bright-red brick-built houses with flat roofs and balconies over their entrances where people are sitting in the shade quenching their thirst and talking to their neighbours opposite. Seeking relief from the heat he slips into shady alleys and strides beside the Thames. Everywhere there is industry, business, purpose: street sellers call their wares, shopkeepers haggle, car-men wheel their carts and curse him for getting in the way, carriages rumble past and spray him with dust. London reeks of coffee, filth and stinking bodies, his own included. After an hour in the heat his shirt clings damply to his body, his woollen stockings are wet and itchy, his head drips under his hat, and his under-linen is so soggy it feels like he's pissed himself.

In a tavern near the Barbican, Titus drinks his ale and considers what he should do. In this city of busyness he has an asset that must be respected. This he's known ever since he was a sulky boy whose whip-thrashing masters tut-tutted at his lack of aptitude for learning. William Smith, his master at Merchant Taylors' School, hadn't even hidden his surprise when they met in a tavern around the time of Bart's Fair two years ago.

'What you, Oates, a clergyman? So you've finally mastered Latin and Greek at last? Never thought you would.'

'What you, Smith, a sodomite?' Titus rejoined when their paths converged again at the Pheasant in Fuller's Rents.

And there were others who had been pleased to kick his arse out of their doors: his Cambridge tutors who'd informed his father that his son was a great dunce, but a plodder, they conceded, as if they cared. His father never acknowledged this latter point, being a preacher whose mouth did all the work for him, but then, Titus, the second son, was always surplus to requirements; a child given to convulsions, the Devil's curse. Even his mother acknowledged that there was 'something unnatural and not quite right about the boy, although a mother's love is a mother's love all the same.' He'd heard her say so to his father when he was a little child hiding in the chimney corner.

Titus surprises himself sometimes, in his self-belief. All the insults, the rejections; hasn't he always coped with these, and coped well where other men would just accept failure? Hasn't he always found a purpose? Yes, he's a plodder. Others might give up on him but he's never given up on himself; rather, he's made himself up, like a character in one of Medburne's plays; rewritten himself again and again. He purses his lips and expectorates his tobacco onto the ale splattered floor. Surely there is employment waiting for him in this thriving post-fire city: this new London that was burned to ashes by... Titus' dull brown eyes turn glassy and bright, he calls for more ale and laughs as he throws the last of Medburne's shillings onto the table. This new city that was burned to ashes... this new post-fire city that was brought down by who else but... the Society of Jesus. Imagination is a marvellous asset for a man with empty pockets, and resentment a mighty furious fuel for a man who does not shun hard work.

And now he is sure, beyond doubt, where he must go, and he knows what to say to make himself welcome. He sets forth to seek a man who loathes the Jesuits even more than he does: the mad old clergyman, Israel Tonge, at his home in the Barbican. He will feed the papist-hating cleric tales of Jesuits and plots, and Tonge will slather at the jowls and lick them up like a starving cur. Titus has lived and worked amongst the Jesuits, as a spy of course – as Tonge had advised him to do when he had nowhere else to go – always, ever, the spy, whose sole purpose was to discover their plotting: Titus Oates, alias Titus Ambrose, alias Samson Lucy, the respected Salamanca doctor of divinity, the discoverer of the Hellish Popish Plot to assassinate His Sacred Majesty, King Charles II, overthrow Parliament and establish the Romish Church here, in England. He will show his father, his schoolmasters, his Cambridge tutors, the Parkers of Hastings, Captain Sir Richard Routh, Matthew Medburne; he will show them all, everyone who has spurned him, what a plodder can do.

29

PLOTTING A PLOT
AUGUST, 1678

Israel Tonge's eyes are shining as if it is the first Pentecost and the Holy Spirit has lit a candle inside him, here, at his home, whilst sitting at his desk. From the depths of his shaggy grey beard the clergyman's lips belch out phrases that Titus doesn't understand. 'They sin against God… dogs stain… pigs all of 'em.'

'Has the old fart heard a word of what I've just told him?' Titus asks himself aloud. 'What? Are you a madman with your ramblings, Tonge?'

'Yes, yes, I heard you and now I must concentrate,' Tonge says, closing his eyes and pressing his fingers on his temples. 'God speaks to me through words and letters and I must rearrange the letters in the words to discover God's message. You say that Father Strange spoke to you at length of how he and others fired London in '66 and you are willing to testify to this? Let's jumble up the letters and see what we make of it.'

He writes *Strange, afire* and *evil* on a paper, takes his scissors and cuts each word into separate letters. Tenderly, he touches the scraps and slides them around in little swirling movements and all the while his lips tremble as if in silent prayer. 'I have it, I have it' he cries, and writes *arranges, rife.* He frowns. 'Whatever does it mean? I need more words; the message is only partly composed.'

Titus snatches the quill from his hand. 'This is no time for women's parlour games; have you listened to a word I've said? A Jesuit plot is brewing and we must staunch it before it spreads.'

Tonge grabs a clean sheet of paper and a new quill and begins to write frantically, dipping his nib into the ink several times and flying it across the paper. 'The Jesuits trusted you, let you discover their secrets?' he asks. 'I told you they would.'

'They gave me fifty pounds to kill you,' Titus declares.

'Ah, so they know of the pamphlet I write and would have me dead before I take it to press. They will easily find me at home here, at the Barbican.' The quill trembles in Tonge's hand and blots the page.

Titus sifts through the pile of papers on the desk. 'God's blood, Tonge, if they knew what a fucking tedious document it is that you write, your life would be in no danger at all.'

Tonge stares at Titus, his eyes ablaze. 'You say they let you into their secrets, and you have knowledge of their covert plans to kill the King, topple Parliament and put York on his brother's throne with the pope sitting at his right hand? I knew it, I knew it.'

'They plotted it all at their triennial Consult in April, here, in the city, under the King's long, whore-sniffing nose, at a tavern in the Strand: fifty Jesuits and their new English Provincial, Father Whitbread, made plans to assassinate the King when he took his morning constitutional in the park. Jesuit lay brother, John Grove, alias Honest William, and Thomas Pickering, a Benedictine lay brother who refused to give me help when I went a-begging a second time, these two have already tried to shoot the King, but they hadn't checked the gun and the flint was loose. Father Whitbread whipped Pickering for his incompetence and they made a second attempt, but on this occasion, Honest William forgot the gunpowder, or pretended to forget it because he lost his nerve. Next time, they will not make those mistakes.'

'You must write it all down. Get to it, get to it, now.' Tonge thrusts a quill and paper into Titus' hand. 'Nothing is evidence unless it is in writing and sworn upon. And we need names of conspirators, and the date, time and place where the deed is finally to be done. The Catholic Duke of York, he's a conspirator in this plot? He's plotting his brother's death you say? Fratricide is it? And His Majesty's popish wife who worships her devilish idols at Somerset House, she's in on it too?'

'If we want her to be, yes.' Titus answers casually, as if they are planning a picnic in the countryside. 'Anyone in York's or the Queen's household; any Jesuit or Catholic; anyone with Catholic employers or friends. We may accuse whoever we like, and as you say, they are all at it, plotting treason, so what's written is evidence. The Queen's physician, Sir George Wakeman; he's in a very handy position to poison His Majesty, wouldn't you say, Tonge?'

'He's a Catholic, of course he's plotting. The Devil cackles heresies into his ears like all the others.'

'The Jesuits will beshit themselves in fear,' Titus says, pulling a face. 'But mind, not a word of this matter to anyone but ourselves. They believe that I am one of them and I have their confidence. Should they discover my real affinities and intentions they will kill me.'

'If we do not inform the Lord Chief Justice of everything we have discovered, we will be guilty of misprision of treason,' Tonge declares, stabbing his quill in the air and letting ink drop like tears onto his paper. 'If the Jesuits do not murder us in our beds, the King's hangman will do it at Tyburn.'

'Do not dare to go out into the city blabbing of treason

like a madman,' Titus retorts. 'I promised the Jesuits that I'd kill you, remember.'

Tonge scowls. '*You* kill *me*? You couldn't watch a butcher wring a goose's neck without spewing up.'

'Open up your lugs, old man,' Titus hisses, 'and heed what I say. There's money to be earned from the discovery of treason, so, we keep our mouths shut until the evidence is properly documented, and when we are ready, we will surprise the King with our proof of the Hellish Popish Plot against his sacred life.'

'Good, good,' says Tonge without looking up as he cuts up more letters.

'We need to plan how to do it. The Jesuits must never discover that it is I who informed on them, or they will kill me.'

'They will kill us both,' Tonge rejoins.

'Listen; I will hide my papers here, at the Barbican,' Titus explains. 'I'll just slip them behind the wainscot somewhere, and later, you will pretend to find them and take them to my Lord Chief Justice or maybe even better, go right to the top, to Lord Treasurer Danby.'

'No, no, no, these men of politics will not heed anything I say,' Tonge cries. 'You know that I warned the Privy Council about the Jesuits and their plotting before Parliament went down, and they smirked at me as if I'm an idiot and shook their heads.'

'They will listen to me,' Titus boasts. 'When I get going with my sermons, the congregation open their ears and listen for hours. And being young they will not treat me like an old fool.'

Tonge snorts. 'Why should these great men listen to you, a clergyman with no parish who begs for his living? We need to speak directly to the King. He takes his walk in the park each morning especially so that he can have a little chat to his people. We can hang around His Majesty and await an opportunity to tell him of this terrible plot.'

'What? Shall we approach him ourselves? In public? Don't you understand that if the Jesuits see me in conversation with the King I am done for. I must hide away, remain anonymous.'

'Oh, I know just the man who will approach the King on our behalf,' Tonge says, excited. 'Christopher Kirkby, a chemist who assists King Charles with his experiments. They're trying to discover the Philosopher's Stone, you know.'

'Can Kirkby be trusted?'

'Yes, yes, yes, upon my oath, he can. He wants rid of the Jesuits as much as we do. I will urge him to alert the King to a terrible plot against his life. The King will listen to him. Finally the papist pigs will get the traitor's death they deserve.'

'Finally,' says Titus, 'as a brave and loyal subject of King Charles II, I will claim the reward that I deserve.'

'And when this is so, and you are a rich man, perchance your father will slap you on the back and congratulate you,' Tonge says.

'Fuck my father,' Titus mutters.

***

Charles is annoyed to find Christopher Kirkby hovering around him in the outer gallery so early in the morning and muttering about a plot. His morning constitutional is his own private time and he will not be pestered with matters of state or any other business. He refuses to think about Lord Treasurer Danby's failure to squeeze more money from Parliament's tight purse strings, nor of his cousin Louis XIV's reluctance to pledge another generous handout. Such concerns are for later, when he has refreshed himself with exercise. Charles merely glances at the paper Kirkby hands to him as he hurries downstairs. When he is about to enter the park he calls for Kirkby to approach him.

'Tell me of this plot, but do be brief,' he says.

'Your Majesty is in danger this very morning,' Kirkby says, trying to catch his breath after rushing behind the King and his courtiers and almost tripping over a dog on the stairs.

Charles cannot help smiling at the nervous chemist despite his annoyance, for his wig is all askew and in his agitation he is jumping about like a grasshopper.

'There is a plot against your life, even now, as you take your walk,' Kirkby stammers.

'A plot to assassinate me? How?' Charles asks, still smiling.

'By shot, sir, this very morning...'

'The ducks have been kept waiting long enough for their breakfast,' Charles says, and he strides into the park towards the pond. 'We'll speak of this in my bedchamber when I return,' he calls to Kirkby, 'unless I am shot dead first.'

'Tell me, who is it who plans to shoot me? You have names, I presume,' Charles asks while he pours water into a bowl for his dogs.

'It is a Catholic plot, Your Majesty.' Kirkby's voice trembles as the accusations tumble out of his mouth. 'Thomas Pickering, a Benedictine, and John Grove, a Jesuit, alias Honest William, have both vowed to assassinate you. Indeed, they have already made two such attempts, but failed. And Sir George Wakeman...'

'What? My wife's physician? Does he hide a great blunderbuss under his bed?'

Kirkby does not discern the ridicule in the King's dry

questioning. 'No, sir. He will use poison if the assassins fail again.'

'The Jesuits are mighty indiscreet to divulge plans which surely they would wish to keep privy to themselves,' Charles says. 'How came you by this information?'

'A clergyman, Israel Tonge, has obtained written evidence of the plot, and has asked me to inform Your Majesty with haste.'

'I suppose I had better see these papers you speak of,' Charles says. 'I will see the two of you tonight, between the hours of eight and nine.'

30

FIVE LETTERS

AUGUST, 1678

'It is disgusting in that Palace, there's dog turds every-where,' Tonge complains. 'We had to step over them before we bowed to the King, and when he dismissed us, I stepped backwards to give my obeisance and trod in one and I had to walk around the park to clean my shoe. Kirkby told me it's always like this, even in the closet where the King does his chemistry experiments. There are more dogs running around than servants to clean up after them. The spaniels even piss and shit in the King's bed.'

'You should have wiped your shoe on your beard,' Titus scoffs. 'Nobody would have been any the wiser. The Devil knows what livestock lives in it.'

'You should have gone to the King,' Tonge snaps. 'It's your plot.'

'Did the King ask about me?' Titus asks

'Only your name,' Tonge replies.

'You didn't fucking tell him, did you?' Titus' words come out in a strangled scream. 'Christ, Tonge, you know that I have to remain an anonymous informer to protect my secrecy. The Jesuits will kill me if they know that I spied on them. Did you tell this to the King?'

'I did, and the King conceded that you needed protection.'

'Whilst we were talking,' Tonge continues excitedly, 'the

Duke of York came in and asked what was the matter, but the King lied, and told his brother that it was merely base business.'

'Secrets from his brother, eh? My discoveries disturbed him.'

'On the contrary, the King was bored. He yawned when I told him that you travelled to Valladolid carrying plans for a Jesuit rebellion in Scotland. He laughed behind his handkerchief when I read about Honest William forgetting the gunpowder, and he shook his head and rolled his eyes when I told him about the thousands of pounds that King Louis was offering to the Jesuits. The King cares about nothing but his dogs, his women and his sport at Newmarket. He didn't give a shit, remember, when that idiot, Thomas Blood, walked out of the Tower with the Crown Jewels hidden under his cloak and the sceptre stuffed down his breeches.'

'Blood got lands in Ireland worth five hundred pounds and a pension for his trouble,' Titus says excitedly.

'The King is a fool.'

'The King and his brother need spies,' Titus cries, 'and who better to do their dirty work than a man like Blood.'

'You are our spy, Oates, our informer. You should have read your forty-three articles to the King, not me. He would have paid more attention to you, asked you questions, and you would not have been stuck for answers; you never are. I had hardly begun reading when he bade me stop midsentence. "I have no time for this," he said. "I am not inclined to believe what you have told me, yet amongst so many particulars, I don't know that there may be some little truth in this. I will leave Lord Treasurer Danby to deal with it." Then he started tapping his fingers on his knee as if he were listening to music that I couldn't hear and he dismissed me.'

'After all my hard work setting out my articles, I hope

Lord Danby takes matters of treason more seriously than the King,' Titus grumbles.

'*Your* hard work,' Tonge cries,' what about *mine*? You forced me to copy each of your forty-three articles to disguise your hand and I had to correct your spellings as I wrote. In his exasperation Tonge spits out the words and sprays Titus who promptly retaliates by directing a gob of chewed tobacco onto the clergyman's crisp white neckband.

'Lord Danby expects me to search the streets and alleys with his servant, Lloyd and Christopher Kirkby,' Tonge complains. 'We are to apprehend assassins carrying knives; that is if they don't kill us first.' He pulls at the stained neckband and almost strangles himself. 'You're fucking scared, Tonge.'

'And you are not? You send me out on errands in peril of my life whilst you hide yourself away.'

'Heed what I say, Tonge. There's a Jesuit plot brewing: you know it, I know it, every Protestant in London knows it except the King, who heeds nothing but his whores. We need to force him to take it seriously — and he will need a lot of persuasion.'

Tonge, who has finally managed to untie his neckband, throws it aside. 'Listen,' he says irritably. 'Lord Danby requires that I ask my anonymous informant to provide more information: what he has is insufficient to make a conviction. These letters you mention from Whitbread, telling Father Fenwick to offer the Queen's physician fifteen thousand pounds to administer the poison if ten thousand pounds will not entice him, and the other one that tells of the burning of Westminster and Whitehall; Danby needs to hold these letters in his hands. He will send his men to intercept Jesuit correspondence at the Post Office, so you have to give me dates when the Jesuits are posting their letters to make it easier for his men.'

'Oh,' says Titus, and frowns. 'It will take time and trouble to provide such detailed evidence, and secret, safe lodgings for myself, in case the Jesuits begin to suspect me. Tell Danby that I want recompense for putting my life at risk.'

'You cannot expect to be paid until there is proper evidence,' Tonge says.

'Then I must cease my investigations and find other sources of income. The Jesuits will pay a high price to get their hands on my papers.' Titus holds out his hand. The old clergyman has to dig into his pocket three times before Titus closes his fingers.

'Lord Danby believes that Mr Edward Coleman must needs be busy in the plot if any be, he having been secretary in both the Duke and Duchess of York's Catholic households, but he requires more evidence to get a search warrant: those were the Lord Treasurer's very words. Do you know anything of this, Oates?'

'We'll leave Coleman to hang himself, for the moment,' Titus says. 'It's the Jesuits we're after. We've exposed the traitor in the Queen's household although the King refuses to believe that his wife's physician is planning to kill him, but he will believe it, certainly he will, as the plot develops. For the present we will target another royal Catholic household.'

'Louise, the French Catholic whore who the King sent for after his sister died,' Tonge cries, 'she who is now Duchess of Portsmouth? Where else would evil reside but in her den of sin? Surely she spies for King Louis.'

'I was thinking of the Duke of York and his personal confessor, Father Bedingfield,' Titus says. 'Let the Catholic whore rot in sin until we need her. York is at the root of the plot, he will become King when his brother is assassinated, so his household is where the conspirators must be found.'

Titus has spent all day writing. He knows that the corre-spondence must be vague, ambiguous, lacking in detail, for the content will be scrutinised by Lord Treasurer Danby. The letters need only give a few hints to what is written in his forty-three articles; too much information could betray them as forgeries and spoil everything. He must attempt to disguise his writing to give a separate, distinct hand for each correspondent.

He addresses the five letters to the Duke of York's con-fessor, Father Thomas Bedingfield at Windsor. 'See what a plodder can do,' he says aloud. He knows no harm of four of the correspondents, except that they are Catholics and Jesuits, and he's finished with that society and their broken promises, but the final letter, this will be his triumph. Yes, he has a good memory and no, he never will forget a man who's slighted him. 'For Father Whitbread, a traitor's death,' he hisses. 'Never gave me a chance to be a schoolmaster to the boys at Saint Omer.'

Titus promised himself years ago that he would conjure something audacious, and here it is: the Hellish Popish Plot. When Danby and the King read these letters they will believe every detail and his Plot will crack open and grow.

In the months to come, nothing will be true or false unless Dr Titus Oates makes it so.

31
DID A CHILD WRITE THESE?
31ST AUGUST, 1678

Charles had been enjoying his summer holiday here at Windsor until the letters arrived. For four years now the castle has been undergoing refurbishment and each time he returns there are more wonderful artworks to admire. He doesn't know what to say to his brother, so he listens and tries to appear more surprised than he is.

'Did a child write these?' James asks. His brown wig curls in costly ringlets down his chest and his eyes are narrowed in anger. 'Father Bedingfield's name is incorrectly spelt, in fact, none of these supposed Jesuit plotters can spell their own names.'

Charles rises from his chair to pour his brother a glass of wine. 'Take no heed. The letters are obvious forgeries. It seems that the same man wrote at least three of the letters, probably all of them, and badly too.' He places two of the letters side by side. 'Look, the papers match. They have been cut from the same quire.'

'But I do take heed,' James says. 'Who is it who so cruelly defames my honest confessor? Father Bedingfield was terrified when he read these letters, not only for himself but for the honest men who are implicated in these preposterous lies. Fortunately, he had the good sense to come to me immediately. The poor man was in a dreadful state; he could barely speak. I will get to the truth of it. The matter must come before the Privy Council. I insist upon it.'

'It would be better to keep this privy to ourselves,' Charles says. 'The more you stir a turd the more it stinks.'

'I didn't know you could be so vulgar,' James tells his brother.

'Let the matter rest,' Charles says, 'unless you wish to have Lord Danby's men sniffing and scratching around your household looking for further evidence of treason.'

'Let them come. They will find none. I want these lies exposed and my honest confessor vindicated.'

This is not what Charles wants at all. Nothing but harm can come to James if these accusations are made public, even though proven to be unsubstantiated. He does not need to tell his brother that since he declared himself to be a full, practising member of the Roman Church he and his household have become vulnerable to all kinds of allegations of treason; naive and bull-headed as he is, James surely knows that this is so.

'Whoever wrote these missives?' Charles ponders, and answers his own question. 'A man who hates Catholics, and Jesuits in particular, that's obvious. The writer is barely literate; a common man of no account. We shall pay no heed; people are always talking of plots against my life but none has come to fruition.'

'How our father would have loved Verrrio's new fresco paintings here,' he says, to change the subject. 'And Catherine is beginning to admire Grinling Gibbons' wood-carvings. The man's work is truly amazing, don't you think? He can carve anything into his wood: foliage, flowers, birds, violins even and so profusely and delicately. And his pea pods are such an amusing way to leave his signature, don't you think?'

James is not to be put off. 'I mean to have this matter

aired in public. You may be unwilling to bring it to the attention of the Privy Council. I am not.' He bundles up the letters and rises to leave. 'I shall personally deliver these to Lord Danby and charge him with the discovery and punishment of their author.'

'No, give me the letters, I'll deal with them,' Charles orders. 'I'll send for Danby immediately. His men will seek out the author. Now then,' he says more cheerfully, 'shall we play tennis this afternoon? It will divert you.'

'No,' says James, 'you always win.'

'Not on this occasion,' Charles mutters to his brother's departing back.

***

Lord Danby makes his obeisance to the King and stands straight and confident before him, elegant in his long fair wig and his silken court clothes. They are of an age, Charles and the Lord Treasurer: two opposing pieces on a chessboard, a king and a knight, the one dark, the other pale.

Charles waves the letters under the Lord Treasurer's nose. 'Your men have failed you, my lord, and you have failed me. You promised that they would intercept this correspondence at the Post Office. My brother is sorely troubled and his confessor also. He need never to have been alerted to this plot, if plot there be, which I very much doubt. What happened?'

Danby takes the letters from the King's hand and frowns, making his eyebrows crawl together like two blond caterpillars. His mouth tightens under the thin moustache. 'I will look into it, Your Majesty.'

Danby strides through the palace and into the courtyard where his manservant, Lloyd, follows him to his carriage.

'My lord, look there,' Lloyd says, pointing to a stout man,

around sixty years of age who hurries in the direction of the royal apartments.

'Whatever brings Thomas Blood here, to Windsor?' Danby settles himself into his carriage and Lloyd sits beside him. 'When Blood returns to London, visit him. Discover whether he waited upon the King or his brother today and what business was conducted.'

'The usual enticements apply, I presume, my lord? A girdle full of guineas hidden about my person?'

'Yes. I can count on you to use your intuition to offer whatever is required?'

'Of course, my lord. By what name is Blood known these days; is he a captain, a colonel, a major or plain Mr Allen, as he was last time.'

He uses the alias Dr Ayliffe, these days. He resides with his wife at his apothecary shop in Shoreditch where he practices. Use the excuse of buying physic, then speak with him privily in a back room.'

'Rather a commonplace occupation, if I may say so, my lord, for a daring sort of man who almost got away with stealing the Crown jewels and who once attempted to abduct the Duke of Ormonde and threatened to hang him at Tyburn if a ransom were not paid.'

'I dare say that he has learned, with age, to earn his living in quieter ways,' Danby says, 'but, beware, he is still the same man. He is neither hot headed nor violent, but he will maim, or even kill in cold blood. And remember, Blood serves many masters. Be discreet, tell him initially only that I wish him to inform me of the purpose of his visit to Windsor today. Take him to a good tavern. He may pretend to be a man who spurns strong drink but he can easily have his tongue loosened by wine and a few treats. I would be interested to know who is using Blood currently, and for what purpose.'

Within a few days Lloyd has some of the answers Danby requires.

'It was the Duke of York who sent for Blood, my lord, not the King. He asked Blood to discover the writer of certain treasonous letters purporting to be from Jesuit priests which were sent to his confessor, Father Bedingfield. York believes them to be forgeries.'

'Just as I thought,' Danby says. 'Has Blood named the authors of these missives?'

'He has discovered nothing to report to York, no evidence that they are forgeries, but if he should, he will contact me to inform your lordship before the Duke is told.'

***

Summer continues dry and hot. A fever is spreading fast and taking away the young, the old, the weak, the strong. On Tuesday 2nd September, every London household fasts in remembrance of the Great Fire, as they have done for the past twelve years. In the church of St Mary Overie, on the south side of London Bridge, Israel Tonge preaches a sermon of fire and damnation. He is at the height of his oratory, propounding God's vengeance upon the perpetrators of the conflagration, when he halts midsentence and stares into the congregation. Titus is amongst the people, catching Tonge's eye.

'I have heard nothing from Lord Danby, not a word. Do you have any new evidence?' Tonge asks urgently as he pulls Titus into the privacy of the vestry after the service has finished and the people have departed. 'What shall we do now?' he asks morosely. 'Nobody important wants to hear about our plot.'

'I know what to do,' Titus says, 'that's why I sought you out. Did you think I came to church to doze through your ramblings in the pulpit for three hours with an empty belly and a bursting bladder?'

'What shall we do?' Tonge asks excitedly.

'We shall find a magistrate and swear upon the Bible that our evidence is true.'

32

UNWELCOME VISITORS
6TH SEPTEMBER, 1678

Edmund wonders why they have come and who recommended him to them.

Surely they lie when they tell him that one of the Secretaries of State, Sir Joseph Williamson, told them to bring their deposition to him. Williamson would never show such poor judgement. The Secretary knows that of all the men in the Commission of Peace, he, Godfrey, is the least suitable to deal with this matter. It is no secret that he has Catholic family members and friends, his cousin, Mary Gibbon and Edward Coleman being amongst them. If Coleman's name is mentioned in connection with this business, as Edmund fears it may be, he will be compromised, surely, between loyalty to his friend and his king.

He should have refused to listen to Israel Tonge yesterday, sent him away to try his luck with another magistrate. Instead, he allowed Tonge to take him to a tavern to meet his *'honourable friends.'* Christopher Kirkby, the King's chemist, had bowed profusely whilst holding onto his wig, which was an alchemy in itself, being of several colours not commonly found in human hair. His temper was as lively as his wig when Tonge spoke of the Jesuits. Lloyd, Danby's manservant, a quiet man without a proper face, just the expressionless countenance of a gentleman's gentleman, spoke very little. Lawyer, Richard Adams greeted Edmund as if it were their first meeting, as if they had not met several times since Adams was released from the Gatehouse Prison several years ago, but somehow he sensed that Tonge was not deceived.

Today, in his home, three men stand before him, unwelcome. Edmund would rather deal with any common rogue, pickpocket or swindler than these two clerical gentlemen and their nervous friend, the chemist.

Tonge introduces Titus Oates, doctor of divinity.

'I have lived with the Jesuits abroad, as a spy, to learn their secrets,' Oates interrupts, stepping closer to Edmund and thrusting papers into his hands. 'It is I who am the discoverer of the information in the deposition we have brought for you. By swearing before a magistrate upon the Holy Bible, I avow that what is written is the truth, in all its Hellish detail.'

Edmund knows immediately that he dislikes this bull-necked young man who does not know how to keep his distance, either physically or verbally. It is unsettling, to say the least, to have that big face with its huge jutting chin so close to his own. Edmund does not respond to Oates' outpouring of information, merely indicates that the three informants should sit on the chairs he has placed for them facing his desk, so that he will be able to read their faces as they speak.

Edmund turns first to Israel Tonge. 'I told you yesterday that I would rather you took your depositions elsewhere...'

Oates leaps to his feet and leans on the desk. 'It is a matter of high treason, you cannot refuse.' Being so close to Edmund, the strident tone of his voice sends a pain into the magistrate's ever sensitive ears.

'Pray be seated, Dr Oates,' Edmund says sharply. 'Dr Tonge brought the matter to my attention, so I will speak with him initially. I will hear you later.'

'My good friend speaks truly,' Tonge says, greatly agitated. 'The Jesuits are plotting, they always are, and you must hear our oaths because if the King and the Privy Council do not heed our warning, the papist dogs will kill us all, for they are here within our city walls with daggers under their cloaks, convening in secret places.'

'I take it that as you mention high treason, you believe that these Jesuits are conspiring to kill King Charles.'

'And ourselves, for discovering their secrets.'

'Who knows of this, besides yourselves?'

'The King has been alerted to the danger.'

'Which of you dared to approach His Majesty with the dire information that assassins are waiting to kill him?'

'Being known to His Majesty, I was able to warn him of the great threat to his life when he walked to the park with his dogs,' Kirkby says in a trembling voice.

'Does the King continue to take his exercise as usual, each day, since he was told of this plot?' Edmund asks, knowing what the answer will be.

'Unfortunately, yes, I believe he does.'

'If His Majesty does not heed your warnings of a terrible plot against his life, why should I be troubled with it?'

'The King has received a copy of my evidence and has entrusted it to a member of the Privy Council,' Oates retorts.

Edmund does not ask which member it is that he refers to: he knows that it can only be Lord Treasurer Danby. He asks his visitors to kindly excuse him for a moment or two while he peruses their document. Conversation always requires a great effort of concentration for Edmund. It is a relief to read the deposition rather than to hear others speak of it.

'I see that the Irish are ready to rise against us and are resolved to cut all Protestants' throats,' Edmund says dryly after several minutes of silence.

'Aye twenty thousand foot soldiers and five thousand horse are ready in Ireland and a further fifteen in the North await...'

Edmund cuts Oates short. 'The people will be terrified when they hear of this,' he says more to himself than to his visitors. He turns to Tonge. 'You mention firing of houses and towns?'

Tonge nods and turns to Oates. 'Tell Sir Edmund what you know,'

'A Jesuit lay-brother, John Grove, alias Honest William, fired Southwark in '76. Fathers Strange and Whitbread, the English Provincials, told me so themselves on separate occasions, in confidence you understand, believing me to be one of them.'

'John Grove lost his own home in that fire, but bravely saved others,' Edmund replies, barely looking up as he scans the deposition. 'I see that you also accuse him of other serious crimes: high treason, in fact.'

'Lord Danby believes Mr Edward Coleman to be involved in the plot, too, but at present we lack evidence that this is so,' Oates says, 'but others are named in the deposition, as you have seen. Dr Wakeman, the Queen's physician...'

'I have heard enough.' Edmund retorts and picks up his Bible from the desk. 'Will you swear upon oath that these matters are known to the King?' he asks Tonge and Kirkby.

'Will you swear that the evidence in these papers is of your own discovery?' he asks Oates.

Afterwards, Edmund will never understand why he underwrote the deposition and why he allowed Titus Oates to take it away.

There is the Bible, there are three men standing before it, and there is himself, the magistrate, rising from his chair.

Between the laying on of hands and the swearing of the oath something happens and Edmund forgets who he is and loses the purpose of his life. He has always known that he has two selves, the one, the man of duty, elated to be pursuing his life's work, God's work, and knowing himself to be happy even beyond all happiness. This is his real identity. His other self, cursed with his father's melancholy, must be fought, kicked to the ground, vanquished for the enemy it is. He has asked himself many times as he shuffles through the midnight of his darkest days, why ecstasy must always be followed by deep despair. The answer is ever the same: it is his temptation, his wilderness to overcome. When he climbs again onto the pinnacle, the euphoria will be all the greater because he knows that once more, he has beaten the Devil within his soul.

This day a man has entered his home, a man he cannot like and would have turned away from his door but that he must do his duty as a justice of the peace. This man, Titus Oates, has not seen the well-respected, God-fearing knight of the realm that he is. He has seen a third self that Edmund has locked away these forty years within a vault in the depths of his soul.

The three men prepare to take the oath. Edmund watches their faces, as is his habit, being often in the position of discerning the truth behind the spoken word. Christopher Kirkby strokes the Holy Book tenderly, with his fingertips, as if he hardly dares to touch something so sacred. Israel Tonge studies it, his eyes full of fire and tears.

Titus Oates holds his hand above the Bible and it hovers there. And this is the image of Oates that Edmund will carry with him: that big hand, casually floating above the Holy Scriptures, and Oates bringing his face close to Edmund's, too close, and speaking, in an odd bleating murmur, words of insolence and venom.

'I know you will do right by me. I see that there is no Lady Godfrey in your home. Men like us... being as we are... we must stick together.'

Edmund recalls that first forbidden intimacy: the touch of masculine hands upon masculine hands; the silky feel of soft brown curls falling onto a young man's naked shoulders. He remembers the snuffing of a candle, the sorrowful farewells, the guilt, the denial: *it did not happen, it never was.* He thinks of the love he has shared in his maturity: a love that passes the love of women. He has become a man he does not understand: a man of tenderness yet a sinner before God. And he is mortified.

33

A MAN MUST BE TRUE TO HIS FRIENDS
EARLY SEPTEMBER, 1678

Coleman's wife ushers Edmund into her parlour and tells the maid to lay another place for supper. Edmund feels suffocated by heavy perfume, bobbing ringlets and incessant conversation. This is not what he's come for.

'Edward will be home in time to change his clothes before our supper guests arrive this evening. I expect him any minute,' she says, smiling as always. 'Prithee, Sir Edmund, do make yourself comfortable while you wait.' Edmund listens and hears. How ironic it is that of all the people with whom he is obliged to converse, this prattling woman manages to be the one person who conveys to him almost the entire meaning. He never sees on her countenance the bemused frown or the suppressed smile which, to his shame, tells him that he has misheard a word or a clause and made an inappropriate response. There are two reasons why Mistress Coleman's conversation is so easy upon Edmund's ears, the first being that she only talks about people: people he knows well. And when she speaks the names of these courtiers and titled people she looks him straight in the eyes, mouthing the names conspicuously. Not that she does this for Edmund because of his deafness. This is a habit of hers. She collects people of quality, invites them into her home for dinners and parties in her best chambers and she likes to show them off, even when they're not there, like his cousin, Mary, collects shells to display above her mantlepiece.

She is talking about the King's French whore, Louise, who has been created Duchess of Portsmouth, and the silver bedstead in her apartments which are grander than Queen Catherine's, when she halts midsentence, puts her hand to her mouth and apologises for forgetting her manners. 'Pray Sir Edmund, will you take a glass of wine while you wait? Or brandy, maybe?'

Edmund declines with a shake of his head.

'I have no idea where Edward's business has taken him today,' Mistress Coleman says, 'but I think he may have been asked to attend Lord Danby; he often is. Did you know, Sir Edmund, that the Duchess of Portsmouth was once Lord Danby's whore? Maybe she still is. When I heard of it, I said to Lady Pratt, "surely, it cannot be true. To think of it: the King having to share his favourite mistress with his first minister." Small wonder that they do not like each other.'

Edmund is desperate to escape the chamber; the house. Behind the pretty face with its fashionable patches, Edmund, the justice of the peace, so used to reading physiognomy to ascertain guilt or innocence, sees a caring woman who loves people. He cannot bear to be there, sitting in her parlour listening to her innocent chatter. It feels like telling a lie, knowing that her husband's name has been linked to a treasonous plot, and yet pretending all is well. Edmund does not doubt that if Lord Danby's men should search Coleman's home, they are more likely to find evidence of guilt than innocence.

'Forgive me, I must take my leave,' he says abruptly, with a bow. He reaches into his pocket and hands her a note. 'When your husband returns, kindly give him this message, for I must speak with him urgently.'

Edmund walks heavily as if through deep snow on this hot September evening. Why do his legs respond so sluggishly to the urgency of his errand? Something other than his usual melancholy is swaddling his thoughts. He is aware of a great worry growing inside him like a canker. What is it that frightens him so? He does not doubt that he is doing right, his way being always to be fair to both sides. Coleman must be warned. A man must be true to his friends.

Someone walks behind him, he senses this; senses that there is more than one person and that they travel faster than himself. Why do they not pass by? He arrives at Weldon's tavern on the Strand and they come closer. When he passes through the door, they follow. Who are they, these men who have dogged him these last weeks? Lord Danby's spies? Or Shaftesbury's? Or an adversary he never knew he had?

George Weldon takes Edmund into an upstairs chamber that the magistrate has used on occasion for private business. 'There is pen and ink, as usual, Sir Edmund, if you need to jot anything down in your pocketbook.'

'When my friend arrives, please greet him with the alias Mr Clarke,' Edmund says in a low voice. 'Our business is of a sensitive nature. I know I can trust you to be discreet as always, George.'

It is not long before Edward Coleman strides into the room dressed handsomely in a green silk suit laced with gold ready for his wife's supper party. He is accompanied by a serving man carrying drinks of ale.

'I came in my carriage; it is too hot to walk.' Coleman unties his neckcloth, throws it onto the bed, and takes a seat at the small table opposite Edmund.

'Your carriage livery will be recognised. You should have come quietly, by the backstreets, and in plain, simple attire, as I advised in my note,' Edmund complains. Has his friend no common sense?

'I do not possess such garments,' Coleman says. 'Whatever is the matter, Edmund? Why do you leave me strange messages asking me to pretend to be someone else and to come here secretly? My guests cannot eat until I return home and my wife worries that the food will spoil. She says you are most welcome to return with me to take supper with us.'

Edmund is surprised that anyone would want to eat one of Mistress Coleman's sumptuous suppers in this heat and gives his apologies. 'I shall take up no more of your time than is required. Something has been revealed to me. I speak of treason, of a Catholic plot to kill the King.'

Edmund watches his friend's convivial countenance, looking for signs of guilt but sees none.

'Oh, that,' Coleman says. 'I have heard of it. It is gossiped on the streets all over town. The Jesuits are at it again, they say. It is all lies, of course. Drink your ale, Edmund, you are very flushed, the heat will overcome you.' He pushes Edmund's glass towards him. 'There are always rumours of popish plots. Unfortunately none of them have come to fruition.'

'I did not hear you speak those last words,' Edmund says. 'Let me come to the point.' He takes out his pocket book. 'I advise you, most strongly, Edward, to tell me anything you know of such plans. Do you have anything to impeach?'

'I know of no plans that would not be pleasing to the Duke of York, his cousin King Louis, and our own monarch, who only pretends to be a loyal Protestant.'

Edmund has to ask him to repeat what he has said for he cannot believe that he heard correctly.

'You think the Treaty of Dover was a deal made between France and England to ally against the Dutch and their fleet. King Louis does not give Charles large sums of money just for this. Listen, Edmund, I have discovered the real reason for Louis' generosity. There is a great secret between

King Charles, the Duke of York and King Louis. And their late sister not only knew of this, she came to Dover as Louis' envoy. Only a few trusted Catholics are aware of it, and when I served York in France, I learned of it too.'

'Do you have anything to impeach?' Edmund asks again.

Coleman laughs. 'Shall I indict King Charles? Shall I indict the Duke of York? Shall they be tried for high treason? For hear this, Edmund. Our King, who prays his Protestant prayers, and reads his Protestant Bible, and feeds his Protestant ducks in his Protestant park while he chats amiably with his Protestant subjects; our Protestant King has promised King Louis that he will repay his generosity by the conversion of our country into the true religion of the Roman Church. This is the real Treaty of Dover: the Treaty of Madame. It will happen in my lifetime, Edmund, in my lifetime, and yours.'

Edmund makes no comment. He should be shocked, he knows he should. Why is he so calm? 'I speak only of what my informers have told me,' he says in the neutral tone he uses to the accused, at quarter sessions. 'Matters of state between kings are none of my business. Your name has been linked to a treasonous Catholic plot and I advise you to wait upon York and to discover whether His Highness has heard anything of this affair. And I ask you again: do you have anything to impeach?'

'We have never had such great hopes since Queen Mary's days.' Coleman's voice is rising in his excitement. 'I speak of the conversion of three kingdoms and the subduing of a pestilent heresy…'

'Be quiet, Edward,' Edmund orders loudly. 'Do not speak to me of such things,' he whispers.

Coleman takes out his pocket watch. 'I must go. My wife will be anxious to seat our guests at table. Listen Edmund, diplomacy is a slow business; far too slow for an active man like myself. If I have done things to hurry it along it has been in the sure certainty that His Majesty and York would approve.'

'Would approve… but had no knowledge of?'

'Maybe.'

'Maybe?'

Coleman sighs. 'Neither the King nor the Duke gave me a commission to do what I have done but…'

'I urge you again, go speak with York,' Edmund interrupts. 'Upon this matter there must be no misunderstanding between us, for my ears, as you know, do not always give an accurate report of what I hear. Tell me again, but slowly, while I take note, for the written word will not lie.'

'Then I shall put it in writing for you.' Coleman grabs Edmund's pocket book, writes a sentence or two and hurries away.

Edmund picks it up and it is heavy. Oh, the weight of Coleman's words.

34

FORCED BY DUTY AND CONSCIENCE
28TH SEPTEMBER, 1678

Godfrey's clerk says that the magistrate has not partaken of his breakfast nor is he dressed for visitors at such an early hour.

'We must see Sir Edmund before we present our deposition to the Foreign Affairs Committee of the Privy Council which we are summoned to attend without delay,' Tonge says. 'You turned us away last night because the justice was abed.'

'Get him out of his bed, give him his breeches, and be quick about it,' Titus orders. The old man shuffles away muttering that visitors at such an early hour bode no good.

This time Titus has brought two copies of his deposition. The magistrate, in his shirt sleeves, without collar or neckband, takes one and reads.

'You have been busy, Dr Oates, with your spying.'

'My additional thirty-eight articles tell of what I have discovered about the Catholic plotters here in London during August and September.'

'So I see. How can the Privy Council not be terrified when they know that twenty thousand Catholics in London, strong men and armed, are ready to rise within twenty-four hours or even less?'

The magistrate is not behaving as he did at their previous

meeting; Titus can see that. He discerns the sarcasm in his words.

'You say John Grove told you in confidence of his further plans to kill the King. The Privy Council will take your word against the word of the lay brother?'

'It is written in the deposition and sworn before yourself, a justice of the peace. How could it not be believed?' Titus asks.

'The committee awaits us,' Tonge says, rising from his chair. 'Please sign our documents, Sir Edmund, we must go.'

'Let the justice read a moment,' Titus scolds. 'He needs to know what he puts his name to.'

Edmund scans the document and finds his friends' names littered throughout the new articles. He comes to article sixty-five: Sir William Godolphin, English ambassador at the court of Spain, is accused of being in on the Popish Plot. Titus has seen him at Mass in Madrid.

The page blurs. Edmund feels sick. Sir William Godolphin is Valentine's brother-in-law.

'I have read enough. It is all hearsay and gossip, and badly written at that.' Edmund dips his quill into the ink. 'Let the Privy Council make of it what they will.'

It is a terrible thing to know that you are doing something that you should not do; indeed, to dread the consequences, but to be forced by duty and conscience to continue upon this course of action.

Edmund has waited all morning. Why does Lord Danby not send for him? He needs to be there when Oates speaks, to explain to the Lord Treasurer how unwillingly he signed the deposition, believing it to be the lies and deceit of one man. Edmund's servants have walked softly around him for days now, glancing at him and at each other the way they do when his melancholy comes upon him. This time it is different. It is not just his usual sadness that hounds him. Too many great worries are tumbling around inside his head so that he cannot focus upon any one of them, being sorely distracted by the others. It pained him to hear Dr Oates accuse gentle John Grove of such terrible deeds. The loyal friend's heart was thumping wildly whilst the conscientious member of the Commission of Peace signed the deposition. As for Edward Coleman, he should have advised him to sort through his papers; burn anything that might incriminate him. Why did he not advise his friend thus?

Late afternoon arrives with no summons. Edmund hurries to Whitehall. Why is the journey so urgent? Danby, the King and the Privy Council: these are intelligent men. He will find them laughing at Oates' preposterous articles. Still, a flood of panic rises in his breast.

In the lobby, Lord Danby strides towards him. His pale complexion is flushed pink and his eyes are angry.

'This has been badly done, badly, I say. You should have brought Dr Oates' deposition directly to me. Instead, you went to that notorious gossip, Coleman, who, upon your advice, told York of the plot before I had opportunity to alert the Privy Council. York is furious that he was kept so long in the dark about a treasonous rebellion that centres around himself.'

'I was told that His Majesty had informed you of the plot after listening to Dr Tonge and Christopher Kirkby,' Edmund says. He is both relieved that Coleman followed his advice and indignant at Danby's reprimand. 'Dr Oates told me that he gave a copy of his articles to the King who passed it on to a member of the Privy Council. That would be you, of course, my Lord, surely? You had knowledge of this plot, if plot there be, before ever it was brought to my attention. It was your responsibility to inform York, not mine.'

Danby's pale caterpillar eyebrows crawl together. His mouth is so tight he cannot speak.

'I understand that you also believed there to be no truth in it, there being no real evidence at all, only hearsay,' Edmund continues, and he pauses, waiting for the Lord Treasurer's reply. Danby can only splutter a splinter or two of words but Edmund knows that he will suffer the full force of his wrath, yet still he goads him, he cannot stop himself.

'When Tonge and Kirkby waited at your door with more of their evidence, your servant shut the door in their faces. You refused to put yourself out to study their evidence because you thought it all nonsense, as I do.'

Danby finds his voice. 'You were informed of a treasonous plot. More importantly, Oates swore to this in your presence, and you did nothing. I repeat, you did nothing. You read the deposition, you signed it, you kept the contents privy to yourself. You should have come to me. Shame on you, Sir Edmund. I shall speak further of this matter with your friend, Lord Chief Justice Scroggs. The Commission of Peace will not suffer its justices to trifle like this with the crime of misprision of treason.'

Somehow, Edmund finds his way home. He knows that he has made a terrible mistake. How could he have been so foolish as to expect the Lord Chief Justice, the Lords, the Commons, anyone, to even consider that Dr Oates has perjured himself; that a clergyman's hand could touch the Holy Bible while his mouth spoke false? How could he not have realised, at that very moment when he put his name to Oates' first forty-three articles, that he was signing his good friend Grove's death warrant?

35

ARRESTS HAVE BEEN MADE
EARLY OCTOBER, 1678

Newmarket has been rather dull these first days with few races and no opportunity for hunting or hawking due to tempestuous weather. Now that the storms have abated, Charles has spent the early morning at his stables with his many fine horses, talking with ostlers and jockeys, inspecting his stud and watching the training. Charles smiles when he remembers a time, seven years ago when he was a jockey himself and won the Town Plate and a purse of thirty-two pounds.

At noon, he saunters through the crowded little streets of Newmarket dressed like every other country gentleman, chatting with a baker, a pedlar, a little child who wants to pet his dogs, a cluster of pretty women in the market square: with anybody who desires to engage him in conversation. His house on the high street with its small rooms and low ceilings could be the home of any common burger. The royal apartments in the courtyard behind are comfortable only, by no means palatial. In exile, in his youth, he lived like a poor nobleman: a majesty with no majesty. At Newmarket he relives this freedom: becomes a man like any other. It is his escape from politics, from being a king whose Parliament will not heed him however sycophantic they may appear to be. But this time there is no respite. Charles fears that Titus Oates with his damned plot has spoiled his friendship with his only living brother with whom he has enjoyed sailing and other sports since they were young. This plot is an ember that must be dampened or it will flare into a great conflagration that will consume his Catholic heir and the Great Secret between himself and Louis.

'Titus Oates is a wicked man,' he complains to his brother while they eat their dinner.'I had to listen to him bleating like an obsequious goat for two days when I should have been here.'

James is angry. 'How can the man lie and lie again and again and have the audacity to expect to be believed?'

Charles knows what it is to live a lie: to sit in a kitchen wearing a labourer's coarse clothes; to turn away and coil his tall frame until it shrinks like a snake while maidservants gossip of Charles Stuart, the dark young prince more than two yards tall, and ostlers talk of a reward of a thousand pounds. How very difficult it was to have to find an excuse when a kitchen maid wondered why he hadn't the skill to wind the jack in the fireplace. 'In Staffordshire," he lied, "we seldom have meat and when we do we rarely use a jack.' He had to pretend to be ill and hide in a bedchamber so that he could escape the dangerous questioning of friendly innkeepers and stable boys. On the long journey from the battlefields of Worcester to the boat that took him to the safety of his mother's family in France, he lied many times to save his life; to save the Stuart Monarchy. He remembers the concentration it required, the attention to detail, the terror of being caught out. 'Odd's fish, James,' he says. 'Titus Oates vomits lies in profusion but he has gone too far in his accusations to be summarily dismissed. His eighty-one articles must be thoroughly investigated: with great circumspection, of course.'

Charles can hold back no longer; the time has come when

he must acquaint his brother with the worst of Oates' allegations. 'Oates claims to have been given a packet of letters from Father Strange to carry to Madrid. This, he opened, and to his supposed horror, read of risings in Scotland and Ireland; money for attack; plans to murder Protestants...'

James cuts him short. 'I do not wish to hear all this. If Edmund Godfrey hadn't given credence to his deposition, Oates would never have been invited to tell such lies to yourself and the Privy Council.'

'He spoke of plans to kill me and... I'm so sorry to have to tell you this...' Charles puts a comforting hand on his brother's shoulder, '... after I'm dead they intend to make you their Catholic King.'

'How dare Oates implicate me?' James declares, glaring angrily at his brother. 'I say again, you should never have given him the courtesy of listening to his lies. You must do something quickly to put an end to Titus Oates and his discoveries. I fear for the innocent Catholics he accuses.'

'You think I don't?' Charles demands. 'Oates' accusations hurt me deeply for the tender feelings I have for our Catholic friends who risked their lives to hide me in their priest holes, their barns and their manor houses: the Penderel brothers, Father Huddleston, pretty Jane Lane: without these brave men and women the sacred royal bloodline from father to legitimate firstborn son would have died bleeding at Worcester.'

'Good God, Charles,' James says sourly. 'If you had been the victor at the battle of Worcester, would you have any interesting stories to tell? You should be thinking of your wife, our loyal Catholic Lords and our Catholic friends at court, all of whom Oates has put in a most precarious position. Mr Pepys is frequently to be seen at Mass in the chapel at Somerset House. He should be warned. He's here for the races. I'll send for him.'

When he's sitting, the King doesn't know what to do with his long legs, Pepys thinks, unless he's on a horse: a big hunter or one of his race horses. He's more at ease walking or sailing one of his ships. Or, most probably, lying abed with one of his whores. It's a common joke around the court that his member is of a size with his sceptre. Well, there's enough women who might verify this. The King knows that he's nicknamed *Old Rowley* after one of his stud stallions here at Newgate, and someone has even composed a ballad about this. It is rumoured that the King, upon hearing one of the ladies at court singing it in her bedchamber, knocked at her door.

'Who's there?' the lady enquired.

'It's Old Rowley himself, madam,' Charles had answered.

Pepys cannot stop himself smiling at this anecdote but today, the royal brothers are in no mood for jollity.

'Do you know Dr Titus Oates?' the King asks.

'No, Your Majesty, I never met him nor listened to him preach but I have heard about the Popish Plot.'

'You will know Matthew Medburne, the comic actor, of course, from the Duke's Company?' the King says. 'Oates has accused him of treasonable talk, at a club, the Pheasant, in Fullers' Rents.'

'I know him well,' Pepys replies, shocked. 'But I never visited that club, which I believe to be one of ill repute.'

'Following Oates' accusations, arrests have been made.'

'Oh dear,' is all Pepys can say.

'Never fear, Mr Pepys, the accused will surely be vindicated, for there can be no real evidence against them: just the word of this one man, Titus Oates. Lord Chief Justice Scroggs will need further verification to go to trial.'

'I fear for the Catholics in our city,' Pepys ventures.

The King raises his eyebrows. 'You have Catholic acquaintances, Mr Pepys?'

'My Italian musician, Morelli, who lives with me.'

'Are you thinking of changing your religion?' the King asks pointedly. 'I hear you attend Mass in the Queen's chapel. I would strongly advise you that this is not a good time to convert to the Roman faith.'

'A man must be true to his religion,' York interjects.

'It is only that I like to listen to the music at the Mass,' Pepys replies, feeling uncomfortable, like a piggy in the middle between the two brothers. 'I am a Protestant and always have been.'

'Is Edward Coleman amongst the accused?' York asks his brother, of a sudden.

'Edward Coleman's papers are to be seized,' the King says.

Pepys has met Coleman in York's apartments on several occasions. People say that it was he who encouraged the Duke to convert to Catholicism. He's a thin man, dark, eager, ambitious. Lord, but if any man should be assisting the Jesuits to plot a rebellion, Coleman would be the prime candidate.

'I rather fancy the young bay in the first race this afternoon,' the King says cheerfully. 'Come on, James, Mr Pepys, let us go and place our bets, and tonight, in the barn, Bart's fair comedians will entertain us with a play.'

Part 5
Where is Sir Edmund?
October, 1678

"… a man of Contradictions…"

Alan Marshall (1999)

36

MASTER OF A DANGEROUS SECRET
MONDAY 7TH–FRIDAY 11TH OCTOBER, 1678

It is strange, Edmund thinks, this feeling that everything is happening outside his own body, even his thoughts. It is almost as if he is watching himself going about his daily business, listening to himself speak, although here he is, inside his clothes, he can see that he is, for he is looking down at his feet wearing the shoes that his maid, Elizabeth Curtis, polished this morning. Today is quarter sessions day for Westminster and Edmund has found it a relief, of sorts, to attend to his business as a justice of the peace, to listen and to concentrate and to make judgements.

During recess he dines, as is his custom, with the head bailiff and an old friend, another justice of the peace, Thomas Robinson. He would fain make his excuses, wanting neither food nor conversation, but finds himself trapped by routine in the certain knowledge that their conversation will be entirely of the latest news of the Popish Plot.

'Ordinary folk are afraid,' the head bailiff is saying. 'They are arming themselves against a Catholic rebellion.'

'Don't you see,' Edmund says, 'that the Popish Plot is all a pack of lies.' Except for Coleman, he thinks. Except for arrogant, rash, misguided Coleman who has finally surrendered himself and been taken to Newgate goal. He should visit Coleman's wife again, offer some comfort. He would, if there were any comfort to give.

Edward Coleman, the traitor and Titus Oates, the liar. Which one will be his hangman? He had always feared that in his melancholy he would take his own life, but now he fears a worse demise. He cannot bear the shame of it. His brothers and his dear cousin, Mary do not deserve such disgrace.

He has not touched the meal of larks' and neats' tongues on the platter before him. Neither had he eaten breakfast. He cannot bear the sensation of food slithering down his throat. If he swallows he will retch.

'I played my part in this affair as duty directed. I let Titus Oates into my home and signed his deposition,' he blurts out in the overloud tone of the hard of hearing.

Robinson nods. 'Of course you did; you could do no other.'

'Parliament looks ill upon me. It is well known that I am a friend of papist families. Some very great men are saying that I have not done my duty.'

'Come on, Sir Edmund, eat up, your food is going cold,' the head bailiff says annoyingly, as if he were speaking to a small child.

'The Privy Council took Titus Oates at his word,' Edmund complains.

'Dr Oates has made a good living for himself from his discoveries,' the head bailiff replies. 'The Privy Council has given him a fine apartment in Whitehall with servants and guards for his protection when he walks the streets seeking popish plotters.'

Edmund thinks of John Grove, imprisoned in his innocence. He puts food to his lips but cannot eat it. Grief, like a huge lump of gristle, sticks in his throat.

'What of your own personal safety?' Robinson is asking.

'Surely, you do not go out at night these days without your man for protection?'

Edmund wipes his mouth with his kerchief again and again. He pushes his platter away and rises to leave. 'I fear no harm in the alleys and streets,' he tells his friend, 'yet I fear for my life. It is neither thieves nor beggars nor Catholics but men of importance who blame me. Old Henry Moor cannot protect me against them.' His voice is raised and men at other tables turn to stare.

'I did my duty and I will not part with my life tamely,' he declares with sudden ferocity. 'No indeed, I will not.'

On Tuesday he visits cousin Mary. Tells her that he must speak with her urgently; alone. She takes him into her parlour and he bolts the door.

'Have you heard that I am to be hanged?' he asks.

She shakes her head and looks at him as if he speaks in a foreign language she doesn't understand.

'All the town is in an uproar about me,' he says. 'Surely you have heard of it? Oh, cousin, I have made a terrible mistake and I will die for it. I took the depositions of Dr Tonge and Dr Oates weeks ago. I dined with the Lord Chancellor and the Attorney General and I kept the depositions privy to myself. I should have disclosed all I knew to them and now… and now they blame me.'

'You will worry yourself to death or else starve if you do not eat,' his cousin says. 'I'm sorry, Edmund, but I must go and tend to Mother. My daughter has sat with her long enough.' She unbolts the door and turns to him speaking slowly and carefully with kindness in her eyes. 'I'll send you a jelly for your better digestion.'

He calls again, early the following day. Again, his cousin excuses herself to go upstairs promising to return very shortly. What is he doing grieving for himself, here, in this house that smells of sickness, where above him an ancient woman is dying? He returns home.

After tending to her mother, Mary Gibbon hurries to Hartshorne Lane. She finds Edmund supping whey, her jelly untouched, and is offended.

'Oh, cousin, it is my father's melancholy that afflicts me so. I have been let blood, several ounces these last days, but I cannot shake it off. Leave me. Go.' He sees the hurt in her eyes and is sorry for it. 'I am best alone, pray, let me be,' he says more gently. 'Your mother needs you more than I.'

Urgency pulls him through his days. A man staggering towards the steps and the rope must tie up his business deals; settle his debts. He speaks with another old friend, Thomas Wynnell, promises to meet him at Colonel Weldon's tavern in York Buildings for dinner on Saturday noon to complete a property sale.

'Edward Coleman will die,' he tells Wynnell, 'and I may not have long to live.'

'Nay, nay,' Wynnell comforts him. 'It is only your usual sadness that makes you think thus, so sorrowfully. It will pass.'

'I am master of a dangerous secret,' he tells Wynnell and walks away.

His pocketbook hangs heavy in his coat dragging him stumbling through London's streets. His is desperate for the comfort of his cousin's company and on Thursday morning he sends Mrs Pamphlin to fetch her. The housekeeper returns with Captain Gibbon.

'My wife cannot leave her mother for fear that the end will come and she will not be there,' Captain Gibbon says.

'Then I will not disturb your household again,' Edmund says.

Elizabeth Curtis looks at him with sorrowful eyes and speaks so quietly he cannot hear her words. She holds out a dish of chocolate and the bitter-sweet smell makes him sick to his stomach. He pushes it away. Mrs Pamphlin tells him loudly that he must eat. The arrogance of the woman; she is his housekeeper, not his mother. And what does she, a mere working woman, know of anything: of the benefit of fasting for a man prone to melancholy; of the laws of misprision of treason?

His neckband chokes him. He tugs at it and throws it into the middle of the room.

On Friday he walks. Come late afternoon he finds himself in Drury Lane. A man and his lady acknowledge him. He does not recognise them and he walks on looking down. Too many people know him. Too many to remember them all, especially today when great worries cloud his mind and he has no list for conversation. One bad decision made in the split of a second in a lifetime of duty and diligence has unmade him. He lifted the quill, he put his name to the deposition, he signed his good friend Honest William into Newgate, the rope and worse. And he himself? He knows that he will die very soon one way or another.

He is sitting by the fire in his parlour when the message comes.

'A stranger brought it; he waits in the passage,' Elizabeth Curtis says.

Edmund reads. 'A stranger you say?'

'He awaits a reply. None of us know him, sir. Not I, nor Mrs Pamphlin, nor her daughter who is with her.'

Edmund is aware that she is watching him, wanting to know the contents of the message. The woman would peer over his shoulders and peek at the letter if she dared. If she could read. It occurs to Edmund that he has no idea whether she ever learned to read.

He has no time for this ill written epistle. If the writer has matters of importance to impart let him show himself in person. Yet it bothers him that the correspondent fails to disclose the nature of the business. The signature is unknown to him, most likely an alias. 'Tell the messenger that I don't know what to make of it,' he says.

The vestry at St Martin's meets tonight but first, he visits Henry Bradbury, a baker, asks him to wait upon him later at Weldon's tavern. 'I have done you wrong,' he says, 'and it must be righted.'

He hastens to the vestry, being late, which he never is, and he surprises himself how little he cares that the vicar, Dr Lloyd, has begun to proceed with the business without him; he, who is known as *the mouth of the vestry*. He speaks only once. 'That will not do,' he cries out when they discuss the poor money that is owed by the King's friend, the Duke of Buckingham and he sees the other men jump at the vehemence of his contribution. Their agreement comes to him in a rumble that hurts his ears. After recent problems with the overseers of the poor, who have each been fined forty shillings for holding onto more than seventy pounds which should have been paid to the vestry, they decide that the overseers should meet the last Sunday of every month after Divine service and give an account in writing to the churchwardens of any extraordinary disbursements made. For a moment, happiness rushes through Edmund, like a drug. Poor people's lives will be the better for what has been agreed today. Duty. That's what is important now, what urges him through his days.

When the business is over, he departs with one of the vestrymen, Joseph Radcliffe.

'I must pay my debts,' Edmund confides as they walk to Weldon's tavern. 'I have wronged one of the overseers of the poor, the baker, Bradbury, and I am resolved to make amends. I will have the matter sorted this very night.'

Edmund bends his tall frame into the tavern doorway

and the heat hits him. He wonders if a fever is coming upon him and struggles to remove his coat.

'But, Sir Edmund, it is cold,' Radcliffe pleads.

'The fire stifles me.'

When Radcliffe has assisted him and he is free of his heavy coat he throws it into the window recess and finds a table at the far end of the room away from the hearth. He sees that other men are wrapped in coats against the cold. Within the quarter hour, surely they too will be sweating like dray horses.

'What is it that troubles you so?' Radcliffe asks.

'I made Bradbury pay his forty shillings fine for a fault that I now understand was not his.'

The baker is sent for and paid. Edmund decides there and then that he will change his baker. The ten shillings he gives each week for bread for the poor shall henceforth be given to Bradbury. He is pleased that Radcliffe is here to witness this so that there will be no misunderstanding in the future.

'I will have every outstanding parish account settled tonight,' he tells Radcliffe. Edmund knows that there are enough funds available from money he has loaned the vestry without taking any interest, and it has not all been repaid. 'I am quiet, now, at peace,' he says when the business is settled.

'Good, good,' Radcliffe says cheerfully and turns the conversation away from the magistrate and his troubles. 'Now then, what news?'

'This you will hear, very shortly, that men will die.' Edmund stands to leave. 'I fear, my friend, that I may be the first.'

At the door, George Weldon helps him on with his coat and asks if he will dine with him on the morrow, Saturday. Edmund takes out his pocket book to check his appointments. All he sees is Coleman's hand, bold and treasonous, jumping from the page.

'I don't know if I should,' he tells Weldon. 'You will not see me so often at your house in the future.'

He must go home. There are affairs to settle this night before he takes to his bed. First, he has an obligation to fulfil, even now. He will visit his good friend, Lady Margaret Pratt, at Charing Cross; she expects him tonight at her social gathering.

***

Mrs Pamphlin is hurting his ears, wailing about the deeds to her cottage that she has mortgaged to him. He tells her to leave him be, but she stays in the passage watching him as he goes up and downstairs tumbling through his chests and trunks, grabbing papers to throw on the fire. He must leave nothing behind that will be misunderstood: disgrace his memory when he is gone. Time, his time, is no longer a lazy river tumbling carelessly towards a distant sea. It is a blind alley. He sees a dark wall before him and all the meaning of his life seeping away on filthy cobbles. Should he wait for the law's slow wheels to drag him to a traitor's death, as surely, Edward Coleman also awaits, or should he take charge of his demise? He has the courage for this latter course, he knows he has. He is a businessman used to making sharp decisions.

So why does he hesitate? Surely, this is the easiest decision of them all. A deep sadness overwhelms him. Death, now that it is following in his footsteps and coming ever nearer, is not what he wants at all. He will never see the new churches fully completed, their spires redefining London's post-fire skyline. He will never see St Paul's rebuilt with the magnificent dome Wren has designed. He will never finally succeed in Chancery against his nephew nor retire to the tranquillity of Ireland with Valentine. His demise, which in his misery he had sometimes craved, will come too soon. These thoughts die in the fluttering of a moment. He thinks of his father, and a wondrous elation floods through him into his very soul. What once he had feared above all things: above the plague, the fire, the hangman's noose; it hasn't happened. It will never happen. The terrible malady of the father was never, ever, to be bequeathed to the son.

37

MISSING

SATURDAY, 12TH –
WEDNESDAY, 16TH OCTOBER, 1678

Sir Edmund is up very early as usual, and calm, which surprises Judith Pamphlin after last night's frantic burning of papers by candlelight. She's desperate to ask him again if he is sure that her mortgage deed is safe, but dare not for fear that he will shout at her again. Anyway, he has already gone out when the first visitor of the day arrives well before seven o'clock. He leaves his name, Richard Adams, and says he will call again later; so the matter must be urgent, whatever it is.

Mary Gibbon's daughter comes around eight, to invite Sir Edmund for dinner, which shows how worried they are about him, their house being a house of death, but Judith supposes a bit of company might cheer them up a bit, although perhaps it is Sir Edmund who needs his spirits lifting after being so morose this last month and more.

He returns during the early morning. Says nothing about whether he will accept the invitation to dine with Captain and Mrs Gibbon. By this time there is another visitor waiting for him in the parlour even before Betty has taken him his breakfast.

'He's a dark man, that's all I can tell you, Mrs Pamphlin,' Betty says.

'Is it the same man who came yesterday evening with the

strange letter that Sir Edmund didn't understand?' Judith asks.

'It might be,' the maid replies. 'You saw more of the man who came last night than I did, standing there with him in the passage.'

'Aye, but it was lit by just one candle. I didn't see his face clearly.'

Henry Moor creeps up behind them and complains, as usual, about their gossiping. One day, when he really annoys her, Judith will tell him that his wife knows how to gossip more than any woman, but then, she's had a good number of years to practise, being as ancient as he is.

'The master has judicial business that is no concern of women,' Moor says.

'So who is the man in the parlour?' Betty asks.

Betty is bold like this with Henry but he doesn't mind because she sneaks him little bits of leftover cheese and puddings from the kitchen to take to his wife. She gets him to tell her all sorts of things she's no right to know and then she tells Judith. But on this occasion he is as ignorant as they are.

Sir Edmund had hardly touched his breakfast, only drank a little and then he went out again. This is how he is these days: in out, in again out again, getting under Betty's feet when she's trying to dust the parlour, or needing to use the privy when she's sweeping it out and scattering new herbs. Wherever he's going this morning, he's not expecting to meet people of quality. Henry Moor got him into his new coat but Sir Edmund changed his mind and sent for his old one. Said the old coat would do well enough. Then he asked for his sword. The parlour door was open so Judith heard everything, even old Henry wheezing with the effort of getting Sir Edmund's long arms in and out of the sleeves. He's out for dinner on business, this much she knows, and his host had better provide whey with bread soaked in it, for that's all he eats these days and then he only sips at it a bit. Something's not right with his insides, she's sure of this. He's needing to rush to the privy several times each day and he's clearing his throat and wiping his mouth all the time now. Next time one of his sisters calls, she'll have a quiet word: suggest that he sees a physician.

'Sir Edmund's out again,' she says as Henry Moor watches his master walk down the path through the woodyard.

'I thought he had forgotten something,' Henry says, more to himself than to Judith, 'for halfway along the path he turned as if to speak to me but thought better of it and went on his way.'

Judith spends the rest of the morning with Betty cleaning the chambers at the top of the house, until at noon, a servant comes from Colonel Weldon's tavern, enquiring whether Sir Edmund is ready for his meeting with Mr Wynnell.

'Mr Wynnell is early, so no cause for alarm,' the young man says. 'I will find Sir Edmund sitting at table with him when I return, for sure.'

'Mr Wynnell is eager to get his business done,' Judith tells Betty with a confidential nod.

In the afternoon Mr Wynnell calls. Judith cannot tell whether he is angry or worried. 'Where is Sir Edmund?' he asks. 'I've waited for more than two hours.'

Henry Moor is sent for.

'I understand that yesterday Sir Edmund told Weldon that he would see him no more at his tavern,' Wynnell tells the clerk. 'If he did not intend to keep his appointment with me, why did he not send word?'

'No doubt urgent business detains Sir Edmund,' Moor says. 'Pray, give my master a little more time. When he returns, I will tell him that you await him at the Colonel's establishment.'

'Sir Edmund is never late for anything,' Betty says when Wynnell has departed. 'Whatever can have happened?'

'I dare say Mr Wynnell has got his days mixed up,' Moor says.

In the evening Judith lights the big lantern outside the house and still Sir Edmund has not returned.

'Nay, woman, leave your foolish worrying,' Henry says. 'What do you know of urgent judicial matters that would detain a magistrate. Where the master goes, and why, is none of the housekeeper's business.'

'Perhaps he is visiting his friends in Richmond,' Betty says hopefully, but Judith knows that Betty does not believe this. None of them do, not even Henry who is surely only pretending that he isn't worried about the master.

It's not yet nine o'clock on Sunday morning when Henry returns from Mr Michael's house. Judith has been watching out for him. 'What news of Sir Edmund?' she asks. 'Does his brother know where he is?'

'You silly fool, he has been gone out these last two hours,' the clerk replies and hurries away into the office.

'What a strange thing to say,' Betty says. 'How can Sir Edmund have gone out when he never came in?'

'It's Henry's way of telling us womenfolk to mind our own business,' Judith says.

Mr Michael and Mr Benjamin come to the house.

'Perhaps he has gone playing bowls with his friends?' Betty suggests to the brothers, 'To cheer himself up, as he sometimes does when he's sad.'

'What, on a Sunday?' Mr Michael says, with derision. They send Judith to Mary Gibbon while the clerk goes with the brothers to call upon Lady Pratt and other of their brother's friends.

Nobody knows where Sir Edmund has gone.

On Monday, the clerk goes out and returns hours later and hides away in the office. Mary Gibbon arrives on Tuesday and very upset she is, Judith can see that.

'The Godfrey brothers are very worried, as are the Captain and myself and all Edmund's friends,' Mrs Gibbon says, 'but that clerk, I cannot understand him at all. He told me that upon his faith, Sir Edmund is as well as I am. Those were his very words. Why would he say that?'

'Yon clerk has been behaving very strangely since the master disappeared on Saturday,' Judith says. 'He's been out in the country searching for the master, I know he has. He came back yesterday traipsing soil and blades of grass all through the house. He won't say where he's been, just taps his nose with his finger and shakes his head.'

'Oh, Judith, do you think he knows something of your master's whereabouts?'

'He would like me to think so, but why would Sir Edmund confide in him, a servant, when he has your good self, his dear cousin, who is always willing to listen to him.'

'Oh, but I could not come when he sent for me and now he has gone away and I do not know when I will see him again. Mr Michael and Mr Benjamin came to me yesterday and asked all sorts of questions.'

Judith looks expectantly at Mrs Gibbon, waiting for more.

'They wanted to know what sort of humour he had been in these last days so I told his brothers that he has been much disordered.' Mary's voice trembles and she lets out a little sob. 'Mr Michael took it very badly. He lifted up his hands and eyes and said, "Lord! We are undone, whatever can we do?"'

'Oh,' says Judith, 'surely he did not mean…'

'He would say no more, only calmed himself and said that he had thought his brother might have called at our house after church on Sunday.'

'Did Mr Benjamin say anything?' Judith asks.

'He said not to worry, that they would come to me again when they had more news. But he has been missing three nights now and there is no more news. Oh, Judith, something is very wrong: I know it.'

'Moor is going to a funeral later today,' Judith says, trying to sound more hopeful than she feels. 'The brothers have asked him to advertise to the crowds that Sir Edmund is missing, as if it isn't being gossiped about all over London. But maybe someone there might know where he has gone.'

'You've been gone a long time, what news?' Judith asks, when Henry returns.

'Someone died and was buried, you silly fool,' the clerk replies.

'But what of Sir Edmund?'

'What of him? Cease your worrying, woman. He is well, I tell you.'

This is not what Moor's wife believes. Yesterday they met on Hungerford market and of course got talking of the master's disappearance. 'It's a clear matter of *felo de se*,' she announced with all the smugness of a clerk's wife addressing a mere housekeeper-cum-laundress. Judith had to ask her what this meant. 'Your master has taken his own life.'

'Did your husband tell you this?' Judith asked. Moor's wife just stood there with her arms folded under her saggy bosoms. 'I know what I know,' she said.

Moor's wife might be right. One of the neighbours has told Judith that a man in a barber's shop has been spreading the news that Sir Edmund has killed himself out in the country at Primrose Hill.

The mayor's mace-bearer calls to inquire if there is news of Sir Edmund. Judith takes him into the office to talk with Henry and leaves the door slightly ajar. If the clerk and the brothers won't tell her what's going on she has no choice but to listen behind doors; she has a right to know what has happened to her employer and is desperate to hear what news the mayor's man has brought. Betty has been out on the streets again today and all the gossip is that Sir Edmund has been murdered.

Henry is telling the mayor's man that when he attended the funeral, Parsons, the churchwarden, told him that he had seen Sir Edmund on Saturday morning at about nine o'clock on St Martin's Lane and that the master inquired of him the way to Primrose Hill.

Dear God, Judith prays. Let not the man in the barber's shop be speaking true.

'This needs looking into,' the mayor's man is saying. 'Have you made enquiries as to whether Sir Edmund was seen in these parts last Saturday?'

Judith ponders on what she has heard. The clerk was out for quite enough time to have walked to Primrose Hill on Monday and on Tuesday. This would explain his dirty shoes.

Another day goes by and still no sign of Sir Edmund nor any clue as to his whereabouts. He just seems to have vanished last Saturday.

'Rumours are spreading that he has run off to marry a widow, or else a woman he has compromised,' Betty says. 'Sir Edmund's nephew is telling everyone who asks that his uncle has been murdered by papists.'

Henry has crept into the kitchen and goodness knows how long he has been listening to their conversation. They don't know he's there until he suddenly announces:

'The master's brothers have spoken to the Lord Chancellor. They want to draw up a proclamation advertising the master's disappearance but the Privy Council will not allow it.'

Judith would rather have had this piece of gossip from one of Sir Edmund's sisters than Henry who has seen more of the Godfrey brothers these last days than a mere clerk should, in her opinion.

'The Privy Council is of the belief that Sir Edmund, being rather more melancholy than usual, has just gone to the country for a few days, to cheer himself up, which is what I've been a telling you women since Saturday. So,' Henry continues, 'now that the Lord Chancellor is saying the same thing, maybe you'll begin to listen to a man talking sense,' and he departs to the office after helping himself to a slice of apple pie.

'If Sir Edmund walks through the door tomorrow in good health, yon clerk will be insufferable,' Judith says.

'Oh, I wish he would,' Betty says. 'If the worst, the very worst has happened to him, no one will ever call me Elizabeth again.'

'Don't you like us to call you Betty?' Judith asks, surprised.

'Sir Edmund always says, "Elizabeth" and it seems so respectful, as if it's a sign that he likes what I do for him and knows how hard I work cleaning the hearths and sweeping the floors and making his dish of chocolate. He's been so very good to me: you know that I was living off the poor basket when he found me.' She starts to cry and Judith knows better than to tell her that the master calls her Elizabeth because that's how her name is written on the household accounts and he's too deaf to hear everyone else saying, 'Betty.'

38

THE YOUNG CLERK
16ᵀᴴ–17ᵀᴴ OCTOBER, 1678

'Well now, young Sam,' Pepys says. 'What have you been getting up to whilst I've been at Newmarket with His Majesty and the Duke. I hope you haven't been debauching yourself like you did last time I was away. You know that I promised to turn you out if you did that again.'

'No, I haven't forgotten, Mr Pepys.'

He hasn't answered my question, Pepys thinks, so he's been in the taverns again, getting himself fuddled. Well, he seems sober enough today. Sam is slight and fair, a good-looking boy who appears much younger than his twenty-one years. He's one year out of his apprenticeship and his position in Pepys' household is lowly but it's a good start for a young man. He's clerk to Will Hewer, the chief clerk, and he does his job well, and Lord knows Pepys needs his clerks now more than ever, his eyes being mighty painful for close work of any length.

'I hope you had good sport at Newmarket, sir?' Sam asks politely.

'I had to keep to my chamber for a day or two,' Pepys says, 'the wet weather having wrought badly with my hip and my knees so I being in greater pain than usual. The Duke couldn't go hunting and the King couldn't go hawking and there were very few races, but when the weather picked up so did the sport.'

'Very good sir.' Sam puts a pile of papers on Pepys' desk. 'Here are the documents you asked me to copy while you were away.'

Pepys thumbs through the papers. Sam is a careful scribe, there are very few alterations in his work, he can see that, even with his poor eyes. It's a mighty pity that he's so easily led to the taverns and alehouses but he'll maybe know better after a year or two. 'Well now Sam, what's been going on in my absence?' he asks. 'What news?'

'A man went missing on Saturday and everybody in the taverns and coffee houses are saying that the Jesuits have murdered him,' Sam replies, excitedly.

'Who is he? Anybody I know?' Pepys asks.

'A justice of the peace, Sir Edmund Bury Godfrey.'

'Oh,' Pepys says, 'I had cause to visit him on one occasion, to prepare a warrant for an arrest.'

'Yes, sir, I remember. It was when you found your butler, John James, in bed with your housekeeper.'

'That was no business of yours,' Pepys retorts.

'No sir, of course not, sir.'

'Sir Edmund might be taken up with some urgent judicial business which has taken longer than expected,' Pepys suggests, 'or maybe gone away for a holiday. He's a lonely sort of man who shuns any company of wit.'

'Or else he is in bed with a whore; that's what some people are saying,' Sam says with a snigger.

'Do not speak so disrespectfully of your betters,' Pepys rebukes, but he cannot prevent a smile from creeping across his face. Sir Edmund Godfrey is the last man in the world to visit a brothel. He wouldn't know what to do when he got there.

39

THE MAN IN A GREY SUIT
17TH OCTOBER, 1678

Dr Lloyd, vicar of St Martin-in-the-Fields, has sent his manservant to Hartshorne Lane and he has been in the office with Henry Moor for a while now. They speak with muted voices and Judith can hear nothing of their conversation. The afternoon light is beginning to fade and outside a storm is brewing as he takes his leave.

'Is there any news of Sir Edmund?' she asks as she hands him his hat.

He dismisses her question with a shake of his head.

She goes straight to Henry in the office. All he will tell her is that the master's brothers are on their way and having said that, he will not look at her.

Something has happened; she knows it.

'Lord Danby is sending his mace bearer, Sergeant Ramsey,' Henry says, almost as an afterthought, as if Lord Danby is just a neighbour, or the pieman, not the Lord Treasurer of England and the King's first minister.

The candles are already lit when Sir Edmund's brothers arrive with Mr Michael's wife, Mary Gibbon and their brother-in-law, Mr Plunknett. The gentlemen go straight to the office with Henry.

Judith takes the ladies into the parlour. 'We have heard something terrible, Judith,' Mary says. 'From Dr Lloyd, the vicar, who had a visit from the curate of St Dunstan-in-the-West. The curate was in a bookshop in St Paul's churchyard, around noon today when a man, a stranger, came to him, tapped him on the shoulder and whispered into his ear that our brother, our dear brother… oh, it is the worst news ever.'

'If indeed it is true, Mary,' Mr Michael's wife says firmly.

Judith can't help herself. 'Whatever has happened to Sir Edmund? Pray tell me,' she pleads.

'The stranger came into the bookshop, walked straight up to the curate and told him that Sir Edmund has been discovered in Leicester Fields,' Mary tells her.

'Then the man just walked away,' Mr Michael's wife says. 'The curate has no idea who he is or how he heard the news. He made enquiries of the booksellers but no one knows ought of him except that he was a man in a grey suit of clothes.'

'And what of Sir Edmund?' Judith asks, her voice faltering.

'I cannot speak of it, it is so terrible,' Mary says. 'The constables are searching Leicester Fields, hard by the Earl of Pembroke's home.'

'It is likely all gossip and lies,' Mr Michael's wife says.

Mary turns to Judith and says in a whisper, 'The man in the grey suit told the curate that dear Edmund lies by the dead wall.'

'Is he… is Sir Edmund…' Judith cannot utter that terrible word, *dead*, not to his cousin, not with Mr Michael's wife giving Mary that dreadful look to shut her up from speaking. Mary takes hold of Judith's hand and squeezes it as if to give herself the strength to speak the words.

'The man in the grey suit told the curate that poor Edmund lies… he lies with his own sword run through him.'

It is ten o'clock when they come banging at the door.

First, Sergeant Ramsey, who heard the terrible news whilst drinking at Duke's coffee house nearby, followed by Constable Brown and several other men, all of them wet and muddy and making a mess in the passage. Constable Brown's voice is velvety and low as he explains to the brothers that Sir Edmund's body has been discovered in a ditch at Primrose Hill and taken to a nearby tavern. Mr Michael and Mr Benjamin are saying, no, it couldn't be their brother, even though the constable says that he knows Sir Edmund well. The White House tavern at Primrose Hill being as the constable describes, a very poor and lonely establishment and not the sort of place that Mr Michael and Mr Benjamin would usually visit, they send their brother-in-law, Mr Plunknett to ride out with the constable to identify the body.

There is something Judith doesn't understand but she dare not ask, for Mary is sobbing and Mr Michael's wife has turned deathly pale in the candlelight.

Why did the man in the grey suit announce that Sir Edmund lay dead in Leicester Fields when his body has been found in a ditch some distance away, at Primrose Hill? The man in the barber's shop had known this two days ago. Yet the other thing he said was right: he knew about Sir Edmund being impaled with his own sword.

40

THIS IS MY BROTHER, GODFREY
THE EVENING OF 17TH OCTOBER, 1678

'Why have they brought it here?' Landlord Rawson's wife complains. 'They'd no right to just turn up at our house with a dead body and put it on our dinner table.'

'We couldn't leave him there in that ditch, in this weather, Margaret. We brought him here so that Brown could look at him properly in better light and see who he is. He's an important man: Sir Edmund Bury Godfrey. He's well known to the King and the Lord Chief Justice.' Rawson is exasperated. He's wet and cold and hungry and still in a state of shock after seeing that dead hand hanging over the ditch. 'Do you think I want him here?' he asks his wife testily.

'That man was murdered, or else he murdered himself.' Margaret's voice is rising to a shriek. 'There's blood on the door posts where they carried the body into the house.'

'That's not blood. It's just brown muddy water, from the men's clothes.'

'There's blood dripping onto the bottles in the cellar through the floorboards from where they first laid him on the floor.'

'I've told you three times and more, it's only rain and mud: we were all drenched in the storm and it was muddy in that ditch. No blood come out of him at all: only a little bit on the sword.'

'It's all your fault, John,' Margaret moans. 'If you hadn't gone out with the baker and the farrier looking for a silver topped stick, which you had no right to do, you wouldn't have discovered this Godfrey man with his sword sticking out of him. When Constable Brown returns with Sir Edmund's brothers tell them I refuse to have a dead body on my table.'

'Shall I tell the constable to lay him on our bed?' Rawson asks irritably. 'Shall we sleep either side of him tonight?'

'Yes, this is my brother Godfrey,' Mr Plunknett tells Brown mournfully. 'My brother-in-law, of course. Sir Edmund is my wife Sarah's brother, as you know.'

The constable suggests that they examine the dead man's clothes, to see if he has been robbed. Mr Plunknett doesn't want to touch the dead body, he steps away and lets the Constable search the dead man's pockets.

'Sir Edmund's pocket book is missing,' he exclaims. 'Surely he would never leave home without it.'

'Of course not,' Mr Plunknett replies.

When he sees what Constable Brown pulls out of Sir Edmund's pockets, Rawson wishes he'd had the courage to climb into the ditch when he had the opportunity: a piece or two of gold or silver wouldn't have been missed. In the first pocket the constable finds four broad pieces of gold and a half crown wrapped in paper and then he pulls out six guineas wrapped in another paper parcel. In the second pocket there are two small pieces of gold, several silver coins, a guinea and two rings, one with a diamond, not to mention the ring on his finger. It wasn't a footpad who put that sword through the magistrate's chest. Whoever did the deed had no desperate need of a guinea or two.

41

THE INQUEST
FRIDAY, 18TH OCTOBER, 1678

The dead magistrate lies ready on the table, the fire is kindled, the eighteen jury members are sworn, two coroners arrive, and then the trouble starts.

It's not what you'd expect at an inquest. Rawson is used to dealing with ill-tempered common men in their cups but to hear these two respectable and sober gentlemen raising their voices over a corpse has shocked him almost as much as when he saw that dead hand hanging over the ditch. And all this is going on in the presence of the deceased's family and friends. Mr Richard Mulys, who Rawson knows well, being a regular at a club that meets at the White House and also a close acquaintance of the deceased, is calling out, 'Pray, sirs, I beg you, such raising of voices is disrespectful to Sir Edmund.' But Mulys is not a gentleman of quality, only a gentleman's steward, and the two coroners are not listening.

'The case clearly comes under my jurisdiction,' Mr Cooper says. 'I being Coroner of Middlesex. He moves closer to the corpse and lays his hand upon it, as if he owns it. 'You have no right, sir, to turn up here and announce that you will preside.'

But Mr White, the Coroner of Westminster, insults Mr Cooper in front of the jury and everyone who has come to watch, and says that there are people in the parish of St Martin's who have asked him to take charge because they don't trust Cooper to do it properly. Rawson notices that Mr White looks straight towards the two Godfrey brothers as he says this. It all ends with Michael Godfrey slipping a guinea into the Coroner of Westminster's hand and then he departs, but the brothers look none too pleased about it.

Before the inquest begins, coroner Cooper and the jury, with Constable Brown, the Godfrey brothers, and Sergeant Ramsey, all traipse off to the ditch in the slush – there had been a fall of snow during the night – to view the place where the body was discovered. Rawson stays behind with the dead man and his sisters who want to see their brother in peace and quiet. They speak very little except to wonder why his clothes are so dry after lying in the ditch in the rain. Rawson explains that he kept the fire burning all night to dry them out.

'That was kind of you,' one of the sisters says. 'We would not like to think of him lying here all wet and cold.'

Rawson smiles wanly.

The coroner and company return with a multitude of folk who have been hanging around the tavern and the fields since before sunrise and the sisters depart. Everyone is cold and thirsty and wanting a drink of warm ale. Mr Mulys stands beside Miles Prance, the Queen's silversmith, who speaks not a word and looks pale enough to join Sir Edmund on the table.

'It was a dry death,' Sergeant Ramsey announces. 'There was a bit of blood and watery stuff on the grass where the constable pulled out the sword, that's all.'

They come to the business of examining the body and then the second argument begins.

Two surgeons arrive: Nicholas Cambridge, who is introduced to the Godfrey brothers, and Zachary Skillarne, who needs no introduction to them because he comes at their invitation. Michael Godfrey tells the coroner that the family do not want the body to be opened but the coroner says that this is the usual procedure and in such a case as this it is necessary in order to establish the cause of death. Michael Godfrey says that he will not suffer his poor brother's body to be desecrated any more, considering the violence that the murderer has already done to him. The coroner insists that it must be opened; it has yet to be established that Sir Edmund was murdered. Surgeon Skillarne takes the brothers aside and they whisper together for some time before they agree, with poor grace, to allow the body to be probed with medical lances, but nothing more, Michael Godfrey tells the coroner, he will not watch his brother's body being butchered.

The surgeons ask for the corpse to be stripped and a stranger steps forward rather too eagerly for Rawson's liking and men are pushing behind the jury to get a better view. The stranger takes the shoes off the corpse's feet and Constable Brown tells the jury that Sir Edmund didn't walk through the fields to that ditch; not in those clean shoes. The coroner concedes that the shoes are clean but he has spotted a few grass seeds on the soles.

The deceased is a long thin man who must have felt the cold keenly because a pair of socks and three pairs of stockings are peeled off him. The black breeches and drawers come off next and the poor dead magistrate lies in all his nether nakedness, with half of London craning their heads to see.

'If I'd known that my tavern was to become a theatre of entertainment I would have fetched a crate of oranges and asked the King to send little Nellie to sing a ditty or two and show a pretty ankle,' Rawson says to Sergeant Ramsey.

'You let these common people in, they've drunk your beer and paid for it,' the sergeant rejoins. 'Why complain?'

Another man comes to assist and they prop Sir Edmund up, stiff as he is, with his knees together and his feet dangling either side of the table. They manage to unbutton the coat and the waistcoat and pull them off without too much difficulty, the coat not being tight at all, as if it was made for Sir Edmund when he was rather fatter than he is now, but his arms are so very long and stiff that they cannot get the flannel shirt off him without fear of breaking his bones, so they have to tear it off.

'Observe the two wounds on the left breast,' Skillarne tells the coroner. 'Here, the wound is an inch deep where the sword hit a rib and could go no further. Here is a second puncture where the sword went right through him, penetrating his heart.'

The sword is brought for the surgeons to examine. Rawson's stomach churns when he sees that weapon and remembers the struggle Brown had pulling it out and the terrible gurgling noise it made. The brothers and a little old man who says he is Sir Edmund's clerk identify it to be the deceased's own sword. Both surgeons agree with Constable Brown that there is only a little blood on the point, the shaft being black where it went into the body. They find a little blood on the magistrate's back, though not much, Rawson thinks, for a man who's supposed to have been brutally murdered by Catholic assassins.

'Sir Edmund was already dead when his sword was thrust through him,' Skillarne says, looking towards the brothers.

'Had he been alive there would have been a profusion of blood on his body and in the ditch,' Cambridge adds.

Rawson can see the brothers sighing with relief although they keep their faces straight to try to hide it. If their brother had fallen on his sword, his estate would be forfeit to the Crown. Michael and Benjamin Godfrey will not want the

King to squander their family's inheritance on whores and racehorses.

'The breast has been beaten with some weapon or other or with blows from hands or feet.' Cambridge says.

'Lord, bless his soul,' Mr Mulys cries out. 'Was the poor man beaten and kicked to death? Sir Edmund was a good man; this he did not deserve.'

'I do not say these injuries caused his death,' Skillarne says.

'Most certainly they did not,' Cambridge says, and he takes hold of the neck and shows how the chin can rest on either shoulder.

Benjamin Godfrey puts his hands to his face and Rawson thinks maybe Sir Edmund has broken his neck in the process of hanging himself and the King will be able to buy treats for little Nellie from Godfrey's estate, after all. At this point Rawson becomes quite confused as to the cause of death and by their puzzled countenances the jurymen feel the same. Surgeon Cambridge has noticed a green circle around the neck as if the deceased had been strangled.

'It may be crucial to discover if the deceased wore a neckband when he left home for none was found on his body,' Cambridge says.

Michael Godfrey nudges the little old clerk and he pipes up that his master was wearing his neckband on the day he disappeared.

'This may have been the murder weapon,' Skillarne says.

'The jury has yet to reach a verdict; we must not presume murder,' the coroner reminds Skillarne severely.

At this point more medical men arrive. Rawson hadn't realised until this moment that Sir Edmund was such a very important man. The King has sent his own apothecary, Mr Chase, who has brought his son along. They make much of a great swelling on the left ear where, they suggest, a knotted cord lay pressed against his ear when he was strangled.

There is a break in the proceedings while everyone goes off to have another beer and something to eat, although it is not a handsome fare that Rawson's wife produces at such short notice, just some cold meats and cheese and the remains of a pie. They leave young Mr Chase guarding the body and when they come back they find that he has been doing his own investigation and he has noticed two great creases on the neck above and below where the collar would have been.

'Could the upper mark and the contusion on the left ear indicate hanging?' he asks his father.

Michael Godfrey frowns at young Chase and steps closer to his dead brother.

'The lower mark is surely caused by strangulation,' he says. 'Most possibly, the one above was caused by chaffing of the stiff collar.'

'More has been done to the neck than in an ordinary suffocation,' Skillarne replies.

Whatever can be ordinary about death by suffocation? Rawson wonders, and furthermore, is the surgeon referring to hanging or to smothering a man to death?

After more prodding and probing the coroner says that the stomach is empty and asks if the magistrate was ill before he left his home on Saturday last, for it seems that he had not eaten for two days or more before his death. Benjamin Godfrey says that his brother had a small appetite and also fasted frequently, which is why he was a lean man.

They come to discussing when the magistrate died.

'Putrefaction has begun to set in,' the coroner explains, but the surgeons disagree. The body does not smell, they say, and the limbs are still stiff. Surgeon Skillarne says he's been dead four or five days so that he died either on the Saturday when he went missing or the Sunday following, and the coroner agrees. He's been out in the cold which is why the corpse is still stiff, they say.

Rawson is asked to explain how he discovered the body and Constable Brown describes how it lay in the ditch face down with the knees bent, the left arm bent underneath and the right arm hanging over the bank.

'The body lay in a position where Sir Edmund could not have fallen, nor placed himself,' the coroner tells the jury. 'Someone put him in that ditch and I observed coach tracks in the fields where no coach ever comes.'

'I observed the tracks also, yesterday evening,' Sergeant Ramsey interrupts. 'They were cart tracks, which are not unusual in a field, surely.' He adds that the tracks were fresh and the fields were strewn with hay.

'Before he died he was beaten in the chest and afterwards run through with his own sword.' the coroner says. 'His body was carried to the ditch after his death.'

It is getting late and the jury cannot decide upon a verdict: whether suicide or murder. The coroner calls a halt and tells them to meet next day at the Rose and Crown in St Giles. 'Thank God,' Rawson tells his wife. He's heard enough of that ditch and he wants rid of the corpse of Edmund Godfrey. Margaret has refused to sleep in the house if it's there for another night. Silversmith Miles Prance has had more than enough, too. He has fled the room and Rawson finds him leaning against the privy wall shaking violently and vomiting onto his shoes.

'Everyone is saying that the Catholics murdered Godfrey,' Prance stammers.

'The jury has yet to decide,' Rawson says. 'The verdict might well be suicide by hanging, using his own neckband.'

'Aye,' says Mulys, who has just exited the privy. 'My friend, Sir Edmund, was worried sick after Titus Oates came to tell him of the Popish Plot. "Some great men blame me for not having done my duty," that's what he told me.'

"So, says Rawson, 'either he murdered himself, or some great lord did it for him.'

42

WHAT YOU NEED IS A DEAD BODY
SATURDAY, 19TH OCTOBER, 1678

'Oh, Titus,' his mother says. 'Oh, oh, oh.' She's walking around his dining room, touching everything: running her hands along the carving on the chair backs and the tall court cupboard, even opening the little drawers and peering inside. 'Oh, what a life you have made for yourself after everything that has happened to you.' And then she has to go and weep.

'Stop blubbering, woman, you'll spoil your new clothes with your snot,' his father scolds.

His mother takes a deep breath, blows her nose, dabs her eyes and brushes her hand down her silk skirt. Titus thinks she looks ridiculous all done up as she is with false brown curls dangling onto her face. He's used to seeing her with her skirts pulled up to her knees and her grey hair flying out of her cap while she scrubs and dusts. Even in church on Sundays she's never been so stiff and starched as she is today. She winces when she takes her seat at table.

'She's got a plank of wood stuffed down her front to push in her big belly, like she was a woman of quality,' his father says. 'It's digging into her cunt.'

His mother's face turns purple and Titus and his father snigger. His father is wearing his ordinary garb and has not even bothered to visit his barber. 'Your foolish mother thought she would let you down if she came a-visiting you here at Whitehall in her old clothes,' he says.

Titus has discarded his woolly wig and now wears a periwig of brown human hair and his mother has had to stroke that too, and his silk gown and fine linen cassock, and the satin band on his new wide clergyman's hat that he'd placed on the settle by the hearth so that his father would notice it immediately when he went to the fireside to warm his backside.

'Oh. Titus, after all your humiliations, that you should come to be so exalted by the King and the Privy Council,' his mother says, still puce in the face. 'Hasn't he done well for himself, Samuel? To have these grand lodgings and three servants to attend to his needs, guards at his door to keep him safe, and a generous allowance from His Majesty.'

His father doesn't answer. Titus snaps his fingers and a boy brings their dinner: venison pasties and a dish of roasted pigeons and ox tongues that he has ordered from a cook shop, accompanied by a large cheese. His father eats noisily and says that the cook has robbed Titus of his money, for what he is eating is surely not venison but beef and rather strong to taste at that.

'It will have walked its way to market, and therefore be much fresher than half a buck that would have been brought stinking in a cart from the country in the dreadful heat of this last summer,' his mother says, 'and the pasty is very well flavoured.' She does not see Titus squeeze the boy's thigh while he serves vegetables onto his plate, but his father, sitting beside him, misses nothing.

'Does your boy pull out his truckle bed in your chamber at night?' he asks.

Titus, with a mouth full of pastry, doesn't reply.

'Why don't you fuck women like other men?' his father hisses into his ear and pushes his plate away before he has tasted the costly Parmesan cheese.

After the meal his mother goes to his bedchamber to refresh herself.

'I hope you didn't shit in the chamber pot,' his father says. He refuses the wine that Titus offers saying that a strong beer is good enough for any man who calls himself a man and not a molly. 'When I was a lusty young man, newly married, young women flocked to me. Naked they were, all of 'em, waiting on the riverbank shivering in the dark, holding their little rushlights and begging to be dipped into the water to be filled with the Holy Ghost.' He laughs lewdly. 'That's not the only dipping they got. A month or two later, some of 'em, having been married divers years and being barren, found themselves to be with child.'

Titus hates it when his father does this: boasts of his exploits with women. It makes him feel like he did when he was a little child hiding in the chimney: the snotty little fool who needed jumbling about. He begins a new conversation about the Popish Plot: his Hellish Popish Plot. 'That papist dog, Thomas Pickering, who refused to help me when I was begging at the Benedictine house in the Savoy will find himself hanging from the end of a rope now that I have told the Privy Council that he is making further plans to shoot His Majesty with Jesuit John Grove.'

'Maybe,' his father says. 'Maybe not. Where's the proof?'

'It was put down in pen and ink and taken to a magistrate to be sworn to. The King and the great lords are obliged to read and take seriously every word I wrote. I have told them that one night, late in August, coming out of the King's Head tavern, I met a Jesuit, one of the men who wrote treasonous letters to Father Bedingfield, and he trusted me so much, he showed me a bag of mustard balls all ready for the firing of Westminster...'

'Jesuits with sacks of fireballs? Letters forged by you?' his father interrupts. 'You, who never learned to spell? The

King and any man in his right wits will give as much credence to your writing as to his own farts. How much longer do you think you can make a living by your scribbles? A week or two at most.'

Titus does not expect this derision. He never does.

'Your plot will come to nothing,' his father proclaims in his fierce, Anabaptist preacher's tone. 'The Law cannot allow a conviction upon the evidence of just one man. I, of all men, know that. Lord Chief Justice Scroggs will tear up your eighty-one articles and use them to wipe his arse. It is all hearsay: women's gossip, not worth a piss let alone the King's pension.'

Will he ever please his father? What else must he do.

'I killed a woman once,' his father says.

'You never told me that.'

'I'm telling you now. She came to me with her two shillings and sixpence in her hand pleading to be dipped like all the others. It turned out that the water was too cold for her.'

Titus is quick to vindicate his Father. 'That wasn't your fault,' he says.

'It was,' his father answers. 'I kept her under a long time so that she could get her money's worth with me. Fucking justices of the peace tried to put me in prison for it.'

Titus offers his father a plug of tobacco and they chew. His father ejects a stream of thick greenish-brown fluid towards the pot by the hearth and misses.

'Your Popish Plot will ignite faster than the baker's house on Pudding Lane, if a Protestant, a man of quality, were unfortunately to be discovered murdered by someone of the Romish religion,' he tells Titus. 'What you need is a dead body.'

'A corpse?'

Does his father expect him to rob a grave, or even worse, murder someone? Is this what he has to do?

'Aye,' his father says, 'a dead body: a very dead one.'

'Very dead?' Titus queries, frowning.

His father stares at him long and hard and waits until Titus has looked away before he says, 'Seven days dead would be just about right, I'd say.'

43

SO LITTLE BLOOD
SUNDAY, 20ᵀᴴ OCTOBER, 1678

Henry, Judith and Betty are waiting at the door when their master's corpse returns to his home in Hartshorne Lane wrapped in a blanket. Betty has prepared cloths and a bowl of water strewn with herbs and as soon as the coroner's men have laid him on his bed she begins to wash his body.

'So little blood,' she says, 'hardly a drop, but so many bruises.' She calls for Judith to assist her to dress him in his night-shirt and morning gown.

'I would have put him in his periwig to make him look more like himself if it hadn't been so filthy from lying in that ditch,' Betty whispers to the housekeeper, 'so I put on his night-cap.'

'Come, Betty,' Judith says, 'you've done the necessary here.'

They tiptoe across the wooden floor towards the door and gently lift the latch; as if Edmund can hear; as if they are ghosts intruding upon the sleep of the living.

In the kitchen they find a sack that the coroner's men have left. Judith pulls out Edmund's old camlet coat. 'A poor man will be proud to wear this after a good brushing down; there's a good deal of silk in the weave and the goat's hair hasn't started to moult.'

'Oh,' Betty exclaims, 'how very strange. There's no

mending to do. Apart from the muck from the ditch, there's no damage to his coat or the waistcoat at all. I thought the sword would have slashed them front and back. And look at the shirt, there's just the seams to sew up where it's ripped under the arms.'

'Yon clerk told me they had to tear it off at the inquest because his arms were stiff,' Judith explains. 'It's easily mended.'

Betty points to white droplets on the clothes. 'Wherever did Sir Edmund go that last Saturday to get splattered with candle wax?'

'Well, it's either the theatre or to visit a person of quality,' Judith says, 'either that, or perhaps from the candles in a church.'

'Henry took me aside this morning and told me look in all the master's clothes for a note Sir Edmund might have hidden about his person,' Betty says.

'If the master had left a note surely the coroner would have found it at the inquest.' Judith doesn't tell Betty the terrible thought that has come into her head: that Mr Michael is afraid that a suicide note might be hiding in his brother's clothes.

'Perhaps Henry is thinking of the note the stranger brought that last Friday evening,' Betty says. 'I keep thinking of that man. Surely it's more than coincidence that he should visit upon such a strange errand the night before Sir Edmund disappeared.'

'We'd better get these clothes washed and brushed,' Judith says, after they have searched all the pockets and cuffs and found nothing. 'It's not for us to ask questions. The inquest has concluded that the master was murdered; strangled with his own neckband. We servants have to keep our opinions to ourselves, but we have them all the same.'

'Please don't ask me to clean his shoes,' Betty pleads. 'I

couldn't bear to do it. There's something about a dead man's shoes that sends a shiver right through me.'

'Yon clerk will do that and he'll take the master's wig to the wigmaker to be cleaned,' Judith says. 'Sir Edmund would have wanted a poor man from this parish to have his old coat, and the new one too and his shoes and all his shirts.'

'He was a good man,' Betty says. 'Oh Mrs Pamphlin, who was it who hated Sir Edmund so much that they took his sword and skewered his body when he was already dead?'

Part 6
Accusations of Murder
October–February,
1678–1679

"On the 12th day of October… at the parish of St Mary le Strand…with a linen handkerchief of the value of sixpence…"

Mr Justice Wild (1679)

44

THERE IS ANOTHER SUSPECT
OCTOBER, 1678

'I believe I've discovered Sir Edmund Godfrey's murderer,' Pepys announces.

'Who is he?' young Sam asks eagerly.

'The mayor of Gravesend has written to me of a very suspicious character who turned up at the fair two days after Sir Edmund's body was found,' Pepys explains. 'A boot and shoe seller who met him on the road as he was riding to the fair thought he was a highwayman. He was dressed like a gentleman, rode his horse hard and carried two pistols, which is what alerted the boot seller, who hastened to inform the mayor, who describes him as well built, wearing a fair wig, with bushy eyebrows, a slight squint and a rough face.'

'What's his name, this highwayman?' Sam asks.

'This is the strangest part of the whole story. You'll never believe this. He's told the port officials that his name is... *Godfrey*.'

'Is he a relative of Sir Edmund?' Sam asks.

'No, of course not; it's an alias. At the fair, he had his beard trimmed and bought a campaign coat to cover his costly clothes. It was a dark night being the eclipse of the moon, but a London stallholder trading at the fair recognised him as a man who works in a tavern on Cannon Street. He's a bad man, a Catholic, maybe a Jesuit even, and it seems that he was fleeing from the murder. The stallholder noticed the initials J. S. embroidered on his handkerchief.' Pepys hands the mayor's letter to Sam. 'Read the rest, please, my eyes are mighty painful. What else does the mayor write?'

Sam peruses the letter for a minute or two. 'Oh Mr Pepys, this is what it says: 'He was drunk in a tavern and there's a toast to the confusion of those in the Hellish Popish Plot. But the man calling himself Godfrey only pretended to drink and then he threw his glass into the fire. He's a Roman Catholic, Mr Pepys, a popish plotter, and if he's Sir Edmund's murderer, who will get the King's five hundred pound reward: you, sir, or the mayor of Gravesend?'

'Finish reading the letter,' Pepys says sternly. 'Has this suspicious man been apprehended?'

'He went out to board the *Assistance*,' Sam continues. 'Oh dear, this is not good news, sir. The *Assistance* sailed illegally without being cleared by the searchers.'

'Letters must be sent immediately to the commander-in-chief of the King's ships in the Downs,' Pepys says. 'Should the *Assistance* come into port, officials must board her and arrest this man calling himself Godfrey. I must also alert the Duke of York and Secretary Henry Coventry to this new information.'

***

While the corpse of Edmund Godfrey lies in state, awaiting burial, a rather strange letter has landed on the desk of Henry Coventry, Secretary of State for the South, older brother of Sir William Coventry who has been such a good friend to Pepys in the Commons; the best he could have. Lord knows how he could have stood his ground against Lord Shaftesbury without him. The Coventry brothers happen to be Shaftesbury's brothers-in-law but the familial bond doesn't stretch to their politics. Henry Coventry has been loyal to the Stuarts throughout his life, having worked in Europe as an agent for the Crown during Charles' exile years. He's just getting into his sixties now and it shows. He sits at his desk with his gouty leg supported on a foot-stool and his cane propped within easy reach. There's a faint whiff of ointment which gives the secretary's office the aura of a sickroom.

'This is the second missive I've received from a correspon-dent who signs himself, T.G.,' Coventry says, 'The writer claims to have overheard a conversation between two men in a victualling house in Whitefriars on 15th October, one of whom was party to Edmund Godfrey's murder. I cannot ignore this evidence, hearsay though it is. Between the lines I detect a ring of truth: the writer names the place where the magistrate was murdered and claims to know details of how the deed was done. Worryingly, two great lords are implicated.'

'Catholics, of course,' Pepys interjects. 'Your informant seems mighty keen to get his hands upon the five hundred pound reward the King has offered for information about Sir Edmund's death.'

'Aye,' Coventry says. 'He was knocking at my door within hours of the King's proclamation of additional assurance of protection to informers, but the urgency of the writer com-pels me to look further into his accusations. Listen to this Mr Pepys:

'I chanced to hear two persons discoursing, the one saying to the other that if he would go down to Billingsgate he would treat him there with wine and oysters, whereupon the other replied and said: "What you are uppish then are you?" upon which words he swore, God damn him, he had

money enough, and draws a bag out of his pocket and says, there were fifty pounds. The other party was very inquisitive to know how he came by it, and did importune him very much, and at the last he told him that if he would swear to be true to him and never discover, he would tell him that last night he with three men did murder Sir Edmund Bury Godfrey and he had fifty pounds for his pains, and said that he believed he could help him to some money if he would go along with him on the night following.'

Pepys is astounded that a man should so readily confide his complicity in a murder to an acquaintance in a public drinking house where he could be overheard.

'I'd throw this letter in the fire,' Coventry says 'except that T.G. appears to be enticing his friend to return to the place where the body lay, presumably to assist in its removal. He all but names the other three accomplices in the murder, two being in the household of popish lords who have been incarcerated, following Dr Oates' allegations. You know, of course, that this day a warrant has been issued to remove these Catholic lords from the Gatehouse prison to the Tower?

'I cannot ignore T.G's information,' Coventry continues. 'Not after what Titus Oates has discovered about the Popish Plot. Not while rumours spread throughout the city that Godfrey was murdered by Catholics. I am saddened by the humiliation that poor, proud Godfrey may have suffered at these men's hands, if truth it be. T.G claims that on the Monday before Godfrey was murdered, there was a court held at Wild House, and there they tried him, and a priest passed sentence of death upon him.

'Father Whitbread, the new English Jesuit Provincial lodges near Wild House, a place mentioned by Oates in connection with Jesuit conspiracies,' Coventry explains. 'Sir

Edmund's murder is being linked to the very top of the Jesuit hierarchy and also to Titus Oates' discoveries of the Popish Plot.'

'Does the writer name any man directly?' Pepys asks.

'Yes, he does. The murderer's friend having asked him how he came to be implicated in the murder, he says that a broker, one Hogshead, spoke to him of it. He lodges in Eagle Court in the Strand but also frequents the Temple and Whitefriars. I do not know of such a man; do you Mr Pepys?'

'No, I never heard of him.'

'The murderer is at great pains to tell where Hogshead will be found,' Coventry says. 'I ask myself: why is this?'

'Malicious intent perhaps, to get the broker convicted?' Pepys suggests.

'T.G. claims to have heard more of the murder of Godfrey than he is willing to disclose in pen and ink,' Coventry says. 'He promises to make a fuller discovery of it: to disclose in what a barbarous manner they murdered him.'

'It is an easy thing to tell a tale for the King's five hundred pound reward,' Pepys says.

'Aye, yet maybe he writes true and is afraid. Of whom? Of the murderer? Of reprisals from this man, Hogshead?'

'I wonder, did T.G. really overhear this conversation or could it be, perhaps, that he was the other party in the murder conversation?' Pepys ventures.

'This we need to discover.' Coventry says. 'I wrote a brief answer inviting him to wait upon me with haste and it was taken to the Rainbow coffee house where he awaited my reply, for speak with him I must, yet strangely, he has not come knocking at my door again.'

'There is another suspect,' Pepys says, and explains to Secretary Coventry about the man calling himself Godfrey at Gravesend fair who carried a handkerchief embroidered with the initials J.S. 'My jurisdiction as justice of the peace does not extend to Plymouth and Falmouth, as you know, so I must beg you to write to port officials in these towns requesting them to apprehend this man if the *Assistance* docks.'

Coventry peruses the mayor of Gravesend's correspondence. 'The House of Lords needs to be given this new information. I shall arrange for you to speak to them, tomorrow, which I know you will do well, Mr Pepys, you being such an accomplished speaker. I shall also inform Lord Shaftesbury. He is heading the committee that has been appointed to look into the Popish Plot and his friend, the Duke of Buckingham, has put himself at the head of the sub-committee that is investigating Sir Edmund's murder.'

Hasn't Little Lord Shiftesbury got enough of his own plotting to attend to with the Duke of Fuckingham and their anti-French Opposition faction, Pepys wonders.

'The Popish Plot has emboldened Shaftesbury,' the Secretary continues. 'You know that he has begun to speak openly of excluding the Duke of York from the succession.'

Lord, Pepys thinks, has Shiftesbury forgotten that the King once sent him to the Tower and could readily find another excuse to do so if he comes between the royal brothers? Does he suppose that he's another bucket in a well, like Fuckingham; the one coming up while the other goes down, at His Majesty's pleasure?'

***

London is in a terrible state of panic but Pepys cannot help laughing. Alderman Player has gone stark mad with fear and stupidity.

'We shall all rise from our beds to find that our throats have been cut,' he had announced to all and sundry.

In the taverns and coffee houses the people speak of

nothing except the murder of Edmund Godfrey by Jesuits and their fears that the Catholics will ravish their wives and daughters, dash their little children's brains against a wall and burn their mothers and fathers at Smithfield. Chains have been put across the streets and cutlers are doing a brisk trade, for men are sleeping with knives under their pillows. Pepys hasn't gone this far yet, but what he is forced to do feels like a bereavement.

His musician, Cesare Morelli, is leaving, for the safety of both of them. Catholics have been banned from London within a radius of twenty miles, although householders who have traded in the city for at least twelve months and who have no other abode may stay. Aye, Pepys thinks, and take the blame for every murder or house fire hereabouts. There's already been a panic about gunpowder discovered in a Frenchman's house very close to Whitehall Palace until the accused man explained that he is the King's fire-work-maker. Then there was a terrible knocking and banging in Old Palace Yard and Parliament was afraid of another gunpowder plot until Sir Christopher Wren assured them that it was the roof of the building that was about to fall down in the next spell of stormy weather.

A boatman awaits by the back water-gate to take Morelli and his lute to his ship and the safety of Lisbon. Pepys had tried to persuade him to change his religion but it was a vain hope. 'My house will be the duller for your departure,' he tells the musician.

'We have made beautiful music together, you and I,' Morelli says, 'but London hates me.'

'I must discover Godfrey's murderers' Pepys says aloud as he watches the little boat diminishing into the distance. 'Only then, when there are nooses around necks, preferably Jesuit necks, will the city calm down and Morelli may safely return.'

45

WANTED FOR QUESTIONING
OCTOBER–NOVEMBER, 1678

Pepys makes his way to Cannon Street to the house of a haberdasher of hats. He finds him in his shop, attaching feathers to the upturned brim of a high hat.

'Yes, sir,' the haberdasher says. 'I have a lodger who answers to your description: bushy eyebrows and a slight squint, and indeed, bears the initials J.S. He's away again, as he often is. Never tells me where he's going. When he's here, he works at yon tavern opposite.'

'Yes I'm aware of this; the taverner told me he resides with you. Colonel John Scott? Is this the name you know him by?' Pepys asks.

'Aye, but I've no idea what he's doing when he's not in town. Wouldn't dare to ask. He's a sullen man, except when he keeps to his chamber reciting his poetry.'

'You won't be seeing him for a while, he's fled to the continent,' Pepys says.

'Fled? What's he done? Mr Pepys, I told you, I never knew his business.'

'He's wanted by Lord Shaftesbury and the Secretaries of State,' Pepys explains. 'In the unlikely event that he returns soon, inform me immediately. You'll find me at the Admiralty Offices at Derby House between Whitehall and Westminster.'

'Of course, sir.'

'I have a warrant here to search your premises.'

The haberdasher adjusts one of the feathers and places the hat on a stand. 'Very good, sir,' he says. 'Come, I'll show you his chamber.'

'What do you know of Scott's religion?' Pepys asks as they climb the stairs. 'Does he attend an Anglican church hereabouts on the Lord's day?'

'Never seen him in church.'

'You believe him to be a Catholic? A Jesuit in disguise, maybe?'

'Not that I know of, sir. I've told you I know nothing of him. Believe me, I wouldn't have had him in my house if I thought he was a papist, but lately, since he's been gone, there's been all kinds of rumours about him and contradictory at that. Some say he's a Jesuit and others that he's doing work for men of quality.'

'Lord Shaftesbury, or the Duke of Buckingham?'

'How should I know?' the haberdasher retorts. 'He has some fancy gentlemen's clothes that he wears on occasion. He likes his costly lace neckbands, sir, and is particular about how they are laundered, but I never thought him to be a Jesuit dressed up in disguise. Now you're making me wonder whether he really is Colonel John Scott or maybe this title is an alias.'

'Oh, he's Scott alright,' Pepys says. 'He's used another alias, which you'd be better off not knowing. Now, get back to your hats and your customers while I do my business here.'

The search of Scott's lodgings reveals a great deal about the character of the man. Pepys finds a trunk full of mathematical instruments, ten guineas wrapped in paper at the back of his closet and the vilest, most nauseating poetry he has ever read. This sits uneasily beside copies of political speeches and a copy of a document Pepys had written for Parliament setting out details of the costs and strengths of England's army and navy. Pepys is astounded. However did Scott get his hands upon this? And why ever would he want it unless his business abroad is with the French or the Dutch? A little worm of fear begins slithering through his insides. His enemies in Parliament, Shaftesbury and his Opposition politicians, lord, but they could accuse him of giving a copy of his paper to this scoundrel.

As for the murder of Sir Edmund Godfrey, there is nothing in Scott's papers to incriminate him on that score, but nothing to prove his innocence either.

'Could you swear that John Scott was here, sleeping in your house between the twelfth and seventeenth of October?' he asks the haberdasher of hats, after he's completed his search and his coachman and the hatter's apprentice have lugged the chest of papers down the stairs.

'Yes, sir, he was.'

'Would you say he was the sort of man who wouldn't hesitate to kill a man if needs must?'

'He's a boastful man, sir, when he's drunk. He told me that he shot a girl dead on Long Island when he lived in America looking after hogs in the woods, but I thought it was the drink talking and took no heed.'

'That's rather a fetching hat for a lady,' Pepys says, 'the low crowned one with white feathers around the brim; may I take a look?'

'With pleasure, sir. It's a quality hat of beaver which is reflected in the cost: four pounds and five shillings.'

'My lady will look handsome in this,' Pepys says, fishing in his coat pocket for the money. Mary Skynner doesn't pester him for things as a wife would, doesn't expect anything of him at all, only companionship and the pleasure of keeping his bed warm now and then. He loves to surprise her with gifts. No matter that her parents are uneasy about their friendship; he's a rich man and he can afford to keep a mistress. He decided after Elizabeth died that marriage was not for him. 'Well, thank you for your help,' he tells the haberdasher of hats. 'I'll leave you to your business. You may have visitors making further enquiries on behalf of the Secretaries of State and maybe Lord Shaftesbury.'

'So you think he really did murder the magistrate?'

'Oh, he's guilty of a worse crime than murder,' Pepys says tucking the hatbox under his arm.

'What's worse than murder?'

'Treason,' Pepys replies. 'It appears that your lodger is selling state secrets to our enemies.'

***

The funeral procession travels from Bridewell into Fleet Street and along the Strand to St Martin's Lane. Pepys has counted more than seventy clergymen preceding the black draped coffin and men from all ranks of society following behind in their black mourning clothes and wide hats with long black ribbon weepers hanging behind. Lord, but the thousand footsteps that rumble through the streets are like an army on the march. Anyone who can read may buy for just one penny one of the broadside elegies that have been hurriedly printed in time for the funeral, telling of a man loved by the people; an upright justice most unjustly murdered; a man of generous charity and public spirit who cherished the industrious poor; a man who was Rome's deadly enemy. Lord, but they've made the miserable magistrate into a Protestant martyr.

When they reach the parish church of St Martin-in-the-Fields men are jostling at the door to get inside. Pepys just manages to squeeze in before the vicar begins turning people away but he has had to reach his hand into his pocket.

'Well, I hope it's worth it, he grumbles to himself. It's a mighty sum of money I've just given to the vicar, solely for the pleasure of hearing the sermon at first hand although scribes will make shorthand copies of the sermon as the vicar speaks and the printers will be busy as soon as he has left the pulpit. Within days the presses will be clanging out copies for sale.

Dean William Lloyd, vicar of St Martin's, a slight man wearing his own grey hair, stands in the pulpit squashed between two strapping great men wearing clergymen's garb, but they are not men of the cloth, this much is obvious to Pepys: they are bodyguards brought in to protect the vicar from the danger of Jesuits who might be hiding amongst the crowd waiting for an opportunity to assassinate him. Dr Lloyd admits that, initially, he had considered that Sir Edmund might have taken his own life, but having seen the wounds on the body he is convinced that he was murdered. He has chosen for his text the murder of Abner, from the second Book of Samuel: innocent blood – Edmund Godfrey's blood – is crying aloud for vengeance.

***

They come without warning in the late afternoon of the day after the funeral: two men who march through the Admiralty offices straight up to young Sam at his desk.

'Your clerk is wanted for questioning,' one of them tells Pepys.

'Concerning the murder of Sir Edmund Godfrey, the other adds,

'How should I know anything about that?' Sam declares. 'Who says that I do?'

'Lord Shaftesbury and the Duke of Buckingham are investigating the murder. They have a witness who says that you have something to confess.'

Sam can't struggle; they've pinned his arms to his sides and demand that he hands over his sword. 'Tell them, Mr Pepys,' he cries. 'Tell them that I know nothing about Sir Edmund's murder.'

'There's a five hundred pound reward for admitting what you know,' they say in unison.

There is nothing Pepys can do except tell Sam to go with them and answer their questions honestly.

'But sir, I know nothing,' Sam protests.

Pepys asks them to wait a moment while he fetches the boy's coat.

46

SEEKING A TRUTH
EARLY NOVEMBER, 1678

Six horses pull the coach along the Great West Road from Bristol towards London. It carries amongst its passengers a rather sharp featured young man but handsome and charming all the same in his dark periwig when he smiles to the ladies, for he has the airs and the confidence of a gentleman. He is being brought to the capital at public expense and has about his person three letters: one from each of the two Secretaries of State, Sir Henry Coventry and Sir Joseph Williamson, and the third from an old acquaintance. He almost laughs aloud as he remembers the ten pieces of eight that the self-appointed Salamanca doctor of divinity was relieved of at their last meeting at Valladolid in Spain.

William Bedloe had only lately been released from jail when he broke the seal of the letter from Titus Oates and read of the five hundred pound reward that Parliament and the King are offering for information concerning the murder of Sir Edmund Bury Godfrey. He's never met the justice, but he and Oates go back a long way: ever since they were employed in the Catholic household of the Earl of Norwich, who is now the Duke of Norfolk.

Bedloe's fingers are tingling for that reward. Five hundred pounds is a vast sum of money and Titus had written that no one has yet come forward to claim it. Bedloe immediately informed both Secretaries of State that he was willing to disclose particulars of Edmund Godfrey's death. He knows himself to be a great rogue, and there can be no profit in attempting to deny this. He has travelled abroad purporting to be a member of the English aristocracy, leaving debts in his wake, and he will do so again when the need arises. Yes, he's a thief, a highwayman, an opportunist, and always will be, and this is one of the few truths that he will tell. He will wear his tailored gentleman's waistcoat and breeches and his laced cravat and cuffs and speak to Williamson, Coventry and the King, and tell them, in his well-practised gentleman's accent, all about the murder of Sir Edmund Godfrey. He has names, a date, a time and a place. He has a motive, and he will tell the secretaries exactly how Godfrey was murdered and how the body was taken to the ditch. But before he gives his evidence to the Privy Council he must visit Titus Oates; get more information. The magistrate's death needs to be presented to the King and the Privy Council as part of the bigger Popish Plot. He wants to laugh aloud again at the irony. What he, William Bedloe, seeking a truth from Titus Oates?

***

'I wonder that the King and the Privy Council did not inquire whether you were detained at His Majesty's pleasure on the very day when you were supposed to be in the Queen's house with Godfrey's corpse and his murderers,' Oates says, with a sneer.

'William Bedloe snatches Titus' knife and opens an oyster. 'Are the Lords or the Commons or the King himself going to make a call upon the keeper? They need someone to blame for Godfrey's murder: Catholics to be precise.

They need evidence and I will provide it. That five hundred pound reward is as good as in my pocket.'

'I want half of that reward,' Titus declares, 'and my ten pieces of eight.'

Bedloe spreads his arms wide to encompass the large chamber. 'You have lodgings here at Whitehall fit for a gentleman, you have servants, you eat whatever you fancy and you dare to ask me for a few filthy foreign coins? I, who was obliged to borrow money from a woman on the coach for my dinner and a bed. She expects me to buy her a ring for her trouble.'

'You owe me,' Titus says.

'Take that sulky look off your visage; you're ugly enough without it.'

Oates snatches the dish of oysters. 'I got you out of trouble more than once.'

Bedloe pulls back his chair and stretches his legs onto the table. 'Call for your boy to bring more wine and a bottle of brandy. And send him to the cook shop for a proper supper.'

'Last time I ordered your dinner you ran away with my purse,' Titus says sulkily. 'You've drunk enough tonight. Lord Treasurer Danby won't like it if you speak before the bar of the House of Lords tomorrow, too drunk to stand.'

'I'll decide when I've had enough. Send for your boy. And while I eat and drink, you, Dr Oates, discoverer of the Hellish Popish Plot, will advise me how to improve my evidence.'

'What did you tell the King and the Privy Council today?' Titus asks when dishes of meat and poultry are spread on the table.

'I told them that I came too late to be an assistant in the murder but that I found Sir Edmund strangled and lying dead on the floor in the high altar of the Queen's chapel.'

'That's good. I've been thinking myself that it's about

time I brought the Queen in on my plot. Some great men in Parliament want rid of that popish bitch.' Titus frowns. 'Isn't the chapel rather too busy to hide a dead body? People are always there saying prayers and lighting candles.'

'I thought I'd add a touch of blasphemy to the murder,' Bedloe says, and laughs.

'Tell Shaftesbury and the great lords that the body was in a little secret chamber around a corner where nobody important goes.' Titus speaks quickly, in the tone of an expert advising a novice. 'Don't worry if you change little details in your story to make it more believable as you tell it to the Lords and the Commons. They probably don't compare notes. You can make some excuse if you get caught out in a lie; you forgot, or you couldn't see properly in the poor light. "Is that what I said? Really, Mr Speaker? That's not what I'd meant to say, but, of course, I was tired after my long journey from the West Country."'

'Oh, I came across as an honest witness today,' Bedloe says. 'I told them I had done some work for the Jesuits when I was a servant in the Earl of Norwich's house but that I am a Protestant now, and so are my friends, and they have been so since the world began. They liked that. I told them that I know I am a great rogue, and will not deny it, but I was never a murderer, and after I was shown Godfrey's dead body and I was asked to help to get rid of it, I ran away, and took a coach from the Talbot in the Strand to my mother in Bristol. But she, being an honest woman, pleaded with me to discover to the King whatever I knew, and so with her blessing, I wrote to the Secretaries and promised that I would swear an oath on the Bible to the discoveries I would make.'

'These men of quality never imagine that a man like yourself would think as much of swearing to the Book as of kissing a backside,' Titus says.

'You should know,' Bedloe retorts.

'Tell me who did it. You gave names, Jesuit names?'

'Two Jesuits, Father Walsh and Le Phaire came to me promising several thousand pounds if I would kill a man that was a great obstacle to their designs.'

'I know of Le Phaire,' Oates says. 'He's one of the Queen's entourage.'

'I described him as an Englishman who names himself a Frenchman.'

'Excellent. The Jesuits like their aliases. Who is this other Jesuit, Walsh?'

Bedloe laughs. 'God knows; I don't. I told them he lodges near Wild House, where Captain Atkins also lives.'

'Captain Atkins?' Titus cries. 'The one who has accused Mr Pepys' clerk? You idiot, Bedloe. You shouldn't have named another informer. They will think you have colluded together.'

'Oh, they liked it when I named Mr Pepys' clerk as one of the murderers standing by the body. The Privy Council cannot argue with two informers giving similar evidence.'

'But they will make you share the reward with this Captain Atkins.'

'I gave them much more evidence than he has. I was rather enjoying myself, getting carried away telling my story: "And standing there, beside the dead body, by the light of a dark lantern, I saw that the dead body's bosom was all open." I paused for a moment or two for effect, then I confessed that I saw Godfrey's murderers.'

'Really?' Titus stares, open mouthed.

'God, Titus, you're a fool, I was never there, remember. I was detained elsewhere.'

Titus turns away from Bedloe's grinning teeth.'You tell such a good story that I forget myself.'

'I've had lots of practice and hoodwinked cleverer men than you,' Bedloe says, slapping Titus on the shoulder.

'You could have been there, in that chamber,' Titus says. 'You could have murdered Godfrey with your own hands. Keepers have been known to let a man slip out of custody if it is worth their while.'

Bedloe laughs. 'This you have told me before, as I remember, having yourself escaped from incarceration in Dover Castle not so many years ago, following events in Hastings.'

'What else did you tell the Privy Council?' Titus asks.

'Oh, I mentioned one or two names,' Bedloe says. 'Not the men who really did it.'

'What?' Titus asks, astounded.

'Forget I just said that, you hear me, Oates? You're right. I need a clear head for Lord Danby, tomorrow.' Bedloe pushes his glass of wine towards Titus and helps himself to the remains of a pullet. Titus leans forward, alert, staring into Bedloe's dark, insolent eyes.

'Who did it? Who killed Godfrey? You know, don't you?'

'One hears things, even in jail. Especially in jail.'

'Who?' Titus asks. 'Do I know them?'

'They know you, and they'll kill you if I tell them I've told you their names.'

47

BY THE LIGHT OF A DARK LANTERN
EARLY NOVEMBER, 1678

'Madam, this man, Bedloe, he's a rogue.'

'A thief.'

'A highwayman.'

'He was only recently let out of prison.'

Catherine's ladies flutter around her with pins, laces, bodices, petticoats and a silk gown, all in her favourite sweet pea colours.

'Oh, madam, the Duchess of York's ladies will speak of nothing else but this man and how the Secretaries of State and the Commons harken to every word he says.'

'Pray, do be quiet and bring the curling tongs, the King will be here shortly and I will not be ready,' Catherine scolds.

'Oh, madam.' Catherine's favourite lady arranges her curls around her face. 'Why does Secretary Williamson believe the lies that Bedloe tells: that Justice Godfrey was murdered in your house on the Strand?'

Catherine lifts her face while her lips are reddened with a crayon. She asks for her rope of pearls. She doesn't know what to say, what answer to give to her ladies. She is a foreigner: a Catholic in a Protestant country. Charles has told her often that the people love her but she doesn't feel loved. Not since Titus Oates and his horrid Popish Plot. Not since Edmund Godfrey's body was discovered in that ditch.

'Madam,' one of the ladies says nervously while she fastens the pearls around Catherine's neck, 'do you think it is possible, perhaps, that in a secret chamber somewhere at Somerset House, they really did drag the poor man there and murder him?'

There is a terrible stillness. If the fire crackles Catherine cannot hear it. Neither a skirt nor a petticoat rustles. The ladies look to their Queen with frightened eyes.

'Nobody has been murdered in my house, and there are no Catholic plotters,' Catherine says, trying to keep her voice calm but hearing it rising. 'Sir Joseph Williamson was very wrong to order Somerset House to be searched without the King's permission, and His Majesty is furious with him, even though I do not stay there very often. Why should I? My apartments here at Whitehall are nearer to the court and the King.'

'It was an insult to yourself, madam,' Catherine's favourite lady says.

I have suffered worse insults, Catherine thinks, feeling the anger rising. 'Take those frowns off your faces,' she tells her ladies. 'It will upset His Majesty. He hates to see women distressed. He always blames himself, even if it is not his fault.'

Charles arrives in a flurry of spaniels, guards and footmen. He is all smiles to the ladies, charming them as always with his low bow displaying a handsome leg.

'One of my bitches is whelping,' he announces.

Catherine hears someone stifle a giggle. Even the footman at the door is trying not to smile, for the stream of nameless young women who are smuggled up the back stairs at Whitehall Palace is no secret. Charles just pretends that it is.

'You shall have a puppy if you like,' Charles says.

'What lies does this rogue, Bedloe, tell Parliament about

the murder of the magistrate in my house?' Catherine asks, when the ladies and the footmen have retired and they are alone. 'I think it is time I was told the full details; everything.'

'Oh, my dear, do not worry yourself,' Charles says. 'It is all lies, as you say. Let us plan some entertainment to cheer you through the winter. We shall have another masque, at Somerset House, perhaps, and you will disguise yourself as a boy again and show off your pretty legs.'

Whenever disaster happens, fire, plague, the Dutch breaking through defences in the Medway, Charles has an amazing capacity to enjoy himself, regardless. Perhaps it is something he learned to do after the murder of his father; a way of distancing himself from the pain. Catherine tells him that she cannot partake of pleasure in anything until her household is vindicated. 'Tell me all,' she says without trying to disguise the anger in her voice. 'Why ever do the Privy Council heed this highwayman's words?'

Charles comes to sit beside her and one of the spaniels jumps up and pushes its nose between them; jealous. 'It is evidence, my dear, and they must listen, and so must I, but there is no need for you to worry about it. Let Williamson, Coventry, Shaftesbury and the rest, make their investigations. We shall have music and dancing to distract you.' He strides to the door where excited spaniels thrash his legs with their tails. 'I'll go now, summon the musicians – do you know, Catherine, there's a young musician, Henry Purcell, who has composed an anthem for Christmas Day, inspired by Psalm 19…?'

'It is my household that is accused,' Catherine interrupts. 'My ladies are greatly worried. Tell me everything, Charles, all the lies about this murder that is supposed to have happened in my house.' She knows that he wants to be away, outdoors, getting his exercise. Charles returns to the settle, ill at ease, with one long leg stretched out, the other bent, ready to jump up at the first opportunity.

'If you're sure, my dear,' he says.

'Where is this chamber where they say the body lay?'

'Oh, somewhere in Somerset House.'

'Who did he see in that room with the body?' Catherine asks in a whisper.

'He names two priests: Walsh and Le Phaire.'

'I know Le Phaire. Who is Walsh?'

'Bedloe says he is one of your entourage. Obviously, he is not.'

'Why should Father Le Phaire want Edmund Godfrey dead?'

Charles sighs. 'Why indeed? Standing beside these priests was a young man who is clerk to Mr Pepys at the Naval Office, whom I know well; Mr Pepys, that is. This young man, Sam Atkins, has already been accused of being an accessory to the murder by another informer and is in Newgate awaiting trial. With them in the chamber beside Godfrey's body was a man wearing a purple gown, whom Bedloe recognised as an attendant in your chapel, although he did not know his name.'

Catherine is astounded at the amount of detail the highwayman has given in his tale, as if he is familiar with Somerset House; as if he really saw the men he describes. A flush of terror rises inside her up to her throat. Pray God that none of this really happened. She will never admit to anyone, not even to Charles, that she believes there to be even a hint of truth in Bedloe's accusations. 'So men from my household are accused,' she murmurs, 'an attendant in my chapel who wears a purple gown. Now, I wonder, would that be the silversmith who cleans my silver and designs little trinkets now and then? I forget his name, is it Prince, or Prance perhaps?'

The spaniel lying between them has fallen asleep. Catherine strokes its silky ears and it makes a little growling purr, like a cat. The other dogs prowl by the door swishing their tails and getting under each other's feet. One of them comes to Charles, rubs against his knee and watches his face. 'You shall have your walk in a minute,' he says, chuckling to himself, as the dog scampers to the door.

'Do you know, Catherine, my dogs heed what I say better than my Parliament. Yes, three of your household are accused: the two Jesuits and this attendant in your chapel. Father Le Phaire lifted the blanket, and Bedloe saw by the light of a dark lantern that the dead man was indeed Sir Edmund Godfrey, although I doubt they had ever met. He says that he agreed there and then to help remove the body the following day, but thinking better of it, did not keep the appointment. Later, however, he happened upon Le Phaire in Lincoln's Inn Fields.'

'What? Quite by chance?

'Apparently so. Your Jesuit rebuked him soundly for breaking his word after which, incredibly, he proceeded to tell Bedloe exactly how the murder had been done.' Charles pats Catherine's hand. 'Never fear, my dear, it is all a pack of lies. You do not need to know the rest of Bedloe's testimony, of how they are supposed to have abducted and murdered Godfrey. It will distress you.'

'Tell me.'

'The dogs are restless.' Charles stands and tickles the sleeping spaniel out of its slumber. 'Walk with me while they take their exercise and you shall hear Bedloe's tale if I can remember every version, for he has made changes to his story each time he has related it; to me and the Privy Council, the Lords and the Commons. But at every telling the magistrate is supposed to have been murdered in Somerset House.'

'This is what Bedloe claims Le Phaire confessed to him of the murder,' Charles says, while they walk arm in arm in the garden with the dogs running ahead and Catherine's favourite lady following at a discreet distance.

'As Godfrey was making his way home on the Saturday afternoon, at around five o'clock, the murderers lured him into Somerset House, telling him that they knew of some persons in the vicinity who were agitators in the Popish Plot and asked him to go along with them, to make an arrest. Sir Edmund, they said, showed great readiness to do so, and sent for a constable and appointed to meet him at Strand Bridge. He was persuaded to walk a little way into the courtyard but he had scarce made two or three turns about, being a man who cannot stand still, before several men rushed upon him and stopped his mouth with their gloves and pushed him into a small chamber. They put a pistol to his head and asked him to hand over Oates' depositions, which is ridiculous,' Charles says, 'because Godfrey did not have them. They are locked away, as the Jesuits would have known. This was never the motive for the murder, if murder it was, which I doubt.'

'Bedloe is a wicked man, to lie like this under oath.'

'Bedloe appears to have received a lesson from Titus Oates after he had made his discoveries to myself and the Privy Council. When he presented his evidence the following day he changed the motive to one that fits nicely into Oates' Popish Plot. Now he says that Godfrey was privy to a secret known only to the Society of Jesus and that the Jesuits killed him to prevent him from revealing it.'

'What secret would Godfrey know?' Catherine whispers. 'Maybe that the Jesuit Consult met at your brother's house.'

'Odd's fish! If that secret gets out there will be trouble. James has confided to me his fears that Edward Coleman may have told Godfrey of the consult. Coleman has ever been indiscrete and boastful and was a good friend of Godfrey.' Charles' features take on a lugubrious frown. 'Edmund Godfrey was the best justice on the Commission but he was a meddling, stubborn, miserable man, full of his own self-importance. He made enemies every time he sentenced a criminal. The Earl of Pembroke had reason enough to kick him to death if we are looking for motives.'

'Perhaps he did,' Catherine says. 'The Earl is a very bad man.'

'How are these men supposed to have killed the magistrate?' she asks, rather more brusquely than she intended.

'Bedloe says that the Jesuits and their men smothered Godfrey with pillows and knelt upon his breast until they thought he was dead, but seeing that he was yet breathing, they took a cravat and strangled him. They waited until the Monday when they carried the body away through the streets in a sedan chair. Later, Bedloe changed the day that the body was removed to Wednesday, somebody, Titus Oates no doubt, having advised him that the body was unlikely to have lain undiscovered in that ditch in the country all those days until the Thursday.'

'Wouldn't the dead body have been rather too stiff to squeeze into a chair?' Catherine interrupts.

Charles laughs. 'Odd's fish, Catherine, I hadn't given it a thought. Godfrey was a tall man with long legs. Imagine these murderers carrying poor Godfrey through the streets with his stiff dead legs sticking out of the door.' They are both laughing now, Catherine cannot help herself.

'And are they supposed to have taken him all the way out to the country in that state?' Catherine asks and holds her stomach which hurts with so much laughing. 'Surely someone would have seen them, even at night, for they would have needed lanterns to see their way.'

'Apparently they had the good sense to transfer the body to a coach for the final part of the journey to Primrose Hill.'

'Just as well, especially with the sword sticking out of it,' Catherine says, and they are laughing as if they will never stop.

'Actually,' Charles explains, when they are calmer, 'Bedloe says that they put the sword through his ribs shortly before they threw him into the ditch, to make it appear that he had killed himself. Odd's fish! I don't believe a word of it, and neither should you, my dear. This fellow, Bedloe, is mighty cautious about his discoveries. He ensures that he himself is neither implicated in the murder nor the disposal of the body. His evidence would be hearsay only and of no account except that he bolsters his tale with having himself witnessed Godfrey lying dead in a little chamber in Somerset house with the murderers standing beside him.'

'Oh what dire times these two men, Oates and Bedloe, would make believe we live in, with their lies,' Catherine says. 'Lady Shaftesbury carries a pair of little silver pistols in her muff for fear of being assaulted by Catholics, even when she's in her carriage.'

'It is in her husband's interests to have her show them off,' Charles retorts. 'Lord Shaftesbury ears are closed to evidence of any other cause of death but murder by Catholics. The Popish Plot is a gift to men like Shaftesbury, who oppose French alliances.'

'My ladies are afraid,' Catherine says. 'What shall I tell them?'

'Tell them that I shall take care of them all,' Charles says, 'as I promised in our marriage settlement.'

Catherine has stopped walking and turns to face him.

'When were you going to tell me that Bedloe accuses me of planning to poison you?' She speaks quietly, keeping her voice level.

Charles says nothing but she can see that he is furious. He stands before her looking like he does in one of his portraits: regal, proud, unapproachable. In life he smiles, charms, laughs – unless something has happened to upset him.

'When, Charles?' she asks again. 'After they have arrested me and dragged me to Newgate and put me in irons?'

'My dear, do not worry yourself.'

'Oh Charles!' is all Catherine can say, exasperated.

'I was too angry to speak of it and I thought it best you did not know.'

'My God, what a weak and silly woman you must think me to be.'

'It is my duty to protect you.' Charles pulls her to him. 'Now that you know, I suppose I had better tell you that Bedloe's lies are also spilling out of Titus Oates' mouth. He also has accused you of plotting my death. Coleman's conviction for high treason has made these two liars bold in their accusations.'

'Bold enough for Oates to be brought to my house upon the direction of your council, looking for a chamber where Oates supposedly overheard me plotting to murder my husband.'

'Brought to Somerset House without my permission,' Charles declares angrily. 'Never fear, my dear. I have had Oates confined to his lodgings under guard, and his papers have been seized.'

'These bad men tell lies about me because they know it is what some men want to hear,' Catherine says. 'The English Parliament want rid of me. They want to replace me with a Protestant Queen with a Protestant baby boy in her womb.'

'I am not King Henry VIII,' Charles says gently. 'I will never divorce you. I will prorogue my Parliament if they try to force me to do it.'

He calls for his dogs. Privy guards appear from nowhere ushering spaniels in the direction of the palace.

'If anyone has designs to raise armies against me it will be Shaftesbury's republicans, not Catholics. Fortunately, Secretary Williamson's spies have found no more seditious activity from Opposition politicians since he nipped their plot in the bud last year.

'My dear, do not worry,' he says kindly, in that beautiful deep voice of his that made Catherine love him, even in the early days, when he had to drag himself from Barbara Castlemaine's bed to come to her to try to make an heir. 'Your nose is all red and cold. You should go inside and take a dish of your tea.'

48

A BAD MAN ACCUSES ME
NOVEMBER,1678

Pepys wafts his handkerchief furiously. 'The stench is mighty powerful, it could make a man vomit.'

'You get used to it,' Captain Richardson, replies. 'Now then, Mr Pepys, your visit is otherwise than at His Majesty's pleasure, so it will cost you.'

Pepys slips a packet of guineas into his hand and the keeper leads him through Newgate prison to the cell where young Sam sits on a stone slab with his head in his knees and his ankles in irons. Pepys feet crunch just as if he were walking on shells strewn on a garden path: lice, a multitude of them, are crawling under his feet.

Seeing his master, Sam jumps up and his eyes fill up with hope. 'Sir, sir, I am innocent. Pray help me, sir, you know that I never knew this man, Edmund Godfrey, but Secretary Coventry took away my sword and I was taken to a house in Lincoln's Inn Fields and Lord Shaftesbury and the Duke of Buckingham and the other great lords, they won't listen to a word I say.'

'Knock hard, Mr Pepys, when you are ready,' Richardson says, and locks him in.

'Here, Sam, I've brought you food and clean linen,' Pepys says. 'Take your dinner later when I am gone. First, tell me how you have got yourself into this mess so that I may try to get you out of it. Are you ill, you look very pale?'

'No, sir, don't worry yourself, I ain't got the plague nor anything you can catch, not even a cold; just hungry, that's all. Let me eat a little, sir, so I may think clearly and tell you all I need to.'

The clerk eats while words spill out of his mouth to the only person who will believe him to be innocent. 'A bad man accuses me: Captain Charles Atkins. I know him well, sir. For name-sake we are called cousins although we are unrelated by birth. He has turned against me for reasons I cannot discern.'

'The reason is obvious. The King's five hundred pound reward. Unfortunately,' Pepys says, 'there is another, more personal reason. I know this Captain Atkins. He hates me and he is using you to attack me. He was once thrown into prison because of me, for accusing him of cowardice when he was in command of a small warship, the *Quaker*. I'm sorry to say that my actions ruined him. He's lived in penury ever since.'

'I know how wretched he is,' Sam says. 'He's half starved; all skin and bones, even his face. I've taken pity on him and given him money when he's come a begging.'

Pepys begins to lower his backside to sit beside Sam on the shelf, it being the only seat available, but seeing a long tail emerging from the straw and the bulging shape of a scurrying rodent, he thinks better of it. 'Did your jailer bring you the brandy I paid for?' he asks.

'Yes, sir, thank you,' Sam says tipping up the empty jug.

'Well, I hope it cheered you,' Pepys says. 'Now, tell me more of the charges Captain Atkins lays against you.'

'He accuses me of seeking out a bad man of courage and secrecy, named Child, and inviting him to speak with you so that you could arrange for him to kill Sir Edmund Godfrey on your behalf.'

Pepys sits beside Sam on the bench. He cannot help

himself, his legs have turned to jelly. 'Lord, we are both done for,' he mutters to himself.

'Captain Atkins has told Lord Shaftesbury and the Duke of Buckingham that Sir Edmund Godfrey has very much vilified you, sir, and if he lived long enough he would be the ruin of you. He says that the quarrel between yourself and Sir Edmund was occasioned by the Popish Plot.'

'What quarrel?' says Pepys with derision. Lord knows, he never liked Godfrey overmuch but he had no disagreement with him. They'd met occasionally these last years, professionally and socially, at suppers with mutual friends, that sort of thing. The man had little wit to bring to a table. Being deaf he never partook of other men's conversations and wanted others to listen only to himself.

Pepys knows that in the present climate of the Popish Plot he is vulnerable. He is far too close to the Catholic Duke of York. He's mighty glad that he was at the races with the royal brothers at the time when Godfrey disappeared. No one is going to accuse him of strangling the magistrate with his own hands when he was standing beside the King and his brother cheering for their horses on the very day that the magistrate probably died. Lord, but it was worth the money he lost in bets to have such an alibi.

'Has Lord Shaftesbury offered you inducements to accuse me?' Pepys asks, knowing what the answer will be.

'I've told the noble lords that I am innocent, and so are you. They think you are a papist, Mr Pepys, and they kept going on about a crucifixion painting in your house. They talked to me sweetly and told me I will be pardoned with a handsome reward and set at liberty to lead a very prosperous life if I will but admit to Captain Atkins' accusations. But if I do that, sir, they will surely hang you for plotting the murder even though you were not at home when it happened.'

'You are a brave boy,' Pepys says, 'and a loyal servant. Eat your fill and then you can tell me exactly what you did on 14th October: the day you are accused by William Bedloe, of standing beside Edmund Godfrey's dead body in a little chamber at Somerset House.'

Pray God he did not do as I charged him while I was away and sit in the office at his work with only my other clerks to vouch for this, Pepys thinks, or that will be the end for both of us.

'I was very much fuddled, by the end of that day, sir,' Sam mutters, through a mouthful of mutton pie. 'I do not remember much of the latter hours.'

'Presumably, you did not get yourself into that drunken state alone. You were with other young men?'

'With two gentlewomen, sir, sisters.'

'Were they also befuddled?'

'I cannot rightly say, sir, I was well into my cups. I cannot remember much of that night.'

'You cannot rightly say?' Pepys glares at young Sam, horrified. 'See what great trouble your debauchery has got us into. I sacked you once for drunkenness, remember, and took you back only on condition that you stay sober. You had better say your prayers, for if the Lord does not save us, I don't know who can. Did you tell Shaftesbury and Buckingham that you were exceeding worse for wear with drink on the very day that you are accused and you cannot remember what you did?'

Pepys regrets his harsh words as soon as they are out of his mouth for young Sam has burst into tears. 'Take heart, and think,' he says more gently. 'Weeping will do you no good. If you can find a couple of witnesses to testify where you were on that Monday night when you were supposed to be standing by Godfrey's makeshift bier, Lord Chief Justice Scroggs will have no choice but to acquit you.'

'Captain Vittles will do that,' Sam cries out.

'Captain Vittles?'

'Of the King's ship, *Katherine*. He entertained me and the ladies on board that night, off Greenwich. And when I came to, sir, next day, my friends told me that we had been deposited at Billingsgate steps by the boatswain very late, half an hour before midnight, because the tide flowed so strongly they couldn't make it to London Bridge. And what trouble they had to get me into a coach, the state I was in. Captain Vittles is a good and generous man, Mr Pepys, sir, he will speak up for me. I've known him ever since I was a boy. He put a Dutch cheese and half a dozen bottles of wine into the boat when he sent me off.'

'Oh thank the Lord, we are saved, we are saved indeed,' Pepys cries. 'My Lord Chief Justice cannot dispute the tides. Here is your alibi, Sam, and your witnesses, so cease your blubbering and take heart. I'll find Captain Vittles and his boatswain and bring them to your trial. Now, take off that filthy shirt, and put on your clean one.'

Pepys tries to scrape crushed lice from the soles of his shoes with his stick. 'Listen, Sam,' he says in a low voice. 'Our best defence is to discover who really killed Godfrey so I shall set to and resume my investigations. You know this Captain Charles Atkins better than I do. Would you say he's the murdering kind?'

'He'll do anything for money, sir.'

49

THE DANCE OF DEATH
3RD DECEMBER, 1678

It is ten o'clock, dry and frosty. A day that begins without colour, only white and grey, with a promise of crimson. The bell of St Sepulchre's Church has tolled for four hours and will shortly cease its death knell; for the one it summoned awaits.

Edward Coleman sits with his knees covered in straw and his back against the prow of the boat shaped sledge that will drag him to his execution. He wears a wide hat atop a long periwig and holds his head down, careless of the rowdy spectators, for he is reading a small book, his Bible, or maybe a book of prayers. Guards with pikes and halberds surround him.

As the horse drags the sledge away, Pepys hears him murmur, 'There is no faith in man.' He means the Duke of York, of course. Coleman never confessed because he expected York to save him but Pepys knows that this would never happen. How naive of Coleman to expect that it would. "Mr Coleman," Lord Chief Justice Scroggs had told him at his trial, "your own papers are enough to condemn you." After he had said this, there was nothing York could do. A dark and suspicious letter had been seized upon delivery to Coleman at his house. He had said there were no more letters. He had lied.

All the way to Tyburn the churches toll. It's a long walk but a slow one and Pepys, struggling with his aching joints, barely manages to keep up. The people pelt Coleman with sticks, dirt, stones, nails, whatever they have collected. When it is time for him to stand and speak he has to shout, but still he cannot be heard clearly because of the noise of the crowd. He keeps sneaking glances towards the executioner, and Pepys, standing there at the front of the crowd, sees the traitor's eyes fill up with tears when he watches the hangman fix the noose to the gallows.

Coleman hangs for fifteen minutes and Pepys, standing below his legs, is close enough to look up and see his lips moving in prayer.

They take him down alive while his legs dangle in the dance of death. They cut off his genitals and pull out his bowels: yards of them. Now the traitor lies upon the trestle, all bloody, red and reeking, neither dead nor alive, with his head turned to make him watch his entrails burn. The horrible ceremony is being acted out like a mystery play to entertain the crowd. The stench of it makes Pepys sick to his stomach. He feels his bowels become liquid, churning inside him with each wave of nausea. They quarter the body, each part with a limb attached, wrap them all up in a white sheet and drag the crimson bundle away in the sledge.

50

AT THE SIGN OF THE PLOW
DECEMBER, 1678

They sit together: four men drinking their ale. When Pepys approaches they remove their hats.

'Good evening, sir,' Robert Green says in his Irish brogue as he slides along the bench to make room for Pepys. He's the cushion-man in the Queen's chapel in Somerset House; very frail and elderly. Another man, Henry Berry, is also elderly. He's a Protestant but he wears the livery of Queen Catherine's porters and Pepys has passed the time of day with him many a time when he is at his post at the water-gate of Somerset House. A third man is also well known to Pepys; Miles Prance, the Queen's Catholic silversmith. Pepys has occasionally bought little trinkets for Mary Skynner from his shop in Covent Garden and often sees him at Mass in the Queen's chapel, where he is a verger, conspicuous in his purple gown.

All three are regulars at the Sign of the Plow and Pepys has come here in order to question them about Edmund Godfrey's murder. If indeed the magistrate was killed in Somerset House, these men may have seen something suspicious: some clue to lead Pepys to the real murderers and thus free young Sam and himself from blame. They introduce their friend, Lawrence Hill, a tall, dark, powerful looking, heavily bearded younger man. He's a Catholic, of course, otherwise what would he be doing here, fraternising with the Queen's servants?

'What news, gentlemen?' Hill asks.

'What news, Lawrence? Why, nothing but the worst, for Catholics.' Miles Prance takes a long swig of ale. 'A man is 'prenticed when he's nothing but a boy, learns a skill, works hard at his trade until he can afford to move his shop from St Giles-in-the-Field to Covent Garden where gentlemen may more readily visit. He's good at his craft, you see, so good that the Queen asks him to make little trinkets in gold and silver. He's mighty pleased with himself, and why shouldn't he be; until Dr Titus Oates comes along, shouting about his dammed Popish Plot.'

His three companions exchange glances; he is slurring his words badly and speaking too loud for comfort.

'For God's sake, keep your voice down, Miles, mind what you say, in company.'

Prance ignores Hill's warning. 'Along comes Titus Oates with his plot,' he says, 'and the King makes a proclamation telling all Catholics to leave the city, and what's to become of a hard-working Catholic man and his silversmith's shop?'

'Catholics who have a shop and have lived in the city for a year or more are allowed to remain,' Pepys says with the authority of a member of the Commons. 'You have no need to fear.'

'Yes,' old Robert Green agrees. 'The Queen is a kind lady. She will take care of us.' 'No she will not and you're a fool if you think otherwise,' Prance snaps. 'Her servants are not welcome in this city that hates Catholics. Don't you know that her secretary, her Master of the Horse and her surgeon have already departed, and more of her Catholic people are packing their chests. The Queen has no power of protecting her servants. Sir Edmund Godfrey told me so himself. in court…'

'Oh, so you knew Sir Edmund?' Pepys asks.

'He told me so at Middlesex County Sessions, Hicks Hall, two years ago and thus accused me, with much unkindness.' Prance's voice has become the self-pitying whine of a man well into his cups. 'These Catholics who leave London each day are my customers. What am I to tell my wife when she goes looking at the new fashions she sees the ladies showing off in the Exchange. I can't even afford to buy myself a new pair of drawers. Two of my brothers are secular priests. My sisters are nuns. What am I? What am I?' He leans against the table, pulls himself up unsteadily and beckons to the landlord for another jug. 'I'm a bloody Protestant now,' he shouts above the hubbub. 'I complied with the new Test Act.'

'Hush,' Hill says. 'Catholics and Protestants drink in this tavern and neither will like the way you speak of your religion.'

'I testified, in the presence of the Anglican God, that in the Sacrament there is no transubstantiation of the bread and wine into the body and blood of Christ, and I swore that adoration of the Virgin Mary is superstition and idolatry. I am a Protestant now,' Miles says mournfully.

'You should be ashamed of yourself,' Green says in a low voice but with derision. 'I'm a true Catholic and I'll be so when I die.'

'Don't you be telling me what to do.' Prance has to hold on to the table to steady himself. 'Who cares about you, an ancient Irishman who cannot read or write. Who cares that you lay out the cushions in the Queen's chapel? She doesn't even know your name. I had no choice, no choice, I tell you. Don't you know that the Queen's servants are not protected from complying with the Test Act.'

Lawrence Hill grabs Prance by the shoulders and pushes him back in his seat. 'Maybe it is time to go home to your wife,' he says firmly.

Prance rests his elbows on the table in the attitude of a man defeated and sips his ale. 'My wife had to cut off her hair to have a wig made for me.'

'That was very good of her,' Pepys says quietly, to try to calm the man. 'My late wife would never have made such a sacrifice for me.'

'I've never seen you wearing a wig,' Green says to Prance.

'Men of quality wear wigs. It would be pretentious of me in my present circumstances. Anyway, it itches: it's crawling with lice.'

'Return it to the wigmaker,' Pepys suggests. 'He'll delouse it for you; for a fee, of course.'

'Listen,' Lawrence Hill says, 'Stop feeling sorry for yourself, Miles. You have a skill that is portable. You could leave London, take your silverware and start your business again quietly, in another place where no one will care about your religion.'

'Yes,' Green says, 'A man can set up a business anywhere if he has the inclination and works hard. Lawrence here has gone from living in servants' lodgings at Somerset House to setting up his own victualling shop on Stanhope Street, and he's doing very well, too.'

'Aye,' says Hill. 'Leaving Somerset House was the best thing to happen to me. My wife was always complaining of the cramped servants' lodgings. Our bedchamber was full of boxes and the household linen. Everyone used to go in there to get things when she was trying to get the baby off to sleep. She keeps her own house now, and I am at no master's beck and call.'

'I would leave London tomorrow, if I could,' Prance complains. 'But there are men here who owe me and I must wait until they pay. My wife plagues my ears day and night to get the rent from our lodgers and buy her a new gown. How can I do it except I steal their purses? The bastards will not put their hands into their pockets themselves.'

'Turn them out onto the street with their chattels; I would,' Lawrence says. ''Tis a weak man lets himself be taken for a fool like that.'

'A fool, is that what you say I am? If I turn them out I'll never get the rent. It's months they owe me; more than a year. There are other men besides who have not paid me what was promised.' He stands. 'I'm going for a piss. I'll finish the jug before I leave. I paid for it.'

'I always thought Miles Prance to be a quiet man with very little to say,' Green says. 'I'm sorry that you have had to sit and listen to his complaints, Mr Pepys.'

'I hardly know him,' the porter Berry says. 'I've seen him coming and going and said, "Good day," in passing, that's all. I never spoke with him until this night.'

'I know you're uneasy about drinking here with us Catholics these days, Henry,' Robert Green says.

'And you, Mr Pepys,' Lawrence Hill asks. 'Why have you come here to drink with Catholics?'

Pepys comes straight to the point, tells them what they probably already know: that Sam Atkins is incarcerated in Newgate, innocent. 'If I can find Godfrey's real murderers, then my clerk will be freed. I wondered if any of you had seen anything suspicious at Somerset House on the evening of 14th October; any lead that I could follow up.'

'If we knew anything, we'd have disclosed it to the constables, or to another justice,' Hill says sternly.

Pepys turns to Henry Berry 'Do you remember who came through your gate on that evening?'

Henry is silent a while, counting the days on his fingers. 'I was not on duty that night. I was at home helping my wife serve our customers in my alehouse.'

'Did you see anything out of the ordinary in the courtyard at Somerset house during the days that Edmund Godfrey went missing?' Pepys asks Robert Green.

'Sometimes I like to sit on a bench by the stables, passing the time of day, but not during the blustery weather we had in October. I passed through the courtyard occasionally, of course, on my way to and from the chapel. I don't recall seeing anything out of the ordinary.'

'Like a dead body being lugged about,' Hill says sarcastically.

When Prance returns they are talking about the conviction, on the previous day of lay brother, John Grove. 'I know him very well,' Prance says. 'Only a few weeks ago he bought two silver spoons for a christening where he was godfather. He's a good man, Honest William: he lives up to his alias. He never plotted to kill the King and start a rebellion.' Prance's voice becomes louder. 'Titus Oates is a liar. John Grove is an innocent man.' He is almost shouting now. At tables nearby, men turn and stare.

'Be quiet, Miles,' Hill hisses. 'Don't you know that it is more dangerous to speak out against Dr Oates' discoveries than to speak ill of the King in these troubled times, especially if you are a Catholic.'

'I'm a Protestant, I told you so.'

A man approaches their table, grabs Prance's shoulder. 'You're a papist, Miles Prance,' he says. 'A fox cannot change the colour of his tail.'

'I must go,' Lawrence Hill says abruptly. 'If the baby wakes, my wife needs me to get him off again. He likes to snuggle against my beard.' He climbs over the back of the bench and strides between the tables to the door without a backward glance.

'I want my rent, John Wren,' Prance demands. His words run into each other but Pepys manages to grasp their meaning.

'I'll pay no more money to a papist dog,'

Prance makes a swing with his balled fist towards Wren's chest.

'You'll regret this.' Wren says, grabbing his arm. 'I know you, Miles Prance. I live in your house. I know everything about you. I know when you go into your shop of a morning and when you come to your supper at night. I know when you shit in your privy and take a candle to bed with your wife. I've seen you walking to your papist club at Primrose Hill hard by the ditch where Edmund Godfrey's body was found.' Wren isn't shouting, rather, he is hissing the words into Prance's ear. He pauses, still holding Prance's arm. 'I know that you were not at home on the nights when Sir Edmund Godfrey was lost and murdered.'

Three days later rumours reach Pepys that upon the evidence of Wren, Miles Prance has been arrested for the murder of Edmund Godfrey. Well, the man has connections to Primrose Hill where the body was dumped and also to Somerset House, where the murder is supposed to have taken place. Furthermore, he has admitted to having a grievance against Sir Edmund.

51

ON THE WAY TO HEAVEN
FROM SATURDAY, 21ST DECEMBER, 1678

Afterwards Pepys would think of the irony of the situation; that Miles Prance was on his way to Heaven when his nightmare began.

Prance was in the lobby of the Commons at Westminster waiting to be called for examination. Dinnertime came and his guards were preparing to escort him to Heaven, an eating house nearby. A terrible commotion alerted Pepys and other members leaving the chamber and there was the informer, William Bedloe, pointing in Prance's direction and screaming, 'Look here, this is the verger in the purple gown who I saw at Somerset House standing beside Sir Edmund Godfrey's dead body.'

Miles Prance being taken straight to the Lords Committee that afternoon, there is no opportunity for Pepys to witness his examination, but later, upon hearing that Prance has been escorted to Newgate prison, he hastens to seek out Sir Joseph Williamson in the lobby.

'Mr Prance denies having any part in Godfrey's murder,' Williamson explains. 'He swore under oath that he never stood beside the body in a little chamber at Somerset House, neither did he assist in the removal of the body.'

'Do you believe him?'

The Secretary of State rubs his hand over his dark stubbly

chin and frowns. 'He needs further examinations. He told us he never met William Bedloe until this day and that he was drunk when he was overheard in the Plow, speaking of lay brother John Grove being an honest man.'

Lord, Pepys thinks, nobody knows better than I how befuddled he was with drink that night. Pray God that he never mentions that I sat with him in the Plow on that very evening that John Wren so publicly accused him.

'Mr Prance tried to wriggle his way out of admitting that he had received money from John Grove,' Williamson says, 'but the Lords hounded him with questions and forced him to confess that he has done some work in his shop for the Jesuit lay brother.'

Pepys sees little Lord Shaftesbury slowly pulling himself towards them with the aid of his two sticks.

'Miles Prance has confessed to making arrangements to leave London. Indeed, he had made arrangements to hire a horse to ride out of town,' Shaftesbury says.

'But I heard he's changed his religion; put his name to the Test Act,' Pepys says. 'Surely he has no need to leave the city if this is the case.'

'The Lords don't believe that he has changed his religion,' Williamson says.

'Aye,' Shaftesbury concurs. 'We don't. The man lies on all counts. He has hired the horse to run away from his complicity in the murder. He was there in Somerset House standing beside Edmund Godfrey's body with your clerk, Mr Pepys. You are surely aware that another informer, William Bedloe, who was also there in that chamber in Somerset House, where Godfrey's body lay on Monday, 14th October, has sworn that Sam Atkins was there also.'

'My clerk is innocent; he has an alibi,' Pepys says in desperation, knowing that Shaftesbury is unlikely to heed a word he says. 'I have witnesses to prove where he was on

Monday the 14th October, when he was supposed to have been…'

'Tell that to Lord Chief Justice Scroggs,' Shaftesbury interrupts. 'As for myself, I have interrogated your clerk and believe him to be guilty. After his trial, Mr Pepys, when he is convicted of conspiracy to contrive the murder Sir Edmund Godfrey on your behalf, it will be your turn to defend yourself.'

***

Pepys finds young Sam in his cell wearing a warm coat and with a belly full of meat and pastry that his maids bring every day.

'I hear that you have been questioned by Lord Shaftesbury again,' Pepys says. 'Tell me what happened.'

'Oh Mr Pepys,' Sam cries. 'I try to remember every question they've asked me and every answer I give, but the great lords worry me so much I might just as well be drunk my brain is so fuddled. But I always say I am innocent. I will never let them make me tell lies about you. sir; never.' He pulls a paper from inside his shirt. 'Here are some notes I made after the last time they questioned me, before Captain Richardson came and took my papers and quills away.'

Pepys scans the paper as well as he can with his poor eyes. William Bedloe's name is scattered all over.

'This rogue, Bedloe, is a thief and a highwayman,' Sam complains. 'Why ever do the lords take his word instead of mine? I have done nothing to deserve this.'

Nothing, Pepys thinks, except being a member of my household and young and supposedly malleable.

'Oh, Mr Pepys,' Sam says. 'I begged Captain Richardson not to bring Captain Atkins to my cell but he brought him all the same and I almost lost heart. Captain Atkins used to be my friend. We've drunk together many a time and I always paid, you know, sir, but he accused me with such anger…'

'Now cheer up Sam,' Pepys says. 'I have some good news for you.'

'Have you found Godfrey's real murderer?' Sam asks eagerly.

Pepys shakes his head. 'Not yet, but I have found your Captain Vittals and his boatswain and they have promised to speak for you at your trial.'

'Then I shall sit here, alone in my cell, and think of Captain Vittals' friendly face and his generous hospitality and it will cheer me,' Sam says.

'Good, good,' Pepys says. 'Allow yourself to have no thoughts other than your innocence and your freedom.'

'Mr Pepys, there's something I've discovered that might help you to find Sir Edmund's murderer.'

'Really?' Pepys asks.

'Yes, sir. Yesterday, Captain Richardson took me to the press yard to take my exercise for an hour or so with other prisoners and there was a man there, a hackney coachman, Francis Corrall, and I got into conversation with him. He told me that under the influence of drink, in a tavern some-where, he confessed to his drinking companions that he had transported Sir Edmund's dead body from Somerset House to Primrose Hill. Well, Lord Shaftesbury got to hear of this and brought him here and keeps sending for him to plague him with questions just like he does with me. Corrall pro-tests that he's as innocent as I am of Sir Edmund's murder; he insists that it was just the drink made him boast to his friends. But I'm not sure I believe him, sir, and neither will you if you talk to him. You'll find him in a filthy cell, though, sir. He knows something, innocent or not, I'm sure of it.'

Francis Corrall lies in a freezing cell with other prisoners. They are shackled together with their coats pulled up over their heads for warmth. The hackney coachman looks to be a good few years younger than Pepys. His eyes are red with weeping and there is blood at his ankles where the irons cut into his flesh. Another of the prisoners is well known to Pepys. He's seen him many times performing on stage: Matthew Medburne, comic actor in the Duke's Company. His linen shirt is grey, his lace cuffs are filthy and his wig hangs tangled and greasy onto his chest. Well, at least it will help to keep his head warm, Pepys thinks.

'Captain Richardson lies to our wives,' Medburne tells him. 'He tells them that we are allowed a charcoal fire in our cell. You can see that this is not the case.'

Pepys' hands are already freezing despite his gloves. 'Captain Richardson allows your wives to bring hot dinners, surely?'

Medburne nods. 'We do not wish to worry our women-folk, so, on the few occasions when we are allowed to speak with them in the keeper's lodge, we do not tell them the worst of what happens in here.'

'Every night one of us is taken down a hatch to a dungeon known as Little Ease: the condemned hole,' Corrall says. 'We spend all of the following day there denied light and fire.'

'God help you all,' Pepys murmurs closing his eyes in prayer. 'Of what are you accused?' he asks Medburne.

'Sedition is the charge. Titus Oates is my accuser. Once we were friends: I gave him money when he was starving, I introduced him to a club for his entertainment: the Pheasant at Fuller's Rents. Now he claims that this club is a den of sedition. I am a Catholic; it fits in tidily with his Popish Plot to condemn me. I am of course innocent of the charge. I beg you, Mr Pepys, pray, speak to the Duke of York. I have entertained him many times with my comedies. He will be kind, surely.'

'However could he help you?' Pepys says more bluntly than he intended. 'The Duke cannot help himself. Being a Catholic and heir to the throne, he is in a mighty vulnerable position thanks to Titus Oates, who claims the papists want him for their king. There is talk of Charles exiling him to Brussels for his safety.'

'Then there is no hope for me,' Medburne says mournfully.

'There is no hope for any of us in this place,' Corrall whines. His fair hair, chubby, boyish face and tearful eyes are at odds with his heavy bulk and large hands. 'Do you hear a man screaming, Mr Pepys?'

Indeed, Pepys can. Somewhere in Newgate a man is in agony.

'It is the silversmith, Miles Prance, taking his turn in Little Ease.'

52

THE CONDEMNED HOLE
SUNDAY, 22ND DECEMBER, 1678

Soon, darkness has spread all over the prison into a night-time pierced by men screaming out their nightmares. Miles Prance's body is frozen, inside and out. Indeed, he never knew a person could be so cold and still be alive. His fingers and toes pain him dreadfully and he worries that they will snap, like icicles, at the slightest touch. The cold has got into his head for he is having trouble thinking clearly, as if he were drunk.

He knows of only one way to get himself out of this place and home to his warm hearth and his wife's cooking: he must do something terrible that God does not want him to do. And Dr Lloyd, the vicar of St Martin's church, has told him that this is what he must do. The vicar had been let down through the hatch with a lantern in one hand whilst the other held his clerical skirts out of the filth in the open sewer that runs along the floor. Prance will never recover from the shame of watching the vicar's white-stockinged ankles and clean shoes stepping cautiously over the turds and urine overflowing onto the straw.

'You must confess to everything of which you are accused and anything else that you know, Mr Prance,' the vicar had declared as if he were chanting a litany, 'out of respect for poor martyred Edmund Godfrey.'

'Edmund Godfrey was no friend of mine,' Prance had muttered. 'And he's no martyr either. He was killed because some people didn't like him.'

The following day Captain Richardson comes peering into the darkness with his candle and asks if the prisoner is ready to make his confession to the Lords. By this time Prance can only focus upon one thought: getting out of this foul hole.

'Send word to the Lords,' he tells the keeper. 'If I have the King's promise of a pardon, I will make a true and perfect discovery concerning the death of Sir Edmund Godfrey.'

He dozes a little. He awakes to candlelight hurting his eyes. Captain Richardson is standing over him. 'Come quickly,' he says. 'Lord Shaftesbury and other great men are ready to hear your confession. They will assure you of His Majesty's promise of a full pardon for your discoveries.'

I will not stay alive for many days in this freezing hole, Prance thinks. It is the Lord's Day. He tries to pray but no words come.

He is taken to Lord Shaftesbury's house. He tells Shaftesbury and the other lords what they want to hear; and Captain Richardson, of course. The keeper is always there, listening to what the prisoners confess wherever they are, even when they are asleep or drunk and don't know what they say.

He returns to Newgate but not to Little Ease. First, he is taken to the keeper's lodge where someone awaits him. The handsome, hard featured man neither smiles nor frowns. Prance turns away but his visitor comes to stand before him, invading his space until he feels obliged to face his accuser. William Bedloe says nothing; only stares and Prance dare not look away, not until there is an understanding between them; a covenant sealed without words, just a hint of a nod, and Prance feels himself dragged into a world of lies.

Having confessed to lord Shaftesbury, Prance is allowed to exercise in the press yard with other men. Below ground there is a drinking cellar run by a prisoner. They buy Prance cheap gin they call, *Kill-Grief.*

'Who killed Godfrey?' they ask when he is drunk. 'You?'

He tells them what he told Lord Shaftesbury. It is easy, second time around; the words just fall out of his mouth, and the names of three men slip out of the cells of Newgate, through the iron bars and onto London's streets.

53

MILES PRANCE ACCUSES

CHRISTMAS EVE, 1678

'Come,' says Captain Richardson, as he removes the fetters, 'His Majesty has appointed a council extraordinary to hear your discoveries, and he has sent for you.' He leads Prance to where his wife awaits him with food and a clean suit of clothes. There is a fire; a breakfast of hot broth, bread and cheese; a bowl of warm water to wash, and his barber has arrived to shave him.

'I had thought that I would have to stand before the King stinking like a night-soil-man,' Prance says, as he hurriedly cleans his shoes with a handful of straw.

'As to those nights when you were not at home, Miles,' his wife says. 'It was on the 2nd and 3rd of October, or thereabouts. Tell this to the King and the great lords.'

'The King will not care about dates,' Prance says, heaving a great sigh. 'It matters not whether I was away or at home.' Our house in Covent Garden, he thinks, is not so far from the Strand for a man to walk the distance to Somerset House, murder somebody and walk back home again, or hire a hackney carriage. 'What matters,' he tells his wife, 'is that William Bedloe has sworn under oath that he saw me standing there, beside the dead body.'

'Do not speak one word, Miles, until you are assured of the King's pardon,' Mrs Prance warns. She puts her arms around him and holds him tight. Prance strokes the light flaxen hair peeping out of her hood, what's left of it since she chopped it off for his wig. She's a pretty woman with her clear, blue eyes. Her fair skin is almost transparent now, with worry, since he came to this dreadful place. 'As to that night when you did not return to your bed until two or three o'clock in the morning,' she whispers. 'Say nought of that, but if you are asked, plead that you were drunk in an alley somewhere, sleeping. Oh, Miles,' she says, pulling back and looking into his eyes. 'I know that you have not been yourself these last weeks. Pray God to give you the courage to say to the King whatever needs to be said to bring you safely home to your family.'

In his few lucid moments in those hopeless hours in the stinking hole, Prance came to realise that any evidence he gives, any new discovery he makes concerning the murder of Edmund Godfrey will be scorned upon unless it fits neatly into Dr Oates' Popish Plot. It has to be Catholics who did the deed. And it has to be Jesuit fathers who organised the murder operation and one of the Catholic lords who offered a handsome reward. Nothing else will be believed. And in his account of the magistrate's death he must corroborate Bedloe's evidence, what little he has heard of it, which is probably enough, the murder of Godfrey being all the talk in the taverns and the coffee houses these last weeks. So, he must affirm that the murder took place in the Queen's house, on the Strand. One thing he has learned from Bedloe: to distance himself from the actual brutality of the murder, the act itself. His hands did not tighten the cloth around Godfrey's neck, neither did they thrust the sword through his chest when he was dead. He must present himself as the victim of seditious priests who worked their evil upon a poor tradesman who is losing good business now that his Catholic clients are fleeing London. He will be honest. He will admit that he has a past grievance against Edmund Godfrey and so it will be readily believed that he was seduced to play a small part in the horrible crime.

'Come, make haste,' Captain Richardson urges. 'The King awaits.'

'If you speak the truth, Mr Prance, and make it good, I will give you your pardon,' the King says, and Prance, having taken his oath, thinks that the King looks so very grave and solemn in his extraordinarily long periwig and all his Privy Council regalia; not at all like the smiling, friendly monarch he's occasionally glimpsed rushing in or out of Somerset House or waving to his subjects from his barge on the Thames.

He promises the King that he will faithfully declare everything he knows concerning the murder of Sir Edmund Godfrey. Despite the King's assurance, he is afraid.

He fears death by hanging.

Even worse, he fears life. He fears living every day until his death-day ridden with a great cancer of guilt growing inside him.

As soon as he begins to present his evidence he sees a man scribbling notes: a dark, serious man, Secretary Joseph Williamson. He sits close to the King and occasionally the King leans towards him and whispers something and this makes Prance nervous.

'About a fortnight before the murder,' Prance begins, trying to keep his voice steady, 'I was spoken to by one Gerald, an Irish priest. I was asked to take part in the killing of a man. No, my lords,' he says, in answer to their question, 'he did not tell me who it was that was to be killed and I did not consent to be a part of it. I thought it was a horrible thing to do, to kill a man like that, in cold blood.

'About a week later, Father Gerald and two Catholic men

of my acquaintance confided to me that they intended to kill Sir Edmund Godfrey because he was a great enemy to Queen Catherine and her servants, and he had used some Irishmen ill.'

They ask him, of course, for the names of his friends.

This is the moment that he will remember, when by the warmth of a charcoal fire, in a cell well away from Little Ease, Captain Richardson tells him that his friend, Lawrence Hill, now occupies that freezing hole, and he will burst into tears with the horror of what he has done and try to recant his confession. But on this day, Christmas Eve, in the presence of the King and his handsome bastard son, the Duke of Monmouth, and Secretary Williamson, and the other lords, on this day that he fulfilled his silent pact with William Bedloe, all he desires is his freedom. He wants to go home.

'One of the murderers is the man who lays cushions in the Queen's chapel at Somerset House,' he says. Williamson raises his eyebrows in a question that Prance cannot avoid. 'Robert Green, is his name,' he answers, surprising himself how boldly he passes sentence of death upon the old Irishman. After this it is easier to name the others. 'And with Robert Green and Father Gerald was Lawrence Hill, who at that time resided at Somerset House.'

'These men are your drinking companions?'

'It is our custom to meet on Sunday evenings at the Sign of the Plow with other acquaintances.'

'You say that you refused to have any part in the murder when Father Gerald first approached you,' Williamson asks. 'Why did you change your mind?'

Prance explains that he consented to take just a small part in the affair because of some malice he bore to Sir Edmund Godfrey, being troubled at Hicks Hall county court some two years ago about parish duties. Sir Edmund had refused to consent to his discharge as another justice did and told him with much unkindness that the Queen had no power to protect her servants. He had quite forgotten this, he tells the King, until these three men spoke to him about the murder and the priest, Gerald, had declared that it would be no sin, but an act of charity to kill such a man. And so he had been persuaded and they promised him a handsome reward from one of the Catholic lords.

'I see that what you would not do in cold blood, you would do for money,' Williamson says, sourly.

'I am struggling to make a living in my shop because my Catholic customers are leaving London,'

'Speak up,' the King says, 'we can barely hear you. Now, explain what happened on the day that Sir Edmund disappeared.'

'They had been watching Sir Edmund for a week or more before his death–'

'Who had been watching him?' Williamson interrupts.

'These three: Hill, Green the cushion-man, and Father Gerald. They were waiting for an opportunity to waylay him. That same morning, Green called at Sir Edmund's house, enquiring for him of the maid, and finding him not within, all three sought him out and dogged him all morning and into the afternoon to all the places he went to, until at about six or seven o'clock in the evening, he visited a great house in St Clements and coming out, at around nine o'clock, made his way towards Somerset House. Lawrence Hill went on ahead and waited inside the wicket gate, which was open, and he called to Sir Edmund as he approached, and told him that there were two men quarrelling in the courtyard who might soon be quieted once they saw him.'

'Did Sir Edmund agree to this?' Williamson asks.

'He was unwilling at first but after some little persuasion he entered through the wicket gate.'

At this, Williamson puts his hands to his face and shakes his head and looks so very sad that Prance thinks maybe Godfrey was a good friend of the secretary. 'Robert Green and Father Gerald followed Sir Edmund,' Prance continues, 'while Lawrence Hill lured him down a narrow passage leading to the watergate of Somerset House and through the lower courtyard until they came to a bench that is in a corner, at the bottom of a steep descent adjoining a rail next to the upper end of the stables.'

'Where were you, Mr Prance, whilst all this was going on?' Williamson asks.

'I was waiting at the bench with Henry Berry, the porter of the other gate, and an Irishman who lodged at Green's House.'

'What is the Irishman's name?'

'My Lord, I never knew his name.'

'So now we have two more murderers who have joined the pack, and yourself also, who has suddenly appeared at Somerset House.' The King asks what part he, Prance, played in these events. Is he saying that he was present at the murder?

'No, Your Majesty, my Lords, I was not.' At this point, Prance's voice begins to tremble. And his hands. And his legs. His whole body has gone into a fit of trembling. He has to pause in his narrative, take a hold of himself before he is able to speak. Sir Joseph Williamson is looking at him eyebrows raised, waiting.

'By the time they were come halfway down with Sir Edmund,' Prance continues in a shaky voice, 'I went up to the wicket to give notice if anybody came.'

'What of the guards at the gate?' Williamson asks.

'I saw no guards, my Lord.'

'Who passed through the gate while you kept watch?'

'I saw no one, my Lord. I stayed at the wicket gate in

great agitation and Henry Berry had gone towards the stone stairs which lead to the upper court, there to keep watch also.

After around a quarter of an hour I came down to the bench to see what was done.' Prance's heart is beating fast and his voice is trembling so much he cannot go on.

'What had been done, Mr Prance?' Williamson asks.

'I came down to them and I found... I found... they had throttled Sir Edmund. But his body remained warm, and he seemed hardly dead. They had dragged him behind the bench into the corner where...' A great weakness comes over Prance. He feels empty inside. The handsome breakfast his wife brought has done little to assuage his hunger after being almost starved in the condemned hole.

'Continue with your evidence, Mr Prance,' Williamson says, impatiently.

After days of solitude in his cell all this talking requires a great effort of concentration. The narrative that he has spent two days contemplating has become muddled in his mind. He must relate to the King and the lords precisely what happened on each day that he was with the murderers, but the days are tumbling around inside his head and he is afraid that he will bring them out in the wrong order. He must try to think of the horrible business one day at a time and let the story emerge slowly. Yes, this is what he must do. But he has lost his train of thought and the King and the lords are waiting.

'What happened after Sir Edmund was dragged behind the bench,' Williamson prompts. 'Did you see for yourself?'

'No, no, my Lord, I did not. Robert Green told me later that he had himself strangled Sir Edmund. Indeed, earlier in the day he had shown me the twisted handkerchief with which he planned to do the deed. Sir Edmund struggled and Green said he had broken his neck with pulling the cloth so tightly. And there,' Prance says, 'in the corner, in the dark, behind the bench, the old cushion-man knelt and thumped Sir Edmund on the breast, until he was sure that he was dead.'

'What did you do with the body?' the King asks, glancing at Williamson who has his hand to his brow. 'Presumably you did not leave it there in the corner behind the bench.'

'We all helped to carry him through a door which leads up several steps.'

'Be precise, Mr Prance. Name the persons who carried the body,' Williamson demands.

'Lawrence Hill, Robert Green, Henry Berry, Father Gerald, the Irishman and myself; we all helped to carry him up the stairs into a long dark gallery which opens into the upper court. There is a door on the left which leads up eight steps to a little closet in the house where Hill lodged. And there we laid Sir Edmund's body with its back resting against a bed. And there he stayed for two days.'

'In Lawrence Hill's house?' Williamson asks.

'Aye, my lord, in Hill's rooms within Dr Godwin's servants' lodgings. Two days later, Hill took me to see the body in another room at Somerset House towards the Garden. Henry Berry and Robert Green were there and they told me that they had carried it there at nine or ten at night being afraid of discovery.'

'After two days? That would be on the Monday, presumably,' Williamson says.

'Yes,' says Prance, 'I believe it was on the Monday.'

'You saw the body?' the King asks.

'It was bended, Your Majesty, as it was before.'

'How was the body transported from the garden room to the ditch at Primrose Hill?' the King asks.

'On Tuesday night, the body was brought back near to the place where first it lay, into a room in the gallery higher up the court, where it remained until nine or ten o'clock on Wednesday night; and then, thinking fit to remove it to another....'

'What again?' the King declares. 'Are you asking this court to believe that you shifted a dead body around the busy courtyards of Somerset House on several occasions without being discovered?' Prance is shocked that the King should let out such a guffaw when they are speaking of the dead.

'Continue with your evidence,' Williamson says. At least the Secretary of State is treating the matter with the gravity it deserves,

'On Wednesday evening,' Prance explains. 'I happened upon the murderers in the long dark alley by the eight steps, shifting the body yet again. Hearing me approaching, Hill and Berry fled in fear, supposing me to be some stranger.'

'Despite the implausibility, there is a ring of truth about this story, don't you think?' Williamson says to the King. 'Tell us more,' he charges Prance, 'and pray, do not stop until Sir Edmund rests at Primrose Hill.'

'Gerald, Green, and the Irishman stood still as I approached but when they saw that it was me, they asked for my help to carry the body into the little closet where it was first laid in Hill's lodgings. And there we waited until after twelve o'clock that same Wednesday night. Hill and Berry came to us when their fright was over and we decided that Hill should go out to fetch a sedan chair, which he did. He left it at the foot of the eight stairs. And when the body was put in the chair, I carried it with Father Gerald. Henry Berry, the porter, opened half the gate to let us out.

'When we came to Covent Garden, we being tired, Green and the Irishman took their turns at the chair. And so we carried it as far as the new Grecian church, in Soho, and there Hill met us with a horse. And we took out the body and… and…' Prance's heart is beating so fast he is too short of breath to speak.

'Mr Prance, pull yourself together; you must tell the court what happened.' Williamson says.

'We are waiting,' the King says.

'We forced open the corpse's legs and we set it… we set it… upon the horse and Lawrence Hill rode behind to hold the body up. The others followed him to Primrose Hill after they had hidden the sedan in one of the partly built houses by the new Grecian church, planning to collect it later when their deed was done.'

'Did you also follow Lawrence Hill into the country?' Williamson asks.

'No, my lord, I returned home when the body was set on horseback, fearing to be missed.'

'To your home in Covent Garden?' Williamson asks.

'Yes, my lord, on Princess Street, where I keep my shop. It was between one and two o'clock in the morning when I arrived home.'

'Where was the porter, Henry Berry, while the body was being removed?'

'He did not depart from the gate.'

'There is a Catholic club that meets in a tavern near Primrose Hill. Are you a member of this company that convenes at the White House?' Williamson demands.

Prance did not expect this question and he stammers his reply. 'Yes, yes, my lord… but I have been busy… I have not set foot in that establishment for a twelvemonth.'

'We are impressed by the detail in your discovery so far,' the King says after talking in whispers with his son and Secretary Williamson. 'You shall be taken immediately to Somerset House where you will meet with the Duke of Monmouth and the Earl of Ossory. A clerk of this court will accompany you to take your evidence. There you will show them the bench where Sir Edmund was murdered and the various chambers where you saw his body. Any further evidence you give will be in virtue of the oath taken before us all this morning. Do you understand?'

'I will give a true and faithful report, Your Majesty,' Prance says.

This Prance had not expected: to be forced to lead the King's bastard son through Somerset House on the murder trail. Up and down to the bench where the deed was done, back and forth through the long dark gallery, up the eight steps even to the very chamber where he had told them the body was first laid against Hill's bed. And he had let himself down. He who is as familiar with the passages and galleries and courtyards of Somerset House as the beads on his rosary. He couldn't locate the garden room. And now, after a paltry dinner of cheese and old bread he is taken back to the King.

No, Prance had not expected this. He had not expected to be made to stand before Green and Hill and Berry and have to accuse each one to their face. He turns to Robert Green prepared to see anger in his eyes. Anger breeds anger and this he could have coped with but there is only bewilderment and hurt in the old Irishman's eyes.

'You went to Sir Edmund's house,' he accuses boldly. 'You followed him from place to place; you told me so. You told me that you had broken Sir Edmund's neck. I was with you when we carried the body away on the Wednesday night. How can you deny this?'

'I deny everything. It is all false.'

'Do you deny that you know me?' he asks fiercely.

'I know you. I don't deny that,' Green says. 'I know you very well, I've drunk with you.'

'Yes,' Prance says. 'We have often drunk together at the

Sign of the Plow, and it was there that I showed you Sir Edmund as he passed by, telling you that he was the man that would not allow the Queen's servants any privilege. Now,' Prance continues, gaining confidence, for he can see that the lords are pleased with this little anecdote, 'what is the name of your friend, the short well-set Irishman who lodged at Berry's alehouse around the time that Sir Edmund was murdered?'

Green answers confidently that the Irishman was Kelly, a priest.

'This is the Irish murderer I spoke of this morning,' Prance declares.

Green is asked if he has ever quarrelled with Prance.

'No, Your Majesty, my Lords, I never had any quarrel with Mr Prance, nor anything to say against him.'

The cushion-layer is presenting himself as an honest man, Prance thinks. Yet it is turning to my advantage, not his.

Lawrence Hill stands straight and tall and broad of shoulder. He glares at Prance; angry, indignant.

'Do you deny that you know Robert Green, or the priests, Gerald, and Kelly?' Prance asks.

Hill turns away from his erstwhile friend and addresses the King and the lords directly. 'Yes, Your Majesty, my lords, I know Robert Green and Father Gerald. I know of no Irishman named Kelly. I never met such a man.'

'What?' says Prance, 'you do not remember the short stocky man who lodged in Henry Berry's alehouse?'

'Yes, I saw a man of that description visiting the Queen's Chapel now and then. I did not know his name.'

'Do you also deny that you know me?' Prance asks.

'I do not deny it. Why should I? We have known each other for five years or more. Not long ago I invited you and your wife to my new home in Stanhope Street and we were drinking together.'

Prance has to pull himself together, remind himself that this situation is none of his making: John Wren and William Bedloe have brought this dire predicament upon him. He has his own wife and business to protect. Where was his friend, Hill, when John Wren accused him in the Plow and all his troubles began; his strong friend who could have ended the matter there and then and sent Wren off with a bloody nose?

'Do you know Mr Prance to be an honest man?' the King asks of Hill and leans forward awaiting his answer.

'For aught I know, he might be an honest man.' Hill lets his words hang in the chamber for just enough time for the King and the lords to turn their eyes away and onto Prance who becomes acutely aware of his stooped posture, caused by many years of plying his craft and made worse these last days in the cramped conditions of Little Ease. How does the King see me? he wonders. As a dishonest man? A liar afraid to stand straight and true before himself and the great lords as Hill does?

'I never saw Sir Edmund Godfrey, except once at Somerset House,' Hill tells the King. 'It was upon the occasion of a pickpocket that was taken there.'

'You saw him on 12th October,' Prance accuses. 'You dogged him all day and led him to his murder at Somerset House. In the days following you helped to move the body several times. You took me to see it in a chamber by the garden and you fetched a horse and sat behind his body all the way to Primrose Hill.'

'No, I did not. Christ's blood, you lie, Miles Prance.' Hill is shouting now. 'The Devil take you and send your soul to damnation. As God is my witness not one word that you have spoken this day is true. You lie before God and the King and before your friends. God damn you for it.'

'Has Miles Prance testified all this to save himself?' the King demands drily of Hill.

'I cannot speak for him, Your Majesty,' Hill says. 'I cannot say what cause a man would have to lie about his friends upon the Holy Book. There was much talk amongst the customers in my shop yesterday that Mr Prance had been pardoned and I was pleased for him, he being my friend. I little thought that I should be brought here to be accused about the murder of a man upon his account.'

'What was the colour of the horse that Lawrence Hill hired for the removal of Sir Edmund's body?' The King asks Prance, all of a sudden.

'Though the night was dark, I did discern the horse to be a brown one,' Prance promptly replies.

'What say you to this?' the King asks Hill.

'I never rode with Sir Edmund Godfrey upon a horse, and knew very little of him. I deny everything, Your Majesty, all of these lies that Miles Prance has spoken against me.'

'I have one more question,' the King says holding up a paper. 'I have here a deposition taken this morning at Somerset House from one Anne Broadstreet, formerly housekeeper to your previous employer, Doctor Godwin. Do you know this woman, Mr Hill?'

'Yes, I do, Your Majesty.'

'Mrs Broadstreet says that you left Somerset House at Michaelmas, 29th September, or thereabouts, going then to a house of your own in Stanhope Street. This morning, Mr Prance contradicted her and swore you left later. When did you leave your lodgings at Somerset House, Mr Hill?'

Hill's answer surprises Prance. Any man with common sense would have told the King that he was far gone from Somerset House by the end of September, well before Sir Edmund disappeared; he has the housekeeper's word written this very morning in a sworn deposition to support him on this. Instead, Hill tells the truth. He puts himself right in the middle of the murder scene on the day that Godfrey disappeared.

'About the middle of October, I was busy settling myself into the house where I now live,' Hill tells the King. 'On 12th October, I was agreeing the lease with my landlord but did not settle matters until the Wednesday after.'

Lawrence Hill and Robert Green being taken to Newgate to await their trials, Henry Berry is presented for Prance's interrogation. The porter is all red in the face with indignation and he talks too fast. If the King were much closer, Berry would spray him with his spittle.

'Do you know me?' Prance asks.

'I have seen you at chapel and never heard ill of you,' Berry says. 'But I never sat with you upon a bench waiting for a murder to happen, although I have sat upon that very bench occasionally to rest and take the air. I never acted any part in Sir Edmund Godfrey's murder with you. I never kept watch while anyone was murdered. I never knew Sir Edmund Godfrey, only I saw him once, as he passed by about a year ago. I never opened a gate to let his dead body out in a sedan and I never saw you and Green or any priest carry a sedan chair out of Somerset House. Your Majesty, my lords, I beg you,' Berry pleads. 'I am a Protestant and upon my oath I speak true. If I had done such a terrible thing, I would not deny it.'

'There was a time when I also denied these things as stiffly as you,' Prance retorts and the King and the great lords nod their heads and send Berry to be incarcerated in the Gatehouse jail.

They take Prance back to Newgate but not to Little Ease. Having confessed, he is allowed a few comforts.

54

TAKE A GOOD LOOK AT HIM
25TH AND 26TH DECEMBER, 1678

Pepys has risen early to go to church. By the time the vicar
has finished his sermon his Christmas dinner will be ready.
His maids have been busy since three in the morning
making his little mince pies the way he likes them and the
whole house smells of bay and cinnamon and the roasting
of a pullet and beef ribs. In the afternoon, he plans to visit
young Sam with the remains of these Christmas treats.

Charles takes Catherine, as he had promised, to hear the
Christmas anthem that Henry Purcell has composed for the
Chapel Royal. He pats Catherine's hand, keeping slow time
with the music, closes his eyes and loses all thought of anything other than his pleasure in the harmony of the male
voices and the words of Purcell's text which was inspired by
Psalm Nineteen.

'Who can tell how often he offends? Cleanse me from my
secret faults,' Charles sings with the choir, in his well-sea-
soned bass.

Catherine has to smile. Her husband's faults are no secret.
The whole world knows of them.

In Newgate, Prance's wife visits him in the keeper's house
with as big a Christmas pie as she could fit into her oven,

full of minced mutton, suet, currants, raisins, orange rind, and tasting wonderfully of spices: ginger, mace, nutmeg and cinnamon. 'There's a little sugar in the mixture,' she tells him, 'but you cannot taste it; rather, it brings out all the other tastes.'

Captain Richardson, having eaten a generous portion, compliments Mrs Prance upon her cooking and she tells him to share the remains with other prisoners.

'Lawrence Hill will get no dinner at all until he confesses,' the keeper replies. 'Prisoners in Little Ease are not allowed treats.'

Prance imagines his friend's huge body manacled and squashed into that little stinking hole. He bursts into tears.

'Take me to the King,' he begs Captain Richardson when his wife has departed. 'I must recant my confession or three innocent men will hang.'

***

'Wear your pattens, the floors are filthy in these places,' Judith tells Betty, but when they arrive at Newgate prison, in the early morning after a sorrowful Christmas Day, they don't have to go into the cells after all. They wait outside by the sculpture of Dick Whittington's cat until Captain Richardson greets them and escorts them to a simple chamber in his own lodging with plain oak panelling and a good fire, and they are told to sit and wait.

Betty is very quiet. 'Are you nervous?' Judith asks.

'I just want to do right by Sir Edmund, that's all, and then get out of this place.'

'Of course you do,' Judith says.

'Do you think the King comes to this chamber when prisoners ask to see him?' Betty asks.

'It would need a good dust first,' Judith scoffs, 'and a

handsome chair brought for His Majesty to put his back-side on.'

After a long wait the keeper comes with two very serious gentlemen in black and a big, dark, bearded man clamped in irons.

'Is this the man who visited your master's house the evening before he disappeared?' one of the gentlemen asks.

Judith shakes her head. 'It was dark in the corridor,' she whispers to Betty. 'I didn't see the man properly. It was you who spoke to him and told him what Sir Edmund had said about that strange note.'

'No,' Betty says firmly. 'It was a much smaller man who brought that note, with a different kind of face.' The prisoner closes his eyes as if he is thanking God for his deliverance.

'Have either of you seen this man in your late master's house?' one of the gentlemen asks.

'I have never seen this man before,' Judith says.

'No, never,' Betty agrees.

The keeper departs with the prisoner. Within a few minutes he returns with a little old man shackled to the big dark man who has been shaved.

The two gentlemen point to the old man. 'Did you ever see this man at your master's house?' one of them asks.

'Take a good look at this man again,' the other gentlemen says, prodding the big man's arm. 'A man can disguise himself with a beard.'

The proud scowling man stares Judith out, but says nothing. Neither do the two gentlemen in black; not until the prisoners are led away again and then they have plenty to say.

'We have a witness who will swear that the old man, Robert Green, a cushion-layer in the Queen's chapel, called at Sir Edmund's home two weeks before he disappeared.'

'And that the other man, Lawrence Hill, called at your master's home on the morning of 12th October.'

'It is a serious business, ladies, to swear on oath,' one of the men says.

'Our witness is hardly likely to perjure himself, you know, ladies,' the other says.

'Take your time, Mrs Pamphlin,'

'Mrs Curtis, you do the same.'

'We will sit here with you and wait while you recall your master's final morning.'

'Are you sure, Betty? Really sure?' Judith asks, as they tread carefully through the frosty streets over icy cobbles. 'Only at first, you said you'd never seen him before in your life.'

'But that was before they shaved him. The more I think of it the more sure I am that the big dark man in irons is the very one I saw sitting in the parlour with the master just before he went out and never came back.'

'But you were only there for a minute or two Betty, how can you be so sure?'

'It must be the same man, it has to be if this witness has sworn on oath that he was there in the parlour with Sir Edmund. And the little old man too. I think I recall a similar man of that age visiting the house earlier in the autumn.'

'You have to be very sure, Betty,' Judith says. 'These men will hang at Tyburn upon your word.'

55

IT IS NOT ME THAT MURDERED
HIM, THEY DID
JANUARY–FEBRUARY, 1679

Twice now Prance has tried to tell the King and all the others that he lied. Nobody wants to hear: not his wife, nor King Charles, nor Captain Richardson, nor Edmund Godfrey's vicar. Prance knows that he has lost everything of the man he once was: his Roman Catholic faith which has been a part of himself since he was a child; his business, which is declining because Catholics are fleeing London; most of all, he has lost his self-respect as an honest man, and a friendly man at that, with a good wit to entertain other men at the Plow or the club at Primrose Hill. He knows that if he tells the truth, or that part of the truth which will exonerate the three accused men, there is a chance he might die for it, one way or another.

Little Ease is colder than he remembers but his body seems to have become used to it and also to the irons and the cramped position. He manages to turn and get onto his knees to pray. 'Oh, God,' he says aloud, 'however did it come to this?' God doesn't answer and Prance knows why. 'I know what I did,' he tells God. 'Forgive me.'

They take him, still in irons, to a room in the keeper's lodge to see an old drinking companion, William Boyce, a glass eye maker. Boyce tries to persuade him to return to his original story.

'No,' says Prance, 'I lied to save myself. Henry Berry, Robert Green and Lawrence Hill, all three are innocent men and so am I. You know that on the very day that Sir Edmund Godfrey disappeared, I dined with you and we were drinking all that afternoon and into the evening.'

'But not all night,' Boyce says, glancing at Captain Richardson who nods encouragingly. 'If you want to save yourself from the gallows, Mr Prance, you must stick with what you swore to the Lords. There is nothing I can say to save you.'

Captain Richardson takes him to Lord Shaftesbury. Oh how keen the great lord is to blame Catholics for the murder. 'Did any Catholic gentlemen of quality come into your shop to buy a weapon or two? Or maybe a Jesuit priest whispered something into your ear about rebellion and regicide while you innocently sipped your ale at the Sign of the Plow?'

Dr Lloyd is never away from Newgate, hovering over Prance like a great black bat, extolling the virtues of Truth, telling him that he must recant his latest recantation. Sometimes they take him to another room and remove the irons before the vicar comes. And why, Prance wonders, even as he shivers in Little Ease and feels his body falling away from his soul, why is Godfrey's vicar so very eager to blame the Catholics for his friend's murder? Does he know more of how the magistrate really died than he pretends?

Captain Richardson uses a different argument.

'I can always get the truth out of a prisoner, one way or another,' he tells Prance.

He can't think about it: the threatened torture. It is too far away, a thing of the future. He can only think of each moment as it comes because, despite the flock mattress and the blanket his jailer has brought, his body is overcome by shivering. He feels wetness running from his eyes but he isn't weeping. Something is biting him. He thinks it is the hungry rats. When he realises that it is the freezing cold that gnaws at his nose and his fingers great sobs wrench his chest. 'I am not ready to die,' he screams.

In the evening, Mrs Medburne and her sister-in-law are leaving the prison by the lodge after visiting her actor husband, Matthew. Captain Richardson hurries them away but not before they hear terrible screams from the condemned hole. At first, they think it is a woman in labour until they discern that it is a man's voice.

'Not guilty, not guilty,' Prance cries. 'Not guilty. No murder.'

In the morning, Mrs Medburne visits her husband again. The voice is weaker but still she hears Prance cry: 'It is not me that murdered him, but they did.'

One night, Prance becomes aware of a hand hovering above him, limp and long fingered, its ring glimmering in the blackness of the cell. A thin voice whines: 'I am so very cold in this ditch. Pray, pull me out. I told you before, Mr Prance, the Queen has no power to protect her servants.'

The shivering stops. His bladder keeps filling up and he just lets the urine flow out of him through his breeches because he cannot think what to do about it; if he moves his hands his frozen fingers will snap. All he wants is sleep and like an answer to a prayer he is muffled in a sudden, almost unbearable heat and he is falling and freezing into a soft featherbed of oblivion.

Voices come to him, over his head.

The vicar's voice: 'He's dead.'

'No, no, he lives.' Keeper Richardson's voice, strained to a frightened tenor.

'There's no pulse: you've frozen him to death.' The vicar, in panic.

'He'll live if he's thawed out.' Richardson again, shouting for the jailers. 'Here, quickly, pull him up through the hatch and carry him to my fire.'

He feels before he sees. Someone's hands pummel his chest. Someone's breath warms his face. He opens his eyes to fire-light and a loud groan of relief from the keeper, and he sees that it is Godfrey's vicar who has brought him back to life with his thumping hands.

'Have I been dead for a long time?' Prance asks.

For him, from this moment on, there will always be his life before and his life after. Between, like a mighty punctuation mark, there is Edmund Godfrey lying dead in the ditch with his sword sticking up through his back.

Before: he was a child. Innocent. He knew what was important: Truth, Friendship, Catholicism. That time has gone. He must accept this; to grieve for its passing would be too painful. The guilt is not his. He did not choose to be the man who did what he did and said what he said. He has suffered enough. He relishes the newness of his life after Godfrey. He becomes the person he has to be.

***

In the press yard where prisoners mingle, coachman Francis Corrall comes limping towards him. The leg irons have rubbed holes in his ankles.

'They took me away to Lord Shaftesbury,' Corrall moans. 'He offered me five hundred pounds, lodgings at Whitehall and musketeers to guard me if I confess that I really did carry the body away for the Catholics. I told him that it was all lies, what I had said about transporting the body from Somerset House to Primrose Hill; the boasting of a man in drink, and I asked his forgiveness, but Lord Shaftesbury wouldn't listen and he put me in his cellar for hours and when I came out I fainted and he had to give me brandy. I don't know what to do, Mr Prance, I don't know what to tell him. He threatened to put me in a barrel of nails and roll me down a hill to make me confess. All he wants to hear is that Catholic priests paid me to do it.'

'Just keep telling them that you lied,' Prance says urgently.

'But Lord Shaftesbury has found a witness to say that he saw me driving along Tottenham Court Road towards Primrose Hill.'

Prance advises him to bide his time; that all will be well. He explains to Corrall that after they hear his own sworn evidence in court, that the body left Somerset House in a sedan chair, Lord Shaftesbury will set him free.

'I dare not tell my wife how they treat me here,' Corrall moans. 'I lie and say they feed me well, that I am warm with a charcoal fire. Captain Richardson has threatened to put me in Little Ease again, you know, if I don't confess. Oh, Mr Prance, I don't know what to tell Lord Shaftesbury. Five hundred pounds is a fortune to a working man. Your wife will not be penniless: she can sell your silverware whilst you are in this place. My wife has no money. If I stay here much longer she will have to sell my horses to buy food for my children.'

'Hush,' Prance whispers.

Keeper Richardson approaches. Saying nothing, he slips a paper into Prance's hand. There is no signature; it isn't necessary. The conspiracy was sealed weeks ago, here in Newgate jail with a paltry nod. Prance reads. There are just a few lines on the page, not even proper sentences, but it is all he needs.

Part 7
Mr Pepys Investigates
January–Spring, 1679

"There never was such a mystery… in the business of Sir Edmund Bury Godfrey… concerning the manner of his death."

Roger L'Estrange (1687)

56

A PUFFED UP LITTLE WREN

JANUARY, 1679

'Nobody wants to hear anything I have to say,' Judith Pamphlin complains, 'not the master's brothers, nor the vicar, nor Lord Shaftesbury; and I knew Sir Edmund and his moods better than any of them.'

'I've known him for longer,' Betty pipes up.

'My dear ladies, I'm a good listener; pray take your time and tell me everything you know,' Pepys says. 'Sir Edmund kept no other servants but you two ladies to cook for him and clean this big house?' He would have expected a knight of Sir Edmund's status to employ at least another maid and a manservant.

'Only yon ancient clerk, Henry Moor, in his office,' the housekeeper says, in a tone that implies that there is no love lost between them.

'Sir Edmund was a man of simple needs,' Betty says.

Pepys can see that. Sitting here in Godfrey's parlour he can tell just what kind of man he was. This is his best room to display to visitors and Pepys would have expected finely panelled walls: not plain oak panelling and the most unremarkable plaster moulding to a ceiling. He would have expected fine furniture to display Godfrey's status and wealth. I've made a better home for myself than this magistrate, he ponders, me, a *prick louse,* son of a poor tailor.

What little decoration there is, however, tells something of Godfrey's character: that he was a man very aware of the presence of evil. Carved in stone above the main entrance and the parlour window Pepys has noticed circular intertwined motifs: a device used by gentlemen of quality and the common sort of people alike, to prevent evil from entering their houses. Lord, but it didn't prevent evil from following him on the streets and out into the country to his death.

'So, Mrs Pamphlin, you say that Sir Edmund was out of sorts before he disappeared?'

'Sir Edmund regularly suffered bouts of melancholy but he was bled and usually got better. This time was different: he was miserable for weeks, and he was poorly. He suffered from spells of catarrh and he had this habit of wiping his mouth, and he was doing it all the time, those last weeks. And his bowels weren't right. I should know, I do his laundry.'

Pepys could have done without this bit of information.

'He was like this ever since Dr Oates came a knocking at the door with his deposition,' she explains.

Ah, thinks Pepys, this needs looking into: Godfrey was shit scared of Titus Oates. Why? Every other man on the street thinks he's the saviour of the nation.

'Now then, tell me about the Saturday morning when he went missing.'

They tell of a lawyer, Richard Adams, who called twice during the day, and of a stranger who was in the parlour with Sir Edmund when Betty took him his breakfast.

'I had to go into the parlour because I'd left my keys there and I saw a man sitting where you are now, Mr Pepys, talking to the master,' Betty explains. 'The very same Catholic man the keeper brought to us for identification in Newgate jail. Lawrence Hill: one of the men who did the murder.'

'He has to be tried by jury before he is convicted,' Pepys says sternly. Lord help him, he prays, for Hill will be in grave trouble if Lord Chief Justice Scroggs calls this maid to give evidence at his trial.

'Oh, Mr Pepys,' Mrs Pamphlin says heaving a great sigh and shaking her head. 'The master's death is a great mystery and there's one thing that I cannot understand.'

'What is it? Pray, tell me,'

'It's the man in the grey suit of clothes.'

'Who is he?'

'Nobody knows. He told the curate of St Dunstan-in-the-West that Sir Edmund's body had been discovered impaled with his own sword by the Dead Wall at Leicester Fields. Then later in the evening the body was discovered at Primrose Hill. This man knew something about the murder, I'm sure of it. He got the place wrong, but he knew about the sword sticking through him. And two days before the body was discovered, another man walked into a barber's shop and declared that Sir Edmund had murdered himself at Primrose Hill.'

'Now Mrs Pamphlin, he asks, 'tell me, has anyone close to Sir Edmund been behaving strangely since he disappeared? I see you are a very astute woman who would notice such things.'

'Well sir, in my opinion, there's something very odd about Henry Moor's behaviour these last weeks. Yon clerk knows more than you or I can imagine and I dare say that he would say a great deal if he is examined under oath. He keeps taking Mr Michael aside and whispering to him and when they see me coming they stop talking.

'And I'll tell you something else. A day or two after the master disappeared, yon clerk went searching around Primrose Hill and he was within a few feet of that ditch where the master's body was eventually found. He has told me so himself.'

'Why was he searching in Primrose Hill before the body was discovered?'

'Because the Godfrey brothers told him to go there. They said that Sir Edmund was last seen between two and three in the afternoon at Primrose Hill, near the White House Tavern.' She leans closer to Pepys and whispers conspiratorially, 'Something is going on between yon clerk and the brothers; a woman has an intuition about these things. And, well, the Godfrey brothers, Mr Michael and Mr Benjamin, they told me and Betty to keep quiet you know, about Sir Edmund's moods, and if anyone asked, I was to say that the papists had murdered him. And then yon clerk comes and says that the master has remembered me and Betty in his will so to keep our mouths shut if we know what's good for us.'

Suicide, disguised as murder? As if she has read his thoughts, Mrs Pamphlin proceeds to tell Pepys that this is what the clerk's wife believes: that Sir Edmund hanged himself and that sword in his chest proved it. Somebody stuck his sword through him like a stake, to give him a suicide's burial in that ditch. 'What a silly old crone yon clerk's wife is,' she declares.

Pepys takes time to consider this new information. The clerk's wife may well be right. Maybe Godfrey hanged himself and Michael and Benjamin Godfrey found their brother's body and disposed of it to save the estate. Maybe the clerk helped to conceal the body and dump it at Primrose Hill. Lord but if he could find enough evidence to prove this, young Sam will be saved. But if the brothers did this, why did they leave packets of money and a diamond ring in his pockets? With the pockets empty, murder by a footpad would be the undisputed solution to the mystery.

'Now, Mr Pepys, If I may be so bold,' the housekeeper says, 'I think you should talk to the master's cousin, Mary

Gibbon. She knew all about the sadness that used to come over him but Lord Shaftesbury wouldn't heed a word she said. She'll welcome an opportunity to talk to a man like yourself who will listen to her. I'll introduce her to you, if you like.'

'Oh, Mr Pepys, Lord Shaftesbury is just a little man with slim fingers, like a woman, and no meat on him at all,' Mary Gibbon tells Pepys, 'but I have never been so insulted by anyone in all my life.'

'These great men will never listen to common sense when it comes from a woman, especially a puffed-up little wren of a man like Lord Shaftesbury.' Judith sips the glass of gin that Mary Gibbon has offered her.

'Whatever did he do to upset you so much, Mrs Gibbon?' Pepys asks.

'No one wants to hear about my dear Edmund, about how he really was in his last days,' Mary complains, 'not even his brothers. I wasn't allowed to speak at the inquest, so I wrote a little bit, a few lines to explain how miserable he was and how afraid he had been that they would hang him for misprision of treason, and I had it sent to Lord Shaftesbury.'

'Oh, so that's why you were asked to attend the Lords' Committee,' Judith exclaims and Pepys is aware of the pique in her voice. 'If Mr Michael hadn't prevented it, I'm sure that I would have been called for too. Having lived with Sir Edmund and put up with his moods and his impatience, I knew him better than anyone, except your dear self, of course, Mary.'

'Lord Shaftesbury sent for me solely for the purpose of insulting me,' Mary Gibbon says. '"You damned woman," he said, "what devilish paper is this that you have given us?" He refused to believe that I wrote it myself and he put me on oath, wanting me to swear that you, Mr Pepys, or some other body set upon me to do it, and when I refused to do this he called me vile names I could never repeat to you, sir, so please don't ask. Then he threatened me, that I would be torn to pieces by the multitudes for saying such things, like a dog worries a cat.'

57

WHAT THE LOCALS SAW
JANUARY, 1679

Pepys has travelled secretly, by hackney carriage. His own coach would be easily recognised on the busy Tottenham Court Road. There will be trouble if Lord Shaftesbury finds out about this journey to the White House.

'John Waters, a farrier and William Bromwell, a baker; these two men set my husband up to find that magistrate's body,' Rawson's wife tells Pepys, and she heaves a sigh and shakes her head at her husband.

Landlord Rawson is apologetic. 'I knew there would be trouble even before the magistrate's body was carried to our house. There was something that Waters and Bromwell were not willing to confide; I knew that even as we trudged through the fields to the ditch where they had seen a good pair of gloves and a gentleman's silver topped stick lying on the ground. I admit they tempted me against my better judgement. The storm abated and it seemed like such a good opportunity to pick up something for nothing: Goods like that don't fall in the way of a gift to a working man every day.'

'There's a newsletter circulating that says Sir Edmund's body was sniffed out by a dog belonging to Edward Linnet, a butcher of St Giles,' Pepys says.

'It seems that Waters and Bromwell met Linnet earlier in

the day when he was exercising his dog,' Rawson explains. 'They knew the body lay in the ditch and they lured me there and then stood back and let me discover it.'

'Well, they've got their just reward,' his wife retorts. 'Bromwell and Waters have been incarcerated. It doesn't do to tell lies to the great lords about dead bodies lying in ditches.'

'The fools should have made sure that they told Lord Shaftesbury and the Duke of Buckingham exactly the same story about the discovery of the body,' Rawson says.

'I suppose you were also summoned to give evidence to the lords, Mr Rawson?' Pepys asks.

'He was,' Mrs Rawson answers for her husband.

A look of impatience passes between Rawson and his wife. 'Aye,' he concurs, 'but they didn't ask much about how I discovered the body with the baker and the farrier. What they really wanted to know was my religion and I told them that I am a Protestant and always have been. Well, between you and me, Mr Pepys, Lord Shaftesbury seemed very disbelieving about this, because of the papist gentlemen who meet here.'

What? Gentlemen meeting here in this shabby place? Pepys is astonished. Some of the windows have no glass and the wind is blowing through the shutters. Three men sitting in a corner near the door are clearly freezing, muffled up as they are with their coat collars pulled up around their ears. Why choose to meet here rather than a warm coffee house or tavern in the city? This seems mighty suspicious.

'It's a club, of sorts,' Rawson explains. 'Nine respectable men of good honest trades. One or two of them attend the aristocracy and even the royal family in the course of their work. And if they spend more than a few groats on a game of dice, what's that to anyone, whatever the law says about gambling?'

'Only a groat or two?' Pepys gives Rawson a conspiratorial wink.

'It's no matter to me that most of them are papist dogs, I need their business, Mr Pepys, and this I told Lord Shaftesbury. They never talk of matters of state. They like to outdo each other with their wit, as gentlemen do, that's all.'

'And thank God the lords were content with this,' Rawson's wife butts in.

'Which gentlemen attend your club?' Pepys asks. 'Maybe someone of my acquaintance?'

'One of them is Miles Prance, the silversmith who has confessed to involvement in the murder of the magistrate,' Rawson's wife declares. 'Well, even if the King pardons him, he won't be welcome here again.'

'Pity,' Rawson says. 'He's a witty man in his cups. The last time he was here he had us in stitches over his tale of a silver beak he made for a gentleman who has lost the tip of his nose to the pox.'

Rawson asks Pepys if he is acquainted with Mr Richard Mulys, a gentleman's steward from Saint Giles who is also a member of the club. 'He was a good friend of Sir Edmund,' he says, 'and he attended the first day of the inquest. Hear this Mr Pepys. This is what Mr Mulys told me Sir Edmund had confided to him shortly before his death:

Some great men blame me for not having done my duty.'

Now which great men would that be? Pepys ponders. Lord Danby? York? Shaftesbury? Buckingham?

'Here they sat, every week, nine men around this table where you now sit,' Mrs Rawson says. 'The same table where they laid the magistrate's corpse and his blood dripped down onto the bottles in our cellar.'

'Will you never listen to reason, woman,' Rawson snaps. 'It was brown muddy water.' He turns to Pepys. 'There was no blood on the body, and none on the sword'

The three men sitting in the corner call for more warm ale.

'Did you tell the great lords that we saw Edmund Godfrey walking towards your tavern, on the Saturday that he went missing?' one of them calls to Rawson.

'Do you think I'm a fool?' Rawson responds. 'The lords didn't ask about whether Godfrey was seen hereabouts, so I didn't bring the matter up.'

'Pray, introduce me to your friends,' Pepys asks.

Thomas Grundy and James Huysman are local men.

'We walked behind him for around twenty yards,' Huysman says.

'We didn't know that it was him, of course,' Grundy adds, 'not until after the body was discovered and everyone was talking about the murder, and we, hearing that Sir Edmund was a tall, stooping, solitary man dressed in black, believed that it was him that we saw looking so melancholy.'

The youth sitting beside them is introduced as Young Baker. He's keen to tell his tale. He saw Sir Edmund Godfrey walking in his father's field, yonder, towards this tavern, on the very day he went missing.

Rawson glowers at the animated young man. 'You can't be sure that it was him you saw, so keep your mouth shut.'

'If it wasn't Godfrey I saw, I swear it was the Devil in his clothes,' Young Baker declares.

'Oh, to think, somewhere around here his murderers may have been lurking,' Rawson's wife says with a shudder.

Pepys doubts that these countrymen had ever met Godfrey yet he is inclined to believe that the magistrate walked to Primrose Hill and to his death on the Saturday afternoon, between two and three o'clock.

'God knows how the murderers brought a dead body to that ditch without being seen,' Rawson says, 'for I don't. In the five days that the magistrate was missing there was a lot of activity near that ditch. Folk were searching for a missing calf on more than one occasion; soldiers were hedgehog hunting all around; and two men went out hunting a hare. Surely their pack of hounds would have sniffed out a corpse.'

'Aye, Linnet's dog found it easily enough,' Mrs Rawson says.

'Around noon, on the morning of the very day I discovered the body, a local man was dressing a horse and washed his hands in a pond hard by that ditch and he claims that he saw no scabbard, gloves or stick, let alone a dead body. So,' Rawson declares, 'it's a mystery to me how the body and the goods were brought to the ditch and nobody discovered them at it.'

'It's a very secret place around that ditch with all the bushes,' Huysman says.

Whoever put the body there knew Primrose Hill well, of this Pepys is sure. He asks Rawson to light him to the lane where his hackney coach awaits. There's no need to linger in this shabby establishment; he's gleaned important information about the magistrate's wanderings on his last day. There's just one more detail he is curious about.

When they are alone he asks Rawson, 'Did Sir Edmund Godfrey visit your tavern on 12th October last?'

Rawson's answer is the ambiguous reply of a man who trusts no one.

'If a man passes my establishment on a blustery afternoon and doesn't even linger to take a pot of warm ale or a bread roll, I don't know about you, Mr Pepys, but I call that very bad manners.'

58

A TRAITOR'S DEATH
24TH JANUARY, 1679

'You are what I have made you: Traitors,' Titus says to himself.

The Jesuit father and the lay brother stand before the gallows.

'We are innocent,' John Grove says simply, his voice steady. 'We lose our lives wrongfully, we pray God to forgive those that are the causes of it.'

Grove had once lent Titus money.

The King has been merciful. The sickening butchery of Coleman's execution will not happen today. These Jesuits will hang until they die.

Titus is counting. He has killed three men already: Coleman, and now these two. Soon there will be more. The Benedictine, Father Pickering, lies in Newgate, convicted, waiting for the execution cart to come for him too. Other Jesuit fathers keep him company there. The Lord Chief Justice has asked Titus to give evidence to support the prosecution at the trial of Godfrey's murderers. Very soon, he will add Lawrence Hill, Henry Berry and Robert Green to his list of victims. And still the names keep coming. The popish lords are impeached and Matthew Medburne lies sick in Newgate, close to death. Titus wonders if he should add Edmund Godfrey to his list. After he signed the deposition, the magistrate told his friends that he would die.

Titus wants to laugh at the absurdity of it: of his own growing ability to turn his fantasies into reality. He, Dr Oates, who has killed and will kill again, without a drop of blood staining his hands.

He, Dr Oates, who will not forgive rejection, who spurns the patronage of strangers and the pity of friends.

He, Dr Oates, the man whose great imagination has redefined Truth.

Yes, of course he should add Edmund Godfrey to his list. He has been the cause of the magistrate's demise, one way or another.

Men and women standing nearby recognise him, doff their hats. A great cheer goes through the crowd. It meanders its way through the din of the hawkers selling their pies and beer, through the angry words bawled at the dying Jesuits. People turn away from the hanging men to look at him.

He, Dr Oates, Saviour of the Nation, he who has come to see the traitors he accused suffer the death he has brought about as truly as if he himself had put the ropes around their necks.

On Sunday, he will mount the pulpit at Israel Tonge's church in Wood Street. There is always a great thronging these days when he preaches, and Alderman Player's wife has offered the use of her coach to get him through the crowds.

59

AT THE BAR OF THE COURT
OF THE KING'S BENCH
WEDNESDAY, 10TH FEBRUARY, 1679

There are so many folk standing shoulder to shoulder that the twelve jurymen being sworn cannot stand together and the crier commands all persons not of the jury to withdraw upon pain of one hundred pounds. Pepys stays. Lord, he thinks, how Lord Chief Justice Scroggs, with all his justices around him, must be enjoying wearing his new courtroom regalia with his heavy chain of office on his chest and costly fur at his sleeves. Many people in the crowd are wearing new medals around their necks depicting Sir Edmund Godfrey on one side and on the other, the pope, who is supposed to have instigated his murder.

The prisoners are called: Henry Berry, Lawrence Hill, Robert Green. They hold up their hands in turn and take the oath. Mr Attorney General informs the jury of the motive for the murder: Godfrey had discovered the names of some of the perpetrators of the Popish Plot and the first witness is called: Dr Titus Oates, all puffed up in his silk gown and cassock and his long rose scarf. He tells the jury that in the days following the signing of the deposition, the magistrate visited him for encouragement because he went in fear of his life by papists. Godfrey had confided to him that he had been dogged by suspicious people for several days. Pepys has heard nothing of this – the magistrate being followed. So, the man had enemies and discovering who these enemies are would surely expose his killers.

The next witness is a magistrate, Thomas Robinson, who's known Edmund Godfrey since they were schoolboys. 'Sir Edmund became involved in the Popish Plot most unwillingly,' he tells the court. Then he contradicts Dr Oates. 'But he had no fear of enemies when he went about his daily business.'

'But did he tell you, sir, that he believed he would be the first martyr?' Mr Attorney General asks, and the dead man's friend looks straight at the jurymen and says, 'On my conscience, yes he did.'

A Protestant martyr, like those who burned in Mary's reign, Pepys reflects.

Silversmith Prance can't wait to start giving his evidence the minute he is called. 'The priests, Gerald and Kelly, said it would be a charitable act to kill the magistrate, so in the morning, on the Saturday...' He's speaking very fast, but Mr Attorney General shuts him up.

'Before you come to that,' he asks, 'do you know of any dogging of Sir Edmund in the fields?'

Prance says, yes, he was told that the priests and Robert Green had dogged Sir Edmund in Red Lion fields and those by Holborn.

Did Sir Edmund wander around this locality frequently? Pepys wonders, for he himself has spoken to a witness from Holborn who claims to have seen him walking in that area on the very day he disappeared.

Mr Recorder, young Sir George Jeffries, wears his bright red gown over his black clothes and silver lace decorates his cuffs and drips from his cravat. 'So why did they not kill him there in the fields?' he asks.

'They had no opportunity.'

Pepys is astounded. What, no opportunity to commit a

murder out in the country, so instead they decide to do it in the busy courtyard of the Queen's palace on the very evening that the King is visiting with his guards and entourage. Have the Lord Chief Justice and Mr Attorney General ever been to Somerset House? Don't they know how busy it is?

They come to discuss the crucial day: the Saturday when Sir Edmund disappeared. Prance says that either Hill or Green, he cannot remember which, called at the magistrate's house but the maid told them he was not up.

At this Hill shouts out, 'What time was this?'

'About nine or ten.'

Mr Recorder won't let Hill speak. He must wait until later to ask his questions. So the wretched man has to stand there and listen to Prance's accusations and keep his mouth shut. How he manages such self-control God alone knows for it seems that Hill is being presented as the orchestrator of the whole murderous business.

It all seems so silly, so unreal, but Mr Recorder's clerk is writing everything down: how little old Robert Green was supposed to have punched the magistrate in his chest with his arthritic old knees after he had strangled him and then assisted Miles Prance to carry a sedan chair with the weight of a dead body inside; how, later, the dead man's legs were forced apart astride a horse and Hill rode behind him on the journey to Primrose Hill. Pepys has to stifle a snigger; lord, but you could make a comedy or a pretty poem out of it: *Ride a cock horse by Charring Cross, to see a dead body upon a brown horse*, except of course, that the best comic actor, Matthew Medburne is dying in Newgate.

A woman beside Pepys clutches a wad of papers to her chest. 'When may I give my papers to my Lord Chief Justice?' she shouts out.

A clerk grabs the poor wretch by the arm. 'Be quiet, Mrs Hill, or leave the court.'

Finally, the prisoners are allowed to speak.

'My lord,' Lawrence Hill says, 'I suppose it is not unknown to you that Mr Prance made a confession that he had lied before the King. Let Mr Chiffinch, the King's gentleman give his evidence.'

The King's Pimp Master General, is how Pepys and his friends usually refer to Mr Chiffinch, behind his back. His main duty appears to be conducting actresses up the backstairs.

'I was present when Mr Prance swore to His Majesty that the evidence he had previously given against Mr Berry, Mr Green and Mr Hill, was all false,' Chiffinch says.

'If a man can swear a thing and after, deny it, he is certainly perjured,' Hill cries.

He is wasting his time. The prosecution does not welcome this testimony. Pepys has noticed Mr Recorder nudging his clerk and they have put down their quills while Mr Chiffinch gives his evidence.

'Nobody believed Mr Prance's denial,' Lord Scroggs tells the jurymen, and Captain Richardson, is called.

'I had no sooner got Mr Prance within doors at Newgate but he begged of me to go back to the King because all he had just told him was false and what he had sworn previously of the murder was true, and if His Majesty would send him a pardon he would make a great discovery.'

'Now you have an account, Mr Hill, of how he came to deny and how soon he recanted his denial,' Lord Scroggs says, to end the matter.

Henry Berry tries to tell the court that he barely knows Prance let alone plan a murder with him and those priests. He never drank with him but in other company, he says, he just knew Prance as he passed up and down in his alehouse.

'Why, what sort of answer is that?' Lord Scroggs rejoins. 'Don't people usually drink as they pass up and down in your alehouse?' Everyone is laughing now at the Lord Chief Justice's wit, even the jury members. Pepys isn't laughing. Scroggs: he's as nasty as his name suggests, looking down on the prisoners and making fun of them.

The next witness for the Crown is William Bedloe, who everybody knows is a great rogue, but Lord Scroggs doesn't care. Bedloe swears that he was there, at Somerset House, with Miles Prance on Monday 14th October, in a secret chamber with the dead body. Pepys' heart is beating fast, now. Pray God he doesn't swear that he saw young Sam standing beside the body.

Prance butts in to describe the middle-sized dim lantern they held over the corpse. Thankfully, Bedloe admits that he was unable to recognise any of the murderers standing by the corpse that night, in the dark, but when he's asked about plans to carry away the body, he says that they took it out in a sedan chair and the porter, Henry Berry, let them out.

Prance interrupts again to say that there were no sentries at the gate because they were lured into Berry's alehouse for drinks while Berry let the sedan chair pass through the gate. Mr Attorney General says he supposes that this could be what happened.

Constable Brown is called to explain how the body was discovered, to prove that it lay in the same manner as Prance says the murderers told him they had left it, with two hand-fuls of sword sticking out of its back.

Two surgeons from the inquest, Zachary Skillarne and Nicholas Cambridge speak next. Surgeon Skillarne says that the body wasn't bloody which proves that the sword wound was inflicted after death. 'His bosom was open and none of his clothes were penetrated,' he says.

'Are you sure that his neck had been broken,' Mr Attorney General asks, 'because some have been of the opinion that he hanged himself, and that his relations, to save his estate, had run him through.'

The surgeon makes it quite clear that the cause of death fits Prance's story that Godfrey was throttled when Robert Green twisted his neck. 'There was more done to his neck than an ordinary suffocation,' he replies.

Pepys is scornful. Whatever is ordinary about suffocations?

'His neck was dislocated,' Surgeon Cambridge says when it is his turn to speak.

Lord Scroggs cuts him short. 'Why, that means broken,' he tells the jury and dismisses Cambridge before he can argue the matter and calls for Godfrey's maid, Elizabeth Curtis.

She is asked to look at the prisoners and tell if she's seen any of them before.

'This man I now hear called, Green, my lord, was at my master's about a fortnight before he died. He said, "Good morrow, sir," in English and afterwards spoke to Sir Edmund in French and I couldn't understand.'

Whenever did Robert Green learn to speak French? Pepys doubts whether the old man can even write his own name in English. Mr Recorder appears to have his doubts about this. 'Consider well, look again,' he tells her.

Robert Green shouts out that he's never seen Sir Edmund Godfrey in his life.

'That is the man I saw,' the old lady says confidently. 'He had a darker coloured periwig when he was there and was about a quarter of an hour talking with my master.'

'Are you sure this was the man?' Mr Attorney General asks, frowning.

'Yes, I am,' she says and then she points to Hill and says that he called to see her master on Saturday, 12th October, in the morning, and had a conversation with Sir Edmund for several minutes before he went out; she saw him there in the parlour while she was stirring the fire.

'Will you deny that too?' Lord Chief Justice Scroggs asks Hill.

'Yes, I do,' he answers boldly.

'Had you seen him before that time?' Lord Scroggs asks the maid.

'No, never before that time,' she says. 'But he's not the same man who brought the mysterious note to my master the night before.'

Mr Attorney General knows nothing of any note and isn't really interested. 'You swear that Hill was there on the Saturday morning?' he asks.

'Yes, he was.'

'But she did say,' Hill protests, 'when she came to see me in Newgate, that she never saw me in her life, and my lord, I hope to have sufficient witnesses to prove where I was that morning.'

'In what clothes was he then, on the Saturday morning?' Mr Solicitor General asks.

'He wore the same clothes then as he wears today,' the maid says.

'Have you shifted your clothes since that Saturday?' Lord Scroggs asks.

Hill admits that he wore the same clothes on the murder day that he now wears.

Of course he did. How many suits of clothes does the Lord Chief Justice expect a workingman to own?

'But he is not the same man that brought the note,' the maid says again, but nobody is listening.

At last the prisoners are allowed to call their witnesses. The first question the Attorney General always asks is, 'What religion are you?' God help them, Pepys prays. Bloody and murderous: this is what Protestants believe all Catholics to be these days. If all their witnesses are Catholics, Lord Scroggs will not believe a word they say.

He doesn't; he makes fools of them, worries and insults them.

Mary Tilden, Dr Godwin's niece, comes first. She's very brave though Pepys can hear how nervous she is; her voice is trembling. She tells them that Lawrence was a very good servant to her uncle and never kept ill hours. 'He was never out after eight o'clock at night,' she says.

'Pray, how can you give such an account of Mr Hill as if he was always in your company?' Lord Scroggs asks.

'I hope you did not keep him company after supper, all night?' young Mr Recorder butts in, and his clerk is sniggering and other people are laughing outright.

'No I did not,' she stammers, and bursts into tears. 'He came to wait at table on that Friday night and did not go out again.'

They ask about the room in Hill's lodging where Prance says the body lay.

'If the body was in the house, as Mr Prance has said it was, I would have seen it, or one of us would, surely,' Mary Tilden says. 'I used to go into that room for something or other every day.'

Mrs Broadstreet, the housekeeper for the servant's lodgings is called, and she agrees. If the body were there she would have seen it, having gone in and out of that room often during that week, there being several keys, and anyway, one was usually in the door.

'It is very suspicious that you went in that chamber where the body lay, yet saw nothing,' one of the justices says. The poor woman puts her hands to her face in horror.

'It is well, madam,' she's told, 'that you are not indicted.'

Hill's next witness is a carpenter who did some work for him on the new house in Stanhope Street. When he's asked about his religion the man hesitates over his answer.

'My lord, I know him,' Prance shouts out. 'He is a Catholic. He was the Queen's carpenter.'

The carpenter insists that Hill was in his company at Stanhope Street from nine in the morning until two in the afternoon on Saturday, 12th October. Lord Scroggs says he lies on this count as he did about his religion. Hill calls more friends to swear that they were with him at noon and also in the late afternoon and early evening of the murder day. Furthermore, on the day that the body was supposed to have been taken away, the Wednesday evening, one man swears that he was with Hill between five and seven o'clock.

'What time was he carried out?' Lord Scroggs asks, meaning Godfrey's dead body.

'Between eleven and twelve o'clock,' the Attorney General tells him.

Hill's wife has heard enough. She walks straight up to the bench with her papers.

Lord Scroggs refuses to read them.

'Now, Mr Green,' he says. 'What have you to say for yourself?'

Robert Green calls for his Protestant landlord, Mr Warrier, to swear that on the evening of 12th October he was at Mr Warrier's house from half an hour after seven until after ten o'clock, but the landlord lets Lord Scroggs tie him up in knots over dates and times and he comes across as quite the comic actor and people are laughing. Each time he is asked how he knows that it is on the crucial day that he remembers the accused being at his house, he says, 'by my work,' and Pepys can make no sense out of anything he says, and neither can Lord Scroggs.

'I never knew the man to be out after nine of the clock,' Mr Warrier finally cries in desperation.

Mrs Warrier comes to speak and Pepys is quite lost in her ramblings of fowl and bread and cheese and pigeon pies, all in an effort to prove that on the crucial night of Wednesday, 16th October, when the body was supposed to have been moved out of Somerset House, Mr and Mrs Green sat down to a meal in her Protestant home. But she gets all her dates mixed up and says it was the Saturday fortnight after Michaelmas. One of the justices is working it out and says that day was 19th October.

Captain Richardson butts in to tell the court that Mr Green had begged him to visit Mr and Mrs Warrier to ask them to speak at his trial but they had been worried that they could do Green no good at all.

'And you have not,' Lord Scroggs retorts and asks Henry Berry to make his defence. Oh, God, help us, Pepys prays. This is our last chance.

Berry calls for the corporal and three sentinels who guarded the Strand gate where the sedan was supposed to have passed out on the Wednesday night. All four sentries swear that on the night of 16th October no sedan chair went out.

'The porter could open the gate as well as you,' one of the justices says.

'We never saw him open the gate that night,' the corporal replies.

'Did you go out for a smoke or a tipple?' the justice asks with a nod and a wink at the jury.

They all swear that they did not.

The trial has turned, Pepys thinks. If it is proven that no sedan left through that gate, the whole of Prance's evidence is shown to be a lie and young Sam will be vindicated.

Henry Berry calls his maid and she swears that on the Wednesday night in question, which she remembers because it was the day the Queen left Somerset House for Whitehall, Berry had returned home at dusk after playing bowls and he had not gone out of the house all night. If he had, she would have known because he had to pass through her room.

Surely now, Lord Scroggs and the jury cannot deny the

truth. Mrs Hill again speaks out to ask Prance a second time why he recanted his confession to the King. 'Let him swear under oath that he was not tortured,' she demands.

'No, my lords,' Prance says. 'I was never tortured. Captain Richardson treated me well in Newgate.'

'It was reported about town that he was tortured,' Mrs Hill cries. 'He was heard to cry out in the night. He knows that everything he has told this court is a lie, and you will hear that this is so when it is too late.'

'Do you think he would swear three men out of their lives for nothing?' Lord Scroggs demands.

'Well, I am dissatisfied,' the poor woman protests. 'My witnesses were not rightly examined. They are modest folk and the court laughed at them.'

'The sentinels were at the gate all night and let nothing out,' Henry Berry cries.

'Why, you could open the gate yourself,' Lord Scroggs rejoins.

'I wasn't on duty that night,' Berry pleads but nobody important is listening.

In his summing up, Lord Scroggs says that it is impossible that a simple man like Miles Prance could invent such a story as he has told of the murder of Sir Edmund and have it confirmed by William Bedloe and other people he did not know.

'Catholic priests,' Scroggs says, in his summary, 'being the preachers of murder, are capable of contriving such a wicked deed.' He tells the jury not to put too much weight upon the evidence of the sentries. In the darkness they may not have seen the sedan going out. And anyway, Pepys thinks, the jury will remember that Miles Prance has already insinuated that they are drunks and liars.

When the jury return with the verdict. It is no surprise.

Guilty of murder: all three.

60

GO YOU AND SHARE ANOTHER BOTTLE WITH HIM
10ᵀᴴ–11ᵀᴴ FEBRUARY,1679

Lord Scroggs has been kind.

'I have lain under severe imprisonment for a long time,' Sam had told the Lord Chief Justice at his hearing. 'and I earnestly desire my trial. My lord, I have witnesses who have remained in town these fifteen weeks to give evidence for me, ever since the last term. I hope my trial may not take up too much time. I hope I shall have occasion to use only a few of my witnesses.'

At this, Mr Recorder told Sam that he would have to wait until the next session.

'But, my lord, several of my witnesses are unable to stay in town until the next session,' Sam had pleaded, almost in tears.

Lord Scroggs agreed to have the trial on the morrow, 11th February, 'but bring him up very early,' he told Captain Richardson. Sam's trial will perhaps precede the sentencing of Berry, Green and Hill. Lord help us, Pepys prays. Is the Lord Chief Justice thinking to save time by sentencing all four of them in one session?

***

Young Sam holds up his hand and answers the charge confidently:

'Not guilty.'

'How shall you be tried?'

'By God and my country.'

Mr Attorney General explains to the jury that because of yesterday's convictions, the accused will not answer a charge of murder but of accessory to murder. Cheered by the knowledge that at the trial of Berry, Green and Hill, neither Prance nor Bedloe had actually named Sam as being there at Somerset House standing beside the magistrate's body on 14th October, Pepys is dismayed when Mr Attorney General declares that there is proof from the testimonies of Mr Prance and Mr Bedloe that Sam may have been there in that chamber with the murderers consulting how to dispose of the body. But first, Sam's erstwhile friend and namesake, Captain Charles Atkins, is called to give his evidence.

'Some time early in October, I visited Samuel Atkins to borrow a little money.'

'At what house was this?' Scroggs asks.

'At Derby House, the naval offices. We stood together by the great window above the stairs next to the office where the prisoner writes and we discussed the Popish Plot and Mr Coleman and other matters I cannot now remember. And then the prisoner began to talk about Sir Edmund Bury Godfrey and told me that he had much injured his master, Mr Pepys, and would be the ruin of him.'

At this Scroggs asks, 'Did he tell you that his master feared that Sir Edmund Godfrey would ruin him by discovering something about the Popish Plot?'

Lord help me, Pepys prays, the Lord Chief Justice is putting words into Captain Atkins mouth. He's accusing me of being a papist plotter.

'Yes,' the captain replies. 'I understood so. He asked me if I knew a man who could keep a secret and who would murder a man. And he asked if I believed a Mr Child to be such a man, for I had once asked Sam to recommend him to Mr Pepys for being purser of a ship.

'The next night Mr Child sought me out and he asked me if I would join him in the murder of Sir Edmund and we arranged to meet at the Three Tobacco Pipes, at Holborn and Child said that by reason of his ill fortune and lack of money he would do the deed and he asked me to join him in the killing. But my lord, I would never do anything dishonest like highway robbery and I wouldn't ever kill a man. Child gave me eight or nine days to consider and promised me a great reward if I would join with them.'

'Them?' Scroggs asks. 'Who were they, these other murderers?'

'He did not tell me who they were.'

Am I supposed to have paid these murderers? Pepys wonders. Lord knows, I'm wealthy enough to pay large amounts and this everyone knows. It occurs to him that Child and Captain Atkins might really have had some involvement in the murder. Somebody killed Godfrey and it wasn't the three men found guilty yesterday. Captain Atkins is giving a very detailed account of his meetings with Child. It makes sense that they know each other well: two desperate men begging their way through their lives, willing to do anything for a price.

'We met again,' the captain says, 'at the Three Cans, or maybe it's the Six Cans, I forget, and Child told me that if I would not agree to the murder I would have a hundred pounds to conceal it. But if I revealed any knowledge of it I would not live.'

'Did Mr Atkins, the clerk, say that Mr Pepys knew of these murder plans?' Scroggs asks.

Pepys is mightily relieved when the captain replies, 'No, not to me.'

Next, Mr Bedloe is sworn. 'My lord, when I asked the priests who was to carry the body off and I was told Mr Atkins was one involved, I thought it would be the captain,' he points to Captain Atkins, 'whom I have known several years. But when I got into the room beside the body I saw several people there and some of their faces I did see even in the dim light of the dark lantern, and seeing a young man I asked him his name and he told me, "Atkins," and I asked if he was Mr Pepys' clerk and he said, yes, he was and he remembered seeing me often at his master's house.'

Pepys is angry. Bedloe has never set foot in his house. How is a man expected to keep his temper amongst so many lies?

'And that was all the discourse that you had with him?' Scroggs asks.

'Yes, for I was only a little while there, in that dark chamber beside the body. I think the man had a more manly face than the prisoner here has, and he had a beard.'

Lord, but is Bedloe describing Lawrence Hill? Did he really see Hill standing beside the body? Pepys wonders.

'My lord,' Bedloe adds, looking in Sam's direction. 'I would not be guilty of a falsehood to take away another's life.'

'You do well to be cautious, Mr Bedloe,' Scroggs says.

'Indeed,' Mr Attorney General agrees. 'Mr Bedloe was never positive at the first trial that young Mr Atkins was standing beside the body.'

'What say you to Mr Bedloe's testimony,' Sam is asked. 'Did you stand beside the body at Somerset House?'

'No my lord, I am so far from it; I was never in that house in my life.'

'Then call a couple of witnesses to prove where you were

on that Monday night 14th October and you need trouble yourself no further.'

'There is Captain Vittals and his whole company. Here is the captain, my lord.'

Captain Vittals comes forward and tells the court that he has known Sam for fourteen years, since he was a boy.

'How do you remember the exact day, 14th October?' Scroggs asks.

'Mariners are very exact and punctual. They keep accounts of every day and have journals of all passages.' Captain Vittals removes his journal from his pocket. 'On 11th October, Mr Pepys went down to Newmarket with the King and the Duke of York and so I could receive no orders from him until he came back. On Monday,14th I went to Mr Pepys' offices and his clerk, Sam Atkins, told me that Mr Pepys had not returned and there were a couple of gentlewomen, sisters, who desired to see a yacht and I told him to bring his friends by and by. So I returned to get my yacht ready and get some provisions.

'It was half past four when I saw the boat approaching carrying Mr Atkins and the ladies. We were in the cabin drinking wine and by eight or nine o'clock, and I beg your lordship's pardon, but I confess we were a little warm. At half past ten, I ordered my men to get ready a boat of four oars that belonged to the yacht, which would go swifter than other boats. Mr Atkins was by this time very much fuddled. I put him and the ladies in my boat, with four of my men, who are here today to give evidence, my lord. I fell asleep and in the morning when my men returned with the boat they told me they had been obliged to put Mr Atkins ashore at Billingsgate at half an hour before midnight because the tide was too strong at the bridge to get the boat through.'

Captain Vittals men having sworn that this is so, Scroggs

tells them they need trouble themselves no more and Mr Attorney General makes it very clear that there is no problem of disproving the King's evidence from the previous trial. He repeats that Mr Bedloe never positively identified the prisoner as one standing beside Godfrey's body.

The verdict is a foregone conclusion.

Not guilty.

Young Sam is on his knees. 'God bless the King and his honourable Bench,' he cries.

'I should be glad if the rest who are convicted had been as innocent as you are,' Scroggs replies and Pepys is astounded when he adds: 'If any Protestant had done such a thing as this it would grieve me to the very heart.'

Has the Lord Chief Justice forgotten that yesterday he convicted Henry Berry – a Protestant? Being the Catholic Queen's porter, maybe Scroggs believes him to be a secret papist, as Pepys is supposed to be.

'Well, well, Captain,' Scroggs says, while Sam embraces the man whose evidence has saved his life. 'Go you, and share another bottle with him.'

Landmarks of Edmund Godfrey's London, 1678

Use this map to follow Edmund Godfrey as he is sighted by friends and neighbours in this area on Saturday, 12th October, 1678.

To Primrose Hill

Tottenham Court Road

Marylebone

Holborn

4

5

Lincoln's Inn & Fields

3

6

St Martin's Lane

Drury Lane

1. Hartshorne Lane

2. Church of St Martin's-in-the-Fields

3. Church of St Giles-in-the-Fields

4. Fuller's Rents

5. Turnstile

6. Wildhouse

Covent Garden

Somerset House

The Strand

2

Charing Cross

1

The Thames River

St James' Park

Whitehall Palace

The Cockpit

Sketch map, not to scale.
From Hartshorne Lane to Primrose Hill approximately 3 miles

61

FOLLOWING GODFREY'S FOOTSTEPS
SPRING 1679

After the sharing of bottles; after long nights of sleep in his own warm bed; after the relief of the verdict; the euphoria of acquittal; after all this, a great sadness comes to Sam and Pepys cannot understand it. He finds him at his desk, lethargic and mournful, the document he's working on littered with errors.

'Those three convicted men are innocent, I'm sure of it,' Sam says. 'Every prisoner in Newgate believed this to be so, even Miles Prance. They had alibis, as I did, but the great lords refused to listen to them. Oh Mr Pepys, it preys upon my mind that I am free and they were hanged. What really happened to Sir Edmund? I cannot concentrate upon my work until I know the truth of it.'

'Then we shall seek the truth.' Pepys whisks away the spoiled paper and unrolls a large document onto the desk. It is a street map of London annotated all over with Edmund Godfrey's name, accompanied by those of other men and women. With the information Pepys had collected when he toured London asking his questions, his clerks have plotted sightings of Edmund Godfrey on the Saturday he disappeared. 'Let us trace the magistrate's footsteps on the day he went missing from his home. Where he went and whom he met will be crucial in seeking his murderers.' Pepys taps his finger on Hartshorne Lane. 'He was up very early and out, so his servants told me, around six o'clock.'

'Whatever did he find to do in the darkness before dawn?'

'All I could glean is that he was seen by three people on St Martin's Lane around eight o'clock; presumably by this time he was returning home for his breakfast. I spoke to Richard Cooper, his sister Mrs Leeson, and James Lowen; obviously people with whom Sir Edmund was well acquainted. They said, "Good morrow, Sir Edmund," and he acknowledged them in what Mrs Leeson described as a grave formal way. It seems that he didn't want to have a conversation, just walked on with his cane dangling before him. "The justice was melancholy," Mrs Leeson told me. Her brother disagreed. "Sir Edmund was studying, that's all, he was a serious man," he explained.'

'He had heavy matters on his mind,' Sam suggests. 'Maybe he couldn't sleep for worrying and he went out walking to think things over.'

'It's well known that he habitually wandered London's streets at night.'

'Out late at night and up before dawn; what was he up to, alone on the streets, when all honest men are sleeping?' Sam asks.

'Seeking rogues, thieves, nose-slitters, is what his clerk told me.'

'Or whores,' Sam suggests with a titter.

'Show some respect for the poor man,' Pepys rebukes. 'Sir Edmund didn't like women and was well known for sending women to a house of correction if he discovered them up to no good.'

'Maybe that's the root of his problem,' Sam says quietly. 'Maybe he was one of those men who seek their pleasure with… sorry sir, but maybe he liked to be with men.'

'He was a deeply religious man, surely it is not possible

that he was...' Even as he speaks, Pepys knows that it is possible. 'Edmund Godfrey was a complicated man,' he tells Sam. 'A Protestant with Catholic friends including the traitor, Edward Coleman. He was generous to the poor in his parish yet vindictive in his punishments of criminals. He even had the audacity to arrest the King's physician for a debt to himself.'

'Would you say he had many enemies?' Sam asks.

'I would say that in the course of his duties as a justice of the peace, many men and women had cause to hate him, including his own nephew whom he took into his business. There was much bad feeling between them: a case in Chancery over an annuity, I believe, so his clerk says.'

Pepys taps his finger again at Hartshorne Lane. 'Now this is an interesting fact to consider. Whilst he was out, a lawyer, Richard Adams, called at his house between seven and eight o'clock. I know something about this man. Around nine years ago he was incarcerated for speaking seditious words. He was linked to Shaftesbury's gang of Opposition politicians.'

'Oh, so was Sir Edmund involved in subversive activities with this lawyer? Was he plotting to remove the King and put his brother on the throne?'

'This is what the Jesuits are supposed to be plotting,' Pepys answers, 'but it would be interesting to know what business Richard Adams had with Sir Edmund. The King believes that if anyone is plotting to overthrow the monarchy it is more likely to be Lord Shaftesbury and his friends than any popish plot.'

Sam picks up a quill and strokes his finger along the feather several times. It's a while before he speaks. 'Oh, so maybe Lord Shaftesbury murdered Sir Edmund because he knew too much about a plot he was hatching.'

'Now then, Sam, do not jump to conclusions,' Pepys says.

'Let us follow Sir Edmund on this map to see where he went and most importantly, where he ended up. After his early morning constitutional he went home for his breakfast. He had a visitor in the parlour when the maid took him his food and he was there for some time. Betty Curtis, the maid, identified Lawrence Hill as the man she saw.'

'So it was a dark man who sat with Sir Edmund. One unknown to the servants by name.'

'Around nine o'clock Sir Edmund was out again. Now listen to this, Sam; his behaviour was quite odd just before he left home. His clerk helped him on with his new coat but Sir Edmund changed his mind and asked for his old one. It would do for the business he had that day, he told Moor.'

'So he wasn't intending to visit any person of quality?'

'We'll come to that later. He set off through his wood-yard but turned back towards Henry Moor, as if he had forgotten something. But then he continued on his way.'

'He's indecisive, as I thought,' Sam says. 'Matters on his mind befuddled his head. Do you think he murdered himself, Mr Pepys?'

'We'll think about this later, too. First we'll follow him on his last walk until the trail ends. I'll explain who he met and what conversations he had. Mr Parsons, a coachmaker and churchwarden saw him on St Martin's Lane, and claims that he asked directions to Primrose Hill and set off walking into the country.'

'Surely Sir Edmund knew the way?' Sam asks.

'That's what I thought, but maybe he was in a hurry and was asking about a short cut through the fields. Judith Pamphlin, Godfrey's housekeeper claims that Parsons told her that Godfrey was asking the way to Paddington Woods.' Pepys shakes his head. 'So many conflicting accounts. Between nine and ten o'clock, a brewer from St Giles saw him in the fields walking towards Marylebone and talked with him a little. This is corroborated by two other witnesses. William Collins, one of the jurymen at the inquest, claims that he saw Sir Edmund on Saturday morning near his barn which is hard by Marylebone Church. Sir Edmund was talking to a milk-woman at Marylebone conduit not far from Paddington Woods which is only about a mile from Primrose Hill. Thomas Mason, another juryman at the inquest, also saw him on Saturday morning, walking from the Paddington direction towards the fields between Marylebone Pound and Marylebone Street. He said, "Good morrow," and they had a conversation, just passing the time of day, that was all.'

'This is good evidence that Sir Edmund went to Primrose Hill that morning where he was murdered, either that, or he took his own life there,' Sam says with some animation.

'No, this is not what happened. It seems that he never reached Primrose Hill in the morning.' Pepys points to Whitehall on the map and moves his finger towards the Cockpit. Lord Danby's daughter saw him walking near her father's house, around eleven o'clock.'

'Why would he wear his old coat to visit the Lord Treasurer?'

'Lord knows, Pepys declares, 'but on the very last day he was seen alive, Sir Edmund Godfrey apparently visited Lord Danby. What his business was I cannot imagine. They did not like each other.'

'They were discussing the Popish Plot,' Sam answers with all the assurance of the young. 'What else do people talk about these days?'

'Around noon,' Pepys continues, 'Thomas Snell of Holborn Turnstile claims that he saw Sir Edmund pass by on his way to Red Lyon Fields. But I question the reliability of this witness. He didn't know it was Sir Edmund he had seen until later when a friend told him it must have been the magistrate who had gone missing. And the time doesn't fit because at one o'clock, oilman, Joseph Radcliffe, met Sir Edmund outside his shop on the Strand as he passed by. He knows Sir Edmund well, being a vestryman, and he had been with him the evening before. He asked him if he had dined and he invited him to dinner but Sir Edmund excused himself due to pressing business.

'Now here's a strange thing, Sam. At noon, Sir Edmund had an appointment with a business associate, Mr Wynnell, to discuss the sale of property. They had arranged to meet at Captain Weldon's tavern on the Strand but Godfrey never arrived. Yet here he is on the Strand around an hour later. Why did he not call in at Weldon's to give his apologies?'

'He was very much disturbed in his mind and had completely forgotten, I suppose.'

'Aye, it would seem so. Radcliffe told me that the previous evening Captain Weldon had indeed invited him to dine at his house on the Saturday and Godfrey had replied that he wouldn't see him in his house so often in future.'

'Mr Wynnell may have got his dates confused.'

'Maybe, or maybe Godfrey was so distressed he couldn't cope with dinners and business meetings. Radcliffe told me that Godfrey looked melancholy that morning. A day or so later, Henry Moor told Radcliffe to keep his mouth shut about this, Sir Edmund's black mood. He didn't say why.'

'Because the Godfrey family don't want the disgrace of a suicide in the family,' Sam ventures. 'But it is looking that way to me.'

'Hold your thoughts; you haven't heard all the evidence yet,' Pepys advises. 'Now we come to the afternoon and it gets even more confusing.' His finger travels north, up the Tottenham Court Road and off the edge of the map. 'Between two and three, Sir Edmund was seen by three local men walking in the direction of the White House at Primrose Hill.'

'So, it's obvious: he died at Primrose Hill.'

'Ah, but this is only surmise, Sam. These men never knew Sir Edmund. But what other tall stooping gentleman in black was wandering in that lonely place late that afternoon looking so melancholy I cannot imagine. Neither can I imagine what business Sir Edmund would have there.'

'Perhaps he went there to arrest a felon?'

'Whatever it was, he didn't stay there long.' Pepys moves his finger back down Tottenham Court Road and east along Holborn. 'Around three o'clock, two gentlemen saw him at the back court of Lincoln's Inn. He went out of the back door and they watched him turn the corner wall by the Turnstile where a barrister of law met him. I wonder, could this possibly be the lawyer, Richard Adams who had called at his house twice that morning?'

'So the final sighting was around three o'clock,' Sam says, 'at Lincoln's Inn Court, although he was also spotted around that time at Primrose Hill. What a mystery we are trying to unravel.' Sam takes a knife from his pocket, takes a quill from a heap on the desk and begins sharpening the nib.

'Aye, his brothers told the Secretaries of State that he was last seen between two and three o'clock,' Pepys says. 'But listen, Sam. I have some very secret evidence which I have promised never to reveal.' Lord, but it would have done Sam no good at all for him to have disclosed this information to him, before his trial. He feared it would have broken the boy's spirit.

Pepys explains that he got into conversation with some of Sir Edmund's neighbours. Elizabeth Deakin a servant to a Mr Breedon of Hartshorne Lane, has claimed that another servant in that household, John Oakley, saw Sir Edmund on the Saturday evening about nine o'clock.

'On Hartshorne Lane?' Sam queries. 'However could this be? His servants never saw him again after he left home in the morning.'

'No, Oakley met him near the Watergate at Somerset House on the Strand.'

Sam puts down his knife and stares at his master, aghast. 'Oh Mr Pepys, this backs up Bedloe and Prance's stories. I don't believe it. Nobody in Newgate, apart from Captain Richardson, believed Berry, Green and Hill were guilty.'

'John Oakley knew Sir Edmund well,' Pepys says, 'their households being neighbours. Oakley told this maidservant, Elizabeth Deakin, in confidence of course, that he saw one or two men standing around Sir Edmund at this time. He doffed his hat to Sir Edmund and the magistrate acknowledged him.'

Sam is quiet for a moment or two. When he speaks his voice is low, almost a whisper. 'Oh, Mr Pepys, that was maybe the last time Sir Edmund was seen alive and John Oakley may have seen the very men who murdered him.'

'Indeed, so promise never to speak a word of this,' Pepys demands. 'Oakley is so afraid, he told no one, only his father and the maidservant and they warned him to keep quiet or the papist murderers will cut their throats whilst they sleep.'

'So nobody important knows of this sighting,' Sam says, 'except you, Mr Pepys, who is good at getting people to tell you their secrets.'

'The trail stops at Somerset House. But what happened there that night was not what Lord Scroggs was told in court. It is ridiculous to believe that a dead body was taken away in a sedan chair by men who had never been trained to carry it, at least one of whom was old and frail. But Bedloe and Prance know something of the truth, I'm sure of it.'

'Yes, that's what I've been thinking all along,' Sam says. 'And what of Captain Atkins and Mr Child? I thought it rather odd that Mr Child wasn't brought to give evidence at my trial.'

'Does the man really exist?' Pepys queries. 'Now then Sam,' he continues, 'here's another strange thing. William Bedloe has sworn that he saw Miles Prance, in his purple verger's gown, standing beside Godfrey's body in that chamber at Somerset House. What I'm asking myself is this: if they were there together, why did they give such diverse accounts of the murder? Lord, but it would appear there were two Edmund Godfreys murdered at Somerset House: one whose body was taken away in Corrall's coach and another who left in a sedan chair and also, two sets of Catholic priests planning the deed.'

'No one has come forward to confess that he strangled Godfrey with his own hands or put the sword through his breast,' Sam says. 'Prance and Bedloe were beguiled by the promise of a reward and a pardon from the King and their evidence is hearsay only.'

Pepys tells Sam of the strange letter Secretary Coventry received from the informer signing himself T.G. who claimed that Godfrey was enticed to a makeshift court at Wild House, tried by a Jesuit priest, sentenced to death and murdered there.

'The Jesuits who are accused, Father Kelly, Father Gerald, Le Phaire; all have fled the country or are in hiding. Does this prove their guilt?' Sam asks.

'Their fear, more like,' Pepys replies. 'And nobody knows who the hell this man Kelly is. It seems to be an alias. In the present terror, no jury would believe a Jesuit to be innocent. I wouldn't rule out that foul mouthed, drunken rogue, Colonel John Scott, as the murderer, despite my having found no evidence; he'd do anything for money. Yes, he is capable of murdering a man, but too slippery to risk getting himself caught dragging a dead body around Somerset House.

'But listen Sam, the strangest thing of all concerning Godfrey's death, must surely be this: that the two Secretaries of State have heard nothing at all about it, except from unexpected sources. If it were indeed a planned murder, and one discussed in a tavern or a coffee house, however could they not have heard rumours of it? Their informers are everywhere, you know: on the streets; in the taverns, alleys and gin shops. They have contacts in jails, in clubs, in private gentlemen's homes. Not one has sniffed out even a scrap of evidence about Oates' Popish Plot and nothing at all touching Edmund Godfrey's death.'

'If nobody knows anything about a murder, then surely it was suicide,' Sam deduces, putting aside his sharpened quill and taking up another.

'Do not jump to conclusions,' Pepys warns. 'Now then Sam, this hackney coachman, Francis Corrall, who claimed he took the body away, well, I wonder if there may be some truth in this even though he afterwards strongly denied it.'

'The poor man has been released from Newgate but is unable to work because the irons have injured his legs,' Sam says sadly.

'Oh dear, however will he feed his family and his horses?'

'A great lord, the Earl of Clarendon, has come to his rescue with a large sum of money to keep him from the poor basket until he is fit to work.'

'In these troubled times of plotting and murder it is easy to forget that there is kindness in men's hearts,' Pepys says, wiping a tear from his eye.

One day, around this time, a great darkness falls over the city of London. In the Queen's chapel the ghost of Edmund Godfrey is seen floating above the altar during Mass iridescent in the candlelight, and seeing him, Louise, Duchess of Portsmouth, the King's Catholic whore, falls to the floor in a swoon, or so the Protestants say. In these early months after his death, it seems that poor Sir Edmund's ghost is wandering around London streets and alleys much as he used to do in his lifetime, for there have been several sightings.

'We cannot leave Edmund Godfrey restless and revenant, waiting for a solution to the mystery of his strange demise,' Pepys tells Sam. 'The magistrate has left a great mystery in his wake, the evidence I have found has guided me, with a bit of intuition, towards the tragic ending of his story.'

Part 8
Whatever Happened to Edmund Godfrey? September–October, 1678

"… imagination is an important component of historical understanding. Such imagination entails trying to put oneself in another's shoes, guided by probability and fact…"

Peter Hinds (2010)

62

THE DUKE AND HIS SPY
LATE SEPTEMBER, 1678

Thomas Blood refuses the brandy that is offered. 'I avoid strong drink these days, Your Highness,' he says.

James calls for a glass of small ale for Blood. They sit at the table waiting for the servant to bring it and leave them alone: England's heir and his spy in a closet in the royal apartments, comfortable in each other's company, chatting about the Duke's greyhound bitch which has got lost again.

'I'll ask around,' Blood says.

'Well Dr Ayliffe?' James asks brusquely as soon as they are alone. 'Do you have it?'

'The opportunity has not yet presented itself, sir. I have been dogging him every day and I have been close once or twice.'

'Damn,' James curses. 'I expected better of you. I wanted it now, before I depart for Newmarket.'

'Sir, you said I was to do it without force. Yesterday, I found Sir Edmund alone walking away from Fuller's Rents. I followed him along Drury Lane into an alleyway and I could have done it easily but he, being aware of some small movement about his person, began to turn his head and I had to flee before he recognised me, aye, and before he called for the constables. It isn't easy, sir, other men are dogging him as well as myself.'

'What?' James demands. He glares at Blood through his lazy, heavy-lidded eyes, 'Do you know them?'

'None of my acquaintance, sir. Common men by their attire. They go about in pairs and follow wherever he goes.'

'This is an unexpected hindrance to our design,' James says. 'Do not fail me, Blood. If these men get to Godfrey before you do, you will suffer for it.'

'I have followed him these few days and he unaware except that one time. I will do it soon, sir, you will see.'

'Remember this,' James says. 'The contents of the pocketbook are not for your perusal. If I find that any secret information I read therein has become known to my Lord Danby or the Secretaries of State, or to every common man on the streets, you know what I will do.'

'Sir,' Blood says quietly, 'you have promised me a generous reward, well befitting the sealing of my lips. You know that I have lived a dangerous life and enjoyed the spoils and thrill of it all and it is only thanks to God's providence that I have lived my three score years. I am nothing these days but the Lord's instrument and your own, sir, of course. I will serve you both faithfully.'

'Listen,' James says, 'forget what I said earlier about no undue brutality. Wait upon me when I return from Newmarket, give me Edmund Godfrey's pocketbook and I will double your reward.'

63

OLD ACQUAINTANCES MEET
EARLY OCTOBER, 1678

Whilst the King and his brother are enjoying their sport at Newmarket with Mr Pepys Captain Charles Atkins is making his way through Holborn fields when he is approached by an old seafaring acquaintance. Mr Child is the opposite of his name; there is nothing innocent or naive in his nature. He's big and muscular. His greying hair and beard flow long and wild and his angry eyes stare over Atkin's head into the distance: Neptune lacking his trident. The captain has no great liking for the man but they share a neediness and an anger that ill fortune has forced upon them.

'I thought I'd find you here,' Child says. 'Walk with me. I have something private to say to you.'

Captain Atkins is uneasy. He makes his apologies. 'I am busy today.'

Child is persuasive. 'I have a proposition that will interest you. There's rich pickings you won't want to miss. We'll meet tomorrow night; somewhere where we can talk secretly.'

He points across the fields. 'The Three Tobacco Pipes yonder will suit our purpose.'

The following night finds them in a shed in the back part of the tavern. Captain Atkins is sitting with his back to the house and Mr Child with his back to the garden and after the master of the house has brought a pot of ale they are alone and Child comes straight to the point. 'I want you to assist me in the killing of a man.'

The captain is shocked. 'What man?'

'A magistrate.'

'Who knows of this?'

'You and I and others who will pay a mighty great reward for the deed.'

'What others? Why do they want him dead?'

Child shakes his head. 'That is not for me to say.'

'You know that I am not afraid to do anything for a good reward, but I could never commit highway robbery, let alone kill a man.'

Child is insistent. 'You will not be required to pull the rope around his neck or thrust the sword through his heart; you will be my assistant only.' He stands to leave. 'I'll give you eight or nine days to think on it.'

Captain Atkins has no intention of becoming involved in the killing. These days he is never really desperate for money. He can nip into the naval offices any time and seek young Sam who is always ready to dip into his pockets, for namesake, even though they are not related. Such charity keeps the captain going. If there was ever a man he'd willingly murder it would be Samuel Pepys who accused him of cowardice, ruined his naval career, caused his father to disown him, and forced him into a life of penury. A great hatred boils inside him. He has promised himself that one day he will get his revenge.

Eight days pass and the old acquaintances meet again at the Three Cans tavern.

'I must decline your offer,' Captain Atkins says.

'If you will not agree to assist in the killing of this man you will have a hundred pounds to conceal it,' Child promises. 'But if you reveal any knowledge of it, I warn you, you will not live.'

'I can keep a secret, as you know,' the captain insists.

'Then you must assist me to do the deed to prove that this is so.'

Captain Atkins has nothing to say. He has no choice. How easily has Child coerced him into becoming an accessory to murder.

64

SATURDAY MORNING,
12ᵀᴴ OCTOBER, 1678

Miles Prance is in his shop on Princess Street, in Covent Garden, at nine o' clock in the morning helping a gentleman to select a gift for his godson's marriage when they come for him, disguised, of course, in dull grey clothes: two Jesuits of his acquaintance, a young priest he knows from Somerset House and an Irish priest, a short stocky man Prance never liked, who lodges occasionally at Henry Berry's alehouse. Nobody knows his name only his alias, Kelly. The Jesuits pretend an interest in his wares while they wait. The gentleman eventually chooses one of Prance's favourite pieces: a silver porringer, quite plain, save for a leafy border around the base and two scroll handles, each topped with a little cherubic face.

'Your godson and his wife will appreciate the quality of the piece,' Prance says. 'The simplicity of the design allows the craftsmanship of the decoration to catch the eye.'

When the customer has departed, the Jesuits charge Prance to be ready. 'There is a man who has ill designs against us; we need your help. Do not stray far from your shop. When it is time we will come for you.'

***

This morning, Edmund cannot make the simplest of decisions. He couldn't even decide which coat to wear. Walking across the yard he hesitates. Perhaps he should send Henry Moor to Wynnell with apologies that he cannot meet him at noon at Weldon's tavern. No, no, there will be time enough for Wynnell and the property sale despite the unexpected visitor this morning, wasting his time with a trivial matter that is no concern of a justice of the peace. He makes his way towards St Martin's Lane, halts beside the church and worries that perhaps he should have sent Henry with a message after all, but he cannot think any more of Wynnell; there are matters of far greater import to settle today. But first, a walk into the country. He needs to think while he walks; clear his head for the confrontations to come. He knows that he will have no peace until he speaks his mind. He knows that his adversaries wait for him. A great force other than his own will is pulling him along London's morning streets and he is powerless against it.

He meets Parsons, the churchwarden.

'I am taking the air to Paddington Woods,' he says, to take control of the conversation, to steer the talk away from Titus Oates and the Plot.

'Are you going to buy the place, to stock up your woodyard?' Parsons jokes.

'What is that to you?' he replies, in no mood for humour. 'I must be on my way. I hope to walk as far as Primrose Hill, time permitting.'

Parsons, obsequious as ever, informs him of a route to Primrose Hill through fields and gates, as if Edmund has never walked in that direction, although he knows that he has. The churchwarden has served his purpose. If ill should befall him today during this unexpected assignation out in the countryside, his brothers will know where to seek him.

In Marylebone he passes people who know him. A

milkwoman, whose name he never knew, delays him with her gossip and he has a devil of a job excusing himself before she pours a dish of milk down his throat. He has no time to walk the further mile to Primrose Hill.

'Bah,' he says. 'This rendezvous is not of my choosing. Let the man wait,' and he retraces his steps. Crossing a field at Paddington Woods he pauses to speak with Thomas Mason, an acquaintance from the vestry. Back in St Martin's Lane several people doff their hats to him and talk briefly of nothing, only the weather, how fair and dry is has become, but getting colder and looking like rain. No one dares to say, I have heard that you are to be hung for treason, but he is sure that this is what they are all thinking.

Reaching Charing Cross he hails a shoeshine boy and rests each foot on his stool while the boy scrapes the countryside mud from his shoes and shines them with a rancid mixture of soot and stale oil. He is ready now, he has to be, he has delayed long enough. His own warm hearth and Elizabeth Curtis' endless dishes of hot chocolate are close but he must wait for these dubious comforts, the better to try to enjoy them when the day's business is completed. As he approaches the Cockpit a clock chimes a quarter hour after eleven. People he knows give him 'Good day.' Lord Danby's daughter recognises him and smiles; he doffs his hat. When she is out of sight he strides to her father's door purposefully, as if he is confident that the outcome of the meeting will favour himself. Afterwards, surely, there will be time enough to walk to Weldon's tavern to meet Wynnell at noon. Lord Danby will not allow him to interrupt his morning for many minutes. It is the Lord Treasurer's way to be brisk, being a busy man who has no time for other men's dilemmas, only his own. Well, Lord Danby will have a serious dilemma when he has heard what he, Godfrey, has to say.

Even as Danby's man, Lloyd, opens the door and he steps inside, he knows that it is badly done, this decision to confront the Lord Treasurer. Danby has his own more pressing worries: the Tower. He has been negotiating a secret deal with King Louis, a bribe worth a huge amount of money but Parliament has got to know of this. Danby has, of course, been dealing on behalf of the King and York, but will they admit this? No: not in the present anti-Catholic, anti-French climate. And Danby must have arranged this deal most unwillingly, he being strongly anti-French at heart. Well, the Lord Treasurer has compromised his personal integrity for political gain and he deserves what is coming to him.

He waits for Danby to call for him. He doesn't carry a pocket watch but he is aware of the passing of time. Lloyd is courteous, invites him to partake of refreshment, 'A glass of warm ale, Sir Edmund, to fight off the cold, or brandy, perhaps?' He came here to talk, he tells the manservant, somewhat impatiently; if he wanted drink, he would go to a tavern. 'But I thank you kindly,' he adds, seeing a flare of irritation flash across Lloyd's usually expressionless countenance.

At least half an hour passes before Lloyd comes again. 'Lord Danby has a moment to speak with you now, Sir Edmund.'

'What is the matter?' Danby asks without looking up from a paper he is reading, as if he does not know what all London knows: that he, Edmund, is living in fear of the hangman's noose because Dr Oates told him of the Popish Plot and he told nobody, not the Lord Chief Justice nor the Attorney General nor the Lord Treasurer: only his friend, the traitor Edward Coleman. He has no choice but to come straight to the point.

'Am I to be called to appear before Parliament, to explain myself?'

'Maybe, maybe not. I really cannot say.' Danby flicks through his papers, quill in hand, adding a quick signature now and then. He doesn't look up when he says, 'You will be informed bye and bye, Sir Edmund, if necessary.'

What did he expect? How ever could he have thought that Danby would listen quietly at his desk while he explained the flaws in Oates' articles: the ridiculous accusations against John Grove – that he had started a fire that burned his own home in Southwark; the laughable failures of the would-be assassins to kill the King; the audacious allegation that tens of thousands of Irish and Catholics are armed, ready to rise against the King? The words he had practised earlier while he walked spill out of his mouth and he cannot stop them.

'I have visited Dr Oates, and discussed certain matters with him. The discoverer confirmed to me that he informed you, my lord, of the Popish Plot before ever he came to me with his first forty-three articles.'

The Lord Treasurer has put down his quill. He leaves his desk and comes close, his blond eyebrows meeting in a frown, his pale eyes slits of anger. 'Ah, but Joseph Williamson and I, we did not read the very lengthy deposition that Titus Oates waved before our noses; we sniffed it and smelled a plot. So we sent him to a justice of the peace, the best we knew, who would give the articles the due consideration for which we did not have the time, and we expected that justice to tell us what Oates had discovered.'

'Dr Oates had already informed the King…'

'The King has a Catholic wife and a Catholic brother,' Danby snaps. 'He cannot involve himself in the investigation of this plot for fear of saying and doing too much or too little; those are His Majesty's very words.'

Edmund walks away from the Cockpit knowing that he should never have let it come to this: the great Lord Danby and himself, two men facing each other in a duel, each accusing the other of misprision of treason.

'God's providence is good indeed,' Thomas Blood says to himself. For having waited in the cold for Sir Edmund to leave his house this morning and followed him out into the country and back again without ever having an opportunity of approaching him alone in a secluded place, he had thought his luck was out. When the magistrate went into the Lord Treasurer's house, he had walked away to warm himself in a coffee house. But here is Sir Edmund, at Charing Cross, passing through the crowds with his stick in his hand and his sword at his side. The magistrate looks down at the cobbles as if to avoid any casual meeting with acquaintances, hidden as he is under his wide brimmed hat. Blood shadows him, ducking in and out amongst shopkeepers' wares laid out on the street and clusters of gossiping housewives with their baskets. When the magistrate is distracted, maybe stepping out of the way of a carriage or a cart or one of the heaps of horse shit that litters the way, it will be an easy thing to creep up behind him and slip his hand inside his coat pockets; a boy with very little training could do it.

But Blood can't do it, not yet. Sir Edmund has a way of glancing to one side, then another, and every so often he turns and looks behind. Ah, thinks Blood, does he know that he is being dogged? Or is he on the lookout for popish plotters: Jesuit assassins who seek an opportunity to murder him because, thanks to Titus Oates, he knows too much about their plans? He prepares himself for a long wait, for the magistrate is close to home and probably wanting his dinner, but he walks straight past Hartshorne Lane and pauses to speak with an oilman outside his shop on the Strand. Blood turns, watches the passing traffic as if he is waiting to cross the road, but he's close enough to hear their conversation. Sir Edmund, being deaf, speaks louder than ordinary and Blood clearly hears him tell the oilman that he has no time to accept his invitation to dine because he has urgent business matters to attend to and must hurry away. Now what business would that be? Blood wonders.

It's a long walk following the magistrate north along Drury Lane in the cold and the drizzle and Blood is missing his dinner. He manages to grab a pie from a hawker and throws his coins into the basket without losing sight of Sir Edmund. Strangely, those two men who have been dogging him all week are not around today. This makes his task much easier, although Blood half wishes that they were here, that he could discover who they are and their purpose in stalking the magistrate. York might reward him grandly for such news.

The opportunity comes suddenly of course, as such opportunities do. Blood has just time enough to pull off his gloves in readiness. Sir Edmund turns into one of the little streets near Wild Street. Well now, Blood thinks, the Duke will be interested in this bit of information. Can it be that this justice of the peace, to whom Titus Oates brought his discoveries of the Hellish Popish Plot, is visiting Jesuits at their residence at Wild House nearby? Godfrey ducks under a low archway into a narrow alley and Blood, coming up close behind slips his hand into Sir Edmund's right coat pocket and feels the hard leather of what must be the magistrate's pocketbook. Sir Edmund is quick, as if all along he has been preparing for the assault. He turns and raises his stick but Blood grabs it and pushes him down onto the ground. Sir Edmund is on his knees, twisting his body around trying to raise himself but the sword in the scabbard hanging by his side is getting in the way. Blood thrashes him with the stick and kicks him in his chest once, twice, thrice, until he lies on his back quite still, blocking the alley.

Blood doesn't care whether the magistrate is dead or alive and Duke won't care either once he is in possession of the pocketbook. He makes a quick search of Godfrey's pockets before he flees. It surprises him that the magistrate carries such a large amount of money on his person wrapped in little paper packets, and also, apart from the ring he wears, there are two more rings in one of his pockets. He's tempted to reward himself with a diamond ring and a packet of guineas but it's too easy: where's the excitement, the fear of being caught, the exhilaration of fleeing with the booty after a daring assault? No, he has the pocketbook, he has done what he has been asked to do. These days he is a reformed man: he's neither a common thief nor a footpad. He is employed in the Duke's service and will be well rewarded for doing his duty.

65

SATURDAY AFTERNOON,
12TH OCTOBER, 1678

Nausea brings him back to consciousness. He shouldn't loiter in this dim, stinking alley where old jettied houses block out the light. This is a place where men go to urinate, drunks to vomit and whores to ply their trade. Passing cut-throats and nose-slitters will rejoice to find a gentleman with money in his pockets waiting for them like a donkey-eared performer at a fair preparing for flying puddings. He drags himself through the pain until he sits resting his back against the wall. Church clocks are chiming half past the hour, but he has no idea what hour it is, two or three? To call for constables would be useless: his attacker has fled. Anyway, he couldn't bear the shame of revealing himself as a victim of crime – he, whose life's work has been to arrest and convict such felons.

He pulls off his gloves and feels inside his coat pockets. The realisation that nothing is missing except his pocketbook hits him worse than the assault upon his body. Yesterday evening he burned every letter Edward Coleman had sent from abroad. He should have thrown the pocketbook into the fire with them. He would have done if he had been thinking clearly. No common footpad has taken the pocketbook, of this he is sure; his assailant is on Lord Danby's payroll or else the Duke of York's: who else would want it? The man has followed him from the Cockpit and will run to Danby with his prize.

He tugs at the linen band around his neck. Suddenly, it is choking him. He straightens his wig, replaces his hat and reaching for his stick manages to stand. Still he hesitates, unsure of what to do or where to go. The loss of the pocketbook with the evidence of Coleman's expectation of a Catholic revolution will be the end of him; this he knows. His lifetime dedication to duty has been crushed by a chain of events instigated by two men: Titus Oates and Edward Coleman. He has dealt with each of them according to his conscience – the one as a conscientious magistrate, the other as a friend. Both will destroy him. Only God can help him now. He closes his eyes in prayer.

Let not my quietus come by the hangman's rope,

Nor let the Thames swallow me into a common grave with the unknown, the unhappy and the murdered.

Let me just slip away and be gone.

God answers the dutiful magistrate with a stab of conscience that pains him more than his physical hurt. He has business to complete this day. Men guilty of great wickedness must be brought to justice.

***

He turns out of the alley and onto Wild Street leaning on his stick and holding himself where his assailant kicked him. Oh, that his friend Valentine Greatrakes were here with his healing hands to stroke away the pain. Minutes later he is tapping on a door. He removes his hat, stoops under the low doorway and slips inside.

He came here, to Wild House, just a few weeks ago to warn John Grove of Titus Oates' lies. The Jesuits will not like what he will tell them today, but for the love he bears his friend he will not shy away from his duty. He will speak of what he has discovered, he will accuse, and the Jesuits will not, cannot, deny the truth of it. A young priest takes him to a chair by the fireside and brings warm ale. Beneath the hospitality, the concerns about his comfort, there is a silence, a sadness. Nay, it is more than that. He senses a deep, unspoken misery stained with the wrath of the accused.

When he has warmed himself he asks to be taken to Father Whitbread. He had expected hostility but the priest only nods and conducts him to the sick English Provincial's bedchamber.

'Sir Edmund Godfrey has something he wishes to discuss with you, Father, if you feel well enough,' the priest says, removing his clerical hat and running his hand nervously through his thin, fair hair which frames his prematurely balding pate.

Father Whitbread tries to lift his grey head from the pillows. There is something childish and trusting about the large grey eyes staring from such a small face. His voice is weak and Edmund cannot hear what he says even when he puts his ear close to Whitbread's mouth and smells sickness on his breath, bitter and putrid. 'Pray, what did your master say?' he asks of the priest.

'He begs you to speak with your friend, Lord Chief Justice Scroggs, to plead on behalf of the Jesuits and the Catholic Lords who are accused of treason.'

Would that I could, he says to himself. To Father Whitbread he says, 'I have grave matters to discuss. I have seen terrible things...'

'Hush, you see how ill he is,' the young priest interrupts, angrily. 'Your business must wait until he is well.'

'When he is well he will be indicted and incarcerated and it will be too late,' Edmund retorts. 'Listen, Father,' he says gently to the man on the bed, 'I have discovered a great evil that is happening at a club in Fuller's Rents, the Pheasant. There I saw Jesuits doing abominable things that I would never have believed of your people whose vocation is to educate young boys, to train their minds and enlighten their souls.'

Father Whitbread's owl eyes stare red-rimmed and ghastly from his grey countenance. He is coughing now, badly. A nurse appears from nowhere with a bowl for him to hawk into.

'Did the Pheasant club please you when paid your visit last week?' the priest says menacingly as he steers him away from the sickroom.

Edmund ignores the attempt to malign his character. 'You were there also?' he asks the priest.

'We are concerned. We are keeping an eye on that den of vice,' the priest promptly replies, but he looks away when he speaks and Edmund ponders that maybe it is Jesuits who have dogged him around London these last days; lay brothers or priests in their disguises who wish him ill because he knows too much.

'I am a magistrate; my life's work is to eliminate lawlessness and evil, and I have never been afraid to do my duty,' he tells the young priest. 'I believed that if there were any truth at all to be found hiding inside Titus Oates' eighty-one lies, I would find it in that place. I confronted Oates twice on this account, but he would talk of nothing but plots and treason, so I went directly from his lodgings at Whitehall to Fuller's Rents. There, at the Pheasant club, to my horror, I was offered, for my pleasure, boys no older than sixteen, some much younger. If I inform Lord Chief Justice Scroggs of this, every Jesuit who remains in London will be accused of these abominable acts. I thought it better for Father Whitbread to deal discreetly with the Jesuit perpetrators of this evil: to cut off the infected branch to save the tree.'

'I see your point,' the young priest says, 'but we cannot trouble Father Whitbread; you have seen how sick he is. I will convene an urgent meeting between ourselves and a committee of priests and lay brothers, most of whom are presently in hiding, of course. Meet us this evening at the watergate at Somerset House. We will be safe from prying eyes inside the Queen's house.'

***

He passes through Lincoln's Inn and inquires for lawyer, Richard Adams.

'You called upon me early this morning while I was out,' he says. 'What is the matter?'

'I called twice,' Adams replies. 'Shaftesbury and Buckingham wish you to wait upon them.'

'I am done with those two lords, and they know it,' he replies tersely. 'When the King is shot dead and the revolution begins, you and I will know who to blame. The Jesuits are but the scapegoats that Titus Oates has fortuitously provided.'

Adams accompanies him to the back door. 'What shall I tell Shaftesbury and Buckingham?'

'Tell Buckingham to cease his lewd behaviour with whores and to pay the poor money that he owes to St Martin's vestry; the overseers need it to pay for medical services and food for the miserable poor of the parish. And tell Shaftesbury,' he adds wearily, 'that I am tired of keeping other men's treasonous secrets. I have more pressing concerns.'

At Holborn Turnstile he goes west. He will walk as far as St Giles churchyard where the mutilated remains of traitors are buried. He will warm himself in the tavern opposite the church, a low establishment, where condemned men travelling to the hanging tree at Tyburn are traditionally offered a glass of ale to fortify them for their ordeal.

It is not for his own sake that he has set out upon this mournful pilgrimage. The afternoon is not a rehearsal for his own death pageant. No, he walks for gentle John Grove and for rash, boastful, Edward Coleman. He walks to prepare their way. When their time comes, their death sledges will drag them over the path he walked today and they will feel that he is with them: that they follow in his footsteps. This is all he can do for his friends.

***

The gentleman is walking slowly from St Giles Church out towards the countryside leaning heavily on his stick. His head is bent into the wind and he is holding one arm around his chest as if in pain. Francis Corrall reins in his horses and waits atop his little yellow hackney carriage with its bright red wheels.

'Can I take you anywhere, sir?' he calls.

The gentleman asks to be taken along the Tottenham Court Road, and as far as the road will take him into Primrose Hill and to wait for him there. 'A strange time of day to take the air, in this lonely place,' Corrall says to his horses as he wraps his coat tightly around himself and buries his nose in his muffler. 'The wind is getting up and soon it will be too dark for the gentleman to find his way back to the road.'

No one is waiting for him at the White House tavern.

'What?' he asks. 'Nobody came today enquiring for me, Sir Edmund Godfrey?'

'No, sir, no one has asked for you. Only a couple of local men dined here, around noon,' landlord Rawson says. 'We're never busy this time of year.'

'He said he would wait. He said he would stay here all day until it was convenient for me to come to him.'

'May I ask the gentleman's name, Sir Edmund?' the landlord asks. 'If he lives in these parts I'll send for him to come at once.'

He takes a crumpled paper out of his pocket. 'I do not know the man,' he tells the landlord. 'He left a message yesterday evening asking to meet me at your house today at a time of my own convenience. Bah, if he chooses not to come it is nothing to me except that he wastes my time.' He throws the letter into the fire and departs.

Ah, he thinks, as he walks towards the lantern light of the waiting hackney carriage. It is clear to me now why the writer of that note failed to keep his assignation at the White House. The man has followed me all day and has taken away what he sought before ever I reached Primrose Hill.

66

SATURDAY EVENING,
12TH OCTOBER, 1678

Miles Prance, only a little the worse for drink, is in a public house near his shop in Covent Garden with his friend, William Boyce, a glass eye maker, when they seek him out again in the late afternoon.

'Something has happened. Go home, fetch your verger's gown,' they tell him. 'Meet us at Somerset House this evening at nine.'

'I don't know what these Jesuits want of me,' Prance complains to his wife as he stuffs his purple gown under his coat. 'And I don't know whether I will want to do it. I don't trust this Irish priest, Kelly.'

'Don't go, Miles,' his wife says. 'You owe them nothing; you are a Protestant now.'

'They say I am a still good Catholic in my heart and there is a service I can do for the Roman Church. It is a great honour,' Prance says, whilst he adjusts his wig, 'and they will pay me well, you know.'

***

Edmund asks the hackney coachman to take him directly to Somerset House. Two Jesuits wearing their ubiquitous grey disguises wait by the watergate illuminated by lantern light. One is the young priest he met at Wild House this afternoon. The other, an Irish priest, short and stocky who goes by the name of Kelly, he had encountered last week in the Pheasant club at Fuller's Rents. Two other men stand with them. Edmund recognises the disgraced sea captain, Atkins, a beggar by trade, and Mr Child, a ship's purser whom he knows to be a rogue living on the fringes of lawlessness. They turn away, refuse to acknowledge him.

The porter opens the wicket gate and the Jesuits lead him through a passage into the great courtyard of Somerset House, and up a set of stairs. They pass a piazza on the left, descend another set of stairs and enter a small chamber overlooking the garden.

There is a good coal fire and the chamber is well lit. He removes his sword and hat and the young priest assists him with his coat. A table is set with inkhorns, pens, paper and new wax candles. The priests pull their cassocks and gold crucifixes over their layman's attire. Another man sits at the table. He wears a purple gown, such as a verger in the Queen's chapel might wear. Edmund realises that this man is not unknown to him. He is Queen Catherine's Catholic silversmith, a most annoying and conceited man who came before him some time ago at Hicks Hall county sessions, arguing that the Queen's servants were exempt from parish duties. The silversmith is nervous. His flaxen wig sits badly and he keeps tugging at it, like a man unused to wearing one.

'Pray, be seated, Sir Edmund.' The young priest indicates a single chair at the opposite side of the table, and before a word is spoken he sees that the three of them have set themselves up as a jury, and himself as the accused.

'Mr Prance will be our recorder,' the young priest says, pushing the writing materials towards the silversmith.

'Now then, Sir Edmund, what is the matter?' Father Kelly asks.

'You know what is the matter.'

'Ah, the little boys at Fuller's Rents. You blame our Jesuits for their depravity.'

'It is you I accuse of depravity, of vile practices—'

'Pray, do not shout, Sir Edmund,' Kelly interrupts, putting his hands to his ears. 'We are not hard of hearing.'

'The boys were innocent and you have spoiled them with your vile acts.'

The silversmith is plainly horrified. He shakes his head and looks to each of the priests, frowning. Father Kelly reaches for a jug and pours dark wine into Edmund's glass. The wine is good. He finds that he is thirsty and drains his glass. Father Kelly refills it. He drinks again.

'You, I accuse, not the boys,' he says, stabbing his finger towards Father Kelly. 'You are culpable, all of you,' he charges the young priest, 'every member of the Society of Jesus. You all knew what was happening. You looked away. You did nothing.'

'I suppose Titus Oates failed to inform you that Protestants also visit that club,' Father Kelly says. 'His own schoolmaster frequents that place. Go to them, the Protestants, and make your accusations. We won't be your scapegoats.'

'You cannot blame others to cover your own guilt.'

'We deny every word that spews out of the mouth of Titus Oates.' The young priest thumps his fist on the table. One of the candles falls from its holder, spilling droplets of wax onto Edmund's clothes. The silversmith rights it before it sets the papers alight.

'Do you call me a liar?' Edmund demands. 'I visited the Pheasant to witness for myself what was happening in that club which Oates described as a den of sedition, and I found a worse evil. I talked to the boys. They told me what you did to them, how you took them from the streets, from their families. A negro they call Black Tom, was stolen from his master, a surgeon I know well.'

The two Jesuits confer with each other in whispers.

'I came here to settle this matter outside of the law,' he says angrily, turning to the young priest. 'I want to save your society from the disgrace, to allow you to punish your priest here, and other guilty men of your society, privately. Where are your superiors? Where is the committee you promised to hear this case?'

'We are here and we have listened, Sir Edmund,' the young priest replies dryly.

'And we do not like what you say,' Father Kelly adds.

He stands. He is dizzy. It was foolish to drink strong wine when he has fasted all day. 'I see no point in continuing this consultation,' he declares. 'You give me no choice. Tomorrow, I shall wait upon my Lord Chief Justice…'

'It need not come to that.' The voice is thin, but strong; taut as a tendon. An elderly father has entered the chamber.

'Good evening Father Strange,' the young priest says.

The former English Provincial shuffles towards the table and takes a seat beside Father Kelly. 'This shouldn't be my concern,' he says wearily. 'I've been living quietly, enjoying my retirement, taking pleasure from my books. And now this.'

'With respect, it is your concern,' Father Kelly says, with derision. 'You let Titus Oates into our Society. It is he who sent this magistrate to snoop around in the Pheasant.'

'Oates was destitute; indeed, he was starving,' Strange says. 'I saw that he was a coarse, vulgar man of low breeding but he professed such an interest in converting to the True Church that I could not deny him. And later, when he returned from Spain, he walked in the snow with holes in his shoes. What could I do?' He holds out his hands in supplication. 'By that time he knew too much. He walked through our doors and he saw everything that we do, even the things that shame us.'

'But Father, everything Titus Oates says is a lie,' the young priest cuts in.

'A few days ago,' Strange replies sternly, 'after Titus Oates had finished telling his eighty-one lies, he directed you, Sir Edmund, to the Pheasant; to discover a terrible truth. Why he did this I can only surmise.'

He believed that I would wish to partake of the sinful depravity I would find there, Edmund says to himself, and thus paid me the worst insult I have ever suffered.

The silversmith has put down his quill and buried his face in his hands. Black lice are crawling through his flaxen curls.

'Oates couldn't have discovered more about us, I tell you,' Strange says, his voice stronger now, 'even if he had followed us into the confessional. He gave me no choice. I had to keep him with us. Sir Edmund,' he says, 'you are known to be a furiously diligent justice of the peace. You could be the ruin of our society; we know that. Pray, let us get this matter resolved to everyone's satisfaction. Do not let the vile actions of one or two men ruin the good reputation of our Society. If my men swear on oath never to visit that den of sin ever again, will you keep your side of the bargain and save us from disgrace?'

'I will,' he replies simply. 'But you must know that I will visit the Pheasant from time to time to ensure that all is well. I will return Black Tom to his master and find honest employment for the other two boys.'

'Have you recorded in the minutes that Sir Edmund visited the boys in the Pheasant?' Kelly asks Prance, grabbing the paper, whist he looks the magistrate straight in the eye and Edmund becomes horribly aware that in his eagerness to seek a wisp of truth from Titus Oates he has made himself vulnerable to shocking accusations of a personal and shameful nature and he realises, too late, that he should confiscate the silversmith's notes. He also realises that he is feeling very sick.

'I need some fresh air,' he mutters and stumbles towards the door.

'It's getting late,' the silversmith complains. 'My wife will be worried.' It is the first time he has spoken.

'We will not detain you much longer, Mr Prance,' Father Strange says. 'Our business is done. Conduct Sir Edmund out of the palace and then you may return to your wife in Covent Garden.'

'Aye,' says Kelly. 'Go to your bed, also, Father Strange. Sir Edmund has expressed a willingness to be kind to our society for his friend, John Grove's sake. Our business here is done.'

The silversmith leads him through the palace, carrying his coat, hat and stick. Father Kelly having removed his priestly garb accompanies them with his sword. They come to a bench in a corner at the bottom of a steep descent adjoining a rail near the stables.

'Leave me here to rest awhile,' Edmund says.

The silversmith gives him his hat and stick and puts his coat around his shoulders. Father Kelly sits beside him and addresses him insolently, without his title. 'You will not disgrace us, Edmund Godfrey, we will not let you shame our society.'

The courtyard is well lit, lanterns hang above doorways and link boys with their flaming torches accompany visitors on their way, but in this dark corner Edmund can barely see the faces of the men around him. It seems that two glasses of dark wine have made him very drunk. Thankfully, the courtyard is busy, for the King is here playing the good husband: visiting his wife. The privy guards are pacing about in pairs and several riders, ladies and gentlemen, are dismounting while grooms run forward to lead their horses to the stables. But the problem is that he is feeling too weak to stand and this is surely more than the effects of fasting and strong wine. He knows now that Father Kelly has drugged him.

Captain Atkins and Child have been hanging around waiting for him to leave; this much is obvious to Edmund. They make their way through the courtyard and stand behind the bench by the railings arrogantly infiltrating his space. It comes to him of a sudden, through the nausea, that he is not wearing his sword and these men wish him harm. He rises unsteadily.

'So, you did not enjoy your visit to the Pheasant?' Father Kelly asks menacingly. 'Let me assure you that never again will you be our guest.'

Leaning on his stick Edmund rises and half staggers in the direction of the porter's lodge. The silversmith walks beside him and the others follow a pace behind.

John Oakley, a servant to a neighbour on Hartshorne Lane passes by while he stands by the watergate waiting for a hackney cab. He doffs his hat and Edmund acknowledges him.

***

Two men assist the passenger into the carriage and sit with him. It's the same tall, stooping gentleman Francis Corrall took north into the countryside earlier.

'He's a little the worse for drink,' one of them says.

The inebriate gentleman utters something Corrall cannot comprehend, but he thinks he is asking to be taken home.

'Wait coachman,' another man says in an Irish brogue, 'you have forgotten our friend.' He grabs a man wearing a purple gown beneath his coat, and pushes him inside.

'Do your work now, Child,' he hisses to the men inside the cab. 'Drive to Fuller's Rents,' he orders Corrall as he slams the door shut, 'but first, make a stop at Covent Garden.'

Edmund hears the din of the blinds being pulled down at the windows. Inside the carriage there is not a pinhole of light and the strange thing is this: the clarity of his hearing.

'Who are you?' Prance asks of the other two men, and Edmund feels the silversmith's fear.

The weight of a heavy man's body is pressing upon Edmund and he smells the foul breath of a common man used to a diet of onions, old meat and bad beer. He can barely breathe for the pressure on his chest, and worse, for someone is tightening the linen band at his throat until his thoughts seem to fly away from his head and he is looking down upon himself in the darkness of the carriage, watching himself die. 'My brothers and my dear cousin Mary will not know where to find me,' he cries before his ears are assaulted by a low keening, and he cannot be sure whether it comes from inside himself or from the silversmith sitting beside him.

They push up the blinds and by the light of the coach's swinging lanterns, Prance sees the magistrate slumped in his seat with his neckband pulled tight in a knot and knows that he is dead. He just cannot stop his legs from jerking and his shoes from banging on the floor and a terrible pain is stabbing inside his bladder.

'Let me out,' he stammers, through chattering teeth, 'before I piss myself.'

'All in good time, Mr Prance,' one of the murderers says, 'when we reach Covent Garden, as planned.' He presses his hands on Prance's knees to try to keep them still.

The Irish priest, Kelly, is waiting for him by the square

in Covent Garden, holding a lantern in one hand and the reigns of a brown horse in the other.

'The magistrate is dead,' Prance wails, while he turns to relieve his bladder beside the horse. 'Those men murdered him.'

'Well,' Kelly says, matter of fact, 'if we could not have enticed him inside the cab, I would have followed him down Hartshorne Lane that leads to his own house, and run him through with his own sword.'

'Where are they taking him?' Prance asks. 'They should throw him in the Thames, and be done.'

'The magistrate will lie in state in an outhouse at the Pheasant club in Fuller's Rents for a day or two. Appropriate, don't you think?'

'These men who strangled Godfrey, who are they?'

'Mr Child did the business with Godfrey's neckcloth and Captain Atkins was his assistant, as are you. You are all in this together,' Kelly retorts. 'But what is that to me? I'll be far from here when the body is found.'

'So will I,' Prance says, almost in tears. 'I don't know why you asked me to come. I have taken no part in the deed except to sit beside a man being murdered by men I did not know. Just pay me what you promised and I will take my business away from London and forget what just happened. I didn't kill him. They did. I played no part in it.'

'Oh, but you are part of it now,' Kelly says. 'You are an accessory to a murder. However, your real contribution is yet to come. Take this horse, you will need it. Go nowhere, Mr Prance, wait in your shop. In a day or two someone will visit you to explain what more you are required to do.'

Before the week is out, Francis Corrall will know, without any doubt, the name of the gentleman he had carried in his coach. Everybody will be talking about it; the dead body of

Edmund Godfrey that was discovered dumped in a ditch at Primrose Hill with his own sword sticking through his chest. And Corrall will fool himself no more. The magistrate was alive when he was helped into his coach and dead when he was carried out at Fuller's Rents with his arms around the shoulders of two men. This isn't something a man can keep to himself in the tavern of an evening with his drinking companions, but he's careful not to tell the whole truth, to keep the Pheasant out of the story. So he boasts to his friends that he had carried the dead magistrate to Primrose Hill. What is worse, as the days go by and further details of the death emerge from the inquest, that Edmund Godfrey was strangled to death, Corrall realises with horror that the murderers left their evidence behind in his coach: Edmund Godfrey's neckband: the murder weapon. When his wife is out, he throws it into the fire.

67

MONDAY, 14TH OCTOBER, 1678

Father Kelly visits Prance, disguised, of course, in his grey suit of clothes. He gives Prance a bag and a silver topped stick.

'Hide these in your shop.'

'No,' Prance says, 'I've done enough. I'll do nothing more. I've not received a penny for my trouble. What I did, I did most unwillingly. I wanted no part of it.'

A man and a woman enter the shop. They smile at Prance and wait politely. The lady draws her husband's attention to a set of folding spoons embellished with figures on the handles.

'You're part of it now,' Kelly hisses into Prance's ear. 'Pray, attend to your customers, Mr Prance,' he says aloud.

'Madam, examine the spoons, if you please,' Prance says. 'Such fine quality pieces. They were crafted before the late troubled times, during His martyred Majesty's reign.'

'Before you receive your payment you must take a ride into the country and find a place to deposit Godfrey's body,' Kelly says after the customers have left. 'Somewhere where it will remain safely hidden until the priests have fled.'

'The Dead Wall in Leicester Fields?' Prance suggests.

Alone in his shop, Prance opens the bag. What did he expect to find? Fireballs? Pistols? It is only a pair of gloves, a sword scabbard and a belt, in all their murderous innocence.

68

WEDNESDAY NIGHT,
16TH OCTOBER, 1678

Prance opens the gates and holds the lantern while the other two lead a horse and cart piled high with hay.

'Whoever drives a hay cart at night?' Prance complains as they make their way through the Primrose Hill fields. 'If someone happens upon us on his way home from the tavern, it will look mighty suspicious.'

'Just get on with the job, and stop moaning,' Captain Atkins chides.

Prance is terrified and he cannot understand why the other two men are so unruffled. 'I know this place and people here know me. All week, soldiers have been hedge-hog hunting and local men have been beating for a hare. They might return.'

They come to a ditch partly hidden by a thicket.

'We had to pay a butcher, Edward Linnet, three guineas for the hire of his cart,' Captain Atkins complains.

'Did you tell him why you needed it?' Prance asks and hears his voice crack.

'Do you think we are fools?'

'He will guess the purpose soon enough,' Child retorts, 'and have the sense to keep his mouth shut.'

'Has the broker, Owen of Bloomsbury, paid you, Mr Prance?' Captain Atkins asks. '

'No. I cannot find the man. Have you been paid?'

'You cannot expect to be paid until the job is complete,' Child declares.

'Throw him in the ditch quickly, cover him with brambles and let us be gone,' Prance urges.

Child tells him to take hold of the corpse's shoulders while they lower it, face down, into the grave.

Prance backs away. 'I can't touch him, don't ask me…'

'Do it,' he growls. 'It's what you're being paid for.'

For a moment, standing there in the twilight, while Godfrey's long nose pushes against his chest, Prance closes his eyes and fools himself that all of this is not happening. He will wake to find himself lying in bed with his wife and she will be scolding him for eating oysters before bedtime and waking her with his bad dreams.

'See here, Mr Prance,' Child says, bringing him back into the nightmare. 'Sir Edmund Godfrey has killed himself.'

He sees that the corpse's coat covers his head and the waistcoat and shirt are all bunched up and several inches of steel protrude out of its back.

'Thank God this is the last of it,' Prance utters, as they throw brambles over the body.

'Now listen. Tell no one, especially Father Kelly, where we really hid the body.'

69

THURSDAY, 17TH OCTOBER, 1678

Father Kelly is knocking on Prance's door before he has partaken of his breakfast. 'It is almost time,' he says. Are you ready? Where did you hide the bag?'

Of course he's ready. He's been waiting for this day. They go through to his shop and Prance rummages in a corner amongst some boxes and brings out the bag.

'Where better to hide a gentleman's silver-topped stick than amongst your wares?' Kelly says, retrieving it from behind a pile of boxes.

'I was worried my wife would sell it to someone,' Prance complains.

'Carry the stick as if it were your own.'

'What? You're asking me to go through the streets with Godfrey's stick dangling by my side?' Prance cries. 'No, I won't do it. You carry it.'

'I'm not coming with you.'

'I won't go alone. Here, you take the bag and the stick and dispose of them; someone will surely see me throwing it into the river.' Prance's eyes fill with tears. 'I want an end to all this. I want my reward. You promised me that Mr Owen of Bloomsbury will be waiting for me at the Queen's Head in Bow with one hundred pounds in gold, for me to leave the city. I have been to that tavern every night and the landlord has never heard of him.'

'Listen,' Kelly snaps. 'You will get your reward when your work is finished. At noon you will be at the Dead Wall in Leicester Fields. You will leave Godfrey's things beside him as if he put them there himself so that his brothers would find him after he had fallen on his sword. Do not go searching in his coat pockets. His little parcels of money prove that he wasn't attacked by murdering footpads. The constables must find a suicide. If they find a murder our Jesuits will surely be blamed. Afterwards you will come home, pack up your chattels, your silverware and your wife, visit Owen at the Queen's Head, take your reward and start a new life with your family away from London. Remember, Mr Prance, be at Leicester Fields no earlier than noon, and no later.'

'Why so precise a time?' Prance asks. 'If somebody is around, I will have to wait a while.'

'At noon, one of our laymen will be in the bookshop in St Paul's churchyard spreading the word that Sir Edmund Godfrey lies by the Dead Wall in Leicester Fields, impaled with his own sword. Thus the constables will be prepared for a suicide, not a murder. Meanwhile, you will spread Godfrey's possessions near his body and stretch out his hand ready to be discovered by the next man passing by. Be quick, Mr Prance. Do not let the constables find you kneeling beside the corpse holding Godfrey's dead hand or dipping into his coat pockets.'

But this is precisely what Father Kelly has planned to happen: Prance is sure of this. For days now, he has been brooding over why Father Kelly dragged him into this affair and now he has the answer. He has been set up to be the scapegoat for the murder; it is his penance for converting to Protestantism. Well, when the constables go to the Dead

Wall at Leicester Fields, Prance will be far away at Primrose Hill.

At noon, a man has finished dressing his horse and is washing his hands in the pond near the ditch where the corpse lies. Prance lays the stick, scabbard, belt and gloves on the bank and it feels good to be doing this: he remembers Edmund Godfrey's cries just moments before he died. Very soon, the body will be discovered and his dear cousin and his brothers will know where he lies. Prance grabs the cold, dead hand and lays it on the bank. He is just about to reach down into the dead man's pockets when, seeing the man at the pond, mercifully with his back to him, he mounts the horse and flees.

Later that afternoon William Bromwell and John Waters, whilst walking from St Giles towards the White House tavern, meet Edward Linnet walking his dog. The dog sniffs around the ditch and they make their gruesome discovery.

SELECT BIBLIOGRAPHY/FURTHER READING

Beales, A.C.F.: *Education Under Penalty: English Catholic Education From The Reformation To The Fall of James II* (The Athlone Press University of London 1963)

Brandon, David: *Life in a 17th Century Coffee Shop* (The History Press 2007 e-book 2011)

Bryant, Arthur: *King Charles the Second* (Longmans Green and Co. 1931)

Carr, John Dickson: *The Murder of Sir Edmund Godfrey* (International Polygonics, Ltd. New York City 1989)

Defoe, Daniel: *A Journal of the Plague Year* (First Published 1722. Dover Thrift Editions 2001)

Elmer, Peter: *The Miraculous Conformist: Valentine Greatrakes, the Body Politic, and the Politics of Healing in Restoration Britain* (Oxford University Press 2013)

Etherington-Smith, Meredith: *The Private Life of a Royal Palace:* A contribution in *Somerset House The History* Edited by Meredith Etherington-Smith (Cultureshock Media for The Somerset House Trust 2009)

Evelyn, John: *The Diary of John Evelyn* Editor E.S. De Beer Introduced by Roy Strong (Everyman's Library 2006)

Falkus, Christopher: *The Life and Times of Charles II* Introduction by Antonia Fraser (George Weidenfeld and Nicolson Limited and Book Club Associates 1972)

Fraser, Antonia: *King Charles II* (Phoenix Paperback 2002)

Harris, Tim: *Restoration: Charles II and his Kingdoms* (Penguin Books 2006)

Hinds, Peter: *The Horrid Popish Plot: Roger L'Estrange and the Circulation of Political Discourse in Late-Seventeenth Century London* (Oxford University Press for the British Academy 2010)

Jordan, Don and Walsh, Michael: *The King's Bed: Sex Power and the Court of Charles II* (Little Brown Great Britain 2015)

Kenyon, John: *The Popish Plot* (Phoenix Press 2000)

Knight, Stephen: *The Killing of Justice Godfrey: An Investigation into England's Most Remarkable Unsolved Murder* (Grenada Publishing Limited 1984)

Lane, Jane: *Titus Oates* (Andrew Dakers Limited London 1949)

L'Estrange, Roger: *A Brief History of the Times, & in a Preface to the third Volume of Observators* (Printed for Charles Brome, at the Gun at the West-end of St. Paul's 1687 Reproduced by Early English Books Online and ProQuest from a copy in the The Huntington Library, San Marino, California)

L'Estrange, Roger: *Selections from the Observator (1681–1687)* Introduction by Violet Jordain (The Augustan Reprint Society California 1970)

Long, James and Long, Ben: *The Plot Against Pepys: Detection and Intrigue in 17th Century London* (Faber and Faber 2007 electronic edition)

Marks, Alfred: *Who Killed Sir Edmund Berry Godfrey?* Introduced by Father J. H. Pollen S.J. (Burns and Oates London 1905 and reprinted by BiblioBazaar Reproduction Series)

Marshall, Alan: *Intelligence and Espionage in the Reign of Charles II 1660-1685: Cambridge Studies In Early Modern History* (Cambridge University Press 1994)

Marshall, Alan: *The Strange Death of Edmund Godfrey: Plots and Politics In Restoration London* (Sutton Publishing Limited 1999)

Mortimer, Ian: *The Time Traveller's Guide to Restoration Britain: A Handbook for Visitors to the Years 1660–1700* (The Bodley Head London 2017)

Norrington, Ruth: *My Dearest Minette: Charles II to the Duchess d'Orléans* (Peter Owen 1996)

Oates, Titus: *An Additional Discovery of Mr. Roger L'Estrange His Further Discovery Of The Popish Plot Wherein Dr. Titus Oates And The Rest Of The King's Evidences Are Vindicated From The Aspersions Cast Upon Them In That Pamphlet* (1680) (Reproduced by Early English Books Online and ProQuest)

Pepys, Samuel: *The Diary of Samuel Pepys: The Complete Edition* Edited by Stephen Algieri (ebookworms 2011)

Pepys, Samuel: *The Illustrated Pepys from the Diary* Selected and Edited by Robert Latham (Bell & Hyman Limited London 1983)

Pepys, Samuel: *The Shorter Pepys from the Diary of Samuel Pepys, a new and complete transcription* Selected and Edited by Robert Latham (Bell & Hyman Limited London 1985)

Pepys, Samuel: *The Diary of Samuel Pepys,* Volumes One and Two, Edited by Ernest Rhys (Everyman's Library J. M. Dent & Sons Ltd. London 1906)

Picard, Lisa: *Restoration London: Everyday Life in London 1660–1670* (Phoenix Paperback 2003)

Pollock, John: *The Popish Plot – A Study in the History of the Reign of Charles II* (First published London: Duckworth and Co 1903: Classic Reprint Series, Forgotten Books, 2015)

Porter, Stephen: *Pepys's London – Everyday Life in London 1650–1703* (Amberley Publishing electronic edition 2012)

Prance, Miles: *A True Narrative and Discovery Of Several Very Remarkable Passages Relating To The Horrid Popish Plot: As They Fell Within The Knowledge Of Mr. Miles Prance Of Covent Garden, Goldsmith* (Dorman Newman Citizen and Stationer of London 1679) (Reproduced by Nabu Public Domain reprints USA)

Thomas, Keith: *Religion and the Decline of Magic: Studies in Popular Beliefs in Sixteenth and Seventeenth Century England* (Penguin Books 1971)

Thurley, Simon: *The Old Palace.* A contribution in *Somerset House The History* Edited by Meredith Etherington- Smith (Cultureshock Media for The Somerset House Trust 2009)

Uglow, Jenny: *A Gambling Man: Charles II and the Restoration* (Faber and Faber Limited 2009)

Watkin, David: *The Architecture of a Palace.* A contribution in *Somerset House The History* Edited by Meredith Etherington-Smith (Cultureshock Media for The Somerset House Trust 2009)

Websites

archive.org *A Collection of Yearly Bills of Mortality, from 1657 -1758 Inclusive* (1759)

books.google.co.uk *A Collection of the most remarkable trials of Persons for High-Treason Murder, Rapes, Heresy, Bigamy, Burglary and other crimes and misdemeanours. Volume 1* (Printed and sold by T Read in White-Fryers, Fleet Street, London (MDCCXXXIV)

books.google.co.uk *Middlesex County Records: Rolls, Books, and Certificates 19 Charles II to 4 James II 1667 -1688 AD* british-history.ac.uk British History Online, *House of Lords Journal. Morgan's map of the whole of London in 1682, Crown State Papers Domestic, Charles II*

gazette.co.uk/archives *Oxford Gazette and London Gazette archives*

vandaimages.com *Playing cards depicting the Popish Plot, by Francis Barlow (1626-1704). Ink on paper, engraving. England, c.1679 © Victoria and Albert Museum, London*

westminster.gov.uk/archives – *Minutes of St Martin's in the Fields vestry meetings in 1678*

ACKNOWLEDGEMENTS

I am extremely grateful to all the authors listed above whose research has provided so much information about seventeenth century London, the Popish Plot and Edmund Godfrey's strange demise and inspired my imaginative interpretation of his mysterious death. If the reader finds any historical errors – and amongst such contradictory evidence this is not unlikely – these are entirely my own.

Thank you to Dr Alan Marshall, associate Professor in History, College of Liberal Arts, Bath Spa University, for allowing me to use a quote from his biography of Edmund Godfrey (1999) to introduce my protagonist in Part 5, "Where is Sir Edmund?" and also for discussing Godfrey's death and seventeenth century life with me via email. Thank you also to The History Press for permission to use Alan's quote. I am grateful, also, to Dr Peter Elmer, senior research fellow, Centre for Medical History, Exeter University, for allowing me to use material from the Godfrey–Greatrakes letters which form Appendix 3 in his book, *The Miraculous Conformist* (2013). Thank you also to the National Library of Ireland for allowing me to use these quotes from the Godfrey–Greatrakes letters. My gratitude, too, goes to Dr Peter Hinds, Associate Professor of English, University of Plymouth, for allowing me to use his very apposite quote from *The Horrid Popish Plot* (2010) to introduce my imaginative interpretation of the events leading to Edmund Godfrey's death, and to the British Academy for giving permission to use Peter's quote.

Quotations from the letters Secretary Henry Coventry received from the anonymous informer, T. G. are excerpts from the Coventry Papers, and are included by kind permission of the Marquess of Bath, Longleat House, Warminster, Wiltshire, Great Britain. Excerpts from the letters of King Charles II to his sister, Minette, are from Ruth Norrington's book *My Dearest Minette* (1996), and I thank Peter Owen Publishers for allowing me use these quotes. I have occasionally made changes to seventeenth century spelling and grammar in these sources. Harper Collins have kindly allowed me to introduce my murder mystery with the quote from the queen of the genre, Agatha Christie, which I came across whilst reading *Postern of Fate.* The quote from the second book of Samuel, chapter 1 verse 26, from the Authorised Version of the Bible (The King James Bible), the rights of which are vested in the Crown, is reproduced by permission of the Crown's Patentee, Cambridge University Press.

For the trial of Henry Berry, Robert Green and Lawrence Hill I used the Google online book, *A Collection of the most remarkable trials of Persons... Volume 1* printed in London in 1734. The trial notes have been invaluable for my imaginative interpretation and I am grateful, also, to the Google Books team for their prompt replies to my emails. I very much appreciate the work done by Early English Books Online and ProQuest to make primary sources readily accessible to researchers of history and I thank them for their permission to use content from Roger L'Estrange's *Brief History...* (1687) which has been an invaluable source of primary evidence.

I have been researching and writing this book for more than five years and I thank Kiran Kataria for her support. I am indebted to my sister, Janet and my friend, Barbara, both aspiring writers and to author and friend, Susan Leona Fisher, for reading a draft copy and reviewing the novel from a reader's perspective. An especial thank you to Paul for his long-term loan of Jane Lane's biography of Titus Oates. Finally, a big thank you to my husband, Geoff, for his geographical help with drawing the sketch map of Edmund Godfrey's London. He has had to put up with a wife living in the seventeenth century during the research-ing and writing of this book and has been the first person to read it and subsequently become intrigued by the mystery of Edmund Godfrey's strange death.